PRINCESS HOLY AURA

Baen Books by Ryk E. Spoor

Grand Central Arena Series

Grand Central Arena
Spheres of Influence
Challenges of the Deeps

The Balanced Sword Series

Phoenix Rising
Phoenix in Shadow
Phoenix Ascendant

Digital Knight
Paradigms Lost
Princess Holy Aura

Baen Books by Ryk E. Spoor and Eric Flint

Boundary
Threshold
Portal
Castaway Planet
Castaway Odyssey

PRINCESS HOLY AURA

Ryk E. Spoor

BAEN

PRINCESS HOLY AURA

A Baen Books Original

Baen Publishing Enterprises
P.O. Box 1403
Riverdale, NY 10471
www.baen.com

ISBN: 978-1-4814-8282-0

Cover art by Morinekozion

First Baen printing, December 2017

Distributed by Simon & Schuster
1230 Avenue of the Americas
New York, NY 10020

Library of Congress Cataloging-in-Publication Data

Names: Spoor, Ryk E., author.
Title: Princess Holy Aura / by Ryk E. Spoor.
Description: Riverdale, NY : Baen Books, [2017]
Identifiers: LCCN 2017042659 | ISBN 9781481482820 (paperback)
Subjects: LCSH: Fantasy fiction. | BISAC: FICTION / Fantasy / Contemporary. | FICTION / Fantasy / Urban Life. | FICTION / Fantasy / General.
Classification: LCC PS3619.P665 P75 2017 | DDC 813/.6--dc23 LC record available at https://lccn.loc.gov/2017042659

Printed in the United States of America

10 9 8 7 6 5 4 3 2 1

✳ Acknowledgements ✳

Firstly, thanks to Toni Weisskopf and Tony Daniel,
for taking a chance on this crazy idea

Secondly, to my Beta-Readers,
who helped guide me through the minefields I was navigating

And third, to Naoko Takeuchi, CLAMP, Go Nagai,
Akiyuki Shinbo, Masaki Tsuzuki, and all the other creators of
mahou shoujo anime, without whom it wouldn't even have been
possible to *imagine* Holy Aura and her allies.

✳ Dedication ✳

This novel is dedicated to the memory of Stephen J. Reed,
one of my oldest friends who passed far too early.
I wish he could have been here to read this,
because I think he'd have loved it.

PRINCESS HOLY AURA

Part I:
THE PRINCESS AND THE RAT

✳ Chapter 1 ✳

The screaming came from the alley to Steve's right; it was high-pitched, the voice of a child in terror and pain. Steve found himself sprinting down the alley before he'd even consciously realized what he was going to do. *This sure wasn't what I expected after leaving work.* Most days he walked home from Barron's Bagels after cleaning up and making sure the shop was set up for the morning crew, and either prepared for an evening of gaming, or just watched whatever happened to appeal to him.

It seemed that tonight wasn't going to be quite so quiet.

There were a *lot* of shapes moving at the end of the evening-shadowed alley, he realized as he shoved his way past a dumpster. He skidded to a halt, frozen for an instant by the macabre nature of the scene.

A little boy—Emmanuel, a boy who lived in the apartment a few doors down from his—was backed into the far corner of the dead-end alley, eyes wide with fear, face bleeding, beating at dozens of feral cats that had surrounded the kid. A large white rat—a pet?—was clinging precariously to Emmanuel's shoulder, balancing as far away from the hissing creatures as possible.

Jesus, that looks like a Halloween diorama. Steve knew that feral cats could be dangerous in packs, but he'd never seen such a mob around here; one or two, yeah, but nothing like this. Still, it was one thing to attack a little kid, another to deal with a full-grown man. Steve didn't *like* fighting, but he'd found that being six foot three and slightly over three hundred pounds with a good deal of muscle could convince most things to not even try.

"HEY!" he bellowed. "SCAT! Get out of here!" He grabbed up a two-by-four from the ground and whacked one of the animals aside. "Go on, *get*!"

All of the cats turned their heads to look at him, an eerily synchronized action that sent gooseflesh rising in chilling waves across his body. Their eyes glinted a uniform green that seemed, impossibly, to be *brighter* than the light in the alley, almost as though they really were *glowing*. As one, the entire pack hissed venomously at him and then turned back to their prey.

What the hell? Steve was taken momentarily aback. Even the one he'd struck was returning to the attack, leaping up a set of crates for a better position. He'd expected the animals to scatter, at least, and really he'd pretty much expected them to run; now that he had a better look, there were only about a dozen of the animals, which meant that he still outweighed all of them put together by more than three to one, maybe four to one. But as Emmanuel threw a panic-stricken gaze toward him, Steve adjusted his grip on the board and struck *hard*. "I said *SCAT*!"

He connected well and truly this time, sending the animal flipping end over end across the alley, caught another on the backswing, and bored in to start flinging the creatures aside and get to the boy.

The hisses suddenly took on a furious screeching note, and then they *deepened*.

Steve fell back, horrified, as the furry little animals swelled to twice their prior size, eyes shrinking to nothing but faint ridges on a black, flat head with a mouth filled with ebony needle-teeth, body distorting to something semi-bipedal, wrinkled batlike wings extending from the shoulders. Blind the things might have been, but they still all faced Steve now, and he had no doubt they could *sense* him.

His stomach churned with fear, his knees shook, and he wanted to run. But there was a little boy in there, in among those monsters, and a tiny furry creature desperately trying to find shelter, and he was *not* going to leave them.

On the positive side . . . the monsters were now all focused on *him*.

One of them lunged, catching the board and ripping it out of his hands with terrifying strength; two more grabbed the board and broke it apart. *Holy crap, they're strong as hell! I need something tougher!*

He saw it almost instantly: a lovely thick steel pipe, probably torn out of some nearby house, leaning against the wall just past one of the things. *Got to try.*

As the creatures started to slowly encircle him, he jumped forward—with a speed that had surprised a lot of people, thinking that his bulk was mostly fat and not merely an overlay of fat on heavy muscle. He raised his iron-toed workboot and *stomped* as hard as he could on the one in front of him; something crunched and he heard a pained shriek, a quick scuttling to get *away* that gratified him. *Whatever they are, they* can *feel pain.* He hadn't been sure until now.

Something leapt onto him from behind, sinking what felt like a hundred burning needles into his shoulder and back, narrowly missing his spine. He cried out but finished the charge, caught up the pipe, and then spun around without slowing; his attacker absorbed the impact of his entire weight against the brick wall.

Two more flew at him—literally, flapping those leathery wings swiftly and powerfully to propel themselves through the air. Steve swung the pipe around like a baseball bat and a double impact shuddered down the steel shaft; the two monsters were sent smashing into the far wall.

But now the others, clearly realizing that Steve was a far more formidable opponent than they had taken him for, attacked in earnest. Teeth and claws slashed at his legs, two of them lunged for his arms and gripped, pulling, trying to disarm him, take him down to the ground where he would be dead in a moment.

Steve heard his own scream of pain and fear and it galvanized him; he shoved himself up against the tearing, wriggling mass and forced his body into another charge, ramming into the steel dumpster a little ways up the alley, bouncing back and forth between the walls, using his mass and strength and the hard city itself as a weapon to stun or crush his opponents. He spun the steel pipe around, brought it down in a piledriver blow that impaled one of the night-black monsters completely through, tore another from his arm and hurled it into the wall, hammered his fist into another yawning needle-filled mouth—feeling skin tear and rip—and then spun about like a top, hurling the stunned and disoriented things away.

The steel shaft felt *right* somehow, balanced in a good way like a fine quarterstaff, and its extra weight was comforting, helping firm his resolve and courage against these living nightmares. A lot of them were down now, but there were still more, six of them, and they were stalking, coordinating—*remember they can fly*—two of them gone, flanking him in the air, the other four trying to hem him in!

The four in the clear space ahead gave him an idea; instead of retreating, he *dove* at them, dropping his weight on two of them, a falling anvil, then rolling to his feet before the others quite caught him. The steel pipe whipped around as he rose, and he nailed one of the flying ones, the heavy strike sending it sailing thirty feet almost straight up before plummeting back down to land, limply, on the filthy ground. Steve ignored the aching agony in his arms and back and set the steel staff to whirling up, down, right, left, smashing at anything and everything that moved, the slightest sign of beetle-black motion drawing his wrath and the hard, cold vengeance of steel.

Suddenly it was still in the alley; nothing moved but Steve and his shaking, bleeding arms. He looked around, wary, fearful, but no attack came. Everywhere he looked, there were twisted, monstrous bodies . . . but there was not a hint of motion from any of them.

Emmanuel had fallen to the ground, and for a moment Steve had the horrific thought that one of the monsters had killed the boy while Steve was fighting them. But after checking his pulse, Steve decided Emmanuel had just passed out from shock and fear. *No wonder; wouldn't be surprised if* I *do, myself.*

But the thought of being unconscious in an alley with those monsters—some of whom might not be quite dead—kept him quite focused on staying alert.

From behind Emmanuel crawled what Steve could now definitely see was a large white rat, fur gleaming slivery in the dim glow from distant streetlamps and the skyglow overhead. Oddly, it was wearing a tiny crown of some sort. *Kids do put all sorts of strange things on their pets, that's for sure.*

The animal sniffed at Emmanuel, then stood up on its hind legs, surveying the area, sniffing at Steve and the air around. Steve, who had had a pet rat himself some years back, gave an exhausted grin. "'Sokay, fella. I think I got them all."

"That you did," the rat said, with a dignified almost English accent. "Well done, Mr. . . . ?"

Steve blinked, then shook his head. "What the . . . *did you just talk*?"

"I did. Perhaps it would be better if I introduced myself first, and then you can provide me with your name. I am Silvertail Heartseeker. And you are . . . ?"

Am I nuts *now? Did I just snap from boredom or whatever and imagine I was fighting monsters instead of cats? Talking rats? What the* hell, *Steve? You write better RPG scenarios than this!*

He decided, after a split second, that if he wasn't going to assume insanity, then *dream* was the more likely explanation, and therefore, being rude to the talking rat—Silvertail Heartseeker—was pointless. "Um, I'm Stephen. Stephen Russ."

He tried to stand, found that it was *really* hard; screaming pain from uncountable lacerations echoed through him. *I've* never *hurt like that in a dream. Tiny pains, referred pain from something that happened during the day, but nothing like that. It's* clear *pain. Not muffled, not dreamed . . .*

". . . is this *real*?"

Silvertail Heartseeker nodded in a satisfied way. "The natural question, of course. Yes, Stephen Russ, I am afraid this is all too real. You answered calls of the innocent and helpless and risked your life to protect young Emmanuel from things far worse than you imagined existed. For that, I must first thank you. Many there are in the world who would have ignored those cries, and far more who would have fled when mundanity turned monstrous before their eyes."

Silvertail bounced up and laid a pink paw on Steve's hand.

Instantly a white shimmer of light flowed out from the tiny hand-shaped paw, light that was cool and soothing and that surged outward through Steve's body. He saw the narrow rodent face wrinkle in concentration, the whiskers quiver, as the light erased pain, eased tension. Silvertail sagged down, looking as though he had just spent an hour running on an exercise wheel.

Steve flexed his muscles experimentally. There was still pain, but it felt superficial—more like the cat scratches he'd initially expected, not the deep, possibly dangerous wounds the monsters had left. "Wow. Um, thanks."

"On the contrary, as I said, I thank you. I could not cure all of your injuries, but you will suffer no lasting ill effects from this battle." He glanced at the boy. "Emmanuel will also recover, though he should receive appropriate mundane care shortly."

He drew himself to his full height—which, standing, was probably all of eight or nine inches—and bowed. "I must formally greet you, who have passed a test that few in your world would have passed—a test of empathy, a test of attention, a test of reaction, a test of courage, a test of endurance, all compressed into this single battle. You are the one, the Heart I have been Seeking."

Steve felt a chill of awe and anticipation, sensing that the tiny figure before him was far, far more than it appeared, and that it was speaking a ritual, a destiny, not merely ordinary words.

From apparently nowhere, Silvertail Heartseeker produced a glittering brooch, three inches across, of gold and silvery metal, covered with an elaborate pattern in gems. Even to Steve's untutored eye, it was exquisitely made, the main body in the shape of a strangely broken-pointed star with a jeweled galaxy across it. Silvertail lifted the brooch in both tiny hands and said solemnly,

"Stephen Russ, you are the Heart that was Sought, the Courage that is needed, the Will that is eternal. It is for you, and you alone, to take up this burden and defend the world against the darkness that now rises to swallow the light. Take you up the Star Nebula Brooch, and become that which is your destiny. Take it, and become your true self—Mystic Galaxy Defender, Princess Holy Aura!"

✴ Chapter 2 ✴

Steve goggled down at the slightly oversized rat with its overly-shiny white fur, tiny golden crown, sitting on his hind legs and regarding Steve with a far too knowing look. "Become *what?*"

"Mystic Galaxy Defender, Princess Holy Aura," Silvertail repeated calmly.

The repetition of the ridiculous phrase left Steve speechless. He would have laughed, but the situation was not, in fact, funny; instead, he stood there, rubbing his broad face and feeling the never-quite-eradicated five o'clock shadow rasping on his palm, looking around at the monstrous, eyeless corpses scattering the alleyway around him, trying to grasp everything that had happened.

As the ebony bodies began to evaporate like dry ice in the slanting sunlight breaking through the clouds, the ludicrous words finally bounced back into his consciousness. "*ARE YOU COMPLETELY BLIND?*"

"While ordinary white rats do often have vision problems," Silvertail replied primly, "*I* can see far better than you—into the soul, in fact, as well as more mundane spectra."

"Then perhaps you can see why the word 'Princess' isn't exactly appropriate," Steve said sarcastically. "Let alone the rest of that hackneyed Magical Girl word salad you spewed."

"You need to have a little more *respect* for an ancient tradition, Stephen Russ, especially as it is now your destiny to take the Star Nebula Brooch and the name of Holy Aura."

"You have *got* to be kidding me, furball. Go find a nice klutzy junior-high or high-school girl—this Holy Aura is like fourteen, isn't she?" Steve had watched more than enough magical girl or *mahou shoujo* anime to know the outline of any plot involving a magical girl and a cute furry animal.

"Well, yes, roughly fourteen in physical—"

"Exactly. Or if you want to avoid the stereotype, find the most awesomely competent schoolgirl you can and give *her* this . . . brooch."

"So, you want me to send a fourteen-year-old child up against the beings who sent *those*?" Silvertail asked quietly.

That stopped him like a sledgehammer. The melting monsters were now night-crystal skeletons of claws and fangs and graveyard wings, and the memory of their savagery had not faded. "You just told me that's how old, um, Magical Defender—"

"*Mystic Galaxy* Defender Princess Holy Aura," corrected Silvertail.

"Fine, *Mystic Galaxy* Defender Princess Holy Aura," he repeated, trying not to laugh at the ridiculous name. "That's how old you said *she* was."

"That is the necessity of the magical girl or *mahou shoujo* manifestation of the power, yes."

"Look, I could, I guess, kinda take it if I was King Holy Weapon or something."

"The matrix was determined thousands of years ago, Stephen Russ. It can no more be changed than you could shift the mountains in their courses, and even if it could, I have good reasons not to do so."

"But why *me*?"

"Because," Silvertail said, and suddenly he was not supercilious at all, but tired and grim, "I have a conscience, and because there are some very practical limitations of the power."

"A conscience?" He remembered the earlier exchange. "Oh. You don't *want* to send a little girl out against your enemies."

"No. I have done so before, and each time it has gnawed at me, eaten at my resolve, no matter what the reasons or the stakes. And even if I felt no such remorse, the requirements are extreme. Can a girl of that age, in *this* civilization, truly *understand* what we are asking of her? What would *you* do to someone who recruited your fourteen-year-old daughter, if you had one, to become the main warrior in a battle against forces that could destroy your world?"

"I think I'd kill you."

"Yes. And you would be right to do so. What would it *do* to such a girl to be placed in that situation? Even if she survived, what would she be like after fighting in a shadow war against such enemies—ones that make those you just defeated look like *gnats*?" Silvertail sighed. "I have tried many options through the eras, Stephen. I have seen so many die. I have seen so much that was *wrong*."

"What are the practical limitations of the power you mentioned?" Steve was starting to realize that, if this wasn't the most bizarre dream he'd ever had, he was on the verge of the most important decision . . . well, maybe in the world.

Silvertail opened his mouth, but there was a slight stirring nearby. Emmanuel was starting to come around.

Steve grimaced. *Dammit. I'd forgotten about the kid in this insanity.* "We'll pick up on this later, okay?"

Silvertail nodded. "I will pretend to be nothing but a pet until you say otherwise." He scrambled nimbly up Steve's pants and worn leather jacket and settled himself comfortably on Steve's shoulder.

"Hey, Emmanuel, you okay?" Steve asked.

Emmanuel sat up, shakily, looking around. Following his gaze, Steve could see that there was barely a trace of the monsters, and nothing that would draw the boy's attention. "The cats! They turned into monsters!"

Steve put his best "concerned adult" face on. "What? No, though they did puff themselves up and fight back. Scary as heck. But they're gone now."

Emmanuel was pale under his dark skin tone, and was wobbling on his feet. Steve caught him. "Hey, take it easy." Picking up the little boy, Steve could feel him shivering, and there were still many scratches and bites visible. "I've got you. It's just a little way to your house. Just relax."

Shaking, the little boy gripped Steve's arms tight as he headed out of the alley. *Good that he's a skinny little thing; wouldn't want to carry someone much bigger very far.*

In a few minutes he'd reached the door to the Ochoas' apartment and knocked. The door was quickly pulled open; Emmanuel's mother stepped back with her hand to her mouth, saying what Steve thought was "My God!" in Spanish. His father shoved his chair away from their dinner table and ran to join her, leaving two other boys and three girls staring with worried eyes.

"It's all right, um . . ."—he ransacked his memory, dredged the name up—"Luciana, I don't think he's been hurt too bad."

He let Luciana take the boy as Alex—short for Alejandro, if Steve remembered right—looked at both of them. "What happened, Mr. Russ?"

He'd already decided how to tell the story on the walk here. "Bunch of feral cats; never seen so many in my life. I heard him crying in the alley, ran down, and chased 'em off. They didn't want to go right away, as I guess you can see."

"Jesus." Alex frowned. "Some of those cuts are . . ."

Steve knew exactly what the other man was thinking. Animals might be rabid, certainly might cause infections, he should take the boy to the hospital, but the cost . . .

Steve sighed, dug into his pants and pulled out his wallet. "Here. I know you've got basic insurance, but the co-pay's what, a hundred for the ER?"

"A hundred and fifty."

Ugh. Well, ramen isn't that bad, I can survive on that and what Barron's Bagels will let me skeeve off them. "Here's two hundred. That should also get any meds they give him—"

"What? No, no, Steve, I can't—"

"Take it. I want the kid taken care of right, and so do you. Maybe you'll be able to pay me back someday, or just do something for someone else, okay? No big deal."

The Ochoas both tried to argue, but he refused to take no for an answer, and they did, after all, really want to have the doctors look at their son. He got out finally, evading the too-effusive thanks with an excuse that he was late for an appointment.

He looked somewhat forlornly at the McDonald's that he usually passed on the way from work. He'd been planning on treating himself to a cheap dinner, but that wasn't happening now. He muttered a small curse as he realized that he'd lost, and completely forgotten about, the small sack of bagels he'd been bringing home from work. Thinking back he now could remember the bag falling and breaking open. Total loss. "Ugh. Well, there *is* ramen. And maybe the gang will bring some snacks tonight."

Finally he got to his house—or rather, the house he rented an apartment from. It was a third-floor apartment, which from his point of view was pretty swanky; at least he didn't have to deal with people trampling over his head at random hours, other people had to deal with *him*.

Have to remember to pay Lydia the rent tomorrow. Which will leave me like thirty bucks. Ascending the stairs, he got to his apartment and shut the door behind him, locking it and putting the chain on. "All right, Silvertail," he said. "You can stop the act."

"Thank you, Stephen." Hearing the refined accent was actually something of a relief; the events of an hour past had been so bizarre that they had started to acquire a dreamlike quality. "I must say, you conducted yourself in a fashion truly worthy of a—"

"Do not go there, not yet."

"As you will." Despite the straightforward reply, Steve got the impression that Silvertail would have been grinning broadly in vindication, if rats could have grinned at all.

"Emmanuel's family never noticed you."

"No. I thought it best that I was unremarked, and I have had long practice at that over the years."

Steve busied himself with digging out some ramen; to his minor gratification, he found that there was still a bag of frozen vegetables in the freezer, so he broke that open and put some into the broth as it was cooking. "You hungry, Silvertail? And if so, what do you eat?"

"Famished, in fact; I used a considerable amount of power to heal you."

Not without a wince at the small but now significant cost, he added a second ramen packet. "Okay, I'll have food for us both in a minute."

Time to focus on this . . . ludicrous situation. I've got guests coming soon. "Now . . . I was asking about the 'practical limitations' that you mentioned?"

"The power you call 'magic,' and that we might as well keep calling that, has the ability to . . . not *violate*, precisely, but to *trick* reality, to make the laws of reality in effect look the other way, to negate reality in specific ways. But that takes *energy*. A *great deal* of energy to negate the very foundations of reality. And one rule we *cannot* violate is that energy cannot be created from nothing. Thus the energy to perform all magic comes from the magical being itself."

Steve untangled that after a moment. "You mean that this Princess Holy Aura burns her own mass to get the energy to do her stuff?"

"Exactly. Why do you think your depictions of magical girls tends to show many of them with astounding appetites? We've worked hard to disseminate the meme, so that it can be recognized, perhaps accepted, because support and belief are also powerful forces for magic to draw upon. But the energy itself can only be drawn from the actual body of the *mahou shoujo*."

Steve looked down at himself and grinned wryly. "Well, it's not like I don't have a few pounds to spare, I'll give you that. Why else?"

"Mindset. You came into that alley determined to protect others, and with the willingness to face pain and injury in combat if necessary. How many fourteen-year-old girls, or boys for that matter, as opposed to adult men, have that mindset? Oh, they can *learn* it, of course, just as young people of all ages have been turned into soldiers, but an adult who has developed it *naturally* is more stable."

"Plus, if this . . . Princess keeps even part of my knowledge, she's got a lot different perspective on the world than someone who's less than half my age."

"Correct. Yet . . . you have a certain . . . idealism, Steve, a belief in the general rightness and justice that is, or should be, in the world, and that, also, fits my needs. Am I correct?"

A part of him wanted to deny it, because it was becoming more clear that the impossible talking animal was making *sense* in a certain twisted way. But . . . "Yeah. I guess. I want to believe that people are good, that the *world* is a good place."

"And if you have a chance to *make* it a good place?"

"Damn you. Look, don't you see this is all kinds of wrong? If I have to be this . . . Princess Holy Aura. Well, okay. Maybe. If I just have to be her when fighting. But . . . Jesus! It's not like I have anything against girls, but this is just . . ."

"I understand your reservations, Stephen Russ. But you may have to wear that form and seek both allies and enemies, for our enemies also understand the same weapons as we."

"Why in the *world* did you guys choose this . . . particular shape for your superweapon?" he demanded, even as he took dinner off the stove and served it into two bowls.

"Thank you," Silvertail Heartseeker said as the bowl was placed before him. "To answer your question . . . psychological warfare," Silvertail Heartseeker said. "Firstly, such a girl will be underestimated in nearly all cultures and times. They will not be seen as the formidable force they are, and even those who *should* know better will subconsciously underestimate her. Secondly, that age is often a representation of innocence and purity on the edge of adulthood. She stands at the border of light and dark, of child and adult, of weakness and strength. Princess Holy Aura stands between the innocence and purity of the world and those who would corrupt it."

Steve thought about that. It made sense, again, in a strangely twisted fashion. If you accepted the existence of magic, the idea that symbolism was part of its power couldn't be dismissed. "So . . . what *are* our enemies, then?" There had been something almost eerily familiar about those eyeless winged . . . *things*, a familiarity that gave him the creeps.

Silvertail eyed him. "I think a part of you has already guessed. You recognized the nightgaunts, did you not?" At Steve's unwilling nod, he went on. "Some of your authors knew or touched upon the truth—Robert Howard and H. P. Lovecraft, among others."

"You've *got* to be kidding me." He suspected that this might become a catchphrase if he kept hanging around with Silvertail. "Nightgaunts? Lovecraft? *Cthulhu*? Wait a minute, let me see that brooch again." Silvertail proffered the jeweled item without comment. "Damn. That's an Elder Sign, isn't it?"

"The broken-pointed star, yes. Though 'broken' is not quite correct. It represents . . . but we are getting ahead of ourselves. Our adversaries are a . . . not race, but assemblage of beings, some of them unique individuals, others various species, who hail from a mystically separate reality that is, unfortunately, compatible with ours in a manner that is inimical to our survival.

"Periodically—'when the stars are right,' as your authors have put it—their agents here can begin the arrangements to open the gateway and let their ruler through; if she were to manifest completely, she would become . . . a catalyst and an anchor, transforming the Earth to something like their own world and providing an almost unbreakable beachhead for their people to enter our world with.

"They first attempted this when I was young; fortunately for our world, that was also when our ancient civilization was at its peak, and we were able to fight them off, restrain them, until at last we created our ultimate weapon."

"This Princess Holy Aura."

"And her four companions, yes."

"You mean you're going to have to find *four other guys* who will even *consider* this insanity?"

Instead of looking amused or defiant, Silvertail seemed to wilt. "If it were only so easy."

"*Easy?!*"

"Oh, not in the sense you mean. In that sense, yes, it would be hard enough to find men with the same basic decency and courage as yourself, let alone ones willing to risk their own personal identity in such a drastic fashion. But that is in fact an irrelevant question . . . if there is no Princess Holy Aura first. The other Apocalypse Maidens, as they are called, will not be *able* to be located and awakened unless Holy Aura is already there and active, if I have not already fired the opening shot, so to speak, in this era's war against darkness."

He rose on his hind legs again and proffered the brooch. "Take the Star Nebula Brooch, Stephen Russ, and become the shield of light, the vanguard of good against ancient evil. Become Mystic Galaxy Defender Princess Holy Aura, and learn the truth of your soul and the power of the innocence you have always sought."

Steve looked down and took a deep breath. Then he heard footsteps climbing the stairs. "Damn. I have other questions, a *lot* of other questions. But . . . I'll think about it, okay?"

Silvertail gazed at him for a long moment, then gave an audible, tiny sigh. "I suppose I can expect no more. But," he said, as a knock came at the apartment door, "the time for that decision is not unlimited. We have defeated the first scouts of the enemy; their troops will not be long in coming."

✳ Chapter 3 ✳

"Hey, he's *kawaii*, Steve!"

Silvertail held himself still as Richard Dexter Armitage reached out a finger to gently stroke his white fur. *Kawaii? Japanese quoted in reference to anime, obviously. Not surprising that Mr. Russ' friends have similar tastes.* He had already noted the multiple posters of science fiction and fantasy shows of all types, reinforcing his impression of Stephen Russ—along with a wall case filled with weapons ranging from the mundane to models of science-fiction devices. *But that is all to the good. At least Stephen understands the essential nature of the mission, and I need not waste time explaining the basic role of the Apocalypse Maidens, even if there are details he does not understand.*

"Gentle, Dex," Steve said; Silvertail saw a quick sideways glance at him, obviously worried about how well the "rat" would handle being treated as a pet.

"Steve, I *know* how to handle white rats," Dex said, rolling his eyes as he picked up Silvertail and brought him nose-to-nose, grinning and making sniffing noises; Silvertail recognized typical "play with cute pet" behavior and simply sniffed back. "My family's had *lots* of them over the years. Where's his cage?"

"Er . . . I ended up getting him today without warning. Long story. So I'm going to keep him in this box for tonight."

Dexter—a contrast in opposites to his much older friend, with long golden-blond hair carelessly combed back, a delicate-featured face, and slender build—made a face. “If he decides he wants out, he’ll get out of that in about two seconds. You’d better get a cage real quick.”

“I know, I know. Now put Silvertail down. The others will be here soon, and I thought you had character work you wanted to get done.”

“Oh, yeah!” Dex returned Silvertail to his friend’s shoulder and sat down, dumping a large collection of books, papers, and a bag of dice of varying shapes onto the large, chipped folding banquet table that occupied a large part of Steve’s living room. “Look, I was going through this supplement, and since I’m playing a wizard I thought . . .”

Silvertail tuned out the details of the conversation; he was aware of how role-playing games worked—in fact, he remembered with a slight pang the similar games that had existed long before this civilization ever rose, games he had played before that had become impossible. He was much more interested in observing the people, and especially Stephen.

The other players who filtered in over the next hour were an interesting group; one young woman, probably ten years younger than Steve Russ, named Anne, clearly paired with another man of her own age named Mike; a rather hefty but energetic boy named Chad, with a scruffy almost-beard and a cheerful expression, who appeared about the same age as Dex; and one much older man named Eli, quiet but with the air of a military man about him.

What most impressed Silvertail was the way in which Stephen directed his game, even though he was clearly distracted by the events of the evening. It was obvious that Dexter was the *smartest* member of the group, although Anne was often more dynamic as a personality. That only applied in the real-life interactions, though; Dexter shed his nerdish uncertainty when playing his character, and his quick mind and surprisingly powerful voice often dominated play. Eli was quiet, contributing to the game with a considered and careful approach that made his comments and characters’ actions stand out the few times they acted; Chad simply played his character with a cheer and verve that echoed his own personality, while Mike always seemed a bit intimidated by the louder members of the group like Dex, Anne, and Chad.

What Steve did—without, as far as Silvertail could tell, making the others consciously aware of it—was to redirect the sometimes overbearing certainty of Dexter to reduce his spotlight-hogging tendencies, bring Mike more into the game by asking him exactly the sort of questions that his character would be most interested in, and direct events to allow, in general, all of the players to get their moment to shine.

After several hours, the game had to come to a temporary end; it was getting late and some of the others had to get up early. Silvertail noticed Steve trying to hide his interest in the leftovers—chips, pizza that Eli had brought, a vegetable plate from Anne. *This is not a luxurious apartment. Did Steve sacrifice more than I realized this evening?*

To his surprise, Dex—who Silvertail had tentatively tagged as a rather self-centered young man—intervened as the others were packing up. "Hey, let's just leave the extras here. Either Steve'll eat them, or we can have them for the next game day after tomorrow."

"Well . . ." said Anne, hesitating.

"Remember, always bribe the game master," Dex said, glancing at the fridge with an expression that told Silvertail that the younger man was very aware of how empty it was.

At that, the others laughed and agreed. Dex was the last to leave, and as he did, Steve touched him on the shoulder. "Hey, Dex," he said. "Thanks."

"For what?" the younger boy asked; he looked distinctly uncomfortable.

"For making sure they left the food."

"Well . . . yeah." Dex flushed visibly. "Figured you could use it. Didn't see your usual bag of bagels."

Steve grinned. "You're sharp. Anyway . . . thanks."

"You're welcome. I mean, it's just smart game tactics—"

"Shut up and get out of here before you make yourself look like a dick."

"Right. See you in a couple!"

The door closed and Stephen sat down with a *whoosh* of relief. Then he glanced at Silvertail. "You can still talk, right?"

"I certainly can," Silvertail answered.

"Still going to take some getting used to," Stephen said. "So, I still have questions."

"I have no doubt of it, Stephen Russ. But it is quite late; I believe you have to work in the morning?"

"Yeah, but right now I'm not ready to sleep. Not without some more answers."

"As you wish." The questions were, after all, inevitable, and it wouldn't matter if they came now or later. The real trick would be to answer them in a way that would be acceptable to Stephen Russ. Mostly, of course, Silvertail intended to be—and had to be, in fact—honest, but there were very delicate aspects of the situation that probably were best left to later.

Stephen sat down, looking at him somberly. "Not that it really makes much difference if the situation's as bad as you say . . . but I'd like to know if I get anything out of this."

"You mean, is there a reward, other than the self-satisfaction of fighting for humanity's survival?"

He looked pained. "I guess, yeah. I mean, it's worth it just for that, don't get me wrong, but . . ."

"Say no more. A hero is still a person, and still needs to worry about their survival. Yes, Stephen Russ. The magic that binds you to the contract once made also binds the world to reward you once Azathoth of the Nine Arms is banished once more to the realms beyond this one."

"Azathoth? I thought that was the, what, 'blind idiot god' at the center of the universe."

He sighed. "Stephen Russ, you of all people should recognize that the common perception is not going to always be the truth. Lovecraft . . . sensed certain things, was exposed to elements of the truth in passing. But they were filtered through his mind, his beliefs, his prejudices and perceptions of the world. This is true of all others who have glimpsed portions of the truth.

"So no, Azathoth Nine-Armed is not a formless mass of chaos. She—for that pronoun fits better than any other—is an alien invader, ruler and director of the forces and beings beneath her. Her *precise* manifestation—and even more so that of her underlings, the scouts and shocktroops who will come to prepare the way—is affected by the human consciousness, the *gestalt* of human perception and the specifics of those that they encounter and of the civilization that they are seeking to conquer. So some manifestations of your adversaries—if you take up your destiny—will be of ancient lineage, while others may seem far more contemporary."

"So they're shaped by, what, our beliefs? Some Jungian collective unconscious?"

Silvertail twitched his whiskers. "To an extent, yes, that would be a reasonable way to view it. A more modern and cynical way might be to say that they are rather subject to meme infection."

Steve laughed, a short and nervous but still genuine sound of amusement. "That's funny. Hopefully that doesn't mean that they'll manifest spouting 'all your base are belong to us' or something stupid like that."

"No, the more *amusing* memes would not be their forte," he replied. *If only they were. But the memes they will likely manifest . . . you do not need to be reminded of now.* "In any event . . . yes, there is a reward, Stephen Russ. If you defeat these enemies, avert the apocalypse, then the world returns to what it was before this began. Even you will not recall it. But you will find that you are . . . well, *fortunate* would be the best term. The success that has eluded you thus far will seek you out; whatever 'happy ending' you might wish for in this world will be made possible. That will be true of you and all the other Apocalypse Maidens."

"So I'll save the world, not know the world ever needed saving, but then have everything start coming up roses?"

"In essence, yes."

"That kinda sucks. I mean, not the everything coming up roses part—I guess you can tell I'm not exactly doing great on my own, though I won't complain, lots of other people are worse off. The having done something awesome and not knowing it, that sucks."

"I cannot disagree," Silvertail said. "But it is part and parcel of the nature of the enchantment and the war. The powers of magic that make the war possible are usually walled off from this world, ever since the first great conflict. So the battle is fought, the world witnesses the battle, but all of this is affected by—is a *part* of—the grand contest. Once the conflict is resolved, the world returns to what it was before the magic appeared."

"That almost sounds as though magic's real source is this Azathoth, or wherever she comes from."

"Not truly. It is more a matter of the fact that the way in which she was sealed away was done *using* all the power of magic we could channel, so that her entry to the world would of necessity bring the magic back . . . and any attempt to bring magic back would, almost certainly, unleash her as well."

Stephen looked at him. "So why do *you* remember?"

"I am . . . the key, you might say. Or the flaw in the prison, an inescapable one given that there were magic-workers on this side of the barrier. I am the one who watches for the cycle to resume, whenever the conditions are right, because I am the only one with the ability to find those who can close the door."

"But *why*?"

He sighed, feeling his whiskers drooping, remembering in the distant, distant past when it would have been human shoulders slumping. "Because I was the one who *created* the Apocalypse Maidens, Stephen Russ. One of thirteen, the most powerful of Lemuria's wizards, and the only one to survive the conjuration that transformed my daughter and her four closest and most courageous friends into the weapon the world needed. As you can see—" he gestured to himself—"it . . . cost me."

Steve looked simultaneously sympathetic, outraged, and pained. "Do you have *any* idea how hard this is for me to deal with? I mean . . . *Lemuria*? A wizard stuck as a white rat? And you did this to your own *daughter*?"

"I did not do this *to* her; she *volunteered*, and . . ." His voice, despite untold centuries of control, threatened to break. "And . . . I have *never* been more proud than I was that day."

"Oh. Sorry." Steve paused. "So . . . what about the other twelve of you?"

"They . . . were consumed by the ritual. We knew the risks, of course—the power we were unleashing was by far the greatest magic ever worked by mankind. I think I only lived because there was, as I said, a necessity that there be a key, a linchpin, a nexus of the enchantment that would remain throughout eternity." Even after all the centuries, remembering the deaths of his friends still hurt.

"But your daughter and her friends . . . they did win, right?"

"They won, yes. And in doing so ripped the foundations of magic from this cosmos, shattered the stability we had enforced upon the world, and wiped out our entire civilization, nearly dooming humanity to extinction."

"Holy *shit*. And this is the *good* outcome if I take this brooch-thing up and win?"

"No, no, Stephen. That was then, when the world was *filled* with magic, when so much *relied* upon magic that to withdraw it was like turning the foundations of a building to water. My daughter and her friends *did* survive, and so did enough of humanity—or we would not be here to speak of it. But in the other repetitions of the cycle . . . while there is great destruction sometimes wrought during the combat, the world is returned to its prior state afterward. Not entirely without cost—if people were specifically slain by the forces of our enemies, they will be found to have died, albeit by more mundane forces, after the victory. But the world will not be destroyed if you win. Only if you lose will it be plunged into a creeping shadow of its old self."

Steve nodded slowly. "Jesus." He looked down at the Star Nebula Brooch, lying on the table between them, and picked it up reluctantly. "And this really is the only way to fight these things?"

He shrugged. "The only one I know of."

Stephen Russ sighed. "Tell you what. I'll . . . carry it for a while. Think about it. But . . . this is all of *me* you want me to change."

"Not *all* of you. I might even say the least *important* part of you. I do not wish to change the sort of person you are."

He bit his lip. "Yeah. I guess. But dammit, my entire life and self-image aren't just something to toss aside, either."

"I did not say they were, and perhaps I should apologize; one's self-image is not at all unimportant, and indeed for a man of your age, that self-image is the rock on which you have built your identity. So, yes, I was wrong, and I do apologize. I ask you to make a very significant sacrifice, of your self-image, of your position in a society that—you know well—values men more than women in many areas. I ask you to, at least temporarily, sacrifice even the respect that age and size have given you.

"But know that these sacrifices will make you, as Holy Aura, vastly stronger; the willingness of the Chosen to take up the battle at great personal cost, this is one of the greatest sources of power in any magic. Your willing acceptance of this price may give us the key to a swifter and more certain victory. And they will certainly make it more likely that one day you will wake up—the same Stephen Russ you are now—and your life will become brighter, and the world will be safe."

Silvertail could see Stephen considering that. "So," he said, "in a nutshell, the more I'm personally willing to sacrifice to the cause, the more powerful Holy Aura will be."

"Correct. If you accept the burden, you are—while Holy Aura, in any event—sacrificing a major portion of your personal foundation and viewpoint; this will make you *immensely* stronger as Princess Holy Aura."

"You say 'while Holy Aura'; does that mean I can change back to Stephen Russ?"

"Yes. You will of course have no access to any of Holy Aura's powers while in your original form, but yes, you will be able to change back. You will *not*, however, be able to change your mind once you have accepted the power; once done, the enchantment cannot be undone."

Stephen surveyed the brooch again, eyes tracing the beauty of the curves absently. Finally he straightened. "Okay. I'll think on it. And not too long. I promise I'll have an answer for you in . . . um . . . a week. Is that okay?"

A week . . . She will have learned of the loss of her creatures soon. She will know that either I chose to act, or that the Princess has been found. Yet . . . I have no right, nor power, to force the issue. "If it must be, then it must be. One week, Stephen Russ. May that time be well spent, for our enemy is already moving."

✶ Chapter 4 ✶

The white rat's warning hadn't faded from Steve's mind in the last few days. Though Silvertail hadn't *said* anything about it since, Steve knew that the one-week deadline was already pushing what Silvertail thought was safe.

But there were still questions . . . over and above the ones he'd already been wrestling with. With a sigh, Steve dumped his laundry basket out on the [illegible]ed before speaking. "Silvertail, I've got another question—one tha[illegible]n nagging at me a while."

The wizard-tu[illegible]dent glanced up at Steve from Silvertail's perch on the end [illegible]d. "Go on, Stephen Russ," Silvertail said, as Steve sorted throug[illegible]olded but clean laundry for a shirt to wear.

"I get why you di[illegible]t to choose a young girl for this gig—and I agree with your reasons, believe me. And most of those reasons apply to choosing a boy of that age. But why didn't you choose an adult woman? Or maybe look for someone who was, well, already going the transgendered route?" He found a T-shirt featuring the entire collection of trolls from *Homestuck* and pulled it on over his head, covering the Star Nebula Brooch which hung from a leather cord around his neck.

"There are several reasons," Silvertail answered after a pause. "Though I certainly did think of simply looking for a woman of the appropriate type and of roughly your age. Certainly they would not have the . . . issues that you may encounter simply from the transformation, although a great many adults—I suspect including yourself—would not look forward greatly to becoming a young high-school student again."

"God, no. My experiences in school sucked until I hit my full growth spurt, which was, like, the end of my junior year. Until then I was pretty short, a little too fat, and a loudmouthed geek, which made me a perfect bullying target. Kinda like Dex is now; he's a little taller than I was, and skinny as a sheet of paper, but even though he's better looking than I was, he's got that unconscious arrogance that sets bullies off. So no way would I want to go back."

"But to answer your question . . . I did keep that as a possibility," Silvertail continued. "In truth, I was only a few days from giving up on searching for a man of your qualities. But I chose that direction *first* because of the potential advantages. If I *could* find a man with the requisite character—courage, willingness to risk himself for others, clear empathy for the plight of those less fortunate, and so on—"

"Okay, you're starting to embarrass the hell out of me," Steve said, and ducked into the bathroom so the potential blush wouldn't be visible. *And I need to go anyway*. "I'm no paladin."

A sniff of amusement was audible through the thin door. "Indeed? Perhaps not, but you certainly have many of the qualities. In any event, if I *could* find such a man, and one who had a firm self-identity—who was, nonetheless, willing to *give up* that self-identity for the sake of the world—then I would have found a Princess Holy Aura who would be far, *far* stronger than any since the very first time the enchantment took hold and made my daughter Aureline and her friends into the Apocalypse Maidens.

"This I explained to you earlier. The important point for the purpose of your question, of course, is that this level of self-sacrifice—and thus potential power for Holy Aura—did not apply to the other categories you mention, other than the possibility of finding a woman who hated her own identity *as* a woman; such a person would, undoubtedly, have at least as many potential issues to deal with as would you."

Steve nodded, then realized that Silvertail couldn't see him. "Yeah, that makes sense, I guess." Another thought occurred to him. "Hey—that doesn't mean you *set up* poor Emmanuel, did you?"

There was an injured tone in the white rat's reply. "Certainly not!" Then Silvertail's voice took on a more apologetic note. "Though . . .

not deliberately, but in a sense . . . yes, I suppose. Not that I directed the events, but the magic that aids me in finding the Heart that was Sought also will tend to draw the opposition to my area. It was, in that way, inevitable that *some* sort of conflict would emerge, and those conflicts are what bring the destined Holy Aura to the fore."

That made sense. Steve stood up and pushed the handle on the toilet; he was rewarded with the sound of something snapping, a jingle of a chain, and almost no sign of anything flushing. "*Dammit!*"

Opening the tank showed that a key piece of plastic had given way; the entire float and flush assembly would have to be replaced. "Wonderful. Hey, Silvertail, I don't suppose you could give me a sort of down-payment on that 'everything coming up roses' reward? Because this is going to really hit my nonexistent budget."

"What happened?"

After a quick explanation, the white rat shook his head. "No, I have no immediate remedy for this situation. What little magic I still wield is not terribly useful for fixing damaged objects. Although getting more resources . . ." He paused for a moment. "Not yet, no. Unless you commit—unless Princess Holy Aura is manifest—my powers remain extremely limited, circumscribed by my mission."

"Then we've got to go shopping, much as it pains me. I really, *really* hate digging into my savings."

"You do have savings, however?"

Steve grimaced as he dug out his backpack. "Such as they are. Three hundred and seventeen dollars. That's five years of savings, and it would barely cover one month's rent."

"I see." Silvertail watched Steve as he strapped the pack on. "Shall I stay here?"

"From what you just told me, that would be stupid, wouldn't it?"

The white whiskers twitched in an unmistakable smile. "I would not consider it wise to be far separated from you, no. That is why I have gone with you to your place of work and hidden nearby during your workdays."

"Okay, hop in; you can ride in the pack."

It was a three-mile walk from the apartment, and Steve mopped sweat from his face with one arm of his T-shirt; the early summer day was already promising to be scorchingly hot. Finally, the broad storefront of DIY Home, the building supply chain, loomed up in front of him. DIY Home sat at one end of the Twin Pines strip mall, the anchor store for a long stretch of shops that ranged from restaurants to office supply outlets, shoe stores, and others.

Silvertail himself probably wasn't having a great time of it either; that backpack, even with the upper zipper open, was going to be awfully hot. Silvertail hadn't said a word of complaint, though. *And pretty soon I have to give him an answer. It's been four days, I'm past the midpoint of my week.*

On the positive side, Steve knew exactly what he was looking for; he'd fixed more than one cranky toilet in the past, and DIY Home had everything set up to make it easy to find. Fifteen minutes later, he handed over almost all the money in his wallet and left the building supply giant with a gray and orange bag swinging from his hand.

I really need to keep some money on hand. With a reluctant sigh, he turned toward the bank sitting isolated in the middle of the mall, separate from everything else to allow space for its drive-through service. The ATM, at least, was free. It only took a few moments, and another wince at the reduction of his savings, to withdraw thirty dollars. *Gotta make that last a week. More, actually. If nothing else breaks, anyway.*

Steve headed for the path that led out of the mall—across the surrounding verge of grass to the main road—but stopped by the far side of the pet supply house, which was a blind wall and out of sight of everything else. "Here, Silvertail, get out a sec; I want to put this stuff in the pack."

"I appreciate the chance to get *out* of that stifling thing," Silvertail said primly. His bedraggled look emphasized his discomfort.

"Sorry about that. Here." He took the water bottle from the side of the backpack and opened it, letting Silvertail drink. "Better?"

"Much, thank you."

The ground quivered.

"Whoa!" Steve steadied himself against the wall as the vibration peaked, then faded away. "Wow. Haven't felt an earthquake around *here* since I was a little kid."

Silvertail was stiff, nose twitching; he said nothing.

Then the ground shook again, more strongly. Shouts of surprise and concern echoed around the mall parking lot, and there were faint creaks and jingles from the buildings. As Steve stepped out to look around the mall, a lone shopping cart suddenly turned and rattled downhill, jarred loose from its prior perch. Everyone else stood frozen, waiting for the earth to resume its normal immobility.

Steve felt a creeping chill working its way up his spine; he looked down at Silvertail, whose red eyes met his levelly. "That . . . wasn't an earthquake, was it?"

"I suspect not," the white rat said grimly. "It—"

The ground *rocked* under Steve, accompanied by a shuddering, crunching sound that transmitted itself violently through his boots; Steve barely managed to keep his footing.

The blacktop in the center of the parking lot *heaved* skyward, sending an SUV and two compact cars flipping end over end like discarded toys. A second tremendous impact, and the dark asphalt gave way, opened up like a malignant flower, and *something* reared up from beneath the earth.

Steve swore, unable to think of anything coherent to say. The thing was huge, fifteen, maybe twenty feet across, an eyeless, gray-stone monstrosity that rose up higher and higher into the air, a worm the size of a freight train with a mouth of whirring, crushing assemblages that had no business being in anything living. It brought with it a hideous stench, a smell of brimstone and decay, and even the brilliant sunlight was suddenly cold and distant, an alien and sharp light revealing an abomination from an ancient and inimical realm. "What the *hell* . . . ?"

"A dhole, sometimes called a chthonian," Silvertail answered, his calm, controlled voice somehow audible even over the screams, the rending of stone, the rumbling snarl of the creature as it turned down, seeking, questing for something. "A creature of the deep earth, but a mystical one, a species allied closely with our enemies."

Steve felt himself shaking. The nightgaunts had been terrifying, but still on a human scale. They were things he could fight, that he could *imagine* himself fighting, creatures that a good hard swing with a crowbar could break.

But *this*? His brain couldn't even *grasp* how huge the thing was, and the idea of fighting it wasn't even laughable.

The dhole turned toward the screaming, running people, and slid forward, crushing cars and the pavement itself with a casual and horrific force. Steve saw distant terrified faces and realized that even though the creature was clumsy and slow to turn, it was only a matter of minutes before it crushed and devoured something much more vulnerable than empty vehicles.

The Star Nebula Brooch pressed coolly against his skin, beneath the T-shirt, and Steve could not ignore it. Swallowing hard, he reached down and pulled the glittering piece of jewelry out. "Okay, Silvertail . . . how do I turn this thing on?"

"Are you sure, Steve? Once done, it cannot be undone."

He risked another glance, saw the dhole crash headlong into the main storefront, punching a hole in the wall, accompanied by a shrieking, grinding noise as the thing's mouth pulverized whatever it had consumed. "Dammit, yes, I'm sure! I can't stand here and let people get killed! I'd never be able to live with myself! Now, Silvertail! I accept this mission, this calling, whatever it is, I'll be this, this . . . Princess Holy Aura! Tell me what to *DO*!"

The white rat bowed his head, then raised it. The golden crown suddenly shimmered, and an argent glow flickered around him. "Then repeat after me, Stephen Russ. To avert the Apocalypse . . ."

He took a deep breath. "To avert the Apocalypse . . ."

". . . and shield the innocent from evil . . ."

". . . and shield the innocent from evil . . ." he repeated. The Brooch hummed abruptly in his hand, a warm vibration utterly different from the monstrous shaking and impact of the dhole.

". . . and stand against the powers of destruction . . . I offer myself as wielder and weapon, as symbol and sword . . ."

The monster froze suddenly, then pivoted. Steve was barely conscious of the motion, as a warm, tingling sensation began to spread outward from the Star Nebula Brooch, and he found himself completing the oath in chorus with Silvertail, now taller, brighter, no longer a tiny creature but a shimmering figure of a man, indistinct and luminous. ". . . mistress of the spirit, ruler of the stars beyond, Mystic Galaxy Defender, Princess Holy Aura!"

The Star Nebula Brooch burned like the sun, and everything—the mall, the charging rock-worm, Silvertail, and even Stephen Russ himself—dissolved into a pure silver luminescence and an echoing note of music that shook the stars in their courses.

✴ Chapter 5 ✴

The silver *burst* from his body and he became the light, flying outward, making a universe of argent and white touched with rainbows, a whirling cyclone of light that chimed and rang and sang a song of triumph and rebirth. Steve felt a body reforming, electric warmth like a hot shower on a cold, cold day curling around and defining every line, every curve that was coalescing from pure light, tingling like a brush of lightest snow on the finest day. He seemed both within and without, part of the body yet outside of it, a slender form a fraction of the prior size, contours smooth and oddly familiar while being strange, almost alien, and he felt a distant spurt of fear.

But elation and triumph pushed fear back, drowned it out with the sound of trumpets and drums as she spun about—

She?

Steve realized that the thought had felt natural, yet at the same time clashed with the deepest reflexes of his mind. *He! That's how I . . . How Stephen Russ . . .*

But I'm not Stephen Russ. Not now. Not exactly.

Now the terror of uncertainty—of his own *identity* being changed, being different and unknown—burst fully in on her. Yet the ecstasy and certainty of the transformation could not be denied or cast aside, and even in her confusion, Steve knew that what he was becoming was *necessary*, that lives hung in the balance, and he seized that horror, that numbing dread, and shoved it away, into the very farthest reaches of her mind. *This must be. This I have accepted. There will be a price . . . but one to be paid later.*

She threw her arms out, feeling the light *blazing* across her body, forming into the raiment that she *knew* must appear, both in the ancient echoes of knowledge from eons past and in the memories of images Stephen Russ had seen many times. Delicate armored gloves nearly to the elbow, glittering white and silver and pearl shimmering into existence as crystal and metal and cloth, shoulder-guards and sparkling boots and a chiming-crystal skirt of diamond-bright gems edged with mystic metal, woven from the purity of magic as she spun through the perfect pearlescent void—or it spun about her.

Now the light drew in, revealing the world beyond, concentrating to twin arcs of light the brightness of the sun and the essence of hope, arcs that bound themselves around her brows with a flash of pain, flame and ice and lightning forming into a glittering coronet.

It was then that she (*he?* a tiny voice within asked, hopelessly) realized the dhole was *speaking*, in a voice lower than anything human, words shaking the ground.

"Seeking, seeking, smell the light . . . *consume* the light . . . tell us *where*!" The thing reared up, looming above terrified shoppers, some trapped in wreckage. "Surface-crawlers, water-life, nothings, *anakh gryll oman'nanql b'harni Azathoth*!" As it finished the last incomprehensible alien phrase, it began to descend, and screams began to rise.

The screams awakened Steve and what he had become to full awareness and acceptance of this impossible reality. ***"STOP!"***

The shout echoed across the lot, a whipcrack of imperative brilliance, and the immense rock-worm halted, curled swiftly around.

Even as it did, he/she felt her mouth open, the hand extend. *Oh my* God, *I even have to follow through with the hackneyed introduction*?

At the same time, she spoke. "I am the one you seek, monster! Mystic Galaxy Defender, Apocalypse Maiden the First, Princess Holy Aura, reborn as sword and shield, weapon and wielder, mistress of souls and stars!"

Steve, trying desperately to hold onto a sense of *him*self, focused on the words. *I am* not *going to have a catchphrase that ends like "in the name of the stars, I will give you a spanking!" I will be Princess Holy Aura—I* AM *Princess Holy Aura—but on* my *terms! I accept you—now* you *accept* me*!*

With that thought Steve found himself fully aware of a body that was not his, but *hers*, but belonged as much to Steve as ever his own had, and the words of Holy Aura belonged to Steve as well. "You have threatened innocents and brought fear to this world," she continued, "and for that, this Apocalypse Maiden says that *you*"—the extended hand pointed, and then turned to a fist with the thumb outthrust, turning until it pointed to the ground—"are going *down*!"

The dhole bellowed its challenge and charged with a speed that belied its immense bulk.

Holy crap, what the hell am I doing?

She saw the monster bearing down on her like a runaway freight train and desperately leapt aside—

To find herself sailing effortlessly through the air, a jump thirty, forty feet high and twice that in length, evading the clumsy charge with ridiculous ease. Another charge, another leap, and her heart began to slow its pounding just a hair. *It really can't keep up with me! And me . . . I'm jumping like Spider-Man on speed!*

The realization that she wasn't helpless—that this thing was wrecking real estate but unable to reach her—finally allowed Princess Holy Aura to accept that she could *act*. And also to become aware of a distant, clear voice:

"Princess! *Holy Aura!* You must stop it swiftly, before it thinks to call to its brethren!"

Stop it? Even if her strength was equal to her jumping ability, she wasn't sure her hand would survive punching the thing. But . . . *I'm a* mahou shoujo *now, so I should have a weapon . . .*

The thought triggered the certainty, and once more the pure silver light shone out, this time between her hands. *What will it be? A wand? A bow? Please don't let it be some kind of Frisbee or anything.*

A long shaft, glittering as argent as the light, grew from pure luminance and extended out, one end a huge blade, the other a massive ball, the entire thing almost twice Holy Aura's height, and she felt a broad, savage grin spreading across her newfound face. *A broad-bladed naginata, a* bisento*! A weapon I actually know how to use!* Despite its great size, the bladed spear felt light as a dagger in her hands, and she spun it around, creating a shining circle of dazzling reflections before her.

"That . . . is rather different," Silvertail's quiet voice said. "But no matter! You will need to invoke the—"

She wasn't listening. Seeing the destruction that the monster had caused, and realizing that there *were* people injured—people who might *die* if this thing wasn't stopped fast—raised the fury and outrage to its peak again. "Here, monster—try *this!*"

She leapt once more, but this time *toward* the dhole, drawing the great weapon back as she did. It lunged to meet her, but she rose above it, then descended, bringing the massive blade down with every ounce of strength she had and a shouted battlecry. "*Ginhikari no Bisento!*"

The concussion blew out the remaining windows around the mall lot. The Silverlight Bisento *sundered* the dhole's head, shattering stone skin, splintering and crushing the mighty grinding jaws, driving the monster's body downward with the same irresistible, absolute force of an avalanche, hammering the multiton creature's body *into* the pavement with a shockwave of power, bowing the surface of the parking lot into a crater eighty feet and more across. The worm-thing gave one tremendous, shuddering convulsion and collapsed.

For a moment, all was silent; Holy Aura landed atop the stony corpse of her fallen foe and gazed out, shellshocked at the abrupt beginning and end, as people rose from the ground, began to stare at her and point, murmurs of shock and disbelief turning to gratitude.

Then she heard sirens approaching fast. Instinctively she gave a smile and a bow to the assembled people, then leapt away, bounding to the roof of DIY Home and sprinting across it.

As she ran, Steve felt the confusion returning, and a new panic. *What happened there? I was doing that . . . but I wasn't! I didn't think about half of that! I just . . .* did *it! I didn't make up most of that speech! And . . . who am I? I'm a . . . a man, but I'm thinking I'm not! I'm Holy Aura! I'm Stephen Russ! I was shouting an attack I never knew! What . . . and I haven't even . . . how . . .*

Thoughts beginning to unravel, the girl in glittering, implausible armor ran faster, streaking through the air, trying to outrun the one thing she could never escape: herself.

✴ Chapter 6 ✴

Silvertail watched tensely as the pact was fulfilled and Princess Holy Aura was finally reborn. *Let it work*, he prayed. *In the name of all we have sacrificed, in the name of all that was and could be, let this not be a failure*.

With eyes that could see what ordinary mortals could not, he watched as Stephen Russ' mortal frame dissolved in light, a core of brilliance forming into a new shape both delicate and strong as a steel blade, head suddenly thrown back, midnight-purple tresses arching up, sparkling with power, coming down in a waterfall of indigo silk, even as the armor formed, different yet exactly as it had always been. Princess Holy Aura's crown materialized in blessed light and sealed itself to her brow, and eyes the color of amethysts and dreams opened for the first time.

Within the small figure, Silvertail Heartseeker could sense confusion and conflict, and for a moment the girl's form trembled. But she straightened as the dhole renewed its attack and threatened innocents, and called it to confront her: ". . . this Apocalypse Maiden says that *you* are going *down*!"

That was somewhat different from the usual, but that was also good. *Stephen must be accepting his mission!* He began to dare to hope, and once more felt his own powers beginning to be unlocked. *If she can triumph . . .*

A jump, evasion, and he suddenly remembered that Stephen—Holy Aura—did not yet understand her powers, or the desperate urgency of this combat. He shouted his warning, saw her shift her stance.

The immense weapon formed without warning in her hands, and for a moment he was taken aback. *Why in the name of the Sunken Lands would* that *be the shape of the Silverlight Weapon*? But that was a minor concern. The important thing would be to guide her in how to use it. The channeling of power through the blade was not a trivial—

Princess Holy Aura, however, did not even seem to *hear* his attempt to instruct her, but lunged to meet the gigantic armored worm head-on. *No! Such a creature cannot be defeated by brute strength, not as you are now! You need to—*

His mind went blank with complete shock as Holy Aura's *bisento* very nearly *bisected* the eldritch creature in a single blow. *By the Powers Beyond* . . . He felt a tiny smile stretching his furry features. *She is even more powerful than I had expected. This is wonderful!*

But then he saw the girl follow her victorious bow with a leap away . . . and sensed the rising turmoil, the confusion and fear. "Oh, dear," he heard himself murmur. With the threat of the monster now gone, Stephen's mind was now realizing the *changes*, the aspects that he had only contemplated in the abstract before, and Silvertail realized he had to catch up with Holy Aura—or Steve—very, very fast.

That was not, however, so simple when you were a small white rat. And even if he could change that aspect of himself, he could not even approach the speed or strength of the fleeing Apocalypse Maiden.

But a fleeing animal—man or woman or otherwise—will in the end seek a refuge. And Stephen has only one refuge.

It took him some time to make his way back to the apartment—not merely because a rat has, relatively speaking, short legs, but because the last thing Silvertail needed was to draw attention to himself or Steve's neighborhood. More than two hours had passed before he made his way up the stairs, hopping up them one at a time and occasionally pausing to make sure that a *creak* from below didn't indicate someone coming up behind him.

The door was open a crack. He sniffed; the scents told him Steve was inside, and further emphasized the confusion, fear, and anger he had sensed before. Silvertail slipped inside and, with some effort, nudged the door completely shut.

Steve sat unmoving on the battered brownish couch, staring at empty space. His hands were dirty—covered with black and gray smears of some sort—and one lay on his jeans without regard for the stains it might transfer. Two empty beer bottles were on the stand next to him, and the other hand gripped a third tightly.

"Stephen," Silvertail said quietly.

The big man started violently, spilling beer over his T-shirt. "Dammit. Silvertail?"

"Yes. I am sorry for startling you. I see you made it home, in any event."

"Yeah," he agreed, and rose, putting the bottle down on the table. His attempt to look casual about it was belied by the way his hand shook and knocked over one of the others. He started, tried to catch it, and only succeeded in knocking all three down, the remaining liquid fanning out across the carpet and almost instantly sinking in. "*Dammit!*" Convulsively Steve threw himself across the room, ripped the roll of paper towels from the holder, and started trying to blot up the mess with a fevered focus on the mundane task.

"Enough, please. Stephen, stop."

"Can't stop, this will *stink* if I don't get it out, and my landlady—"

"*Please*, Stephen, *stop*."

Stephen Russ froze in midscrub, then slowly sat back, his massive frame collapsing like a deflated balloon as he sagged against the wall, eyes closed, hands shaking and clenching.

Silvertail sighed, smelling the stench of fear and anger mixed with the hops and alcohol. "*Eleitai, halama, meritami,*" he muttered, and light streamed from his outstretched paw; the broad brown stain faded away, leaving the carpet clean and dry.

That roused Steve slightly. "That'd be real handy on laundry day."

"No doubt." Silvertail still wasn't sure how to approach the current—very delicate—situation. "But in my current state it is not, I am afraid, something to do casually. Why not wash your hands, at least, in the more usual way?"

The man looked down at his hands as though he had never seen them before. "Oh. Yeah, they're pretty filthy."

Unsteadily, Steve got up and made his way to the sink, scrubbing away at them. "At least the transformation doesn't, like, disintegrate my clothes or anything. When I turned back, I even had the backpack with me. Good thing; I just got the toilet repaired, works like a charm now. But that's how I got all dirty, you know, even when you try to keep things clean, things get a little dirt on 'em, then you're working with water, and—"

"Steve—"

"*WHY THE HELL DIDN'T YOU WARN ME?*"

The bellow was so loud and unexpected that Silvertail jumped back in alarm before the furious, blotchily terrified face of Stephen Russ. "We *had* discussed the changes, Stephen," he said finally.

The outburst had exhausted Steve; he sank into the couch and put his face in his hands. Finally he swallowed audibly, looked up. "You didn't *tell* me that she . . . she had an *identity*. I thought it would be . . . well . . . sort of like playing dress-up, a cosplay where I had real powers and had to deal with really having a different body."

"That was—to an extent—rather what I expected as well, Stephen. What are you saying was different?"

Silvertail could smell some of the immediate anger fading as Steve realized that Silvertail honestly did not understand the problem. "Well . . . when I became . . . Holy Aura, it was like . . . like I already *knew* I was a woman. Except that I still *knew* I was a man. But in that body, it was . . . *real*. I *felt* this . . . this impression of memory, I guess, of *self*, knowing how to move and run and everything, and it was all *filled* with the absolute . . . not even thought, just *knowledge*, assumption, that I was a woman. Not even a woman, a girl, a teenage girl. I . . ."

Understanding burst in. "Oh. Oh, by the stars and the Light itself, Stephen, I *am* sorry. There is the basic template of Holy Aura, yes, and it has been . . . well, affected, *refined* one might say, over the many centuries by those who wore the title. None of their souls, or their memories truly remain, but something of their essence must linger. For another girl who takes up the mantle, of course, this is not an issue at all; it merely helps make them more certain of themselves, of their role as Holy Aura. But for you . . . Stephen, I *do* apologize, completely and abjectly I beg your pardon. That certainty and knowledge permeating the template would be in direct conflict with your own personal self-knowledge. You did extraordinarily well, then, to push it aside—as you must have—in order to deal with the threat at hand."

Steve extended one shaking hand and stared at it. "And . . . and that's not going away, is it?" he said finally. "Whenever I . . . change, that remnant, whatever, is going to be there. It's not disappearing as I, well, get used to it?"

"No. I am sorry, but now that I have thought on it, no, it is an essential *part* of the magic. In a sense, it can of course help you in your mission, give you some understanding of a body so utterly different from your own, but in other senses it will be a great trial."

"I'm not sure I can do this."

Silvertail closed his eyes and sighed. "Stephen—"

"I know," he said, and his voice shook. "I know, I accepted it, it's not reversible, I don't have any *choice*. I *made* the choice. To save people." His voice lightened for a moment. "To . . . save people." He looked up. "I did, didn't I?"

"You did indeed, Stephen Russ. As Holy Aura, you confronted a monster that would most certainly have destroyed that entire shopping mall and killed many of those there, and continued to do so until stopped."

"And nothing except Princess Holy Aura—or one of these other Apocalypse Maidens—could have stopped it."

"In *this* case that is not entirely true. It was an extremely dangerous and powerful creature, but the more formidable mundane weapons available to your civilization could deal with it. But many would have died, and much destruction would have ensued, before those weapons could have been brought to bear. It *is* true, however, that many of the foes to come will be ones beyond the power of mortal weapons to affect, and some will be ones on which your powers, even when you have learned to wield them, will not be very effectual without the assistance of the other Apocalypse Maidens."

"Right." The dark-haired man looked at his hands for another long moment, then clenched them into fists and stood up abruptly. "I'll have to deal with it. Somehow. It's not going to be easy, Silvertail. I'm going to need help from *someone*, and there's no way I can talk about *this* to a shrink. Not without getting locked up. And maybe I'm paranoid, but I kinda think it could be a bad idea to just go to the agents that'll be investigating this afternoon's freakshow and tell them what's going on. Though it'd be really nice to have the National Guard on standby."

Silvertail allowed himself to relax a tiny bit. *He is a strong-willed man, and his focus is still on helping people. That may just allow us to get past this.* "I am afraid your instincts are correct. Besides the obvious mundane issues of their reaction to the sudden appearance of the supernatural, the fact is that at least some of the authorities will undoubtedly be under the influence of our adversaries. You . . . no, *we*, for you are correct, we must be a team, and I must help you as best I can . . . must for the most part perform this work alone, with only the other Maidens as our support."

"Okay. Kinda goes with the whole meme anyway, right? You don't generally see your magical girl or *sentai* team running over to the feds and asking them for help. Or when they do, it turns out the officer's another eldritch horror out to eat their souls." The humor was forced and Steve's voice was still strained . . . but he was *trying*, and Silvertail felt a twinge of admiration. *Would I have done so well in his place? I have to wonder. I might well be trying to run away even though I knew I had committed myself to the cause.* "So, next step is to start finding the other Maidens, right?"

And we start on the next delicate part of this problem. "Yes, that would be our main goal. The sooner we can gather the full Five, the sooner we will be able to prepare to confront our adversaries, and the more practiced and skilled all of you will be with your powers. This will of course vastly increase our chances of victory when the time comes."

"You didn't specify when, exactly, the time will come—that is, when the Stars will be Right. Do you know?"

"Not exactly. The conditions that make it happen are tied to events here and in that other realm. The appearance of certain agents, and their activities, tells me the cycle has begun anew, and I can *estimate* it; no less than six months, no more than one year from now. As time draws onward, I will gain a better estimate. For now, of course, it is best that we assume it will be sooner rather than later."

"Right. Assume it'll be a very Cthulhu Christmas, then." Steve's voice had steadied. "Well, I guess it's about time to have some leftover pizza. And I've got work tomorrow." He went and got one piece out of the refrigerator. "So, how do we go about finding these others. You said it wasn't going to be as 'easy,' if you can use that word, as finding four more guys willing to do the job."

"Alas, no. While I am permitted the latitude—with, I should add, not inconsiderable personal effort—to shift the choice from a girl of the appropriate age to any other person I find satisfactory, the rest of the spell proceeds once triggered without any control by myself or anyone else, and the other four will follow the ancient pattern set by Holy Aura herself."

Steve froze in the middle of punching in the heating time on the microwave. "Oh, *Christ*. You mean that the other four *actually have to be teenage girls*?"

"I am afraid so, Stephen."

Steve closed his eyes, and Silvertail could hear him counting quietly to himself; the count reached sixty before the man's eyes opened. "Let me get this clear. There are four other Apocalypse Maidens to be found."

"Correct."

"They're particular individuals out there somewhere. That is, I can't just find some teenage girl *I* think would make a good choice and say 'Hey, you're going to be Apocalypse Maiden number two' or whatever."

"Also correct. The magic is already at work. In the original spell, we had the opportunity to select the Maidens ahead of time, place them within the circle, and so on. Ever afterward, the spell, upon being triggered, seeks out . . . well, *appropriate* vessels for the power and links them to the destiny of the Apocalypse Maidens. But I cannot actually see these links until they are close to manifestation."

Steve rolled his eyes. "Do we have *any* idea of where these girls might be, or am I supposed to just start wandering the world, hoping I'll bump into the right ones somewhere between here and Cairo or something?"

Silvertail managed a laugh at that. "It is not *quite* that bad, Stephen. They must be within a relatively short distance of your initial manifestation, and in fact will be found regularly in relatively close proximity in locations where children of their ages gather."

Steve's eyes narrowed. "Just *what* locations?"

"Well . . ." Silvertail found himself very hesitant, yet there was no help for it but to simply move forward. "In prior eras they might be regularly gathered to perform work of some sort, or gather for church, or . . ."

"Christ on a pogo stick. A school. They'll all be going to the same goddamned *high school*, won't they?"

"If there is one such near the area of your first transformation—"

"Yes, there is, dammit, about half a mile off is Whitney High." Steve stared at him accusingly. "You *knew* this from the start."

"Well . . . yes. But it did not matter until now." He could not quite restrain a whisker-twitching smile. "And you should have, given that I mentioned how your world's memes strongly direct these events and phenomena."

Steve grimaced. "Okay, you got me there. I *should* have known. So . . . I have to somehow winnow out four girls from an entire high school. You know, a thirty-five-year-old guy hanging around a high school watching the fourteen-year-old girls closely is gonna end up spending a lot of time behind bars, not saving the universe."

"I understand the implications."

"So . . . oh, my *god*. That's why you *mentioned* high-school students before. You *knew* I'd have to—"

Silvertail nodded. "I see no alternative. You, Stephen Russ, will have to enter the high school in the only acceptable guise—that of a fourteen-year-old girl—to locate, befriend, and ultimately activate, the other four Apocalypse Maidens."

"Son of a—" Stephen stopped, frozen.

When Steve turned back to face Silvertail finally, he wore a smile so cold that it made Silvertail shiver involuntarily. "All right, Silvertail. I remember you saying something else—that you couldn't do much to help me *until I committed*. That means you *can* help me now, *right*?"

"That is true—"

"And you know something, I got a different view of you when I changed. Now that I *have* committed, I'll bet that you *also* have another form you can take. A *human* form. Am I right?"

His perceptions must be astonishingly acute as Holy Aura. He would have been seeing my spirit—and remembering what he saw, even during a most emotionally straining moment. "You are."

He concentrated, and felt the familiar *rush* of power, the triggering of the remnant of the ancient pact in the manner that directly related to him. The light gathered about him, drew him upward, built him up. Silvertail opened his eyes, and for the first time in centuries looked *down* upon the world around him, even upon Steve. "This is my true, original form, Stephen Russ," he said, hearing his own deep voice again. "Varatraine Aylnell, at your service."

"At my service? That's great, Varatraine," Steve said, and slapped him on the shoulder, still wearing that disquieting grin. "Because you're *just* what a fourteen-year-old girl is going to need . . . *DAD*."

✳ Chapter 7 ✳

Steve had to admit there was a *vast* satisfaction in seeing the patrician features of Varatraine *nee* Silvertail go slack-jawed with shock. "Er . . . I *beg* your pardon?"

I need something to keep my mind off the other issues. This conversation hasn't fixed them, just . . . temporarily reduced my panic mode. "You haven't thought this part through, Silvertail. Oh, if it's easier for you, you can pop back to your rat form."

"How . . . kind. What do you mean, I have not thought this through? I have spent a great deal of time thinking of this approach, rather than the prior one."

"In your *prior* approach, your girls all had parents or guardians, I'm betting. Me, though—your Holy Aura is being created out of nothing, or at least nothing you *ever* want to admit to the school administration. Assuming they'd believe you. A fourteen-year-old girl is not an independent adult in this culture. She's expected to have parents or at least a guardian who registers her, looks out for her welfare, tracks whether she's doing her homework, and generally has responsibility for her."

Varatraine blinked, then closed his eyes as though he had a headache. "Ah. I see. You do have a point, Stephen."

"Like they say on TV, but wait, there's more! Where we are right now? Not in Whitney High's school district. You have to get almost over to DIY Home's little mall before you cross into that district. And my hours working at Barron's Bagels, they overlap with school hours.

Now, we're lucky at the moment—school's about to let out for the summer this week, so we don't have to solve these problems this very minute—but the way *I* see it, you're going to have to help me solve at least *three* problems: being Holy Aura's parent, getting an apartment or even a house that's in the Fullertown district, and figuring out how we're going to *live* there when I won't be able to keep working at Barron's."

Another thought occurred to him. "Oh, and we'll have to figure out how to do all the documentation. Which means we need a name for me . . . or her . . . other than Holy Aura and we'll need a social security number and, well, a lot of other stuff."

Varatraine had slowly opened his eyes as Steve continued his narration. Once Steve stopped, Varatraine nodded slowly. "You are correct, Stephen Russ. There is indeed more to do than I had thought. To your latter problem . . . can you show me, or find me, examples of the needed documentation?"

"Ummm . . . Probably. I'll have to check on things like dates and form changes. Like, my social security card was issued when I was born thirty-five years ago, and I'd bet that the cards didn't stay the same up until fourteen years back, so you couldn't use a duplicate of mine. Plus they'll probably check background . . ." It started to become clear to him that this could be a major problem. *Holy Aura, or whatever name we end up using, never* existed *before. We have to fake up her name, probably birth records, and prior school records, employment records and stuff for Varatraine or whatever* his *name will be . . .* "And even if we get past that, I just realized that I won't really be able to work at all. If Holy Aura's going to actually make friends, she'll have to meet up with them outside of school, hang out, really get to know them. Plus actually do her homework and stuff. Yeah, that will *probably* be easier since I've already done the whole high-school thing, but I'll bet they've changed even the curriculum stuff since I was there."

Varatraine shimmered and turned back to the white rat. "I find that I *do* need to stay in this form more," Silvertail said in a peeved tone. "I will need to weave the transformation spells carefully to permit longer-term stability. A considerable annoyance."

He looked up at Steve, a tiny white face with a far-too-wise expression. "However, I believe I can put your other immediate concerns to rest. As you have seen, I still have some significant magic at my disposal. In terms of raw *power*, of course, it does not in any way rival that of Princess Holy Aura or any of our likely adversaries. However, given my rather extended age, I believe I can claim to be more *skilled* with magic than any other mortal being has ever achieved, and one can often substitute skill for power; moreover, most mortal problems are *better* solved through subtlety and caution than through the application of a sledgehammer of power.

"If I understand correctly, in this era as in others, money is a powerful lever."

"Is it ever," Steve said with feeling. "Especially for those of us without it."

"Very well. I can give us access to very significant funds quite easily."

"What? You can . . . what, summon cash or something?" Steve was somewhat ashamed at how eager he felt at the thought. *I have a cosmic mission and here I am thinking that I could maybe afford to have a nice roast chicken for dinner.*

Silvertail laughed. "Not so *outré* a power, no, something rather more mundane. I have been around since the beginning, and over the many, many centuries I have accumulated a little wealth here, a little there, each time the cycle repeated, before I had to return to my small form and remain that way. With practice I have become most proficient at assuring the resources are available in various locations. Just a few touches of magic to assure, shall we say, proper provenance of the resources, and money will cease to be an issue. This will, of course, solve both the problem of your employment and that of where you shall stay."

"That . . . yeah, if by 'cease to be an issue' you mean we can live in decent style, yeah, that solves those problems. But—"

"Yes, the *bona fides* for both Holy Aura and myself as 'Dad' will require some thinking." Silvertail twitched his ears and somehow managed a grin. "And while I admit to being . . . taken unawares by the suggestion, I confess I can think of no better way to provide your civilian self with a proper guardian.

"Still, once I *fully* understand the requirements of documentation, I believe that I can establish background credentials of sufficient solidity, and then we can do whatever the appropriate registration activity is in the proper, mundane manner. This should suffice for a year, which is the longest I can see this having to hold."

Steve couldn't help but grin. "So you can just . . . magic the documentation into existence that shows, oh, I was born in 2001 in Nebraska or something, and moved around until I got here?"

"I certainly believe I can. The great advantage of papers and, once understood, electronics is that it takes very little *energy* to modify them. If your documentation had to be carved into giant stone tablets we could have a serious issue, but for this? I am reasonably confident—if you can guide me in determining *all* of the factors that must be addressed, including the appropriate seals, signatures, forms, and so on."

Wow. "Lucky you're on the side of the good guys. Being able to magically forge documents would be power with *major* potential for abuse."

"In my era, there had to be significant security magic enacted to prevent exactly that, so yes, I am very familiar with the potential implications of that use of my power. In this case, though, I do not see any moral issues; while the identifications and records will be placed retroactively, they will not be used for nefarious purposes, merely to allow you to enter the school for a mission that will save the entire world."

"Yeah, I guess I can give us a pass on that." Steve glanced hesitantly down at him. "How long would it take to deal with the money side of the equation?"

"A few days, no more. As I said, the wealth involved is quite *real*, I merely need to arrange access to it. Why?" Before Steve could answer, Silvertail shook his own head. "A foolish question. You are in economic distress already and this concern will not assist you in focusing on the problems at hand. I will address this issue as quickly as I can, Stephen. And that will not be long, even as you think of things."

"So . . . my savings . . . ?"

Silvertail did not laugh; his tiny face showed great sympathy. "Stephen, for all you are sacrificing I will not begrudge replenishing—indeed, increasing vastly—your own resources. As I said, if we succeed, you shall find yourself improving your position. If we do not . . . I see no reason to force you to live in less than pleasant circumstances."

"Thanks." The little rodent-who-wasn't really did seem to be a decent guy.

But I don't want to be played for a sucker either, so . . . "A couple other questions, Silvertail."

The tiny head tilted, whiskers twitching. "Your tone is serious. Go ahead, then."

"It might be a little late, but . . . I want to know if there's any catches in this arrangement you haven't told me."

"Catches?"

"Yeah. You mentioned you know the memes—that you *promoted* the *mahou shoujo* memes. So you also have to know how some of those things *don't* go so well for the girls. Sure, the outline's usually the same, whether it's *Sailor Moon, Dynamic Avatar Akane, Zenkai Millennium Symmetry*, or *Madoka Magica*: Girl gets chosen to fight evil of some kind and gets a neat new outfit and shiny new powers, usually has a cute sidekick, and usually gets one or more companions along the way, yada yada. *BUT* the *details* vary—and they can be a real screw-fest for the poor girl in the middle. Like, turns out the girl's destiny is to be sacrificed at the end of the show, or that she'll end up turning into one of the monsters, or she's sold her soul as part of the contract and will burn up at the end, et cetera."

"Stephen, I—"

"Hold on. I just want to make it clear I want to know *all* of the 'provisos and quid pro quos.' I know I'm committed to the course—I can *feel* it, really, if I think about it, and that still scares the hell out of me. But if there's any more surprises, I want to know them *now*, even if you're really the bad guy. I'd rather just deal with the betrayal up front."

Silvertail *did* laugh then, long and loud. "Stephen Russ, isn't this something you should have asked *before*?"

"Yeah, probably. So?"

The silvery rat stood on his hind legs and gave a very humanlike shrug. "Stephen, if I were the 'bad guy,' do you think I'd just tell you like that?"

"Might, since you've already got me suckered. But sure, you could still lie, I guess."

"I could. But I will not. Stephen, I have to admit that I probably won't *think* of all of the . . . 'gotchas,' so to speak, in this most unique situation. But I will tell you the remaining . . . well, not traps or tricks, but key aspects of the situation as they may pertain to you."

"Better than nothing, anyway."

"First . . . no, I am in no way the 'bad guy,' at least as you and I would view it. I am not *perfect* by any stretch of the imagination, but the mission I have for you, and the others, is exactly as I told you. It is not in my plans, and certainly would in *no* way please me, for any of you to meet an untimely end during the final, or any other, battle. It is my most fervent hope that you will all succeed and emerge alive from the conflict, and I believe that all of you can; your predecessors mostly did, and all of them *did* succeed—obviously—in the main mission.

"Our enemies, of course, are aware of my existence, although they cannot trace me directly. They will be preparing a response to your presence. That, too, will be affected by the *zeitgeist*, the memes of your era."

"So I can expect not just monsters but demon generals, dark magical girls, something like that?"

"Something of the sort. Exactly what I cannot predict, but there will definitely be coordinated assaults as well as random perils." He twitched his whiskers. "Each of the Apocalypse Maidens will have their own . . . psychological issues. Overcoming adversity—sacrifice, in other words—is as much a part of their existence and power as it is yours. We already know much of your challenge, and undoubtedly there are aspects of that which we have yet to understand."

"But my new friends are also going to have some kind of baggage they have to deal with." Steve sighed, but that didn't actually bother him as much. *Helping kids deal with their issues, well, I've done that before. This'll be a lot* different, *but I actually like helping people work out their problems.* "I can live with that."

"Good. The power of our adversaries will of course increase as we get closer to the time when Azathoth Nine-Armed manifests. I will get a better idea of when that time will *be* after a few months." He looked down thoughtfully, then looked up. "I believe I mentioned this, but I should emphasize—any people killed directly by our adversaries will remain dead in the . . . repaired continuity. This makes it very important to fight efficiently and well; there truly are lives at stake in this world and the one we hope will exist."

Steve nodded. *That* part didn't make him happy, but it did, as Silvertail said, make this a lot less of a game, something with real stakes. He wasn't just marking time until the Big Bad showed up, what he . . . well, *she* did was going to matter right from the start.

For the first time since the transformation, he felt himself smile with wonder. "My god, I really *did* turn into a superhero and beat the hell out of a monster, didn't I?"

"You did indeed, Stephen Russ, and did so in a way . . . most uniquely your own."

"What? You mean my catchphrase?"

Silvertail snorted. "Well, yes, there *was* that, but I meant in the more . . . direct approach you used. The Silverlight Weapon can *channel* the power of Holy Aura into a powerful attack. I admit I had underestimated just how powerful you are—I would *not* have expected a direct physical assault to work on a rock-worm of that size."

"So I've got signature attacks too."

"As you said, Stephen, the outline of the meme is very well known. But we will discuss these when next you are ready to transform. I think that can be left for another day."

Something *much* more urgent suddenly occurred to him. "Oh, one more thing. How often can we expect attacks?"

"Initially, not very frequently. But once more than two or three of the Maidens have been gathered . . . once a week, on average."

Well, of course. One episode a week. I should have guessed. "So I shouldn't be needed in the next few days?"

"No, I would not think so."

"And you'll have money for me in the next few days?"

"Yes. I will promise you that much."

Steve stretched, finally feeling *one* set of tensions slowly starting to fade away, replaced by a much more mundane and urgent demand. "All right, then—I'm going to order us some *real* food!"

✳ Chapter 8 ✳

"You're *leaving?*"

A sharp stab of guilt made Steve wince. "Yeah. I'm sorry, guys. I'll really miss our games, getting together to hang out, all of that."

Dex looked particularly shellshocked by the sudden announcement, which only made it worse. *His parents aren't* bad, *but they just aren't on his wavelength, and I'm one of the few people that really gets along with him.*

Anne, on the other hand, looked excited. "You've gotten another job?"

Have I ever. "Yeah, from a friend of mine from my Air Force days. He's started his own company and he wanted someone willing to run his security."

It *really* rubbed him raw to lie to his friends this way. But there was no reason to drag them into it; none of them were the right age, nor had any daughters or sisters the right age, to be the Apocalypse Maidens. So he and Silvertail had figured out this story as a decent cover. *After all, it only has to last a year at most . . . and after that, either I'll be dead, or things will go back to the way they were, but start getting better. Who knows; maybe this story will turn out to be the truth afterward!*

"How much is he *paying* you?" asked Eli, the ever-cynical.

"A *lot* more than I've made anywhere else. I guess he's got a bunch of investors, and he's paying for the fact he trusts me as much as anything."

Chad grinned ruefully. "Well, I'm happy for you, Steve—I'm sure we all are—but *damn* I'll really miss not knowing what happens in the end of the campaign!"

"Who knows; maybe I'll be able to come back and run it once in a while, once things get settled down out there. Maybe a few games a year?"

"That would be awesome," Mike said. "But, hey, you do what you have to. Working at Barron's Bagels, that really wasn't much of a career, right?"

Ain't that the truth. Except I never really had the drive to go elsewhere. I . . . always felt I was waiting for something.

Now I wonder if I really was.

The others filtered out of the apartment. Dex, as usual, hung back. "So . . . you're really leaving soon?"

"Moving out tomorrow, actually," he answered, and saw his friend's expression drop even more.

"Um . . . you need help?"

"No," he said. *Don't think I could stand to keep lying the whole time.* "I've got everything pretty much set; not taking the bed, I've packed up most of the other stuff."

"Yeah, I should've noticed. Thought things looked more empty. But you didn't pack—"

"I'll finish that tonight," he said, following the high schooler's gaze to the wall of weapons. "Won't take all that long. Thought the room would *really* have felt bare without it and the posters."

Dex's expression was so forlorn that it *hurt* to look at him. *I used to be like that. What would I have felt like if old Lee had left on me when I was that age?*

Steve stepped forward, opened the case and pulled out a futuristic handgun. "Here, Dex; you take it."

Dex's eyes widened. "The *blaster* from *Lucky Starr*? No, Steve, I can't! That's an *original*. The most valuable thing you—"

"What makes it valuable is people who want to own it. I know that's been the one thing in my collection you've wanted, and . . . well, I want you to take care of it for me. If I come back, you can give it back to me. Because you're more valuable than any old model."

Dex suddenly threw his arms around Steve, a startling display of emotion from the usually controlled, unconsciously sarcastic boy. "I'll take care of it," he said, then let go as suddenly as he'd started the hug.

Dex's eyes were wet. "Steve . . . look, I'm glad for you. I really am. I *hated* seeing you living like this, day-to-day worries. I couldn't *do* anything about it, but I hated it. If you're going somewhere where you can live better, I'm happy. Really." He scrubbed at his eyes furiously, wiping away the tears.

"Dex . . ." For an instant he *really* wanted to tell Dex the truth. Almost did. But Steve had no intention of putting a friend that good in danger. "Thanks."

"Welcome," the boy said, voice a little thick. He took the blaster model, looked at it reverently, then tucked it carefully into his backpack. "Well . . . email me, anyway, please?"

Steve grinned. "You bet."

The smile faded as he heard the footsteps diminish away and the lower door shut. "Dammit."

"I know, Stephen," Silvertail said. "There are few mundane tasks more difficult than saying goodbyes to friends."

"Especially when I'm lying to them."

"We did—"

"Yeah, yeah, we agreed, you're right." Steve looked out the dark window, made out the slender figure walking away; he saw Dexter turn, look back; his shoulders sagged, then he turned away, shrugged, and walked out of sight. "Still felt like I was a total dick, though."

"Perhaps. Anyone might. But if I understand correctly, the item you just gave Dex in the name of your friendship was worth enough that you could have paid a year's rent with it."

"More than that. Even given that I'd never actually get what it's worth. Yeah, it was, but if I ever sold it, I'd never get one again. A friend of mine gave it to me years ago; I guess it's just *right* that I give it to one of mine."

"Odd that a boy so young seems your closest friend."

"Closest one *here*, maybe; almost all of my old buddies are scattered around the country, a couple of them are dead. Why Dex? Because he's so damned smart he sometimes seems older. And sometimes I guess he just appealed to my older brother side. Dunno, we just always seemed to *mesh* well, especially for gaming.

"Anyway, we *are* set for the real move, right?"

"Everything has been arranged. You did *very* well in your trips to the library and various government agencies. I was able to understand all of the various requirements to make us 'real people' in the eyes of the law."

"You really got us into the system? For real?"

"I did." The white rat produced—from the same nowhere that it hid the golden crown in whenever there were visitors—a large manila envelope, which almost tipped the creature over. "Mphhh . . . Take a look."

Stephen carefully opened the envelope. There were two slightly smaller envelopes inside. One was labeled "Holly Owen," the other "Trayne Owen."

"Holly Owen. *Holly Owen? Seriously*, Silvertail? You couldn't think of a better alias for Holy Aura than *that*?"

He swore there was a smug smile on the rat's face. "It fits with your world's memes, and if I cannot have some amusement in this job, what in the world is the *point*?"

"Great. I join the ranks of second-rank heroes and villains everywhere." Still, he had to admit it was a perfectly *reasonable* name, and would be pretty easy to remember. Opening the envelope, he found a social security card—of the right design—a birth certificate showing Holly had been born in Los Angeles (conveniently all the way on the other side of the country), medical records showing all her immunizations were up to date, educational records showing she had done well in school up through junior high, and more. "Holy . . . I know you *said* you could do this, but *seeing* it is something else. Even a valid *passport*?"

"While unlikely, it is *possible* we may have to travel some considerable distance, so having a passport seemed prudent."

Mr. Trayne Owen's envelope was fatter because it contained records of his work career and showed that Mr. Owen was a well-paid independent consultant for multiple high-profile technology firms. "This will explain both the fact that I have considerable wealth, and that I do not have to go to an office regularly," Silvertail said. "It will be important for me to be available for you in our search for the other Maidens, and to advise you in the event of new conflicts."

"I see you've got a driver's license. Can you actually *drive*?"

Another ridiculously smug look. "Indeed I can, Stephen."

"How the *hell* did you manage that?"

"I have observed drivers at length, and learned all of the

requirements. The *arcana* of proper clutch use and shifting might remain beyond me, but I will be using an automatic."

"Just *watching* does not teach you how to drive, Silvertail."

"When you augment it with *magic* so that the reflexes and motions are transferred to yourself with repetition, along with perceptual reaction . . . yes, it does."

"Well . . . damn. That's sort of cheating."

"It *is* cheating in that sense, yes. And we may be doing a lot more 'cheating' in addition to my inventing us identities that are no more real than a mirage."

"I guess. Okay, you *do* need to be able to drive around here, so that's good."

He began packing the remaining weapons into a box. It only took a couple of hours to finish packing all the other stuff he wanted to take. "I'm ready."

"Make sure, Stephen. Once you've left, we will not return."

"I'm sure. Not like I had all that much stuff to bring with me."

He looked once more around the little apartment, looking forlorn and dingy now that it was emptied, posters removed, weapons gone, just some battered furniture and appliances. Still . . . it had been home for years. "Goodbye," he said.

Carrying the last box, he walked down the stairs; the door swung shut behind him.

✶ Chapter 9 ✶

Steve looked around the huge furnished basement again, trying to distract himself from what he was about to do. "Dang, I still can't believe we're living in this place. *Thousands* of square feet, including this, what, cut-price Danger Room?"

"Call it a practice room or perhaps dojo," Silvertail, who was now in the shape of 'Trayne Owen'—a tall, slender, distinguished looking gentleman with black hair touched with pure silver at the temples, lightly tanned. His eyes were brilliant blue, a startling contrast to the hair, and his voice was not the tenor that Steve generally associated with the *mahou shoujo* spirit advisors but a deep, warm bass. "Neither your technology nor my limited magic is up to creating a 'danger room' as you envision it. But making a room that is secure and reinforced enough to survive some abuse, that can be done." He raised one dark eyebrow. "You seem particularly nervous, Steve. What is it today?"

"Kinda silly, I guess," Steve answered, feeling embarrassment trying to well up. "I mean, I know I'm committed to the course, but what I'm about to do . . . it's really sort of sealing it."

"I admit to not seeing it that way, but your perceptions are your own. However, is there any point in delaying?"

"No . . . guess not." He swallowed, grasped the Star Nebula Brooch, and focused on the need to protect people—his friends, family, those who could not defend themselves. "To avert the Apocalypse, and shield the innocent from evil, and stand against the powers of destruction, I offer myself as wielder and weapon, as symbol and sword! Mistress of the spirit, ruler of the stars beyond, Mystic Galaxy Defender, Princess Holy Aura!"

Once more the echoing words called forth argent luminance that erased him in a chime of victory and renewal, rebuilt that which had been and would ever be in tingling silver sunshine, formed into a girl slender and strong as steel. She opened her eyes, already in the battle pose that she knew was the ending of the transformation. "Wow," she said. "I mean . . . I did this before, but I was so scared, angry, confused . . . I couldn't *see* it, *feel* it like that. Was it so . . . beautiful before?"

"It is *always* beautiful, more beautiful each time than the last," Silvertail—Trayne—said, his voice rough with emotion. "I am glad you can see it that way . . . Holly?"

"Holy Aura right now . . . but yes, I guess you'd better just call me Holly." She stared in wonder at her arms and hands. "Well, that's *one* way to lose weight."

"Technically, of course, it is not lost, merely . . . displaced, turned to potential rather than actuality. Was your trepidation due to the simple fact of the transformation?"

She laughed, hearing the sound echo back like a golden bell. "No, that wasn't it. It's that I'm not changing *back* for a long time. Maybe not for a year."

Trayne Owen—*since that's how I'd better think of him when he's human*—frowned. "That is not at all necessary, Ste . . . Holly. I had assumed that you would spend a great deal of time as Stephen Russ, whenever possible."

"That *was* my first thought," she said, walking, feeling the *shift* in weight and motion that was at once completely *wrong* and . . . somehow . . . exactly *right*, and that was scary enough that she stopped and focused only on talking. "Umm . . . yeah. I thought that at first, but then I realized I'd be setting myself up for total disaster.

"I need to get *used* to being Holly Owen/Holy Aura, being her for a *long* time, because I'm going to be spending *hours* around teenagers every day when school starts, and if I'm going to have *any* chance of making contact with the right people, and making friends? I can't be clueless about how to *live* like this."

"Hm. You have a point. But I am still not clear as to why you would have to—as you implied—never turn back until the task is done."

"I might change back once in a while, for various reasons . . ." she conceded, and swallowed hard again, "... if for no other reason than to remind me who I really am, because you know, I still find the fact that I'm a girl and absolutely *accepting* that to be really creepy. Because the other part of me isn't accepting it *at all*, you know."

Holly could see real concern on Trayne's face. "Are you all right?"

"Of *course* I'm not! This is completely freaky! But I have to be all right with it by the time I actually meet the other Apocalypse Maidens. And I absolutely *am not* going to be that cliché, where the guy who gets his sex changed doesn't even learn the *basics* about being a girl, gets surprised by having her first period, walks into the boys' room without thinking about it, all those low-comedy tropes. Thanks, I'm going to be the lead in a *serious* Magical Girl show, not a joke."

Trayne rubbed his chin. "This could take considerable time, Holy Aura. We do not—"

"We are *not* going to rush this and screw it up," Holly said with as much finality as her soprano voice could manage. "School won't be in session for a couple months. If I practice living like . . . *being* Holly Owen for that long, I won't blow my role the first time someone startles me. I have enough female relatives and friends to know that I'd damn well *better* know if having my period's going to—do you *know* how weird it sounds to say that phrase?—having it's going to just annoy me, or lay me up for a day or three. I'm *assuming* that this is a real honest-to-God fourteen-year-old girl's body and that means it *will* have a monthly cycle, yes?"

"I am afraid so, yes. You are as real as any other young woman, including the annoyances that may incur."

"Right. So I have to learn how to deal with that. Have to figure out how to *dress*—I assume I can't just summon regular clothes out of nowhere to replace this useless-looking sparkly magical girl armor?"

"No. We can . . . tweak the transformation so that you switch between Holly Owen and Holy Aura rather than between Stephen and Holy Aura, and in that case changing back to Holly would also put her in whatever clothes Holly was wearing at the time, but Holly would still have had to dress herself beforehand."

"Man, I'll have to learn so much. How to dress right and *wear* the stuff right." Holly shook her head. "Freaks me out, really." She *tried* to make it come out light, but the trembling in her voice gave her away. *Not nearly as relaxed about this as I want to make myself think.*

She was seized by an almost irresistible urge to change back, become *Stephen* again. *No,* she told herself, *this will* not *get any easier if I put it off. If I do . . . I might even hesitate the next time a monster comes calling, and that could get me—and a lot of other people—killed. I made this decision, I have to stick with it!*

"It strikes me," Trayne said slowly, apparently unaware of the conflict within her, "that you are . . . oddly nonchalant about the whole idea of dressing in girls' clothing. Or is that an act?"

She seized the question like a lifeline, a focus of something to think about. "No, no, not really. I mean, my being all *calm* is sort of an act . . . actually, totally an act, I want to run around screaming or just change back *right now* . . . but the wearing girls' clothing? Well, I *will* be a girl, so it's not like Stephen-me walking around in women's clothing. And I've been in plays—tried out for Dr. Frank N. Furter in *Rocky Horror* one year, in fact . . . anyway, I can play the role. But I *do* have to get used to it, or I'll blow the role at the worst possible time."

"Well, I do have the simple outfits you asked me to pick up. Having seen many young women of your age, I believe I was able to do reasonably well in terms of size."

"Guess I'd better go change. How's this going to work with the armor outfit?"

"Let me think a moment." Trayne suddenly shrank back to the white rat. "I cannot perform much magic unless I am in this form; most of it is being used to hold the human shape otherwise," said Silvertail Heartseeker. "Now let me see . . ."

The little animal scurried around Holly's feet three times clockwise, three times counterclockwise, and then stopped before her, intoning something in what she had to assume was ancient Lemurian. "*Aiylen ta vrayna, hai embreisan!*" he finished, and a brilliant fountain of rainbow light enveloped her, sent a tingling electric shock through her body. "There. I believe that if you now simply *will* yourself to become Holly Owen the accoutrements of Holy Aura will vanish."

"Okay, I'll try it when I go to change." She picked up the bags Trayne had indicated. "Be right back."

Steve made it into the bathroom and collapsed to the floor, shaking. *Part of me really* thinks *of itself as Holy Aura. I hear "Holy Aura" or even "Holly" and part of me's already saying "Oh, that's me." Jesus. Am I going to lose* myself? She visualized herself as a man, and shuddered at the realization that it was almost as hard to do that as it had been before to visualize himself as a woman.

It really was too much. She knew she *had* to accept this, could *not* yield to the temptation to change back, not now, not so soon, but she . . . Steve . . . also felt she couldn't bear another second of this alien-yet-absolutely-right body. Tears began to stream down her face and she gave a scream of fear and frustration and slammed her arm against the tub.

The porcelain-coated cast iron shattered like candy glass, the impact a cannon shot that shook the house, showering her with debris, cracking the ceiling above. The shock snapped her out of her panic. "Holy moley, as the Captain used to say," she murmured, staring in disbelief at the slender arm and delicate, long-fingered hand which were not damaged—not even *scraped*—by that titanic impact.

"Holy Aura! Are you all right?" Silvertail's worried voice came through the door.

"Okay. Yeah, okay for now. Sorry about that. We'll have to replace the tub and get the room fixed."

"Are you *certain* you are all right?" Silvertail asked again. His concern was unmistakable. "I am not worried about repairs. I am worried about *you*. I have placed a nearly intolerable burden on you, Stephen, and—"

"It's *done*, Silvertail," she said, not without a touch of anger, but controlled this time, controlled, not running away. "I have to deal with it. I was freaking out, yes, but my superhuman tantrum snapped me out of it. I'll finish changing and then get out of here."

She brushed away the debris and opened up the bags carefully. *Panties—nice simple ones, thank God . . . jeans . . . T-shirt . . . bra? Jesus, yes, I'm going to have to wear one. Don't want to think about that. But no avoiding it.* Even without looking down, she could feel that she was . . . well developed for a fourteen-year-old girl. Not ridiculously so (*thank* GOD *that part of the meme isn't applying*) but more than enough to make a brassiere a normal part of her clothing in this here and now.

She concentrated on reversing the change, and in a flash of light the crystal boots, sparkling skirt, and other elements of Princess Holy Aura's *mahou shoujo* existence disappeared. *Aaaaand now I'm naked. Does that make me automatically now a peeping tom? It's my body, but it's not.* She tried to avoid looking *down* too much as she dressed, but the contours that were, once more, alien yet familiar tried to draw the eye . . . and the panic.

Finally she was dressed and stood, shakily, to leave. A movement caught her attention and for the first time she looked at the mirror . . . and froze.

A waterfall of shining deep purple, eyes that shimmered with the depths of the twilight sky, a face drawn from legends and a form from the dreams of angels, wearing a simple black T-shirt and jeans. Holly Owen stared back at her, eyes haunted with unnamed fears, yet with a face filled with utter determination and a strength Steve had not imagined.

Her mouth was dry and her eyes stung, and she realized she had been *staring* in utter disbelief for . . . minutes? "That's . . . *me*?" she whispered. "Oh, crap."

"What is it, Steve? You sound . . . worse."

"Just realizing that this *is* worse," she said, finally tearing her gaze from the impossibility in the mirror and yanking the door open.

Silvertail blinked in surprise. "I see nothing wrong."

"I don't look like 'a teenage girl,' Silvertail! I look like . . . like . . . like some idealized *image* of a teenage girl! I haven't TOUCHED a makeup case and I look like someone took four hours and Photoshop to make me look perfect! Half the girls are going to hate me just on looks alone, and the boys are all going to act like complete *idiots* around me, when they're not following me around!"

Silvertail sighed. "The meme of the magical girl—and for that matter, the superheroine—makes much of that rather inescapable. Your appearance is something of a trial for me as well, I must confess."

"Why? Do I look like some fantasy of yours?" As he said that, Steve-Holly knew that had gone too far. "Sorry. Sorry. I didn't mean that."

"I should hope not. Holly . . . you look almost identical to my daughter, as I have remembered her throughout the centuries. Holy Aura always *echoed* Aureline, of course . . . but only you have ever *duplicated* her." The pain in the tiny voice was all too real, and it reached Holly through her self-absorbed conflict. "Now she stands before me again, reborn in you . . . and once more, I must send her—you—into the dangers that I cannot face."

"Oh. Jesus, I'm sorry, Silvertail." She felt the pain of the older man acutely, remembering her losses as Steve. *Imagine seeing someone that looked like Mom, exactly like her, and knowing I had to send her into, well, what* I *am going into.* "I . . . well, I guess there's not much I can do about that, but . . ."

"No, there is not," he said. "But perhaps . . . perhaps it is *right* that it be so. I must act like your father; seeing you like this, I realize that will be far easier than I had thought." A wan, tiny smile crossed the furry face. "And I do not think you will do less than honor to her memory."

"Thanks, Silvertail." As the other shimmered and turned back to the tall human form, she corrected herself: ". . . Dad."

He chuckled, though there was still a note of tears in his voice before he cleared his throat. "You are welcome, of course."

There was a pause of uncomfortable silence. Holly looked back, seeing the wreckage of the tub. "Ugh. That *has* to get cleaned up. I guess we could at least put all the pieces into what's left of the tub." She stepped back into the bathroom and reached down to pick up the largest chunk of cast iron—and nearly fell over. "What the heck . . . ?"

"Ah. Yes, that is an obvious consequence."

"What? I just broke this thing like it was made of saltine crackers a second ago—"

"*Princess Holy Aura* broke it. *Holly Owen*, like Stephen Russ, is a normal human being," Trayne Owen said. "I transposed, or rather added, the transformation to a female form, as you indicated, but the conversion to, well, mortality remains an integral part of the enchantment. And as a fourteen-year-old girl, even one in excellent physical condition, you have nothing even close to the physical strength that Stephen Russ possessed."

"Oh, I get it. Makes sense, I guess. And that does keep me from accidentally doing something that blows my cover. I won't have Clark Kent's problems."

"No. But I see now that your determination to take significant time to accustom yourself to this life was even wiser than I had thought; you have many assumptions in the way you conduct yourself that are predicated on your size and strength, as well as your sex. You will need to recognize and address all of them."

It was a little disconcerting to realize that she couldn't even *lift* things she-as-Stephen would have moved easily, but Silvertail was right. And the fact was that their conversation had stilled—at least for the moment—her panic and confusion. She straightened. “Fine, I’ll leave it to *you* to clean up. For now, I guess I’d better get started on that practice!”

✳ Chapter 10 ✳

"Nice to get out of the house!" Holly said, probably for the fourth time in the last hour now that she thought of it.

But it *was* true. The last few weeks had been spent mostly indoors, practicing the many different aspects of just being a teenage girl . . . and learning the pitfalls. These included mundane annoyances like finding that a five-foot-seven-inch teenage girl couldn't reach shelves that Stephen Russ at over six feet had no trouble getting to, and more involved and disturbing problems like dealing with menstruation.

At least I don't *have crippling cramps most of the time. It* hurts *sort of like having eaten a really gas-producing burrito—though not exactly like that—but it doesn't put me down for days.*

Silvertail hadn't replied, probably figuring that there was no reply he hadn't already made. "Are you ready to look for new outfits?" he asked, looking around the bustling mall with its dozens or hundreds of shops, and the constant flow and curl of people eddying through the broad walkways in front of the stores.

"Sure am!" Holly felt a touch of anticipation at the idea, and while a part of her was thinking *Well, that's stereotypical, isn't it?* the other part knew that much of the reason was perfectly obvious: as Stephen Russ, he'd been stuck very, very rarely buying clothes, and almost always the cheapest, most straightforward clothing he could get—jeans, T-shirts or an occasional inexpensive polo shirt, simple white or black socks, sneakers.

Now, with Silvertail's resources, Holly could buy pretty much anything she wanted to wear . . . and while the thought still sometimes gave her a bit of a jolt, she actually looked good enough to make buying the right clothes really worthwhile!

But, fortunately, not *too* good. "Oh, and Dad? Thanks for, um, toning down my looks a little."

"You're welcome, Holly," he said with a flash of a smile. "That must be a unique event—being thanked for making someone *less* attractive."

"Still a good thing," she said, glancing in the window of *Current Memes* and seeing her reflection. The black-haired girl with wide eyes was still going to always attract attention—Holly Owen remained beautiful, no doubt about it—but not the incomparably mesmerizing, Photoshop-shaming perfection that had been. Princess Holy Aura might—probably would—always look like that, but that just made it more important to have a little mundanity in Holly Owen's appearance.

"Yes, I concur," Silvertail said. "And I should thank you for your insistence. You were right in more ways than one."

It belatedly occurred to Holly that they maybe shouldn't be talking about these things in public, but then she realized that in some ways, this was the most secure place to talk outside of the house; a thousand conversations rose and rustled about them, murmuring a thousand concerns mundane and vital, and no one was likely to ever overhear more than a word or two of anyone else's without being obvious in their eavesdropping. "Right? About what?" she asked, trying to decide where she wanted to shop first. *Current Memes* was actually a good candidate for later, but right now she wanted more straightforward clothes.

"For insisting that I was viewing the past—and especially my daughter—through a filter of guilt and nostalgia, elevating her to perfection. You were entirely right; she and her friends were not the vision that Holy Aura is; they *became* that vision, and symbolized the ideals represented, by their transformations, but in life they were no more perfection than anyone." He looked at her again and smiled with a fondness that looked beyond the present. "Indeed, in this form you truly look very, very much like her, now that I have cleared the haze from memory. And that will certainly make it easier to play the part of a proper father."

She smiled back. "Well, I'm glad. You're welcome!"

Suddenly Holly spotted another clothing store—*Youth At*

Heart—and she *loved* the look of the deep electric-blue top in the window. "Oh, over here!" she said, and turned, striding quickly toward the entrance, which was across the hall and down.

Wham!

Holly found herself on the ground, having cannonballed off a big man with a bushy red beard streaked with gray. The man looked at her with a combination of concern and annoyance. "You okay?"

She felt Silvertail's hand helping her up. "Um, yeah—"

"Good. But watch where you're going." He looked at Silvertail. "She ran right into me!"

Mr. Owen nodded. "A bit too focused on her destination. Watch yourself, Holly."

"But—" she saw a warning glint in Silvertail's glance, dropped her own gaze. "Okay. Sorry," she said to the man.

"No problem. Glad you're okay." He continued on his way.

Dammit, what the hell's going on? I know *I was perfectly clear to head where I was going!*

It wasn't worth arguing with Silvertail about, especially not at this point, and the two of them entered the store and browsed without further incident. Besides the electric-blue top, there were two others, one black with a deep-violet lace front and another a brilliant red, that really appealed to her.

I think I'm seeing colors *differently. More intense, and more differentiated.* "Hey, Dad, is there really a difference between male and female color vision?"

"There is, in fact. It appears to be at least partially mediated by hormonal development and related changes; even here, those who change their physical sex from male to female have often reported a clear increase in their color perceptions, and in Lemuria it was well-demonstrated. It is not quite so . . . drastic as your culture's stereotypes might make it, but it is a very real effect."

"Wow. Learn something new every day."

She continued looking around. Some new jeans were definitely indicated, as well as some other pants. Holly wasn't sure she was quite ready to try skirts, outside of the *mahou shoujo* outfit, but shorts, definitely. Another store caught her eye and she immediately headed for that one.

She found herself brought up short when a path she thought was clear enough . . . suddenly wasn't. *Second time. Which means it's* me, *not them.*

Okay, what the hell *is going on?* "Silver . . . Dad, am I nuts, or did those people all just *ignore* where I was going?"

He sighed. "Not precisely. Observe, Holly. You *must* observe the world around you, through eyes not blinded by what you were used to."

It suddenly dawned on her what Silvertail meant. She remembered how *he*—Stephen Russ—walked. Just the way she was trying to, confident, focused, and certain.

But the people around here *towered* above her for the most part. It was like walking through a mall mostly populated by members of championship basketball teams. "Oh. It really *is* me."

"I am afraid so," Silvertail answered. "You are used to being a very large man, and—entirely without your conscious intent—you *know* that people tend to give you a fairly wide berth. You are now far less visible, and thus far less subconsciously intimidating, than Stephen Russ."

Holly didn't like that thought, but it made sense. "So I've been an asshole all my life?"

"Knowing your personality, Stephen, I am quite sure you never consciously thought about it—and neither did most people you have encountered. They simply saw a tall, very wide man approaching and gave said man, who looked like he knew exactly where he was going, the space he needed. Admittedly, I think it will do you no harm to learn to watch where you are going more carefully and observe others around you with greater consideration."

"So it's not because I'm a girl now."

"No. Oh, there *will* be difficulties you will encounter from that change, especially in the way individuals interact with you, but at this level your perceived sex, as such, is not truly relevant. Your size and your age and perceived *position* is much more on-point."

Still sounds like I was being a self-absorbed dick before. But I'll let Silvertail be the judge on that. "But if I'm walking right next to a six-foot-something dude who's clearly my dad, instead of running on ahead without looking, I won't have that problem."

"True enough."

As they continued shopping, she paid more attention to the people around them, and the way salespeople behaved. *They always talk to*

Mr. Owen first, and Holly second. Which makes sense with what Silvertail said, because Mr. Owen is the adult, and presumably the guy who will be deciding if Holly can actually get the shoes, dress, whatever. I'm not an adult any more. I'm a teenager, a young *teenager, and that means I'm still mostly a kid.*

The obvious exception to that attitude was boys Holly's age, or a bit older, who often stared at her. *And sometimes guys a* lot *older, which is getting into creep territory.* But *that* change she'd already expected. *Even with the changes Silvertail made, Holly Owen's going to turn a lot of heads.* The more direct stares *were* pretty annoying, though.

Still, after another hour or so she'd found a lot of clothes of all types that she needed, and she took some slight pleasure out of having the taller, stronger Silvertail/Mr. Owen carry most of it. "Can we get lunch?"

"Is it really that time?" He glanced at the watch on his wrist. "I suppose it is. Yes, let's get something."

The nearest decent location was Hearty's, a sort of upscale burger place with other family-type meal selections. The place was crowded, and the two of them found themselves seated in the back, not far from the restrooms, at the only remaining two-seat table. Despite the busyness of the hour, the waitstaff were prompt, and Holly ordered two triple-decker Chipotle Challenge burgers with a large order of Hearty's steak fries. "Plus I want one of your honey-barbeque wing appetizers, and a salad with ranch!" she finished.

The young man taking their order failed to restrain a raising eyebrow, and he glanced at Mr. Owen. Silvertail smiled and nodded. "And I will have the Classic Combo, I think."

The Classic Combo was a single-patty regular burger with a medium fry and drink. Holly grinned at the server as he walked off still looking confused. "I guess a lot of people are going to look at my appetite funny."

"That they will. Not only are you eating to sustain a body they cannot see, one that has an adult man's metabolism, but also you will be expending more energy in transformations and battles—whenever we have them."

"It's been quite a while. When—"

He shrugged. "Soon, probably. But until you start to seek out the other Apocalypse Maidens in earnest, there will be little to draw them out. They will be active, and there will be incidents in the next month or two before you enter school, but where and when? That I cannot predict." He looked at her with a faint smile. "Still, I am not sure that you need *that* much food."

She stuck her tongue out at him. *And am I just playing the part, being immature naturally, or changing? This whole thing is still bizarre and scary, even when it's getting to be almost mundane.*

As Holly was plowing through her second burger, a customer came out of the bathroom and went to the front desk. A moment later Holly caught a fragment from one of the other people going by: ". . . clogged, so Brent, go clear it out. And mop up after."

Ugh, thought Holly. *Sure hope that doesn't mean we're going to get the stink of a clogged toilet* here *while we're eating.*

Even as she thought that, Brent went by them and into the bathroom; she could distantly hear the sound of someone getting out a plunger and starting work.

There was a wet *SPLOOSH!* noise, and suddenly Brent came tumbling out into view, eyes wide. He skidded to a stop on his rear, staring back the way he'd come.

Laughter rippled around the restaurant, which intensified as the plunger then followed, describing a lazy circle in the air before landing with a hollow *thonk* in front of Brent, and finally a blue-and-white scrub brush flipped through the air and bounced ineffectually off Brent's forehead.

Holly was not laughing. She saw goosebumps rising on her arms as though the air had turned to ice, and Silvertail was slowly easing out of his seat.

Then, as Brent scrambled to his feet, there was a deep, sucking, *muttering* noise, as of a set of air-filled sewage pipes the size of the New York City sewers, and the laughter cut off . . .

And turned to screams as something black as night thundered from the bathroom corridor.

✳ Chapter 11 ✳

Holly dove reflexively to the side, rolling and pushing herself up against the wall, and saw Silvertail—Mr. Owen—already in the corner.

The black mass flowed, an avalanche of night, and abruptly red and blue and yellow *eyes* appeared along the shapeless flanks, uncountable mouths opened, and a gibbering laughter echoed from them all, in voices from ear-piercingly high to *basso profundo* growls that shuddered through the air. The tide of obscene black slime split around tables and patrons frozen in midflight, rose up around them, staring with mocking, chilling hunger at each person caught in this flash-flood abomination.

What the hell *is that?*

The thing continued to run, a river of living tar, glistening and with a foul, sulfurous odor, out the doorway. *This has* got *to be one of our enemies! I have to—*

Even as she started to rise, she felt Silvertail's hand on her shoulder. "Not yet," he said, and she could hear the leashed fury and tension, the desire to say instead *Yes, now*.

But she understood, now that he'd stopped her from just *acting* on impulse. *We have to be able to* hide *from our enemies. If I change here, in front of both human* and *monstrous witnesses, they'll know who I am in both guises. They'll be able to trace us. And we can't keep making new identities.*

The wave of leering, mad-eyed corruption passed out the doorway, leaving the floor blackened and warped by its passage. Screams and curses echoed back from the rest of the mall, but the remaining patrons in Hearty's first cautiously, then with terrified speed, began to flee. *Judging by the direction they're all turning, the thing flowed off to the left; everyone's running to the right. That direction will take it straight to the center of the mall.*

"Why isn't it *killing* anyone?" she murmured, hearing her voice shaking. *I'm terrified,* she realized with a strange, breathless abstraction. *Absolutely sweaty-palmed shaking terrified. I know that thing's evil. I know it* wants *to kill. Why isn't it?*

Silvertail's answer held no comfort. "Oh, it shall," he said grimly. "But first it will sow panic and terror. And it has in all likelihood already sealed the doors of the mall; there is no escape from it, so it can kill at leisure."

The last of the mob disappeared out the door; Silvertail glanced around, then made a subtle gesture and whispered words that Holly couldn't quit catch. The security cameras suddenly sparked and smoked. "*Now,*" he said.

Holly took a breath. "To avert the Apocalypse, and shield the innocent from evil, and stand against the powers of destruction, I offer myself as wielder and weapon, as symbol and sword!" The words came easily, naturally, and despite her fear her voice had steadied, rang out with an echoing power beyond that of mere speech. "Mistress of the spirit, ruler of the stars beyond, Mystic Galaxy Defender, Princess Holy Aura!"

The silver light exploded about her again, renewing and rebuilding, summoning forth the armor and weapon that were hers, funneling into her a nigh-limitless strength and certainty that helped drive back the fear of that immense amorphous *thing* that waited outside. "What *is* that creature, Silvertail?" she asked as she sprinted through the doorway.

His answer—as before—reached her easily, even though the screams were louder and incoherent, panicked announcements were now booming from the speakers above, accompanied by the many-voiced chorus of mad laughter. "A shoggoth, Princess."

A shoggoth*? Holy* shit. "That's a *lot* scarier than I thought they'd be."

"Alas, most of these beings shall be; Lovecraft and his peers, for all their mastery of language, were limited by their perceptions and their own beliefs. You do not face a mindless mass of protoplasm, but a hostile and malign intellect with vast control over a body made to consume and destroy."

The shoggoth's black mass glinted with a gelid, wintry sheen, as though it were both molten and frozen; the surface heaved and flexed and pulsed, and the huge, glowingly inhuman eyes flickered with malice. It nearly filled the three-story rotunda at the center of the mall, flowing around the escalators and elevator, a whirlpool that rose rather than fell; dozens of people were trapped on both levels, surrounded by walls of oozing, malodorous chaos. Holy Aura could see men and women, teenagers backed against a wall, a family with a baby stroller in the center of a slowly shrinking circle of vileness.

"Iiii fffeeeel yyoooouuu, chchchaaaaammmpiiiiooon," it said, a hundred voices speaking in a terrifying chorus, just enough out of synch to be eerie and repellent. "Ssshooowwww yyoursselllff . . . oorrrr Iiii wwiiill *FFEEED!*"

The flowing ebony about the family heaved up, transformed to a mouth filled with fangs of polished night, a mouth that lunged and cut the stroller in half; Holly was struck speechless for a moment with horror, until she saw the mother, holding her child in a deathgrip; somehow she had snatched her baby literally from the jaws of death.

With a burst of silver speed, Holy Aura leapt to the top of the second-floor railing. "Then here I am, monster!" she shouted, trying not to show any sign of the panic that was beginning to rise within her; the template of her predecessors helped, encouraging her, supporting her actions and words, and for the first time she was grateful for that wordless yet powerful semipresence. "Mystic Galaxy Defender, Apocalypse Maiden the First, Princess Holy Aura, reborn as sword and shield, weapon and wielder, mistress of souls and stars! You have threatened innocents and brought fear to this world, and for that, this Apocalypse Maiden says that *you* are going *down*!"

Hey, it even let me get through that whole speech, she thought, Steve's analytical attitude also helping to distance herself from the terror the shoggoth's nearness brought forth. *If they're influenced by memes, I guess they have to take the whole package, not just the parts they want.*

The mouths coalesced into a single gigantic maw, and the thing's voice was thunder. "And now I *will* feed!"

Princess Holy Aura leapt backward, a spurt of pure fright powering that jump as a fanged night-dark mouth the size of a garage door *squirted* forward on a column of ebony hatred. But the fanged lunge missed, carving a fifteen-foot chunk of floor out instead, and with her mouth dry but her grip firm, Holy Aura spun the Silverlight Bisento around and sliced completely through the column of blackness.

Smoke burst from the cut and the thing hissed from a dozen new mouths. But the hisses were also laughs, as the severed part was swallowed by and rejoined the main body. "Dammit, Silvertail, what do I do *now*?"

"I told you that such a simple approach would not work on many of your enemies. To kill a shoggoth even with that weapon? If it could be done, it would be a work of hours, carving it apart again and again until finally even its reformed parts were all sufficiently injured by your holy power. You must channel your power, find its expression within you and unleash it. Unfortunately this was not something we could practice before."

She bounded from point to point, evading the thing's increasingly vicious jabs and slashes and grabs as Silvertail spoke. "Yeah. If I have a power that could wipe out something *that* powerful, I'd probably have taken our *house* down."

"That is not the issue; the issue is that only adversaries of true corruption will allow you to call the power forth, recognize how it works. The power is vastly less effective against ordinary beings and structures of mere matter—which is a good thing in such a crowded building as this."

"What?" She parried two more lightning-fast jabs and skidded around the corner of the second wing of the mall, still running. "So I have to call it up only in battle and 'recognize how it works' while something tries to kill me for *real*? Your training plan *sucks*!"

She heard a distant, rueful chuckle. "I cannot entirely disagree. But that is what you must do."

"***How***?"

"The coronet is your Apocalypse Seal—the channel and control for the power that is Holy Aura's, and that will connect you to the others. You felt it seal to you, in pain and power, in your first transformation. Now reach out to it, call *to* it."

"That's hard to *do* when something's trying to *kill* me!" she retorted. She whirled the *bisento* like a propeller, and three writhing segments of tarry hunger fell just short of her and wriggled, smoking, away to rejoin the pursuing red-eyed ebony tsunami.

"I know, but you *must*. Holly—Holy Aura—if you do not begin to battle in earnest, and soon, it will turn its attention back to the people trapped here!"

She bit back another protest. *He's right. This monster* can *do more than one thing at a time, and if I don't keep it focused on me, it'll be* more *than happy to keep chasing me around the mall while it eats everyone I'm supposed to protect!*

She flipped around, bounced off the thick glass of the local Apple store, and caromed between support pillars, leaping straight past the thing as it tried to adjust its flow. "*Ginhikari no Bisento!*"

The silver-shining blade laid the shoggoth open, a cut sixty feet long, and Princess Holy Aura felt a grim smile on her own face at the multivoiced howl of pain and rage. *Maybe that doesn't* really *hurt it, but that stung enough that it'll stay with me for a little longer.*

If I can only figure this out . . .

She remembered that first transformation, twin crescents of light that burned themselves with pure-ice chill across her brows, and felt that pain and comfort echo as she thought of it. *Please, Apocalypse Seal, open, unseal, whatever, at least show me what I can* do—

There was a flash of light *within* her head, and for an instant she leapt, not above a crowd of terrified people, but into the limitless depths of space. She *soared* through a void dusted with numberless points and smudges of light; below her, a mighty whirlpool of stars and dust, turning with a motion so ponderously grandiose that even the rise and fall of the dinosaurs took less than a single turn to complete, and yet she could *see* it turning, could sense the majesty and power of that cosmic pinwheel, of the hundred billion stars encompassed in its light, see how it and its surrounding brethren dwarfed her world and all its people to utter insignificance, of less import than the loss or gain of a single grain of sand in the Sahara.

Yet . . .

Yet . . .

We are not *insignificant*, she thought to herself. *We can't be.*

The vision flickered, and she cannonballed into the railing, slipped, plummeted to the ground floor. Before she could rise, ebony hunger swirled around her, caught at her legs, fought to prevent her from rising. She felt the nauseating pressure combined with a vicious, gnawing pain rising up her calves. Desperately, she tore away, whirled the *bisento*'s blade and crushing ball around and over and through, leapt away, not even a tenth of a second separating her from onyx, burning hunger. Her legs screamed silently, the flesh red and raw, and though she sensed her silver power trying to counter it, that dark malevolence clung to the wounds, contesting bitterly with any cleansing or healing power that dared try to reclaim what it had touched.

The Apocalypse Seal is still the key! But how is insignificance *the point?*

The monster was barely a breath behind. She knew if she entered that vision again, the shoggoth would *have* her.

But if I don't . . . For a moment she wasn't Holy Aura; she was Stephen Russ, someone older, someone *used* to accepting bitter, mundane truths, and yet, somehow, refusing to let it take him down, make *him* bitter and angry. . . . *if I don't understand what my power means, what it can* do, *if I can't figure out how to tap it—I'll fail anyway. It'll catch me sooner or later, and everyone here will die, and that will be the end.*

If I'm insignificant, fine. Just show me what the answer *is for this insignificant mote.*

The vision returned, redoubled in force; almost instantly, Princess Holy Aura felt her body—seeming so distant it lay beyond the horizon of the universe—stumble, be caught up.

But now she saw *beyond* the galaxies, beyond the void itself, and her universe *itself* was puny, less than the merest *atom* adrift between the stars, and *things* waited there, in the spaces beyond and between universes, *things* that hungered for form and power, for the chance to reshape a reality to their incomprehensible and malevolent desires. The places between pushed and probed at the boundaries of all universes, seeking an entrance, a foothold, a beachhead, and all too often found it, encircling and crushing what lay within.

Far, far away she thought she heard a shout of fear, of her name cried by Silvertail, a cry cut off as even her head was enveloped and distant burning hunger began to crush in on her.

She was alone, and both of her were enveloped in alien hunger and malice. There was no light, there was no hope, there was no escape for her or the world, for they meant nothing, and never had. That which waited beyond the paper-thin veil of their puny reality was infinitely more vast than all the dust-mote worlds that deluded themselves into thinking they were anything other than just that, dust beneath the feet of beings more ancient than their universe.

No.

It was a simple, visceral, primal thought, a denial.

But what point the denial? She had *seen* how microscopically trivial, how utterly insignificant not only she, but her entire world, her galaxy, her *universe* was. What was this but a refusal to accept truth, a comforting and threadbare lie?

No. We are not *insignificant.*

A glint of light. A sense of presence.

She seized upon that tiny dot of luminance, even as she felt in the far remoteness of reality her breath cut off, an acid flame scorching away her breath.

Light.

And *now* she saw herself, a single point of thought, of consciousness on that puny speck, that drifting dot of nothingness, but she was not alone. There were *billions* of other points, each one almost imperceptible, but together a brilliant luminance that shone *through* the boundaries of reality—calling the darkness to it, yes, but also *resonating*, not with the spaces beyond, but with something *above* and *below* and *around* all of it.

We are not insignificant. Those things *sought our world, and were cast out, and have been cast out before. They have been defeated again and again by this microscopic dot within the cosmos.*

The cold-metal crescents were warm now, warm and comforting, and she understood. *Matter has resisted them here, and elsewhere, and it does so because it also has* spirit, *has will, to resist.* The limitless universe *was* the power of spirit, the magic she was bound to—as were, in their own way, her adversaries—was the *foundation* of all reality, and she was the first, the living representative of that spark: the power of the spirit that underlay the existence of the cosmic all, of the other mythic elements that made up the world, earth, air, fire, and water. They all were part of, and partook of, the spirit, the *will* of humanity—in both creation and destruction.

And now Holy Aura—and Stephen Russ—understood what it meant to be an Apocalypse Maiden.

A detonation of pure argent light burst from her body as Princess Holy Aura's consciousness returned. The shoggoth's viscous form was blown away from her, water before a depth charge, and scattered, smoking, reforming but painfully, as her acid-burned, eaten flesh renewed itself; she felt the pain ebbing away, *driven* away by her understanding of what the power of the Apocalypse Maiden meant.

"Almost you caught me," she said, standing unmoved in midair atop nothing but an aura of light. "Almost."

Spirit. That's why I'm the first, why he said I had *to be the first.* "Your shape, your terror, you touch both mind and soul. It was *you* guiding me to my insignificance. But that was a lie, all a lie."

"A lie?" it echoed in a voice that made the mall shudder. "Truth, truth, truth," it said, now with a dozen dozen voices, laughing, mocking. "*Ph'iagnik,* insignificant, a speck of refuse within a—"

"Bullshit!" she said, feeling that she was both Holly Owen and Stephen Russ. "Why keep coming *here*, then? We kicked your asses off our planet, and we've done it again and again, and *that's* why you're afraid of us, that's why you can't ignore us, can't leave us to grow again. Because we have the power to *beat* you."

With the certainty came the thrill of the power, the light, gathering into her hands, charging the Silverlight Bisento so it glowed, casting shadows away from her, eradicating any sign of darkness about her. She remembered the vision of the galaxy, of the numberless stars, and the one Sun that was theirs, out of all in the universe. "I am the Apocalypse Maiden, cataclysm and creation in one, and you—you're getting the cataclysm *right now*!"

The shoggoth gave an inarticulate scream and lunged for her, an attack from all directions, a thousand needles of lethal darkness.

She reached out, yet *in*, within and behind and above herself, to the symbol of the spirit—the stars themselves—and chose *destruction.*

Warm, exhilarating fire burned through her veins. Gold-white starflame coalesced upon the blade of the Silverlight Bisento, and the living tar of the shoggoth shrank back, the red and green and yellow points of eyes wide and afraid, but it was too late. "Light of Apocalypse—*Solar FLARE*!"

The auric-argent luminance blasted from her, driven by her will and certainty, and fountained on and across the shoggoth. The hard-driven ebony needles of the thing's substance dissipated, some mere inches from her skin. Its mouths froze in motion and crumbled before the intolerable light, its eyes were blinded and then blown away, dust in a star-wind. The light expanded outward, mercilessly seeking out the dark-flowing thing as it tried to flee, to escape the burning, destroying light, but it had sealed the mall itself. There was no place to run *to*, and the light pierced wall and door and floor like glass. There was a thin, horrified scream, a shriek of disbelieving agony that echoed from the entirety of the world about . . . and then silence.

The light faded, and only a trace of coal-black dust sifted down, to fall on the faces of the people throughout the building, whose expressions were slowly changing from terror to hope and relief.

Thank God. I thought *that the light wouldn't touch other human beings . . . but I couldn't be sure.*

Suddenly realizing that all were staring at her, she recovered herself and bowed.

Can't show how scared I was. How scared I still am, *even after winning. My knees want to give way, but I've got to get out of sight!*

She leapt through the air, forcing her shaking legs to obey, and ducked through the doors which were now open. Three more gigantic steps and a bound and she was in the narrow belt of forest preserve that surrounded the mall on two sides.

Now I can be Holly again.

Even as she changed back, the shock, fear, agony, and elation caught up with her in a startlingly nauseating fashion.

And so she found herself, in the middle of her triumph, on her knees in the forest, wondering if she was about to lose both of those triple cheeseburgers.

Not exactly what I expected after the heroine's victory!

✳ Chapter 12 ✳

The door opened. The shape that stood outlined in the faint light from the hallway was subtly *wrong*; something about the length of arm, joints, stance, said this was nothing that belonged in so mundane a place. But despite its alien nature, it hesitated, unsure.

"What news?"

The voice from within the room was a warm contralto. At first, a human might have found it welcoming. But beneath the voice was something else, as inhuman as the figure that waited in the doorway. "Come," the voice said again, "speak."

The creature in the doorway bobbed low, almost groveling on the floor before rising and stepping forward. Its features were stretched and hairless, with a crest that rose and fell like a fish's fin, eyes huge and dark. Broad, clawed, webbed hands twitched nervously. "Bu'lekau is defeated. Its screams were heard and it speaks no more, and human responders are evacuating the building."

"And do they speak of what destroyed a shoggoth?"

"A woman-child, of silver and light, so they say."

"Tch." The speaker arose, a figure nearly the color of the shadows surrounding her; a brilliant white smile, disconcerting in its brightness, flashed out. "Fear not, Arlaung. I had *expected* this failure."

"I do not understand, Great Queen," he said. "The powers move deeply on this world; a shoggoth of such power is far greater than any adversary the prior First Enemies have faced. I was . . . certain it would work."

The Queen laughed; it was a sound that Arlaung found comforting, but a human would have heard cruelty and hunger. "You do not remember the other times, Arlaung. But there is a pattern, a *way* of these things. Surely, we attempt to change that pattern—and sometimes, we have succeeded—but it is by far its strongest in the beginning. As the others appear, their total power is greater . . . but so are their vulnerabilities. Our best chances of victory have always been when we took advantage not of simple combat, but the opportunities their weaknesses provided."

She surveyed herself idly. "And this cycle may offer us some . . . most interesting opportunities."

Without warning, a lurid purple-and-green glow emanated from farther within the room.

"Ah!" she said, and turned toward the light.

The luminance came from a strange, multifaceted stone within a box covered with alien runes in shapes that human eyes would have found difficult to observe without confusion or even maddening pain; for Arlaung and his Queen, the symbols were clean and clear and strong. "What does the Trapezohedron say, Great Queen?"

"It begins to clear, Arlaung. Soon it will be time for you to carry it."

"Can I not be chosen? Let another carry it in the seeking, Great Queen! I would serve you well as one of the Cataclysm Knights!"

She shook her head, shadows moving like long tresses about her. "You must serve as you were made, Arlaung. The Knights must reflect the Princesses; you know this. You are no more human than I. Be the seeker of the Knights, guide them to me, and be content; for when Azathoth of the Nine Arms comes finally to this her throne, you shall be rewarded with the dominion of Y'ha-nthlei and rule the seas under her, and all your people will bow before you."

Arlaung bowed again. "As you command, Great Queen. I merely wished—"

Another laugh. "Be not eager to take the field of battle, child of the depths. Better far to use humans—for their strength is nigh the equal of their folly, and far more easily bent to our needs."

Her hand caressed the stone and it flickered like a candle for a moment. "We will gather the Knights, and through them find the weapons of *this* world that will defeat the Apocalypse Maidens."

She straightened and looked up, past the ceiling to a limitless distance. "Yes, we have failed before, Arlaung. It is possible we will fail again. But numberless defeats mean nothing, for we will never die . . . and they need only fail *once*."

✳ Chapter 13 ✳

"Holly? You need to go to sleep!" Mr. Owen said, looking in and seeing her sitting at her computer.

Holly sighed, tried to smile and failed. "I can't sleep, Dad . . . Silvertail." The confusion that had made her change the name she used threatened to overwhelm her. *Sometimes I almost forget being Steve Russ, and that terrifies me beyond words.*

He sat down in one of the other chairs, pushing back the graying black hair that needed a trim. "But you *do* need sleep, Holly. Big day tomorrow."

"Why do you think I *can't* sleep, Silvertail? I *know* what tomorrow is. Tomorrow school starts. Tomorrow I'm a fourteen-year-old girl in her first day of high school, trying to look perfectly normal while I secretly scope out my classmates to figure out which of them is going to get thrown at a shoggoth or a dhole or whatever hideous thing our enemies bring out next." She looked down, saw she had the armrests of her chair in a deathgrip.

His dark eyes showed lines of pain and sympathy. "Holly . . . Stephen . . . believe me when I say I understand."

She was silent a moment, realizing the truth of that gentle reminder. "Yeah. Yeah, of course you do. You've done this so many times. How did you manage it, Silvertail? Because I've been around you long enough so I'm sure you're not faking it; you care what happens to us."

Silvertail's human guise dropped its gaze to the floor. "How? By constantly reminding myself that if I do not, those exact children—and all they care for, all they are, all they could ever be—will be destroyed as well. The only way to save them . . . is to imperil them, much as I—as *we*—hate the very thought. I have done all I can in choosing *you*. All I can do is pray this was the right choice. But it never becomes easier, and I pray also that it never *shall*."

His eyes came up and there was a clearer look in them. "But something else bothers you as well."

He's sharp as ever. Guess you have to be if most of the time you're a white rat. "More than one. See, I called you *Dad*. Not the first time. But it's gotten . . . more natural. I *think* of you that way, sometimes, when I'm really comfortable as Holly."

"Ah. And that frightens you?"

"Hell yes!" she said, heard her own voice just a tiny bit too high, too nervous. "I'm starting to *think* like a teenage girl. Like I *really am* Holly Owen. Okay, sure, that's great for our cover, I'm not, like, going to screw it up so easy now. But *that's not the real me*, and I . . . I really don't think it should've changed for me that fast. It's that . . . template thing again, isn't it?"

"I'm afraid so, Holly. All the previous Holy Auras were teenage girls, no more than your current apparent age. It is, in all truth, *necessary* that you become, at least to some extent, Holly Owen as the world will see you. I explained to you the symbolism that made choosing such a person, standing between childhood and adulthood, a vital part of the weapon that is the Apocalypse Maiden."

"Yeah. You did. I'm just . . . scared. And scared like I was when I was little, not like when I was Steve." She got up, walked to the bed, hesitated, turned around, sat down, got up. "See? I can't even figure out where I want to be when I'm talking. Too nervous."

"I wish—"

"I know. I know." She closed her eyes, concentrated. *Now to the hard part.* "But there's something else."

Mr. Owen nodded. "I rather thought as much."

"It's about those other girls, what we're going to do. Now I get it, we *need* all five Apocalypse Maidens to do the full job of kicking these monsters back where they came from and locking the door behind them. We have to find them, we have to awaken them, we have to work together. I got that. But I've been thinking . . . you remember what you told me about why you chose me after all this time?"

"How could I forget?" The front teeth flashed in the smile, reminding her of the incisors natural to a rat. "I was tired of choosing children for this job."

"More than that. You were trying to do the *right* thing by not forcing this on a child. And you were right. But what that means is that we have to do the same thing here."

"We can't choose adult—"

"Right, right, I know, we went over that; the enchantment's already engaged, it will have *already* found the four others, even if they're not active yet. But what I mean is that you made a moral, an *ethical* choice, to not dump the leadership, the key of the whole world's salvation, onto a girl who shouldn't have to deal with it. So that makes it my duty—and yours—to try to keep the *whole thing* as ethical as we possibly can."

The narrow gaze was as piercing as it had ever been from the beady eyes of a white rodent. "Yes . . ." Silvertail said slowly, "of course. But exactly what are you getting at?"

"I mean that maybe they'll have to get it dumped on them in the middle of combat—I know the memes, believe me—but after that? We can't drag a fourteen-year-old girl out into this and keep it secret from her family."

"Lemuria's *Memory*, Stephen! You cannot seriously mean—"

"I mean *exactly* that. How can we be doing the right thing if what we're going to do is make children lie to their parents and sneak out to maybe get themselves killed—or come back broken in their heads? Sure, I'll bet these Apocalypse Maidens are supposed to be strong and all, but half the people who were in the *mall* that day are probably gonna be in therapy for months or years; at least *I* had thirty-five years of life to help me deal with that fight. These kids aren't going to have even half of that."

"And what if their parents say *no*? Or try to have us arrested? Or shoot at us? Steve—Holly—your current culture is *highly* protective of your children, in some ways stultifyingly so. You know what sort of reaction any threat to children will create."

She ran her fingers through her hair, realized she had better brush it again before going to bed, then shoved that trivial thought aside. "Yes. I know. But I know this is the *only* way I could do it."

The form of Mr. Owen wavered, and suddenly Silvertail was

sitting on the chair, staring at her with desperate concern. "You *know* we have no choice in this war, Holly. Even if they say no, we would have—"

"If they say no, it's no." Seeing the half-furious, half-panicked twitching of the whiskers, she forced a smile and went on. "But I think we have to assume there's *some* way to convince them. After all, there really *isn't* any going back, from what you said. The meme demands the super-team get formed, I just have to try to work it so our super-team has super-duper parental support. And between Holy Aura and you, Silvertail, we've got quite a lot of force of personality and evidence that we're not crazy."

The silver-white rat paused, tilting his head, seeming to contemplate. Then a tiny hop of assent. "You . . . make excellent points, Holly. Yes, the imperatives of the enchantment and our ultimate confrontation will tend to smooth our way through such mundane problems. But it will still not make the results *certain*. We still run a great risk."

"But risk and sacrifice, that's part of the *power* of the spell, right? And if the families are aware—"

A squeaking laugh. "Stephen Russ! For that is *your* mind at work, I will swear to it! Indeed, you are correct; *if*—and I emphasize *if*—we succeed in convincing these families to support us, it will symbolize a great deal of willing sacrifice and faith. All the Apocalypse Maidens will be stronger for that." It was astonishing how the little furry face and body could manage to convey such a wide range of emotions; now Silvertail looked at her with a wry cynicism. "However, to *achieve* that will *also* require an astonishing amount of faith, possibly sacrifice, and most certainly luck."

"But it's the *right* thing to do."

Silvertail took a breath so huge his sides visibly swelled, then sighed explosively. "Yes. Yes, Holly, Stephen, you are completely correct. I began this cycle with a determination to take a higher path; I can hardly fault you for insisting I hold to my course. I *cringe* at the thought of how much danger we may be placing our cause in, but I will not argue."

With a flash, Mr. Owen reappeared. "And now, having convinced me of your correctness, can you *please* relax enough to go to bed? The last thing either of us need is for you to try your first day in school as Holly with half a night's sleep."

Holly felt a small loosening of the tension in her stomach. *He agreed. I was right. Or I hope I am, anyway.* "Yes . . . Dad, I'll try."

"Good. Then . . . good night, Holly." He watched as she turned off the computer and got into bed, then switched off the light.

Holly rolled over, and tried to relax. *I think I can, now.* Her eyes *were* feeling heavy, and she drove out thoughts of the future. *Tomorrow will take care of itself. Now that I know Silvertail's supporting me . . .* She smiled. *This just might work after all!*

Part II: AWAKENING THE MAIDENS

✳ Chapter 14 ✳

She stood in the cool September morning, watching as the yellow school bus grumbled its way up to her driveway, and felt an eerie sense of frightened *déjà vu*. It had been almost twenty years since the last time Stephen Russ had boarded such a bus, and the memories of that and earlier bus rides wasn't a pleasant memory to recall. *Maybe I should've talked about* that *with Silvertail.*

The faint whiff of diesel washed over her along with the muffled *crunch* of gravel under broad tires and the pneumatic *hiss* of the door opening reinforced the memory; she looked up, half expecting the blue-eyed, wrinkled face of old Bill to be looking back.

Instead it was the brown eyes of a woman in her thirties, looking—as most bus drivers do—somewhat harried, but she gave a bright smile. "You're Holly Owen?"

"Yes, I am. That's my dad," she pointed to where Mr. Trayne Owen stood at the door, waving.

"Good. Get on, Holly."

She waved back to Mr. Owen and then climbed up the steps.

Thank God it's not too crowded yet. She looked up and down—sure her nervousness was visible—and chose an empty seat. *I'll have to make some friends somehow, but right now, I have to get through the first couple of days and figure out what it's like to be in high school now.* There were the usual faintly curious glances from the other passengers at seeing a new face. Some of the boys looked a hair longer—again, no surprise.

She sat down and the bus started with the same lurch she remembered from two decades back. *And still no seatbelts. Some things never change.* The massive size, height, and cushioned interior of a modern schoolbus were supposedly safer than any other vehicle, but Holly had Steve's ingrained expectation of a seatbelt in any vehicle, and she found herself unexpectedly nervous at the unsecured swaying as the bus continued its rounds.

Okay, that's probably just fine. Be nervous. Lots of the other students will be. You've just gotten here, you don't know anyone, you don't even know the area well since you came from the West Coast. That *will probably be my big stumbling block. Can't be too familiar with this area.*

The bus arrived and disgorged its passengers. Holly paused, looking up at Whitney High; as Steve, he'd had a friend or two that had gone there, but Whitney had become the center of the district; with the other three high schools shut down, it had undergone a major expansion and refurbishing a couple of years back and looked nothing like it had back then.

Well, almost *nothing like.* The central part of the school was still the massive, respectable three-story brick with an old-style belfry that looked something like a watchtower above the columned entrance; that, and the tall chain link fence that had always surrounded the grounds, had given it a prisonlike appearance which led his friend and others to refer to the school as Whitney State Correctional Facility.

That unified and intimidating appearance was gone, however. Extending to either side were two-story expansions in brighter, glass-and-concrete materials; from the quick tour she'd taken with Mr. Owen, Holly knew there was a third extra wing behind the visible front. Behind *that* were the sports bleachers and tracks and other phys ed–related spaces.

Entering the school was a *lot* different. The doors were thicker, heavily reinforced, with cameras observing everyone coming and going. *And an actual couple of police officers on duty.* Steve remembered people just coming and going from his old school—old students visiting their favorite teachers, parents dropping by to pick up a kid for a sudden appointment, and so on. Here, anyone entering who wasn't a student had to go through a separate screening entrance.

The intimidating security suddenly made his friend's old joke much less funny. *Boy, if one of the attacks happens* here, *I'll have a hell of a time keeping it off the video, especially if Silvertail's not with me.*

As she made her way to her homeroom—A207, which meant in the right-hand wing, with Mr. Coyne—the impression grew stronger. The cameras weren't just at the front of the building or the entrances; there were cameras watching the hallways, too. *I* definitely *need to sit down with Silvertail and see if he can put some kind of, I dunno, contingency on the cameras here, so that if I need to transform it'll blank* all *of them. Our enemies will know Whitney High's the center soon enough, but if we can force them to have to keep guessing which of the thousand students is their target, it'll help.*

It was a tiny shred of relief that there were no cameras actually *in* the classroom. *Yet.* And while there were more high-tech screens and such, the classroom didn't look *that* different from the ones she remembered from Steve's pass through public education.

Mr. Coyne was a tall dark-haired man with a long, lined face that held the weariness of the career teacher along with a still-present humor. "All right, sit down, quiet everyone, I know it's just after summer and we'd all rather be outside, but there's going to be a lot to go through."

Holly chose a seat and listened with half an ear to Coyne's quick summary of the way things would work in the school. Silvertail—as Mr. Owen, naturally—had attended an open house and gotten the summary then, so she was aware of the schedule and how everything was organized.

She was *much* more interested in trying to guess which of the students might be the other Apocalypse Maidens—although admittedly there was no reason to assume they were all going to be in the same classroom, or even necessarily in the same grade.

Still, the tropes practically *demanded* that at least one or two of the other Maidens be in classes with her. Who would it be? The shy-looking pale girl with uncontrolled curly brown hair sitting in the corner? The tanned girl with a stack of books next to her that nearly reached her pin-straight hair dyed deep purple with white edging? Maybe one of the two Latina-looking girls who were busy in a whispered conversation on the far side of the room? Or the black girl with poofy black curly hair, whose face was almost completely obscured by the book she was reading?

Holly got no sensation of rightness, or wrongness, from any of them. Inwardly she shrugged. *Silvertail said there probably wouldn't be any way to tell until a crisis. Might as well stop thinking about it and focus on being a fine young student.*

It was true that ultimately it didn't *matter* if she did well, or poorly, in school; after all, either the Apocalypse Maidens would succeed and send the bad guys back to the darkness, at which point Holly would become Steve again and no one would remember any of this, or they'd fail and the world would fall to Lovecraftian horror, at which point no one was going to care about her grades in history. But Steve's pride wouldn't let Holly screw this up. *I did pretty well the first time through; with almost twenty more years of living I'll be damned if I'm going to do anything less than the best now!*

Her schedule turned out to be annoying as hell. *My first class is in B-Wing, then I go back to A, then to C, then I get lunch, and then A, B, C again.* That meant that she would have to walk *very* fast to manage to get to all her classes on time—and they emphasized being on time a *lot*. Being late anywhere could have consequences up to and including suspension, which didn't make sense to Steve-Holly. *So I'm late to class a lot, so you'll punish me by taking me out of the classes I'm apparently not wanting to go to? Brilliant plan, guys.*

On the positive side, the crisscross scheduling, from Biology with Mrs. Rizzo to English with "Doctor, not Mister" Beardsley, Social Studies with Ms. Vaneman, and so on, made sure that she would get *really* familiar with a lot of the school, and see a lot of the students every day.

And boy, did I make the right decision to get a big backpack. I'm almost never going to get a chance to get to my locker, unless I do it just before homeroom or during lunch.

Homework was going to be a pain in the ass. Holly, seeing through Steve's memories, could tell she could probably do a lot of it faster than most people would ever manage, but still . . . *They're saying they'll assign a* lot *more stuff than I remember from back in the day, and boy, they're* hardass *about it. No more handwavy extra-credit slide for me.*

Suddenly she realized the last class was over, the bell had rung. *Okay, first day, fine, but I've got to start talking to people. I've been just half-here all day.*

The students filed out to where the buses were waiting, a huge line of idling yellow boxes. She looked around, figured out where hers should be, and started over. As she did, she glanced idly around, still surveying the people, her eyes skipping over most of the boys, since they—

She froze so suddenly two people bumped into her and she staggered and fell. The hot, rough burning sensation of a hand scraped raw on pavement shot through her. "Ow!"

"Sorry!" said one of the two apologetically. The other muttered, "Why be sorry? It was *her* fault she stopped like that!"

But Holly barely registered the apology or cynical retort; automatically she said "It's okay, I'm fine, sorry, my fault," but she was rising, backing away at the same time, trying to find a route that *didn't* take her past that next bus, but really, there wasn't any choice, was there?

There wasn't. She had to continue, her bus was just on the other side of the one she was approaching. She kept her head down, looking from beneath her hair. There was no mistaking the tall, slender form, the long uncontrolled fall of gold hair.

Richard Dexter Armitage.

✳ Chapter 15 ✳

"Holly, calm down and tell me what is *wrong*!" Trayne Owen struggled to keep from losing control and reverting to Silvertail. "You walked in the door and started talking so fast I can't make heads or tails of—"

"Dex is *at my school*!" she said, voice unsteady. "He was right *there*, getting on the bus, my *God* I was so lucky he didn't look at me, but he *could* have and someday he *will* and—"

"*Holly!*" he shouted. She jumped and fell silent.

"Thank you, Holly. Let's look at this slowly, please. You said that 'Dex' is at your school. You refer to your—to Steve's—friend Dexter Armitage, yes?"

"Yes. I—" At his glance, she managed to stop with great effort.

"I see. An interesting coincidence, if it is indeed coincidence. Though it is, in honesty, not *that* surprising a chance; there are after all only five high schools in reasonable distance of your old residence, and your friend Dexter walked from your house."

"Yeah. Yeah, I should've thought of that. Never asked him exactly where he was going to school, or if I did it was a couple years back and it never sank in. But—"

"But? Try to focus on your *thoughts*, Holly, not your feelings. Why were you so panicked, so 'freaked out,' by this discovery?"

"It's a *secret*! I don't want him to see me like *this*, it's not . . ." She trailed off, and flushed a deep rose. "Oh, *God*, I'm being an idiot, aren't I?"

"I wouldn't say *idiot,* but you—"

"He couldn't recognize me unless I came up and *introduced*

myself—and then I'd have to give him some real evidence before even Dex would start to believe it. As far as he's concerned I'm just one more freshman in the sea of students. I could've done a 'crash-into hello' with him and he'd never have a clue." She smacked herself on her forehead. "Idiot, moron, clueless—"

"Holly, *stop* it!" He put a hand on her shoulder, feeling how small it was—especially in comparison to the massive shoulders Steve had once had. "You have two . . . personas, I suppose we could say, and it is inevitable that the responses of both will cause you problems at times. Dex is a very important friend to you-as-Steve, and it is thus only natural that you might find the idea of him unexpectedly discovering this secret upsetting, and not recognize the other aspects of the situation.

"Add to that your new body and mind's hormonal changes and your lack of experience in *controlling* a set of responses that are very different than those of Stephen Russ, and this reaction is entirely natural. This doesn't make you stupid, it makes you *human*, despite whatever superhuman capabilities Holy Aura may have."

He watched as Holly closed her eyes, hands balled into fists at her side, and stood there, breathing, not moving, for long moments.

Finally she opened her eyes and looked up sheepishly. "You . . . you're right, Dad. Silvertail. As usual, I guess. I remember being a teenage guy and my impulses getting all mixed up and out of my control. This is like that. But it's not the *same*."

"Of course not. Each body reacts differently, and as the proportion of hormones is different, it will cause different general responses. But I suspect you would find it nearly as difficult to deal with even if you were a teenage male. At your age you have *memory* but a long, long interval in which there has been little *experience* of the process of puberty."

Holly grimaced. "*This* part of being suddenly younger I could *really* do without. Along with the whole 'go back to high school' thing."

"I suppose that includes homework?"

"Yeah, there'll be a *lot* of that," she said with a sigh. "I can probably whip through a lot of it faster than most people, but still, it's gonna take time. Don't have much today, but I can see it coming." She sniffed the air. "Wow, what's for dinner?"

"Pot roast," he answered. "Something warm and filling after the first day, and I think you'll need it."

"I *love* pot roast. Hardly ever got a chance to make it myself, though."

"So anything relevant to our mission today?"

Her smile wasn't reassuring. "Oh, yeah." She told him about the security cameras.

"I saw them at the open house," Trayne Owen said.

"I'll bet you didn't quite get how *extensive* the system is. Every single hall has a two-way view, and the long halls have cameras spaced close enough together that they'll be able to identify anyone in the images. All the big spaces—gym, auditorium, and the outside areas of the grounds—have 'em too. The only places they don't have cameras are the bathrooms and the regular classrooms. If I have to change anywhere in the school, they'll either *see* me transform, or they'll know what classroom I came out of."

Trayne nodded. "You are correct; I was busy trying to understand the operation of the facility and the people I was meeting. This does pose a considerable threat to your anonymity."

"So can you *do* anything about it?"

"With this advance knowledge?" He thought for a moment, recalling both long-ago studies of enchantment and far more recent investigations into the workings of technology. "Yes, I believe so. There are several possible ways of addressing this problem; I may go there in my less-obtrusive form and test a few ideas."

"If there's a *chance* of our enemies already being around there, is it going to be smart of you to go anywhere near the school like that?"

He laughed. "It should be perfectly safe, Holly. I am no match for them in combat, true, but I am *very* experienced in avoiding detection and escaping threats. And I do not expect them to be terribly active there yet."

"All right. Just . . . be careful. I'm sure not going to make it through this mess without you."

"I appreciate the concern."

Past her crisis, Holly picked up her backpack and headed to her room, while Trayne Owen went back to the kitchen to see to dinner.

An hour and a half later, they sat down together. Trayne hadn't finished two bites when Holly asked, "So what's *your* problem today, Silvertail?"

"*My* problem? What do you mean?"

"Your expression hasn't changed much since resolving my silly panic attack; you still look really worried. So I figure there's got to be something else bothering you."

She is perceptive—as she must be, I am afraid—and a human face is, alas, much easier to read than a rodent's. "I had hoped to leave the subject for later," Mr. Owen said slowly. "But . . . yes, there is no point in dissembling. There *is* another matter of concern. Your people's investigative forces will become an element of increasing challenge to us."

"Huh?" She looked honestly puzzled. "I mean, sure, I get that the cops will be looking at these things and there's a *lot* of buzz after the first two events. But they don't show up until way after."

"They have not *yet* done so, no, but they may respond more quickly than we have seen thus far. Your own description of the school tells me that you have at least two law enforcement officers present on-site."

Holly bit her lip. "Oh. Hadn't thought about that before. You're right. But if our opponents are going to be things like the shoggoth or that rock-worm—"

"They will not," Trayne said, with conviction born of too many ages of experience. "Our adversaries will manifest in a variety of forms. Ultimately there will be battle, yes, but that battle may be presaged by far more insidious and subtle attacks and manifestations."

"But," Holly said after a moment, "they're still mostly going to be things that the cops can't *find* easily, and when the fighting starts most of 'em won't be things they can fight, right? So basically the police aren't really any different than civilians in this."

"In one sense you are correct, but in another you are terribly wrong, Holly. Physically, in many cases, they will be no more capable of acting than the ordinary people, but this era is vastly different than most of those which have preceded it. The interconnection of communications, the ability to instantly transmit information from one point to another, and—most worrisome to me—the organized and powerful ability to collate and analyze in detail masses of information, all provide a tremendous power for not your police as such, but more pervasive organizations such as your intelligence agencies, to use in ferreting out our identity and location. I do not believe our adversaries have grasped this as much as I, and will have relatively little hold on such organizations at first."

"Crap," Holly said, in a voice that somehow echoed Steve's. "But once they *do* get a clue, they'll be actively trying to use those agents to find us."

"I am afraid so. It was unlikely, though imaginable, that such agencies would drop investigations into the first incident, as isolated oddities are extremely difficult to probe and the nature of the event is so far outside of normal experience that they have few even speculative scenarios to deal with such an investigation.

"Now, however, they have a second data point, and one showing significant commonality with the first—a close geographic correspondence, the appearance of a creature both hostile and utterly unrelated to anything known to your science, and the defeat of the creature by what is obviously the same individual or one of a group of very nearly identical individuals."

"Yeah, yeah, I'm getting the picture, and my gaming brain doesn't like it any more than the rest of me. Forget surveillance cameras, we have to worry about their ability to monitor the net—phones and stuff. Shit, shit, shit . . ." She repeated the word several times like a mantra. "Silvertail, we're going to have to figure out how to keep them from tracking us down that way. I *have* to use the net for all sorts of stuff, and I'm sure that for some of our missions I'll be doing research that way—or maybe one of our Apocalypse Maidens will be a hacker. It'd sure fit some of the memes. But that big whistle-blowing on the NSA showed they can sort through a *lot* of traffic to get what they're after, and now they know to start looking around here."

He nodded. "Yes. Which drastically reduces the amount of information they need to sort, and thus increases their chance to extract relevant information. Fortunately, of course, supernatural beings generally are not communicating via cellular networks or e-mail, but in this era . . ."—he smiled wryly—"in this era I would expect that the Apocalypse Maidens may well be texting each other about crucial information. Yes, Stephen . . . Holly, this is the problem that has concerned me."

"Well, like they say," she said with a grin, "at least now we know. And knowing is half the battle!"

He found himself laughing aloud, knowing precisely the reference to memes so relevant. "Precisely so. The simpler half, unfortunately."

"But," Holly said, waving her fork as though raising her finger for emphasis, "we haven't done much to draw attention to *us* yet. As long as your ID work will hang together—"

"It will. Oh, if they for some reason truly develop a suspicion of you and me *personally*, a *physical* background check will show a mysterious lack of people recalling our existence, but there should be no lack of researchable details . . . and such people are often very satisfied by paperwork that aligns properly." He thought for a moment. "However . . . hmmm . . . yes, that *will* be a problem. I may have to find a way to insert some sort of prior indicators of electronic communication into their databases, ones that show, at least, Trayne Owen as having been sampled as any other citizen by their data-collection systems."

"Jesus. That's . . ."

". . . ambitious, yes." Despite that thought, he felt his heart lighter than it had been in a few days, and smiled. "Yet while their reach is great, and I am but one man . . . I also am a man old as all of them put together, and with subtle and powerful magic they suspect not at all." He nodded decisively. "You are right, Holly. Now that I know, I can at least cover our presence well. It will be up to us, going forward, to hide ourselves from these agencies."

"What's the real problem if they *did* find us, though?"

He blinked in startlement, as she went on, "I mean, if we fail, the world's gone blooey, and if we succeed, all that stuff gets erased and set back. So even if they do get a file on me a foot thick, it's gone once we're done."

He felt a frown creasing his face. *That* is *an interesting question. But I know that this* is *a problem.*

After a moment's thought he had the answer. He also suspected that in his original form, Steve would have quickly come up with the answer, but as Holly, Steve's memories were somewhat separate, and the trains of thought different. "The concern is that if they do manage to figure out, for example, that Holly Owen is associated with Princess Holy Aura, they could try to take you in as a 'person of interest.' The excuse—or rather, in this case, the fact—that you may be a threat to national security would justify doing so, and they would have no requirement to do so publicly or with due process."

"Could they *hold* me? I mean, I *am* Princess Holy Aura, right, and they can't shut that off, can they?"

"Without help from our opposite numbers, no. But they may well *get* such assistance, and even without it . . . Think about it."

He could see her expression go from puzzled to grim. "Oh. Sorry, I wasn't thinking along the right lines. Sure. First, all that'd have to happen is *bad timing*—them grabbing me up and having me, say, flown to Washington, just when the bad guys decide to unleash their next monster in downtown Schenectady or something. You said people killed by these things are going to be really, really dead in both timelines."

She glanced at him, and he nodded gravely. "And . . . ?" he prompted.

"Aaaand . . . if I have to bust out of their custody, I'd probably have to hurt people, which is like the opposite of my job. And I'd become a criminal from their point of view."

"Worse, you would represent a power they *cannot control*."

"Bugger, as one of my friends used to say. Sure. And if they can't control me, even if they accept I *mean* well, they can't be sure how I'll act. What if Princess Holy Aura turns out to be a radical activist? What if she decides to take her superhuman powers out to intervene in some foreign country or whatever? She's one teenage girl; she could do something perfectly well meaning and still trigger a war."

"Indeed. And of course that assumes that such agencies are basically benign. Some try to be . . . but there are others, or organizations *within* such agencies, that are far from benign. Those, especially once contacted by our adversaries . . . those will be malevolently interested in either securing and containing you, or manipulating you for their own purposes."

"Whoa. Are you telling me that there are actually *evil* intelligence agencies? I mean, yeah, I don't trust ours and they do things I'd consider evil, but—"

"There are, in fact, very old organizations—some tied in sidewise means to our adversaries, others quite independent—whose nature is secretive and whose goals are very much what you would consider evil. While magic, as such, is very weak in this world when the cycle has not come, it cannot be banned from the world entirely."

"Great. So not only am I going to be looking out for the monster of the week, but I have to worry about the cosmic Illuminati?"

The comment brought a brief smile to his lips. "Something of that nature, yes. Though even they, for the most part, would *not* want the triumph of Azathoth of the Nine Arms. And there are other forces of lighter motivation."

The smile faded. "But all of them have the potential to interfere . . . and even a small interference, at the wrong moment, could spell disaster—not merely for us, but for humanity itself."

✳ Chapter 16 ✳

"Hey, um, Holly?"

Holly looked up to see another girl looking uncertainly down at her. *Black girl, average height, just a little heavy, big poofy hair she's forced into two huge ponytails . . . dammit, brain, give me her name!*

Steve knew he was usually bad with names, so he'd been working on trying to do some mnemonic associations with the classmates he'd heard the names of. *Hair wasn't tied back, looked like a starburst first day, name was strange, and like stars . . . Japanese name . . .* "Hi . . . Seika, isn't it?" *Let me be right, please . . .*

The dark brown eyes lit up. "That's me! Look . . . um, this might sound a little weird . . ."

"I've heard weird before, I'm from California," she answered. *And you have no* idea *how much weird I've heard.*

"Okay." Seika glanced around the library almost guiltily, then sat down in one of the chairs near the computer terminal Holly was using. "My parents . . . well, they keep bothering me about, you know, talking to people at school, having friends? And they made me promise to talk to three new people this week."

Holly burst out laughing, then immediately cut off. "Sorry! Sorry, not laughing at you, just . . . that's so *parents,* isn't it?"

Seika, who had looked momentarily mortified, gave a relieved grin. "I know, right? But I promised."

"Totally okay. So why me? I mean, there's lots—"

"Your shirt, really."

Holly looked down, to see the colorful assortment of human and trollish characters splashed across her current T-shirt. "You're a Homestuck?"

"Yes!" Seika looked almost unreasonably overjoyed.

"I just got into it," Holly admitted. "It's, well, like one of the only *new* things I'm into."

"Really? Why?"

She rolled her eyes in what she hoped was a properly embarrassed fashion. "This is the first school I've been in and I didn't know many other kids before now."

"First school . . . oh, you were *homeschooled* until now?"

"Right." Holly-Steve was proud of that idea. Homeschooling would easily explain most of the gaps in Holly Owen's "teenage-ness" and any inconsistencies in the kind of knowledge she had and whatever media or books she liked.

"I wish *I* could've been homeschooled. At least then people wouldn't bother you for reading books all the time."

"Well, yeah, but I sometimes wish I *had* been going to regular schools. I wouldn't have been so, um, freaked at my first day."

"Religious homeschooling?" Seika asked, then suddenly clapped a hand over her mouth. "Ohmigod, I'm sorry, I shouldn't poke into things like that, it's not my business—"

Holly grinned. *That's actually pretty sweet.* "Don't worry, it's cool. No, my dad moved around a lot and didn't like regular schools much, so he decided he'd rather make sure I was educated at home and not have to worry about yanking me out of schools every couple years."

"So why're you here *now*?"

"I kinda insisted once he said he was staying here for at least five years. And he agreed that I had a right to at least try public schooling and see what I thought about it. Dad's pretty reasonable, actually."

"So you got *yourself* into this mess?" Seika suddenly shifted her voice to a high-pitched, rough, angry tone: "What the *fuck* kind of *fucking moron* would fucking *choose* to come to a fucking *high school*?"

Holly instantly recognized the voice and its pattern of constant swearing. "Holy *crap* that's a good Karkat, Seika! Oh, wait, I should say that's a good *fucking* Karkat!"

Seika giggled delightedly and looked a little embarrassed. "I practice a lot of the Colab *Let's Read Homestuck* voices, but that's the one I do best."

Holly kept talking with Seika through the period (*Well, there's some more work I'll have to do at home!*) and learned that she really was a lot like Steve's usual friends, a science-fiction and fantasy geek who even did role-play in her spare time. *Have to ask her if she's got a gaming group or something. That's a social activity I understand, and if I can get a social "in"—even a very geeky one—that'll be a big help in establishing myself here.*

Silvertail, currently in his Trayne Owen form, shared her enthusiasm when she got home. "That really is a stroke of luck. Or fate, I suppose, in that you will need to make friends for this to work at all." He rubbed his chin thoughtfully. "You know, I think as your father that I would recommend *you* follow Seika's example. Speak to three new people this week."

She squirmed uncomfortably in her seat, but unwillingly came to the conclusion that Mr. Owen was more right than he knew. "Okay, yeah. I guess. With the homeschool excuse I can even be straight-up curious about stuff that I've read about but never was clear on."

"Speaking of that, how was your first gym class?"

She felt her face go red. "Embarrassing, but not anywhere *near* as bad as I thought. The *class* isn't the problem, of course, it's the changing rooms and showers. There's stalls you can use to change clothes and you're not forced into a big communal shower like they used to do when I was a kid in school. So I didn't feel *quite* so much the pervert as I thought I might be. Still . . . there's not much chance to avoid sometimes looking in the wrong direction, no matter how shy I make myself, especially since I'm not pretending to be some weird religion that would give me an excuse for running in first and waiting until everyone else is gone."

"You actually *are* a fourteen-year-old girl, of course. It is not like you will somehow get caught and arrested."

"Sure, but *I* still know that I am, or was, or will be—you know, this is like *totally* hard to talk about!—a thirty-five-year old guy. Who remembers being a teenage guy, so I can't completely ignore the whole situation. Even though I'm not a guy right now."

Mr. Owen's smile had a wry edge to it. "I understand the problem,

Holly. And undoubtedly this will be an uncomfortable conversation to have at points in your career. But your cover depends on *being* a teenage girl, and I cannot think of a reasonable excuse for you to not be included in the general run of physical education activities."

"No, I know there isn't one."

"The fact is that it is not possible to prevent you from looking, nor from thinking things that may be inappropriate for your society, given your most unique situation; even if Holly Owen is inherently interested in the opposite sex, you have twenty years of learned responses in an entirely different direction. The question is whether you *act* on those thoughts. I know you now well enough to be certain you will not. And that, Stephen—and Holly—is all that matters."

She gave an embarrassed snort of laughter. "Stop it, you make me sound almost like a saint, and that I am not."

"No saint. A basically decent person—which in some ways is better. Someone who can be completely detached from temptation and corruption has a great difficulty *understanding* it, and understanding is vital."

"I guess that makes sense," Holly said, picking up her plate and bringing it toward the dishwasher.

"Speaking of which, I understand now some of your reasons for wanting your room and mine well separated, but I still have the hearing of a rat. The soundproofing may require improvement."

"*SILVERTAIL!*"

✴ Chapter 17 ✴

“Wow,” Seika said, looking around. “Nice house!”

“It’s a little big,” Holly said. “I mean, for me and Dad. But everywhere we’ve lived we ended up finding some way to fill the space, so Dad said—”

“—this time we’ll make sure there’s always enough space,” Trayne Owen’s voice finished.

“Hey, Dad,” she said, noticing how that phrase was actually becoming *normal*, and trying not to let the Steve part of her freak out, “This is Seika, Seika, this is my dad Trayne Owen.”

“Hi, Mr. Owen! Thanks for letting me come over.”

“It’s my pleasure, Seika. I’m glad to see Holly’s made a friend already. Holly, have you got homework today?”

“I did it all last period, Dad, so I didn’t have to worry.”

“We both did,” Seika confirmed. “Otherwise Mom wouldn’t have let me come either.”

“All right. You two go have fun; I’ve still got a little work to do before dinner.”

“So what does your dad do?” Seika asked as Holly led her toward her room.

“Technical consultant. Means he comes up with ideas to make things work that aren’t, mostly. He’s really good at it.”

Seika paused, staring at the wall of weapons in the living room. “Wow, are those your dad’s?”

Holly almost corrected her, but caught herself. *Remember the cover story.* "Mostly. A couple are mine, but most of them are Dad's. Same for the posters and a lot of the books."

"Pretty cool."

The wall wasn't set up identically to the way it had been in Steve's apartment, and Silvertail had in fact added some keepsakes of his own which looked very exotic. The extra space had also allowed Steve to unpack pretty much everything he owned; someone like Dex might have noticed some similarities, but the setup and number of items was different enough that it probably wouldn't immediately set off alarm bells. *Not that I'm going to be bringing Dex here anyway. He's not part of this and he doesn't have any need to know.*

The latter was a good thing, despite the fact that Steve occasionally really missed Dex. If Dex had a flaw, it was that he *wanted* things to be magical and special so badly that Steve suspected it'd be very difficult for him to know the truth and not really, really envy Steve, despite the . . . challenges presented by becoming Princess Holy Aura.

"So, um, Holly, can I ask you something?" Seika said as they came into Holly's room.

Why does she sound so nervous? "Sure, what?"

"Well . . . you've never mentioned your mom, so I was just wondering . . ."

"Oh." She found herself dropping her gaze to the floor, without even thinking about it. "I . . . well, we lost Mom back when I was pretty little."

"Lost? You mean—"

"She died. She'd said she was feeling 'funny' and out of breath, and then she . . ." Holly heard her voice trembling, and swallowed, stopped.

"Oh. Oh, fu . . . I mean, I'm sorry!"

"It's okay," she managed. *Using the truth the right way works. Doesn't make it hurt less.*

Because that was the truth, even though it had happened to Stephen Russ, not Holly Owen, and almost thirty years ago, not seven or eight. But thinking about it now, *as* Holly, he *saw* it all too clearly. He could remember watching his mother just collapse to the kitchen floor, and the paramedics arriving, and eventually having his father take him aside to tell him that Mother wasn't ever coming home.

She blinked hard, wiped away a couple tears. *Convincing, anyway.* "'Sokay," she repeated. "Just don't talk about it in front of Dad."

"I won't! Promise!"

"I guess I'd better be ready to explain for a while," Holly said after a moment of thought. "I mean, that's a question people are going to ask."

"You're probably right," agreed Seika. She looked around the room. "Wow again. I think your room's bigger than our living room. And is that a Powercom Shine Pro?"

"Yeah, maybe you can help me learn more about it. You use Powercom computers, right?"

"Yeah, but we don't have a Shine Pro!"

Holly began to relax again. Seika really *was* a geek of the kind she knew well. They spoke the same language. There were still hidden verbal landmines all over the place, of course—evading the discussion of why she'd been previously using a computer ten years out of date took some mental gymnastics, for instance, given that Trayne Owen could obviously have afforded to buy her a new computer every year if she wanted.

With a little effort, though, she kept their talk mostly focused on learning about the geeky subjects that interested *young* members of that intellectual group. *Homestuck* had been a stroke of good fortune, but Holly was all too aware that she didn't have a clue about most things the younger crowd did as a matter of course.

I'm really *going to have to practice my texting,* she thought. *Even while we've been here, Seika's texted three different people. It's completely habitual with her, and I guess everyone else our age.*

"So, Holly, what do you think about this Princess Holy Aura?"

Holly started and barely got hold of herself. *Don't look* guilty, *for chrissake!* "Princess who?"

"Well, that's what people say her name is. You *did* hear about the two monsters, right? That rock-worm and the huge blob-thing that people saw at the mall?"

"Oh, that! I didn't hear about this princess thing, though."

"Well, look!" Seika expertly tapped out searches into the computer.

Wow. Even more stuff than I thought. That's not a half-bad picture of Holy Aura, either, though it's a little blurry. "Dad was wondering if it was some kind of weird publicity stunt for a movie or something."

Seika gave her a look reserved for idiots. "What's your dad *on*? The one parking lot was totally trashed, there was damage to half the mall, and people like my friend Alyssa are in *therapy* after what they saw!"

Holly raised her hands defensively. "Hey, I was just saying what Dad said! I didn't know anything about it!"

"Then it's time to teach you how to get the truth out of the Web! Never listen to the news—I'll bet your dad thinks they tell the truth! Look, here's what I do . . ."

Holly was impressed. *When* I *was a kid, I don't think teenagers knew what politics* was. *She's fourteen and already looking for her own news sources. And* boy *is she sharp.* This just reinforced her conviction that trying to hide the truth from anyone who *did* get involved would be worse than useless.

"Dinner, girls!"

She glanced up, startled. Light had faded to twilight as they talked. "Coming, Dad!"

"What's for dinner?" Seika asked.

"Sushi. I hope you like sushi?"

"I *love* it. So does my little brother Van, so he's gonna be jealous."

They came into the dining room where there was a variety of sushi on elaborate display. "That's really pretty, Mr. Owen. I didn't hear the delivery guy come, when did it get here?"

Holly saw Silvertail's human form give a broad grin. "No delivery guy, Seika; I made these myself."

Seika stared as Holly shot Silvertail a "*seriously?*" look. "You *made* this? Awesome."

As they sat down, the phone on the wall rang. Trayne picked it up. "Hello, Owen residence. Who? Oh, Mr. Cooper. Yes, we were just sitting down to dinner. They've been getting along just fine. I could bring . . . certainly, if you'd rather . . . That would be fine. It's a Friday so I don't require a fixed bedtime for Holly, so the time's entirely up to you. Of course. Thank you for calling!"

"That was my dad?"

"It was. He says he will pick you up at around eight-thirty to nine; they're going to watch a movie with Van."

"Great!"

Time passed quicker than Holly liked; she was genuinely sad when she heard the bell ring downstairs. "That'll be your dad."

It was indeed Seika's father; in contrast to his at-best-average-height daughter, Dave Cooper was a mountain, at least six foot three and built like a linebacker. "Hey, Sei, you have fun?" he said as they came down the steps.

"*Lots* of fun! Dad, this is Holly, Holly, this is my dad ——"

"Hi," Holly said. *Crap, I'm still not used to being this* small. *Shaking his hand feels like I'm a kid shaking hands with my Uncle Pete.*

"Hello, Holly, nice to meet you," Dave said, then turned to Trayne. "So, did Seika behave?"

"I sincerely doubt you ever have a problem with her behaving. I hardly heard a peep from either of them except at dinner. Oh, here." He handed Mr. Cooper a snap-top container. "Seika mentioned others in her family might want some, so I've packed the leftover sushi in there."

"Oh, now, I can't take—"

"I insist. Consider it a hello present from someone new to the neighborhood who's glad to see his little girl's made a new friend."

"Well, that's kind of you. Have to reciprocate next time, then. Seika, would you like to have Holly visit us?"

"Can she? Tomorrow?"

Mr. Cooper laughed. "That's short notice, so I'd have to check it with your mom. But if it's okay with Mr. Owen?"

"I have no objection."

"All right, then I'll give you a call tomorrow and let you know."

After a few more goodbyes the door finally closed. "That seemed to go well," Silvertail said, reverting to white-rat form.

"Were you worried?"

"Of course I was. You are hardly a professional at deception, Steve, and in fact your basically honest nature makes it difficult for you."

"Not much deception," Holly said. "I'm . . . well, not really *Steve* so much anymore. He's *there*—it's not like I'm *forgetting* him—but the longer I live as Holly the more I *am* Holly. I just have to watch for the places where Holly's . . . blank, filled only by whatever Steve has."

"Yes. But I must give you credit, Steve—Holly. Your decision to spend considerable time accustoming yourself to *being* Holly, even at the risk of more attacks, was indeed the wisest possible course of action. You can pay attention to what is happening around you without risking betrayal of your basic nature."

"Good thing, too. If I was still really thinking as *Steve* all the time, I don't think I could *possibly* have relaxed around Seika."

"I suppose not." He looked at her, beady red eyes suddenly narrowed. "But you have something else to say."

"Yeah. Remember how you said these adversaries are shaped by the modern perceptions and beliefs? Would it be more likely to be things relevant to, well, *my* age group? My peers? Or to the adults?"

The little rat's face became visibly thoughtful. "An interesting question. In many prior civilizations the . . . memes, so to speak, were less fragmented. While children might have different interests, they rarely had completely separate mythologies, so to speak. Are you saying there is a separation?"

"Ohhhh yeah. Millennials and younger kids have a whole new set of, well, urban legends, stories they tell each other, invent whole cloth and pass around. Some of them don't go anywhere, others go viral. And after a while, some start to be less stories and more actual internet mythology. Seika was touring me around all the sites she visits and where her online friends hang out, and boy, there's a *lot* of this stuff. Tumblr legends, creepypastas, all sorts of stuff that's . . . well, partly ironic, partly just stories, but you can tell reading some of the forums that some of it may not be."

Silvertail shimmered, becoming Trayne Owen again. "Show me."

She watched as Trayne skimmed page after page, and saw his expression growing darker every moment. Finally he closed the web browser and turned toward her.

"What is it, Silvertail?"

"I am *very* much afraid," he said after a moment, "that your generation's fascination with the insidious and macabre may serve as the foundation for the most horrific and implacable manifestations ever faced by mankind."

✳ Chapter 18 ✳

"I push the door open slowly," Seika said, miming the action across the broad table. Her voice echoed in the mostly deserted cafeteria, giving an appropriate overtone to her words.

Holly glanced at the other three members of the Steampunk Adventure Club. "Any of you doing anything while the Countess opens the door?"

Caitlin Modofori shrugged. "Iron Jake's got his flux baton ready, but other than that he's just watching."

"By my calculations," said Tierra MacKintor in a deliberately hollow, flat tone, "there is a ninety-two point six percent chance we are about to enter combat. The Argent Automaton is prepared." The startlingly redheaded girl pushed back the gear-encrusted silvery mask and shifted to a more normal tone. "That means I'm holding my speed boost ready for action at the first sign of a fight."

"Got it," Holly said. "If there's combat, you'll start already at full speed. Good thing you told me; I'd assumed you would be going with the strength boost."

Tierra grinned. "Speed *kills*."

The third member, Nikki Hand, closed her eyes. "The Mystic is opening the Third Eye!"

"You'll get a chance to see any supernatural influences. Good thinking, if it turns out there's something beyond the mundane involved.

"As you open the door, you can see a huge, shadowy figure at the far side of the room . . . an immense, monstrous statue. There are many robed figures in front of it . . ." Holly continued describing what the Countess could see, and saw the others exchanging glances.

The fact that both she and Seika liked role-playing games had suggested the possibility of forming a gaming group to both of them. The school required a minimum of five people for any club that met after school hours, and though they'd found both Nikki and Caitlin fairly quickly, they'd been stuck for a couple of weeks looking for a fifth.

Holly knew, of course, that Dex would've been willing to join in a flash, but she honestly wasn't ready to take that risk. Sure, visibly there was nothing to link her with Steve Russ, but long-term social interaction was a lot different than just passing someone in the hallway.

Finally, though, Tierra heard them discussing a *Spirit of the Century* adventure as a possibility and immediately spoke up about the art and fantastic *costuming* possible. Once she agreed to join, the Steampunk Adventure Club began meeting.

Just as well that we chose this genre, Holly thought. *Steve never ran anything in this kind of setting, so I had to invent a new world. If Dex ever does join, or even hears about it, this isn't going to remind him too much of what we used to do.*

But there still were similarities—in the group, if not in the campaign. Seika was by far the smartest, though she wasn't nearly as loud or clueless as Dex; Nikki was the cheerful supporting player who would take whatever role the others left open, reminding Holly poignantly of Chad; even her brown hair and broad figure echoed Chad's own. Caitlin was more serious and thoughtful in play, a strange maturity that echoed the vastly older Eli—although her wavy honey-blonde hair looked nothing like Eli's close-cropped black-and-silver. Tierra's constant support of the campaign with little sketches, bangles, and costume props was certainly a lot like Mike, who used to make portraits of everyone's characters.

Are these four the Apocalypse Maidens? Are any of them?

The thought always intruded, whenever she was talking to a girl near her own current age: *Are you one of us?* And she was never sure if she wanted the answer to be yes or no. As she was getting more used to being Holly Owen, the strain of being the *only* person who knew the secret was getting worse.

The players started discussing the tableau Holly had described, deciding how they wanted to approach this. Holly looked up, saw that the windows were almost pitch dark. "I think we'd better stop it here, everyone."

A faint murmur reached their ears, and Seika grimaced. "Yeah, the teams are all coming back in."

The girls' sports teams practiced on the same days that the Steampunk Club currently met—as did a couple of other clubs. That was partly for the very good reason that if the teams were practicing, there were enough kids to justify keeping some of the buses available, saving parents trips while still getting the students home safe.

They started packing up the dice and books—or, in the case of Holly and Caitlin, tablets. "Darn, I was looking forward to kicking some heads in!" Seika said.

"I know you were," Tierra said. "But it can get tedious. I'll be glad to start that battle completely fresh."

"Tedious? But . . ." Holly bent and picked up her backpack as the two began arguing mechanics versus dramatics and, Holly thought, preferences. *Heh. You can't please even all the players all the time, all you can do is hope to keep them happy MOST of the time.*

"Come on, guys, we'd better head to A-Wing. Get better seats in the buses before the whole volleyball and football teams get in."

Tierra had just opened the cafeteria door when the lights went out.

Nikki jumped and gave a tiny scream. "Sorry! I just . . . *really* hate that."

They waited a few seconds, but the lights didn't seem to be coming back on. They could hear the distant protests of the athletes. "Come on," Tierra said after a moment. "It's not *that* dark, and the buses won't care. I just hope it's not out back home. *So* boring."

A bright white light appeared; Nikki had activated the light on her phone. "It may not be 'that dark' but isn't this easier?"

They all laughed, and started down the corridor, steps echoing loudly in the deserted corridors. "There's the door to A-Wing," Caitlin said. "Why's it closed, though?"

"I don't know—*ooof*!"

The "*ooof*!" was forced out of Holly as she'd tried to push through and the door had refused to budge. "What the heck . . . ?"

"Some idiot's *locked* it?" Tierra shoved against the door, but it wouldn't move. "They *know* we're here, right? We'll have to go all the way to the other end and out the fire doors—and that'll set off the alarm."

Hurrying their steps so that they could still (hopefully) beat the teams to the buses, the five girls headed back toward one of the red fire exits; these were never locked, but any attempt to open them would set off a loud-screaming alarm (something that, invariably, someone would do at least two or three times a quarter). Holly saw the dully-gleaming bar come into view, strode forward, and—

"*OOOF!*"

She bounced off the door so hard she sat down on the cold granite floor.

"What the *fuck*?" Seika demanded in her Karkat voice.

Holly rose slowly to her feet, and suddenly the darkness around her was sinister, filled with amorphous menace. A chill stole down her spine. *A bunch of girls locked into a place with the power suddenly out . . .*

"There's a back door through the cafeteria," Caitlin said, sounding a little nervous. "We could go through there."

"Fine," said Nikki, "But I'm calling my dad anyway. It's *illegal* to lock a fire door on the inside! People could get killed!"

She lifted her phone a bit higher as they walked. "Huh. I'm not getting any bars. How about you guys?"

Wow. It's true. The hairs on the back of my neck are *starting to stand up.* The gooseflesh marched down Holly's arms. "Shouldn't Mr. Jefferson be in back of the cafeteria anyway?"

"Duh, of course. *He'll* have the keys."

Holly had been concentrating furiously, but apparently Silvertail couldn't do his telepathic-talking trick to mere Holly Owen. *Still, he's gotta be nearby. He'd follow me. I'm not actually without any backup.*

A rumble of thunder came from outside, and a flicker of lightning vaguely illuminated the hallway for an instant; they could see the black square of the open cafeteria doors up ahead. The tapping hiss of rain on the roof became audible.

"Wow, this is creepy!" Tierra said, in a cheerful voice. "Maybe we should be telling ghost stories or something." They headed across the empty floor of the cafeteria. "Mr. Jefferson! Mr. *Jefferson*! Someone's locked the doors to the wing!"

"Is the roof *leaking*?" Caitlin demanded. "It *dripped* on me!"

"Boy, I hope not," Nikki said, turning the white light upward to look.

All five of them screamed, a sound that momentarily drowned out the growl of thunder.

Directly above, at the very peak of the ceiling, Mr. Donald Jefferson was spread-eagled, hands and feet impaled by something that glittered, a wide-eyed silent scream of horror showing above a red, dripping gash in his neck.

✳ Chapter 19 ✳

The first thought that came into Holly's head after the shock was a crushing sense of guilt. There was no doubt in her mind now that this was the next manifestation, and that meant that Mr. Jefferson was dead in either reality. *I managed to stop the first two without deaths. I . . . I hoped I could save everyone.*

"OhshitOhshitOhshit . . ." Nikki was mumbling from behind her. Caitlin was simply frozen, staring in utter shock.

"Let's get the hell *out* of this place!" Tierra hissed.

Even as the five of them turned back toward the hallway, the kitchen doors behind them flew open and a shadowy figure strode out, an unhurried, implacable stride clicking menacingly on the polished floor beneath it. Lightning flashed off the edge of a red-dripping axe.

"*Run!*" Holly shouted. She was already trying to think how to deal with this. *I don't know if any of these are Apocalypse Maidens yet. I can't just change in front of all of them; "three can keep a secret if two of them are dead." Got to buy time somehow . . .*

Seika grabbed one of the last chairs as they passed it, dragging it with her rattle-banging up the three steps to the cafeteria exit.

"What do you want *that* for?" demanded Caitlin. "That's not going to stop his—"

"The *doors,*" she said urgently.

Holly suddenly understood what Seika meant. "She's right! If we can take it apart we can use the legs to bar the doors! Come on, everyone, help break this thing!"

The figure was halfway down the cafeteria aisle, boots rapping out a remorseless countdown, as the girls hammered the chair violently against walls and floor, yanked at it.

A quarter of the way to go, but there was suddenly a sharp metallic *crack* and the weld holding the front pair of legs to the underframe snapped, leaving a U-shaped piece of metal—two chair legs formed of a single tube of bent metal.

"Shut the *doors*!" Seika said, voice cracking in panic. Holly and the other three yanked the cafeteria doors—hollow steel with small windows—around, forced them shut.

The metronome precision of that stride altered abruptly, hurrying, not a run, but the sound of someone understanding that a situation has changed. Seika tried to slide the steel curve through the two metal door handles, but something struck the doors heavily, almost forcing them open. Nikki screamed but pushed *harder*, Holly following suit; on the other door Caitlin and Tierra shoved with all their strength, and the doors closed once more—

—and Seika slipped the steel U through the handles.

The door rattled viciously, but the steel held it firm; more, because of the U shape, it couldn't dislodge from someone just jostling it. The five girls grinned at each other for an instant.

Then a tremendous thudding *chop* echoed through the dark hallway, and the door dented outward.

"Come *on*," Holly said. "We've got to get the hallway doors open somehow, before he gets out!"

"Who *is* he?" Caitlin demanded in the panicky tones of someone trying to hold onto a thread of sanity. "Why's he doing this? That . . . that was a real body, wasn't it?"

"Maybe it wasn't!" Nikki said, grasping at a thread of hope. "It's a prank, like that murdering clown-thing we saw on YouTube!"

"Trust me, that was a real body and this is no prank," Holly said. "That axe was real and he's actually chopping through the lunchroom doors. You think anyone pulling a prank here is going to wreck the school like that?"

The doors to the central hall were still closed, and as the five girls ran toward them, they suddenly shuddered with a crashing bang that made all five skid to a terrified halt. *What the hell? How'd he get ahead of us? Or are there* two *of these things?*

But even as they stood frozen in indecision, there was another tremendous crash and the doors flew wide.

Framed in the doorway were two extremely tall girls; one was so dark-skinned she was a shadow against shadows, but her brilliant *chunni* headdress, visible even in the dim light, outlined her clearly.

From that, Holly recognized her instantly: Devika Weatherill, captain of the girls' basketball team. With that hint, Holly could make out that the lighter-skinned, brown-haired girl next to her was Tori Murstein, likewise captain of the volleyball team. Silhouetted behind them was a crowd of other girls, presumably the teams that had just finished practice.

Seeing their expressions, Devika grimaced. "Let me guess, doors down there are locked too."

"Never mind *doors*, run!" Tierra said. "There's a psycho with an *axe* back there—"

"What?" Tori looked amused. "Are you joking? I—"

She was cut short by an echoing impact from down the corridor, an impact that combined with the shriek of ripping metal.

"Not joking! *Run*!"

Reverberating down the shadowed hallway behind Holly and the others, rhythmic, unhurried footsteps were approaching.

That sound—calm, purposeful, and utterly out of place—convinced the others that *something* very bad was coming, and the slow backing up turned into a jog, and then a run as something sang out from the darkness,

"*Hippity-hey, hippity-hop*
Who's next to get the chop?
Hippity-hop, hippity-hey
Who's getting the axe today?"

The voice was a cracked tenor, the sound of madness on the edge, and the tune was a cheerful one . . . in a minor key that turned its macabre cheer to a graveyard threat.

"We *have* to get the front doors open somehow!" Holly told them. "This guy's locked everything!"

"Shouldn't be *possible*," said someone from the volleyball team. "My dad's a fire marshal and he told me that fire doors *can't* be locked from the inside!"

"Well, they *are*," Tierra snapped. "We tried!"

"So did we," said Devika. "But let's get these doors open!"

The front doors of the school *looked* like they should be easier to open, glass fronted as they were—but Holly was pretty sure the glass was thick and reinforced.

But everyone's focused on the door . . .

Without giving herself time to think, Holly backed quietly away from the crowd, and headed down the B-Wing corridor (whose doors showed where the teams had come from). *One girl separated from the rest. That's the trope, right?*

She prayed to whatever powers there might be that she was making the right decision. *If I'm wrong . . . an axe-wielding monster's going to plow right into a crowd of high-school girls. And* monster *will be literally correct.*

B-Wing was silent, her footsteps and the faint echo of her breathing the only sounds. It suddenly struck her that it was *unnaturally* quiet; she wasn't so far away that she shouldn't be able to hear the others trying to get through the front door—or their screams, if the thing caught them. They'd been able to vaguely hear the noise of the teams coming back into the school all the way over in C-Wing!

It's here.

From somewhere—she couldn't tell which direction—the singing began again:

"*Hippity-hi, hippity-ho*
Who will be the next to go?
Hippity-ho, hippity-hi
You're the one about to DIE!"

She drew a breath and reached up to touch the Star Nebula Brooch—

One of the classroom doors slammed open scarcely ten feet from her, and a towering figure came forth, seemingly born from darkness and thunder, a long coat flapping behind it, axe rising for a strike, lightning flashing off the white-grinning clown mask. Her breath caught in her throat and she knew that she had no time for the invocation.

No time at all.

But even as the axe began to descend, a small form barreled in from the left and slammed into the axe-wielding figure with a diving lunge just at the knee. The figure gave a grunt and lost its grip on the axe, the weapon spinning through the air to *thunk* harmlessly into the wall a foot to the right of Holly's head.

"What the *fuck* is wrong with you?" demanded Seika, even as she scrambled to her feet and the figure rolled to a halt, starting to rise. "You *never* break up the party!"

She came to save me. And there's no one else here but us and . . . it. That's got *to be my answer.*

The two girls were backpedaling as the thing rose to its full height and strode toward its weapon. "Seika," Holly said, "I hope you can keep a secret."

"Huh? What? A *secret*?"

Holly's fingers gripped the brooch and the invocation came to her now without conscious thought. ". . . Mystic Galaxy Defender, Princess Holy Aura!"

The pure-crystal light detonated like the Sun in the dark hallway, and the monster threw up a hand to shield itself, momentarily cowering before the Light. Seika, too, tried to shield her face from the light, but Holy Aura could see an expression, not of fear or incomprehension, but wonder and understanding. "Wow," she whispered.

"I am the one you seek, monster!" Holy Aura said—for the Challenge, too, was inviolable. But it would not end the same. "You have slain the good and brought terror to the innocent, and for that, this Apocalypse Maiden says that *you,*" she pointed straight at the shining clown mask that suddenly looked much less terrifying, "are going *down*!"

It gave a mad giggle and suddenly whirled its axe so swiftly that it became a silver and red circle of death.

"*Hippity-how, hippity-hill*
That's what you say *you will*
Hippity-hill, hippity-how
Time to die for you is NOW*!*"

It swung and Holly parried with the Silverlight Bisento, and a shockwave shuddered out from the point of impact, rattling doors, cracking windows. *Crap, this thing is* strong, she thought as she felt her arms give a fraction under the blow. *I thought something this much smaller would be* weaker *than the others!*

But it *was* still a lot taller than she was, and she ducked the next swing and *rammed* the *bisento*'s blade straight through the creature. She heard Seika backing away with faint murmurs that were probably curses. But she wasn't running; she was trying to stay out of the way, yet remain close enough to see . . . maybe close enough to help.

It gave a keening snarl and a backhand blow with the axehead sent Holy Aura tumbling away, feeling blood trickling from her scalp. *Crap! It's a good thing he couldn't turn the blade around that fast, or he'd have split my head in two!*

But even though she felt a little dazed and her weapon was still stuck in the thing's body, she rolled to her feet with more confidence. *Silvertail?*

I am here.

Take care of Seika.

An impression of a nod. *Count on me.*

The thing ripped the Silverlight Bisento from its chest and hurled it at Holy Aura, but she caught it easily. "You can't hurt me with my own weapon, monster—" she began, but cut off when it *sprinted* forward, axe swinging in a dizzying and lethal geometry of cuts that drove her backward. She managed to catch the weapon with the shaft of hers momentarily and bring the ball of the *bisento* around to smash it full in its masked face.

The mask split.

Holly found herself screaming, backing away from the thing while desperately raining unaimed but powerful blows at it to keep it back.

To call what was revealed a "face" was an offense to the word. Yes, there were eyes—glaring, gleefully mad eyes, one green as poison, one red as blood. There was a mouth, with broken, yellow teeth raggedly sharp in an insane grin. There was even a nose, half eaten away by acid or fire. But the repellent, monstrous whole was hideous, ridged with scar tissue, living maggots wriggling through the pus-oozing flesh, holes in the cheeks showing the muscles and fangs from the sides as well as the front, and despite the decaying appearance there was no impression of weakness, of frailty, but of unnatural, unquenchable, abominable life. It stank of old blood and rot and rusting steel, of gangrenous wounds and creeping infections and burned flesh, and it *smiled* with a crazed good cheer that infused it with even more horror than a savage grin or implacable immobility would have.

And it was moving *fast*. Holy Aura could barely fend off its blows, even as she managed—with the help of ancient power and the stabilizing memories of Stephen Russ—to gain control over herself. *It's no worse looking than the shoggoth was.* That wasn't *quite* true, but Steve had seen plenty of horror movies—including the slasher films this thing was drawing on. This was worse . . . but only because she was letting the thing's aura, its *essence*, bring home the reality of its malevolence.

She somersaulted backward, vaguely conscious of Seika and Silvertail now to the side, in one of the classrooms—*got to keep it focused on me*—spun her weapon around, concentrated, saw the corridor brightening with white-silver radiance. "*Ginhikari no Bisento!*"

The broad blade of the immense weapon caught and carved *through* the haft of the bloody axe, and continued its irresistible course through obscene head, neck, and body, cleaving the stalker-manifestation almost entirely in two. The thing collapsed, arms twitching, eyes rolling in their separate sections of skull, the pieces of the axe tumbling to the floor.

Now, I just have to finish it off. But even as she reached within her, looking for that transcendent connection to the power beyond, the slasher-monster's body pulled itself together, the horrific head sealing itself, and even the *axe* mended itself, wood fibers reversing their sundering and merging to become, impossibly, whole again.

Holy Aura parried, but her arms almost buckled.

It's getting stronger, and I haven't been able to kill it!

She needed *time*, and *that* was one thing her opponent was never going to give her.

✳ Chapter 20 ✳

Take care of Seika.

The words had been thought to Silvertail simply, but he was used to seeing what lay behind the words; Holly would not tell him to do, or not do, anything else, but she knew, or thought she knew, what had to happen now. *Count on me*, he replied, and knew that she understood completely.

Seika cooperated by backing away quickly from the two combatants, placing her back against one of the classroom doors. It was simple to use his magic to cause the door to unlock and open; the stalking-monster's magic was focused on Holy Aura now.

The door popping open caused Seika to stumble backward, off-balance; she managed to recover and came to a stop leaning against one of the desks, pushing her springy hair out of her face, shaking, staring . . .

"But not running," he said.

She jumped away from him—a creditable leap, which shoved two desks onto their sides. "*Shit!* I mean . . . Ohmigod, you can *talk?* You're her . . . spirit animal, familiar, I mean, the cute animal that guides the *mahou shoujo* to their . . ."

She trailed off, but the disbelieving wonder in her face showed she'd already made the leap. "No. No *way*. Not me. Not fat, slow, clumsy—"

"Holly—Holy Aura—needs help," he said simply. "You came here to help her. You *did* help her, despite what must have been absolute terror, because she was your *friend*. You are not running. You are a warrior at heart, Seika Lynn Cooper, and your 'slow clumsiness' has already served to rescue Holly once. Will you take up the sword for real? Will you become one of the Apocalypse Maidens and fight at her side?"

"*Will* I?" She opened her mouth with a shaking joy writ clear across every line of her young face, even as the building shuddered to another clash of light and dark.

"Wait!" Silvertail wished he could simply take her obvious acceptance . . . but he had agreed with Steve on the course they must take. "If you do, there is no going back, Seika. Lives will depend on you. And your family and friends may be in more danger until the ultimate enemy is overcome."

Seika hesitated. *She is* very *bright, this one. Even in these circumstances, she understands what I say . . . and I think even some of what is meant beneath the words.* But then another crash, a muffled shriek and curse from Holly, reached their ears. "If I don't . . . she's going to lose, isn't she?"

"I cannot be certain. But . . . yes, I would guess so. That is the way of the enchantment, the course of destiny. The second Apocalypse Maiden is now needed."

"Then do your magic, rat! My BFF is getting *whaled* on out there!"

"My *name* is Silvertail Heartseeker, and you, Seika, are one of the Hearts I have Sought, bearer of the Courage that is needed, the Will that is eternal. Take you up the Apocalypse Brooch and become one of the Maidens who will stand against the ending of all things!"

Seika's brown eyes were wide with wonder, a touch of fear, and a hint of anticipation as the broken-pointed star materialized before her. She swallowed so hard it was audible in the empty classroom, even with the echoes of the battle reverberating through the air, and then reached out and grasped the Apocalypse Brooch.

Ruby-bright light flared from the brooch, and Silvertail knew now who was being called forth. Seika raised the brooch over her head and the light blazed like a fiery star; her eyes reflected both realization and shock as the enchanted necessity took over.

"To avert the Apocalypse, and shield the innocent from evil, and stand against the powers of destruction, I offer myself as wielder and weapon, as symbol and sword!" Seika said, and her voice was the roar of a bonfire. "Mistress of the flame, bane of winter, I am the Apocalypse Maiden, Princess Radiance Blaze!"

Fire ignited around her body, floating her up, and she spun—or the world rotated about her, as she remained still. The luminance burned away her clothes, her body, and formed them anew, Silvertail now seeing a taller figure with hair that enhaloed her head like a dark sun, a figure bound in chains of flaming light, chains thick and heavy enough to restrain an army, not one mere girl.

But beneath the heavy mane of hair, the new face was undaunted, filled with certainty and joy; she strained against the bonds and the chains parted, *shattered* under the obdurate and irresistible power of fire unleashed.

Dark hands caught the silver-glowing chains, spun them about, and they *answered* her call, became a writhing circle of flaming steel into which she settled. Like Holy Aura's, Princess Radiance Blaze's armor was brief and stylized, but it shimmered with reds and oranges and golds like the fire that was her power.

Scarcely had her feet touched the ground, though, and she was off, a blur of crimson light almost beyond Silvertail's ability to follow.

Holly—Princess Holy Aura—*was* in trouble; the implacable stalker refused to give her room, a moment to focus and find the key to power she had learned in the depths of the shoggoth's embrace, and as Silvertail looked she was being forced backward by the thing's immense strength.

But a red-gold meteor streaked through the hallway and slammed into the creature with such absolute might that it flew straight and true down the rest of the hall to smash with earthshaking force into the door at the far end. Had its own power not sealed the doors, Silvertail was certain, the monster would have continued on out and across the rear parking lot like a cannonball.

But even *that* impact barely slowed it. The stalker-thing rebounded from the door, staggered, then reached out, and its axe slid across the floor to its hand.

"*Hippity-hue, hippity-hee*
You need more to finish off me!
Hippity-hee, hippity-hue
Who the hell are you?"

The magic bound Seika to answer, but she showed none of Steve's initial reluctance; she whirled her chains eagerly as she answered, "I am the one you fear, monster! Apocalypse Maiden the Second, Princess

Radiance Blaze! Reborn from the fire, mistress of the eternal flame, defender of life and ruler of the inferno below!" She grabbed one of the chains and snapped it tight between her two hands. "You've hurt my friend and threatened innocent lives, and for that, this Apocalypse Maiden says that *you* are going *down!*"

Silvertail could see that Holy Aura was rising, staring at the cocoa-skinned warrior of flame in awe. *Silvertail . . . is that what* I *am like?*

Exactly like that, yes. You are an Apocalypse Maiden, and so is she. Now, Holly, do what you both must—for the sake of the lives that even now are trapped within this building!

"R-Radiance Blaze, thanks for joining the party!" Holy Aura said, and her smile was more than a greeting.

For the first time the stalking monster gave vent to a sound other than the macabre singing, a growling, hollow snarl; it was a threatening sound . . . but the very fact that its pattern was breaking showed its uncertainty. *It must not escape, Maidens! It knows enough to report who you truly* are *to its mistress!*

It did not seem in the mood to retreat, however, for it raised the axe and began its metronomic stride again.

"He's not going down with one hit," Holy Aura murmured. "I need *time* to get focused."

"You mean your super-attack's gotta charge," Radiance Blaze whispered back. "So I have to keep him off you, right?"

"He could kill—"

"—everyone here, Holly, and you know it, so now that I've got it, let me do *my* job, right?"

Silvertail could feel the pained reluctance echoing from the core that was Stephen Russ, the fear that he would be sending a child to die as a distraction. But as Holy Aura, she knew her duty . . . and could see the eyes of Seika, Princess Radiance Blaze, shining at her with a fearsome eagerness.

"Then . . . go. But *watch out*!"

Radiance Blaze leapt forward, arm curling back, then whipping forward, and silver-flaming chain *streaked* from her hand, straight and true as a rifle shot. The chain's heavy links battered the monster full in the face, and the axe rebounded from the chain. Its eyes were narrowed, squinted in pain and fury, and it made no more taunting songs, but shrank away from the rattling metal that was yanked back to its wielder and then cast forth again, an arch of blazing iron flame that almost twined around the handle of the axe and *did* catch one hand, sent smoke up from the leathery skin.

The manifestation of stalking horror growled again and tried to charge, to close the distance, but in a flash of fiery light Radiance Blaze was *behind* him, wonder writ large on her face as she realized that the speed of fire was beyond human realization, wonder that became a fierce joy.

The creature's own inhuman speed was now put to the test as it began to dodge a barrage of battering chains that zigzagged across the floor and through the air like bolts of volcanic lightning. But dodge them it *did*, and Radiance Blaze began to back up, looking uncertain, as it dodged or parried, one to the left, one to the right, front, back, each one allowing it to take one more step, and its dead clown face grinned anew.

"*Hippity-hend, hippity-hosst*
Now for sure your battle's lost!
Hippity-hosst, hippity-hend
Then I'll finish off your friend!"

Radiance Blaze suddenly straightened, and the tight smile beneath the huge halo of hair was chilling. "Well hippity-hong and hippity-hap, you've just stepped into my trap!"

The monster froze, aware only now that it had not been repeated strikes of two chains but a *succession* of many chains it had deflected . . .

. . . chains that now *surrounded it*.

"*Radiance Blaze—CIRCLE of FIRE!*"

It tried to raise its vicious axe, to protect itself, but eight separate chains rose, arcing up like fiery cobras, and struck, twining themselves together around the monster and igniting into a metallic inferno. The creature screamed and struggled, but for a moment it was held fast, unable to break the chains, unable to slip free.

Unable to *dodge*.

Holy Aura's voice chased after the echoes of her fellow Apocalypse Maiden, and the pure white light eradicated all shadow from existence. "Light of Apocalypse—*SOLAR FLARE!*"

The world went pure white and a ripping, gargling growling scream was torn from the thing. Like a doll in a blowtorch it sizzled and burned, still struggling, snarling, desperate to escape and destroy its attackers, but it was weakening, decaying visage turning to ash, leaving bone, and even the bone scorching, melting away, skeletal hands crumbling, the axe itself tumbling to the ground and blackening before the imperative force of the Apocalypse Maidens.

The light faded away, the chains clattered limply to the floor, and both Holy Aura and Radiance Blaze sagged against the wall, holding themselves up, staring tensely at the remains of the thing: a half-crumbled skeleton surrounded by ash, wisps of smoke slowly trailing up from it.

"That's . . . got it." Holy Aura said finally.

"Yeah." Radiance Blaze stared, then her face lit up. "*Yeah*! Boo*ya*! Kicked *your* ass, huh! Teach you to pick on *this* school!"

"Oh, god, *school*. Silvertail, by now they'll have noticed we're gone, and if—"

"Holly, Holly, trust me, I already have taken care of those issues," Silvertail said, hopping to her shoulder as the two girls started to hesitantly make their way up the corridor toward A-Wing. "Temporary simulacra of both of you have been with the group, and of course we already discussed the cam—"

Without so much as pause or warning, Holy Aura and Radiance Blaze spun around, and a twin blast of flaming spiritual power *roared* down the hallway, catching the axe-wielding, only half-healed form and slinging it back to the fire door, pinning the screaming, writhing thing against its own immovable barrier. "Do you think we're *idiots*?" Holy Aura demanded, and Radiance Blaze finished, "The monster *always* gets back up for one more shot after you think it's dead!"

A thundering stream of apocalyptic energies kept the thing irresistibly trapped between its insubstantial hammer and the fire door's mystically-sealed anvil, and the being's furious screams grew weaker as the combined power of Princess Holy Aura and Princess Radiance Blaze *eroded* it, turning it to ash and the ash to dust and the dust to a mist that dispersed into shadow that faded to nothing before their luminance. The two Apocalypse Maidens kept the power streaming out, their bodies shaking from the strain, faces tense and growing white with the effort, until a final, whispered scream rose and fell to silence and the door blew apart, the spiritual cannon continuing thirty yards before boring a hole straight through the rear parking lot.

Silvertail managed to clear his throat. "Um, yes. Well done, and well read. The memes, that is. You knew it would rise once you had declared it dead?"

"Like there was *ever* a slasher movie where that *didn't* happen," Seika said.

"Of course. As I was saying, we already discussed the cameras. Now, if you two will change *back* . . ."

"Oh." Holly reappeared in a flash; after a moment, Princess Radiance Blaze also disappeared, replaced by Seika.

"Ohmigod, ohmigod, ohmigod that was *so cool*," Seika said immediately. "Holly, my *God* you were so totally awesome it was like—"

"*I* was awesome? *You* kicked so much ass and you were—"

"*AHEM!*" The two girls jumped guiltily. "My apologies, both of you, but we *do* need to get you back quickly. The doors will all be opening in moments as the rest of the enchantment fades, and you must be back with the crowd." He looked at Seika. "You *must* come and visit Holly as soon as you—"

Seika's jaw suddenly dropped. "That voice . . . *Mr. OWEN*?"

My goodness *she is sharp indeed*. "Yes, Seika, you have penetrated my disguise. But listen, please. You *must* come to visit as soon as you can. There is much we have to tell you and discuss and, at least for now, you *must* keep this secret."

She nodded emphatically. "Count on me, Mr. . . . Silvertail? *God* that's going to be *so* weird. But yeah, I can keep the secret! I promise!"

"Good enough, then. Let's get you back to the group. Now follow my directions carefully and you will merge with your doppelgangers . . ."

Two Maidens awakened, and they already work well together. He felt himself starting to relax, then cursed at himself. *That is well and good, but this is still but the beginning.*

And now . . . now the enemy knows where to look.

✶ Chapter 21 ✶

"Daddy!"

Holly jumped up from the stiff-backed plastic chair that sat on one side of the simple table and leapt into Mr. Owen's somewhat startled embrace with such force that even the much taller man was almost knocked over.

She was disconcerted to realize how *little* of her joy and relief was feigned, and how much of it was real. *For a moment . . . it* was *like having my father show up when I needed him most.*

She couldn't dwell on that now; this was a *good* reaction, the *right* reaction for the circumstances. *Too bad he couldn't have just stayed with us, but there was no reason for Dad to be at the school, and every reason for Silvertail to head back home as fast as he could so no one else saw him.*

"Holly, are you all right? When the police called me I thought—"

"I'm fine, I'm fine, but oh, God, Daddy, Mr. Jefferson, and there was a man with an *axe*, and—"

"Slow down, slow down, Holly." Trayne Owen looked up at the detectives with what seemed genuine confusion and worry. "An *axe*?"

"I'm sorry, sir, but you *did* come down here without even waiting for us to explain everything," said the redheaded woman.

"I suppose I did. My apologies. Trayne Owen, and you are . . . ?"

"Detective Dana Kisaragi," she said, showing her ID, and shook Mr. Owen's hand. "And my apologies for having to call you down here, but this is a serious matter."

"Can you explain? Is Holly in trouble somehow?"

"No, nothing like that," Detective Kisaragi said. "Please, sit down. Coffee?"

Holly studied her covertly as her father accepted a cup. Despite the name, Dana Kisaragi had no sign of Japanese ancestry; she *did* have a wedding ring, though, so probably she'd married someone with the name. Tall—maybe a hair over six feet—her hair was clearly pretty long but was pulled up and tied well back, out of her way. Suit was immaculate even though she'd been here since the police had first showed up to get the girls out of the school. Sharp grey-green eyes; using a small recorder, not bothering with physical notes.

Holly's gut sense was that this was a *very* competent officer . . . which made her *really* dangerous for the masquerade.

"First, Mr. Owen . . . I assume you have heard of the two . . . rather extraordinary events that happened near here in the last few months?"

"You mean the reports of . . . well, some sort of *monsters*? One in the mall? Yes, I could hardly miss them."

"Well, it appears—I have to emphasize *appears*—that another such incident has happened at this school. Unlike the others, this one has resulted in at least one fatality."

"Fatal . . . someone's been *killed*? In my daughter's *school*?"

"Yes, sir. Which is why we need your permission to interview your daughter. We're interviewing all the girls who were in the school at the time in hope of making sense of what happened. *Something* happened there, and it wasn't just an ordinary murder."

"How do you mean?" Trayne Owen's eyes were narrowed, studying Dana Kisaragi as though *she* might be responsible for endangering his daughter.

"I am not at liberty to discuss details with anyone at this time," she said. "But it is *vital* that we get information from all the witnesses as quickly as we can, before memory fades or they start talking over what they saw between each other—as they inevitably will once they go back to school."

Trayne turned to Holly. "Holly, I don't know what you saw, but . . . are you up to talking about it?"

She swallowed. She still *was* a little shaky, even after an hour or so, so it didn't take much to emphasize it. "I . . . I guess. You'll stay here?"

"I certainly will." He looked at the detective. "I trust you have no objection?"

"I would *prefer* to interview her alone, but if you insist—"

"I do. You will speak with my daughter in my presence, or not at all."

"Very well." She sat down across from Holly at the little table in the interview room. "Holly, do you need anything? More water? Something to eat?"

She shook her head. "Nothing to eat . . . I'm not . . . hungry yet. A little more water, maybe."

One of the other detectives—Hughes, she thought his name was—opened a small fridge and brought out another bottle of water. "Thank you, Hughes," Kisaragi said. "You and Gilbert can wait outside. No, wait. Go check on the others and see how the interviews are coming; maybe the two of you can take a couple of the other girls or we'll be here all night."

"Yes, Detective," said the one named Gilbert, while Hughes just said, "Yes, ma'am." The door closed quietly behind them. A distant rumble of thunder echoed through the building, showing that the storm had not yet passed.

"Now, Holly, I need you to tell me everything that happened tonight. Start with what you were doing before you noticed anything odd, and then go from there."

"All right. Um, we were sitting around one of the cafeteria tables—"

"Who was 'we'?"

"Oh, our Steampunk Club. Me, Seika Cooper, Nikki Hand, Tierra MacKintor, and Caitlin Modofori."

"Got it. Go on."

"Well, I was running our game . . ."

She told the truth up to the point that they finally made it to A-Wing and the front doors. There wasn't any reason *not* to tell the truth, after all. "All right, so your club, along with the girls from the sports teams and two other clubs meeting that evening, arrived at the entranceway. What then?"

Damn. I can't talk to Seika and our stories have *to match.*

Trayne Owen touched her hand. "Relax, Holly. Just think about what happened and tell the detective."

Suddenly she was aware that there *were* memories of that time—strangely phantom memories, but clear, and she knew somehow that they accorded with what the other girls would have seen and heard. "Well, um, we all tried to get the doors open but they were locked. A couple of the bigger girls grabbed one of the big benches near the office and tried to break the glass in one of the doors, but it didn't work no matter *how* hard they hit it."

"Really? Do you remember which door?"

She thought a moment. "If you're looking from the inside out, the second door from the left-hand side."

The redheaded woman nodded, looking thoughtful. "So what next?"

Holly consulted the ghostly recollections again. "Well, they'd just given up on beating on the door, and even Devika and the older girls were starting to look scared for real, when we hear this voice shouting from down B-Wing."

"A voice? What kind of voice?"

"A girl's voice, I guess. But it was . . . really powerful, like it was through a loudspeaker or something. But it wasn't—not through the school loudspeakers, anyway. You could tell it was coming from down B-Wing's hall." *Boy, this is* freaky. *I'm remembering this perfectly . . . except I know it's not a* memory *at all.*

"Could you hear what it said?"

"Not *all* of it, but at the end of the first time, I'm sure it said something like 'Princess Holy Arrow.'" *Close enough, anyway.*

The *faintest* quirk of Detective Kisaragi's eyebrow showed that she recognized something. "I see. You say the *first time*. The voice spoke more than once?"

"Oh, yeah. Right after that there was a little pause and, well, it sounded like this princess was threatening something, I guess the . . ." —she shuddered, remembering now as an ordinary girl the hideously creepy sing-song voice—"the . . . killer, the stalker? Anyway, I couldn't make out the whole speech but she definitely said that the thing was going *down*."

"Interesting. And then?"

Holly related what those shadowy memories told her—fragments of words, bomb blasts of distant combat shaking the room, the screams of the girls near her. *This must be Silvertail's doing. Of course he'd have made sure we knew what the others had seen and heard. I just have to hope Seika catches on and plays along.*

She was sure Seika would. The smaller black girl had shown she was sharp as a box of razors already, and she'd had the courage to come help her friend even *before* she'd found out she was an Apocalypse Maiden; Seika wouldn't lose her head in interrogation.

". . . and then the doors just suddenly opened, after everything we and the fire department outside had been trying before had failed, and we got out and you guys picked us up and I guess that's it," she finished.

"Yes, that does bring us up to date," agreed Detective Kisaragi. There was the slightest flicker of her gaze, as though she was considering saying something and then reconsidered, or as though she had thought of something and wanted to hide the thought.

Trayne Owen had been staring from one to the other with an appearance of increasing perplexity. "Detective, does . . . I mean, is what she saying true?"

"Do you think she isn't telling us the truth, Mr. Owen?"

"No! No, of course not. But some of these . . . things she describes—"

"It does seem to fit with those prior anomalies. What it *means*—why these events have started happening, why here, and what the ultimate purpose of these monsters or this 'princess' may be? We don't know, sir, and at the moment I can't even speculate. But we've kept you long enough. We *may* have to interview her once or twice more, but we'll call you well in advance. Will that be all right?"

Trayne Owen nodded after a moment. "Someone's dead, and something tried to kill my daughter and her friends. I assure you we will cooperate with whatever's necessary to put a stop to this."

"Thank you, sir." She got up and opened the door. "Let me show you out. And Holly, thank you. You've been a *great* help."

"Thanks, Ms. . . . er, Detective Kisaragi. Umm . . ."

She raised an eyebrow. "Yes?"

"Well . . . is the school closed? I mean, *will* it be closed?"

She and Trayne Owen shared a small chuckle. "It *may* be closed tomorrow, but we will try our best to do all our work and clear out before morning. If not, the next day for sure."

"So it'll be bedtime for you after we get home," Trayne said. "Sorry, Holly."

"Do I . . . have to go?"

"No," Trayne said immediately. "That will be entirely up to you. And I am sure the counselors will want to see all you girls anyway. But we'll talk about that later."

"Good night, Mr. Owen, Holly," the detective said, letting them out of the police station door.

"Good night, Detective," Trayne said.

They walked quietly to where Trayne had parked the minivan and got in. Mr. Owen started the car, put it in gear, and pulled out onto the road.

Holly saw him making a few tiny gestures with his hand and murmuring something very, very quietly.

After another minute, he leaned back slightly. "Holly, you did *very* well. That was a very dangerous situation."

"Dangerous? You mean, if they learn too much they could get killed, right?"

"To an extent, yes. But I sensed . . . some odd indications about our interviewer. My senses, as you know, are not limited to human, and the *smell* of her identity card was slightly different—too new, for one thing. And some of her reactions to the story were less of surprise or puzzlement than I would expect."

"You think she's one of the *enemy*?" Somehow Holly found that hard to believe. Detective Kisaragi struck her as sincere in her concern.

"Enemy? Not . . . precisely. I *believe* she is with the OSC."

"OSC? The Office of Special Counsel?" Holly was confused.

"Eh? No, no. In this general era I believe they have used a number of aliases, but in actuality it is the initials of their organization's motto and goal: Obtain, Secure, Counter."

"Obtain, secure, and counter *what*?"

"Supernatural or super-normal threats," Mr. Owen said.

"Oh, crap. One of those groups you mentioned."

"Yes. I cannot say I am very surprised. There was no subtlety in our enemy's first two assaults, as they are uninterested in stealth as such, and such high-profile paranormal events would naturally draw some of their investigators. With luck, however, the events of this night will actually serve to eliminate you and Seika from consideration as candidates for the two Apocalypse Maidens."

"Dad? I mean, Silvertail, they don't *know* about the Apocalypse

Maidens and all that, right? All that gets erased when the Maidens win."

He was silent for a moment. "I cannot say for certain, honestly. If they were a purely mundane organization, no, they would not, but they are not purely mundane. Over the centuries they have captured numerous paranormal objects, beings, and so on, and some they are capable of controlling and using. So they may possibly have some idea of the existence, though not the details, of the Cycle, and possibly of the fact that there is truth behind many of the worst legends."

"But they're not our friends, either?"

Trayne's face was grim. "No. Their position is that such powers are threats in and of themselves to mankind and must be captured and neutralized, regardless of how those threats might regard themselves, unless and until the OSC decides how they may be used 'for the greater good' . . . without revealing too much to the world."

"And so if they catch up with me—"

"—you will be just one more paranormal phenomenon to be Obtained, Secured, and Countered."

"But they can't actually *do* that . . . can they?"

"Can they truly overpower Princess Holy Aura? No, not as things stand. Magic has not truly, fully reentered the world—and we hope that it never will. So their ability to act against the one remaining full manifestation of mystical power, the Apocalypse Maidens, and of course our adversaries, that is severely limited."

She remembered a prior conversation and shuddered. "But they don't need to *defeat* me. Just interfere with me at the wrong *moment*—"

"—and these well-meaning defenders of Earth will cause its utter, and final, destruction."

✶ Chapter 22 ✶

"Seika's been looking forward to coming over so much," Mr. Cooper said, with a broad smile. "She could barely wait to get into the car. Thought she might just run over here herself!"

Holly smiled back, as did Trayne Owen. But inside, Holly felt roiling nervous tension that was taking everything she had to hide. *I'm so worried . . .*

Worried that Seika would run away when she learned the truth. It *shocked* Holly how much that thought hurt; as Steve he'd been close to Dex, and losing Dex had been painful, but that had still been . . . oh, a sort of *parental* thing, or at least a big-brother interaction. The anguished worry that was burning in her gut now went way beyond that.

Still, they managed to get through the usual parent-dropping-off-kid discussions. The two girls waited, listening, until they heard Dave Cooper's car pull out of the driveway and head off down the street.

Words burst from Seika in a torrent. "Guys, guys, you have to tell me, that was all real, right, I wasn't dreaming, because, O-M-G, I went to bed that night and when I woke up I couldn't be sure, but then there was the damage at the school and all the rumors going around and—"

Despite the sour tension in her stomach, Holly laughed. "No, Seika, it was *real*." The smile faded; she couldn't keep it going, not as things were. "Too real."

The other girl's smile didn't *disappear*, but it did shrink, and she toyed with the huge poofy ponytails on the right side of her head. "I . . . guess I get it. I think."

Trayne Owen made her jump by shrinking to Silvertail. "I believe you do . . . to some extent, at least. Seika, you are now *bound* to the destiny of the Apocalypse Maidens."

"You *are* a magical animal! Wow. And . . . yeah, that bit with the transformation was weird. I mean, seriously freaky, I even knew what to say without knowing it."

"Yet you seemed . . . ready to go along with it."

Seika gave the white rat a look reserved for *very* stupid people. "Who turns down the chance to be a superhero?"

"Many people, in fact, and of those who would accept it, even fewer are suited to the role. And perhaps when you learn the entirety of the situation you may understand *why*."

"Seika, I really wish we could've told you everything *before*—"

"—But that's not how it works, right?" Seika's eyes were narrowed in concentration. "That . . . thing, it was like every slasher movie squished into one. And the new *mahou shoujo* getting chosen in the middle of a battle, that's . . ." The eyebrows came up. "Holy *fuck*," she said in that high-pitched affected voice, "it's a fucking *battle of the memes*."

Holly glanced at Silvertail, whose furry face echoed her own surprise. "You've . . . kinda nailed it, yeah. It's more complicated than that, though."

"Tell me."

"We might as well sit down to dinner while I tell you," Silvertail said, morphing back to his human form. "It will not be a short tale."

They were well through most of dinner by the time Silvertail finished describing the background—Lemuria, the original Apocalypse Maidens' creation, their enemies, the cycle. Seika looked deadly serious by that point.

"H. P. *Lovecraft*? That creepy old writer was *right*?"

"Say rather that he learned much of the truth, but it was of necessity filtered through his own knowledge and experience. And—as we saw a few days ago—as our adversaries adapt more and more to the current *zeitgeist*, their manifestations will be farther and farther from those imagined by your prior generations."

"*Boy* is this going to be hard to keep secret," Seika said after a moment.

As good a segue as I'm going to get. "We don't actually *want* to keep it a secret. At least, not from everyone, not from your family—or the other Maidens', whenever we find them."

Seika screwed her face up. "What? I mean, isn't that *part* of the whole meme?"

"It's one of the really *problematic* parts of the meme," Holly said. "I mean, really, we're not adults, and our parents worry about us going out alone to the store down the road, so don't we think they'd like to know if their girls are going to be fighting monsters?"

"I . . . guess, yeah. But you said we're *stuck* with this, so what if my dad or mom says, 'No way!' You can't just switch me out for a substitute, right?" Seika's anxiousness was almost funny; obviously the idea of having the awesomeness of being Radiance Blaze taken away and given to someone else really bothered her, and in a lot of ways Holly couldn't blame her.

"No, alas, I cannot," Silvertail admitted, returning to his normal form. "And choosing this path means it is difficult and potentially perilous. But in addition to the fact that your parents obviously have a right to know about your activities, there is also the fact that as time goes on, it is possible the rest of your family will be in peril as well. Our adversaries are not at all averse to attacking the Maidens through their friends and family. Holly and I agreed that they also must know this so that they will be alert to the danger and possibly even be able to avoid it."

"It's kinda like the way we finished Mr. Stalker back at the school," Holly said. "We're taking the parts of the meme that we *know* are stupid or dangerous and punching them in the face first."

The smaller girl bit her lip, then nodded. "Okay, I get it. So we're here to figure out how to break the news?"

"Partly," Silvertail said. "But also to let you in on *all* the truth. Some of which may be disturbing, even frightening, in a way that you do not yet guess."

Seika looked suspiciously at Silvertail, then to Holly. "We're not really working for the bad guys, are we? Or stuck in some terrible time loop where we're all going to get killed?"

"No to the first," Holly answered, then paused. "But . . . the second . . . maybe sorta kinda? Not the going to get killed part, but sort of a time loop. I mean, we *could* get killed. Those monsters aren't playing games, Mr. Stalker would've cut us in half if he could."

"But a time loop, yes?"

"More a . . . side branch in time, if all goes well," Silvertail answered. Holly let him summarize the situation.

"So I might help *save the world* and I *won't remember it*? That *sucks*!"

"To an extent, yes. But on the other hand, you will not have to recall encounters with terrifying beings that truly do not belong in this reality—and neither will any of the less-well-protected victims. If people *die* in this continuity due to their direct actions, then they will, unfortunately, die in the main continuity as well. *But* if they have suffered any consequences *other* than death, those consequences will be undone if the Apocalypse Maidens are victorious and Azathoth of the Nine Arms is once more banished to the other side of eternity. Your world will return to what it was . . . only better, not merely for you and yours, but for a considerable time better for many others associated with you and even this area of the world. You in particular will find your life following a path of your dreams; each of the Maidens will have a life that rewards them for their risks."

"Still not sure I like the idea. But I guess if I don't remember, it won't be bothering me *then*."

"Yeah," said Holly. *Time to bite the bullet*. "But there's one other really important thing you need to know." Seika looked at her, and the concern in her eyes showed that she could hear Holly's tension. "This whole deal—about telling your parents, not hiding stuff from them—comes from Silvertail and I agreeing we had to do this *right*—that we couldn't take kids and throw them into life and soul-threatening danger without their parents even *knowing*."

Seika nodded. "Right, I get you. And . . . ?"

". . . and that's partly because Silvertail decided when he started this cycle that he was very unhappy with the whole *mahou shoujo* thing where he was taking half-grown kids and making them weapons. So . . . he decided that for at least one of them, the first, he *wouldn't* do that."

Seika froze. Then her gaze drifted around the room, looking at pictures, displays; she got up without saying anything and looked at the weapons, posters, and other things displayed all around the house. "These . . . most of these aren't Mr. Owen's. Silvertail's. They're *yours*."

Holly swallowed. "Yeah."

She turned back slowly. "You're . . . you're a *lot* older than you look. Right?"

"Well . . . yes and no. The person Silvertail *chose* to be Princess Holy Aura is a lot older. But the longer I've been Holly Owen, the more . . . well, I really *am* fourteen, just with really *strange* memories added in. But I *feel* fourteen. And I'm not . . . I was *never* pretending around you. I mean, pretending to be your friend."

Seika looked nervously around. "Really?"

"Really. They're . . . I mean, I have all the *memories* of the other me, but the feelings are different. It's been . . . pretty scary, actually. I've been moving away from who I was to begin with ever since I started, and sometimes I'm *terrified*."

"Which is part of the reason for Holy Aura's strength. And, I believe, will contribute to yours as well," Silvertail said. "One of the key factors for the power of magic, especially the magic the Apocalypse Maidens wield, is *willing sacrifice*—the ability of the Maiden and those around them to accept that they must give up or at least risk something vastly precious to themselves in order to achieve the goal of defending the world. If your parents accept your destiny, for instance, they are willingly risking their own child for the sake of the world—a very powerful symbolic sacrifice and one that echoes through the enchantment to reinforce your power as Radiance Blaze."

"Well, wait, just *hold* it a sec, if you did that with *her*," she pointed to Holly, "why didn't you choose some adult for Radiance Blaze? Ms. Vaneman, maybe, if you're stuck around the school."

The white rat's whiskers drooped. "As I told . . . Holly, I wish sincerely that I *could*. But while I am permitted—even, to be accurate, *required*—to select the one who will be the vessel of Princess Holy Aura, once that selection is made the enchantment proceeds of its own accord to trigger the selection and, at the right moment, activation of the other four. I have no ability to control that, or I assure you I would have done so in this era."

At least she's not panicking . . . yet. Or freaking out too much. But we can't keep dancing around. "So he got to choose me," Holly said. "And decided he wanted that selection to be the right *person* for the job. I . . . still sometimes think he chose someone not nearly as awesome as he needs, but what he wanted was someone who could handle the demands of protecting the world, fighting the monsters, and adult enough to really, *really* understand what Silvertail was asking them to do. And, if possible, someone who if they agreed would be sacrificing as much as possible in order to do it, so that they'd be the strongest possible Princess Holy Aura."

Seika's eyes widened. "No . . . way. You're . . ."

Jesus, she's smart. "Yeah." She stepped back, to the other end of the room, so as to be as nonthreatening as possible. "He chose . . ."

A blaze of white-crystal light enveloped Holly, and suddenly he felt the height and *mass* returned. ". . . me."

Seika stared at him, immobile. He stayed where he was. "Steve Russ. That's my . . . well, real name. The name I was using before Silvertail chose me, and what I'll be using afterward. If we win. Holy *shit*, now it feels weird being . . . me." The voice he used to accept sounded completely wrong in his ears. The way his body felt—slow, heavy, ponderous—was actually repellent. "Dammit. But . . . you needed to know the truth. We decided that if the whole point of choosing *me* was to make the right choice, then we had to make the moral and ethical path we took the right one all along, as far as we could manage it. I . . ."

Steve concentrated, and felt the weight and mental heaviness fade away, replaced by the lightness and far heavier worries of Holly. "I . . . hope you can understand, Seika."

The other girl said nothing for long moments, and Holly swallowed. *It could all fall apart right here, right now. And yet she'll* still *be the second Apocalypse Maiden, and how will we ever deal with that?*

"Holly . . ." Seika finally said. "You . . . you're real, right?"

"Now? I think I'm more real than Steve right now, and that *scares* me. But that's part of the sacrifice thing, I guess. I'm risking . . . me. All of me. All the choices I made, the *person* I was."

The black girl's gaze suddenly transferred to Silvertail. "So a guy becoming a girl is a big sacrifice? Isn't that pretty sexist, rat?"

Silvertail gave a squeaking snort. "In a sense, I suppose—because there is still much sexism in your society. But in truth, no. The sacrifice is in what you perceive as your *self*. If Steve had possessed a desire to be a woman, it would be less of a sacrifice. Had I chosen a transgender man—one who was born a woman, physically, and was forced to present as one, but who preferred to be seen and thought of as a man despite this—the sacrifice would have been equally strong, because their self-image and personal identity was in opposition to the one I asked them to take on. Yes, as a culture there is still a stronger stigma against a man choosing to take on feminine traits, but the sacrifice is purely a personal one, not a societal one. Steve has of course internalized some of the societal attitudes, but this simply makes his sacrifice of his own self-image, and even his physical form, as well as the respect and position granted by being an adult, more powerful."

Seika took a slow, hesitant step forward. "What about the power—strength, all that?"

Holly grimaced. "It's sort of a sacrifice and sort of not. As Holly Owen, I'm basically what you see. I'm pretty strong for a girl my age, but compared to Steve? He could tie me in knots without even thinking much about it. *But* . . . Princess Holy Aura could kick his fat ass even easier. Steve gets none of that."

Seika toyed with her ponytail again, then looked back at Silvertail. "And you *can't* take this away from me."

"No. Even if you were to reject Holly because of what she was and leave this house, never to speak to us again, you would remain the living vessel of Princess Radiance Blaze. That would of course carry with it the risk—the *inevitability*—that our enemies would eventually seek you out. And while Radiance Blaze is powerful indeed, I believe you understand that, alone, you would eventually fall."

Seika looked searchingly into Holly's eyes. "You . . . you're really my friend, right? I mean, I said you were my BFF before, but—"

"No *but*!" Holly heard her voice come out sharp, tearful, pleading. "Seika, yes, you're my friend. What Steve . . . was, is, whatever, it scares me but he's not really *me* anymore. I'm not *him*. I'm *Holly Owen*. And I'm your friend, I've . . ."—the truth slowly dawned on her in wonder—"I've been happier the last few weeks since we've been friends than I think Steve was in like *years*. I'd . . . I'd miss you *totally* if you left."

Seika stared at Holly for a long, long moment . . . and then without warning her bright smile flashed out again. "I'd *really* miss you too."

Holly was suddenly crying, feeling a fear she'd barely understood seeping away, relief bursting through her, as Seika gave her a hug and she returned it fiercely.

Seika pulled back and looked at Silvertail. "I've seen weirder stuff in some of the things I like reading, you know. But you think this was a hard thing to tell me? Let me tell *you*, if we can't figure out how to do this *just* right—my dad's gonna *kill* you!"

✳ Chapter 23 ✳

"Well, Trayne? You called this meeting, it's your show," Mrs. Cooper said. "Little Van's over with one of his friends for the night." Marilynn Cooper was almost as petite as her husband was huge, but she had her daughter's sharp gaze and an adult aura of responsibility. *Both parents are formidable,* Silvertail thought. *And both must be our allies in what is to come.*

He thought of how badly this could end, and cringed internally. Yet Steve-Holly had been *right.* This *was* the right way to handle the situation, to bear the standard of light. *Truth.*

"Thank you, Marilynn."

"Oh, just call me Lynn, please."

"Then thank you, Lynn." He looked around the moderate-sized living room of the Coopers and made sure his thoughts were arranged precisely; Holly looked nervously at him from her nearby seat on a floral-print chair. *And at least the youngest child is not here; I suspect Lynn recognized there was some serious aspect to this meeting.* "This has to do with that . . . incident at the school."

"You know something more about it?" Dave Cooper asked curiously. "Because all I know about it is what Seika's told me and the say-nothing press releases. Which scares the hell out of me and Lynn."

"Yes, I do," he said. "And we're right to be scared. This and those . . . other monster sightings, they're connected, as I am sure you've guessed."

"Cop we talked to . . . Gilbert, I think? . . . anyway, he as much as said so. But you *know* they are?"

"I do. And . . . this is going to be very, shall we say, challenging to explain."

"You aren't *responsible* for these . . . events?" Lynn asked pointedly.

He laughed; it was a small laugh but real enough. "Rather the opposite, actually. I am involved in trying to put a *stop* to them."

"You're with the police? Or some other government agency, the FBI?"

"I am afraid not. For the most part law enforcement has neither the knowledge nor the resources to oppose these things, and the few that have any of either do not fully understand what they are dealing with, or have mistaken ideas of the proper way to deal with them, and so are unfortunately prone to making the situation worse rather than better."

The two were now regarding him with the wariness often accorded those that were suspected of being less than sane. *Or who are saying things that speak to fears that one would rather not face.* "Holly, Seika, I think you two girls should go somewhere else," Dave said slowly. "Why don't you—"

"This involves us, Daddy," Seika said in a small voice.

"We were there," Holly added.

"I'm not sure—" began Dave.

Lynn held up a hand and her husband stopped. "Girls . . . you know what he's here to talk to us about?"

"Yes, ma'am," Holly said; her nervousness was unmistakable.

"Yes, Mom."

David and Lynn rose from their seats simultaneously. "You talked about . . . this to *our daughter* before you talked to *us?*" Lynn's eyes were narrow below her short-cropped hair, and Silvertail could see her—quite justified—anger rising.

"It was not something I had choice in. As you will see if you will allow me to continue."

Both Coopers looked at him very carefully, then at the two girls. Finally they both sat down, slowly. "All right. Go ahead, then. But I am *not* comfortable with this."

"If you were, I would be most concerned. You *should* be uncomfortable about this, and I am afraid it will not grow easier." He took a breath, let it out slowly, trying to breathe tension out of himself as he did so. "First, I want to make sure you understand this: those reports—of the rock-worm monster at that shopping center, and of the creature at the mall—are not exaggerations. They are not delusions, ill-considered publicity stunts, or any form of mistaken identity. In those two events—and the one that took place last week at Whitney High School—mankind was confronted by supernatural adversaries. If you cannot at least accept that as a possibility, my explanations will be meaningless."

The Coopers looked at each other, shifting uncomfortably. Finally Dave nodded. "Friend of mine was at the mall that day. He's still pretty freaked out. I believe you, that much anyway. So you . . . what, hunt these things, like that show *Supernatural*?"

"In a sense, yes. It is not that simple or direct." He considered how to continue. "Under normal circumstances, these powers cannot enter our world for more than the most fleeting of moments. Every so often, in intervals generally measured in centuries, however, conditions permit them to attempt to enter this portion of reality."

"You mean 'when the stars are right'?" Lynn said with an eyebrow that was raised in a half-humorous, half-frightened expression.

"That is as good a phrase as any, yes."

Lynn closed her eyes; Dave looked slightly confused. "And you try to . . . what? Make the stars not right?"

"Say rather that I am charged with finding a way to shut the door that the stars have opened, before what lies in wait *behind* that door can pass through fully. Thus far . . . I have succeeded."

"Whoa, hold on," Dave Cooper said. "*Centuries*. You . . . You're saying you're—"

"—much, much older than I appear. Yes. I am in fact old enough to have watched not merely this country, but all of the countries you have ever *heard* of rise and fall." He had decided there was absolutely no point in minimizing this. The Coopers—and whatever other families might follow them—*had* to understand the stakes and the sheer *scale* of the threats that loomed over them.

"That . . . do you understand that you're sounding, well, crazy, Trayne?"

"I understand very well what it sounds like. But consider my words in the context of the monsters you concede *do* exist, and the fact that this threat has reached the high school your oldest child attends. There are uncountable lives at stake here, and I have neither time, nor honestly the right, to dissemble overmuch on this situation."

The two were again silent. Lynn finally said, "All of these things . . . they've happened here. Near here."

"And will, in general, continue to do so. Although there are indications that the rest of the world will begin to see sporadic events as well. There are other . . . powers, shall we say, which are becoming active with the gateway beginning to open. But they will be far less common than events here, and if—I must emphasize, *if*—my efforts are successful here, the mundane world that you remember will return."

"So we could just . . . move. It wouldn't be easy, but we could pack up, Dave could transfer to—"

"I am afraid it is too late for that," Silvertail interrupted. "Was too late some months ago, in fact. Oh, you could move . . . but that would not release you from your involvement in this."

"What *involvement*?" Lynn paused and shook her head. "No, wait. First I want some evidence, something to show me why I shouldn't be calling CPS to get your daughter away from a lunatic."

"Very well. My powers are relatively limited when not directed against my particular adversaries. Nonetheless . . ." He smiled wryly and gestured, muttering words he remembered from childhood.

The serving tray, with its assortment of cheese, crackers, and other little snacks, suddenly lifted from the table, floated up nearly to the ceiling, and then described a smooth arc all the way around the room before returning to its place directly in front of the wide-eyed Coopers. "*Cool*," Seika and Holly breathed.

"Obviously," he said, "this does not prove my essential benevolence or other points of my narrative, but it certainly should show that my contention of being something other than an ordinary human being is true. If you want proof that these monsters exist, or that I fight them . . . I must confess that you *will* get that eventually, but the exact moment of such proof lies beyond my control, alas. I can neither predict nor direct their manifestations, and you should really be more prepared before confronting such things in any case."

"I'm not sure I was prepared for *that!* Holy *shit*, Lynn, did you *see* that?"

"I saw it, Dave." She reached out, touched one of the crackers as though to verify that it was still there, withdrew her hand and then picked up the iced tea she'd brought with her, sipped at it in silence for long moments. "All right, Trayne. Tell us what you have to. I'm convinced you're not crazy."

Thank goodness. He had hoped they would be basically rational people—given Seika's overall levelheadedness, it had appeared likely—but even very rational people did not always deal well with the apparently irrational.

"The story begins many thousands of years ago, in a land that you would call Lemuria," he began. He carefully summarized the background, including how he and the others of Lemuria had finally devised a weapon capable of defeating and sealing away Azathoth of the Nine Arms, but left out—for now—the details of exactly *what* that weapon was. He finished with a description of how this had led to the repeating cycle of confrontations.

I am so *sorely tempted to use just the slightest of enchantments to make them receptive, willing to believe and trust . . . but I must not. Steve was unfortunately all too right; either we do this the right way, or we weaken ourselves in the very way we can least afford.*

Lynn's eyes sharpened their gaze and darted from him to Holly to Seika, and the resemblance between mother and daughter was incredibly strong. "Your daughter and ours . . . we can't just move away because *they* are connected to this somehow. Tell me I'm wrong."

He tried to smile, but the weight of worry prevented it. "I wish I could, Lynn. But you are correct. Holly and Seika are a part of this, and that is why there would be no point in your moving. Danger would follow you wherever you went."

Despite his dark complexion—even darker than Seika's—Dave visibly paled. "My *God*." He pointed at Holly. "Holly Owen . . . *Holy Aura*."

"What?" Lynn said, puzzled.

"That's . . . my friend, Martin, he said that's what the girl that took the monster down called herself, Princess Holy Aura. And so . . ."

Holly bowed her head. "You're as sharp as Seika, both of you."

Lynn shot to her feet. "Oh, no, you did *not*! Your weapon is *not*—"

"Yes," he said quietly. "It is, I am afraid. And the first to carry that terrible responsibility was my own daughter, when Lemuria was lost.

I know *exactly* what you are feeling, Lynn, David. Believe me, I do. My daughter . . . and her friends . . . knew what they were volunteering for, and we knew it was the *only* way to save the human species from extinction. And still it tore out our hearts to do it, and I am the only one living who remembers what it was to first forge my child into a weapon." He tried to keep his tone quiet, level, but he heard his voice tremble, as it always had . . . and, he thought, always would . . . at the pride and pain of that memory.

"*Seika*? Honey, you aren't—"

"We both are, Mom," Seika said. And with just a glance between them, the two girls stood up.

"To avert the Apocalypse, and shield the innocent from evil," they began, and a glow started up about them, one white as sunlight on water, one red as gold in fire, "and stand against the powers of destruction, I offer myself as wielder and weapon, as symbol and sword!"

"Mistress of the spirit," Holly said, the light beginning to rise about her form.

"Mistress of the flame," said Seika at the same moment, red-orange light burning its way up her body, the two perfectly synchronized.

"Bane of winter, I am the Apocalypse Maiden, Princess Radiance Blaze!"

"Ruler of the stars beyond, Mystic Galaxy Defender, Princess Holy Aura!"

The double transformation detonated like a silent bomb of light, shaking the house, and when the fire-touched white light faded, both Apocalypse Maidens stood before the stunned Coopers.

Lynn was the first to speak. Taking a shaky step forward, she stared at the taller, slender figure before her. "Seika?"

"It's . . . me, Mom," Radiance Blaze said hesitantly. For those who *knew* Seika, the similarity was clear in the voice, yet it was a voice with more power and clarity than Seika Cooper herself could ever have mustered, and no one who did not know Seika well would ever associate the two voices.

"It . . . *is* you. My God. And . . . yes, that's Holly. But the two of you are so . . ."

"I know," Holly said instantly. "It's kinda . . . annoying. But the power works that way, hooks onto what people expect and believe."

"I see." Both Lynn and Dave stared for a few moments, then turned back to Trayne Owen. "Why?"

He didn't pretend to misunderstand. He told them: the symbolism of the half-child, half-adult, the power of willing sacrifice and courage, the prices that had to be paid, the cycles that repeated and were wiped from the memory of the world. During the narration, the girls dismissed the Apocalypse Maiden forms and returned to their mortal selves. *Best that way. Now that the point is made, no need to push it farther . . . and even with my preparations, it is possible our adversaries might have detected the transformations.*

Lynn nodded slowly; unwillingly, so did Dave. "So," he said after Silvertail had paused, "so, what did *you* sacrifice?"

"Besides having to allow my daughter to make this choice, and help her make it, you mean?"

"Yeah. 'Cause to be honest, Trayne, that's really mostly her sacrifice. No matter how much it hurts a parent. Right?"

"You are absolutely correct, Dave. And I am pleased to hear you say it that way. What did *I* sacrifice?" He smiled with an unavoidably bitter edge. "Most of my humanity. Literally. What you see in front of you . . . is magically maintained. Most of my remaining power goes into keeping this false front working. If I need to work any significant magic, I have to let it drop."

"What do you mean?" Lynn and David shifted slightly backward, away from him. "What are you, then?"

"Nothing . . . horrific. Though there are people afraid of what I am, it's nothing to do with looking terribly dangerous. As you ask . . ." He allowed his false front to dissolve.

Seika's parents simply stared, as Silvertail bowed. "This is what I am reduced to. And at that, I was fortunate; of the thirteen in the circle, the thirteen most powerful magicians in all Lemuria, I am the only one who survived at all, and that because the enchantment required a living, constant lynchpin to keep it active. My friends and I understood we would be consumed by the power we summoned."

He let them stare a moment longer, then resumed his human form. "This is . . . a *real* form, in the sense that it is physical, but most of my remaining strength is used in keeping it real."

They were both silent for moments, then Dave finally stirred. "Well . . . Trayne . . . I . . . I think we really need to think this whole thing over.

You said there's *several* of these Apocalypse Maidens? So you're going to have to do this with *other* parents?"

"I believe you begin to see our problem, yes."

"Hell, I wouldn't want to try to explain this to anyone. And they're all students at Whitney?"

"In all vast probability, yes."

"Can you—"

"—remove the enchantment? No. Unfortunately while I can select the first Maiden, the remainder proceeds utterly out of my control. I will attempt to guide and train them as they emerge, but I can neither select which girls will be the next Maidens, nor shift that selection if the chosen girl attempts to reject it. Seika Cooper *is* Princess Radiance Blaze, and there is no power on Earth or the heavens that can change that, nor that could have prevented her awakening when she came to the assistance of her friend."

"Wait, what was that?"

"Well, Dad, we didn't *tell* the police the truth about *that*!" Seika said with a hint of tense exasperation.

Holly and Seika then summarized the *true* events behind that battle at the school. Silvertail caught the Coopers' eyes. "Be proud of your daughter, both of you. She made a choice to protect her friend, a choice of great courage and personal risk, and it is undoubtedly *that* spirit that led to her being chosen as Princess Radiance Blaze."

He could see they *were* looking at their daughter with a new perspective, and felt himself relaxing. *There is of course one more great hurdle, but these people, at least, understand the idea of choice and responsibility, and are glad their daughter does as well.*

"Holly's not actually your daughter," Lynn said suddenly.

He raised an eyebrow. "You are correct. But might I ask—"

Dave Cooper answered. "'Cause we could hear what losing your real daughter did to you. I can't imagine a decent man then being able to go out and *have* another daughter and raise her into this. Hard enough to pick kids for the job, I'd think." His voice was tense and his phrasing clipped.

"You . . . understand me well, it would seem. Yes. Though in truth I rarely have had the opportunity; the power to return my old body to reality long enough to be useful is rarely available unless the cycle has begun again, and then I hardly have time for dalliance. But on the occasions it was possible . . . no, I would not have done that to either a new wife nor to any child we might have had. I would not raise a child to be a tool, and in the end that is what it would be if I allowed it to happen."

"So what *happened* to your parents, Holly?"

Silvertail saw Holly set her jaw in a very Steve-like manner. *Yes, this is the time.*

But may the gods protect us if we cannot get through this *part of the tale.*

✳ Chapter 24 ✳

"Both died a while back, honestly. Look, I know this is all crazy and you're going to need a lot of time to adjust, but there's one more big bomb we've got to drop on you."

"*Another*?" Dave looked torn between amusement and outrage. "More than changing the whole world we've known and telling us Seika's some kind of . . . magical soldier-girl?"

"Sorry, sir, but yes, and if we don't tell you . . . it's all about the willing sacrifice, right? I mean, you understood that part?"

"That it's what the girls . . . and maybe us parents and people like Trayne . . . have to give up, and choose to give up, that gives you the power to fight the monsters? Yes, we understand, I think," Lynn answered.

"Well, it's also about doing the *right* thing. And constantly choosing kids to fight the war, Silvertail . . . I mean Trayne . . . he knew it was wrong and he finally decided he had to change something. He could choose *anyone* to be Holy Aura, the first Apocalypse Maiden."

Lynn closed her eyes and rubbed her forehead. "Then . . . Holly, are you . . . yes, you must be. You're saying you're not what you look like either?"

"Well . . . yes and no. I'm not like Dad—Trayne. This isn't some phony form that's being kept up, I'm really like this now. And I *think* of myself as Holly most of the time, and I *feel* like Holly, and . . . I *am* Holly Owen." She swallowed and repeated the strange self-discovery she'd made when trying to explain to Seika. "I've been happier *as* Holly than I was . . . before, and that . . . kinda scares me. But that's what the bargain *was,* like Silvertail said. Sacrifice. The more you give up—the more you *willingly* risk for the sake of the world, the more power you have as an Apocalypse Maiden."

"So you're . . . an adult, really?" Lynn said, studying her. "Transformed, but originally much older?"

"Someone who could truly *understand* what was being asked of them," Silvertail confirmed. "I had grown heartsick and weary with having to choose half-children for a task they could hardly begin to grasp. And it finally—after far too long, but then I, too, was caught in the snare of assumptions and, as your modern world calls them, memes—finally dawned on me that I could, at the least, make the *ethical* choice with the first Maiden, even if there was no way to change what would play out—"

"Shit." David Cooper's curse was quietly spoken, but he had risen from his seat and was staring *hard* at Holly. "You wanted someone who could be a fighter, and who'd be giving up as much as possible to become this warrior-girl."

Lynn blinked, then her own incredulous gaze focused on Holly. "Oh, my *God.* Trayne . . . you aren't saying . . ."

Holly swallowed. "You guessed the punchline, huh. Silvertail chose an adult man this time."

Before the others could recover, Trayne Owen said, "An adult man who risked himself to protect others—a child and what he saw as a helpless animal—from a pack of unearthly monsters. A man who showed himself not merely willing to endure pain, and horror—"

"*Silvertail,* don't—"

"It may offend your humility—another good point—but I need to emphasize this. As I said, not merely willing to endure physical pain and horror, but able to recover quickly from the shock of having his worldview shattered when there were other lives at stake. A man who, as well, showed himself willing to subject himself to privation in order to spare others. It was a fearsome test to which I subjected him, and one very, *very* few would have passed . . . but Stephen Russ passed it with flying colors. And then, even knowing what it would cost him, when others were in peril, he chose to take up the Star Nebula Brooch and become—irrevocably—Princess Holy Aura."

Holly felt her face flaming red, the heat burning in her cheeks so intensely that she thought her whole *head* might melt. Seika looked at her. "Wait, you never told me about this test or whatever!"

"Seriously," Mr. Cooper said, still staring, "you . . . Holly . . . you're actually a . . ."

"I'm *actually* what you see." Couldn't hurt to emphasize that. "But I *started* as Stephen Russ, and yes, I can still go back to that . . . to him. To the old me. Crap, how do you even *discuss* this? Anyway,"—she braced herself, both for their possible reactions and for the old sensations that she was no longer looking forward to—"heeeere's Stevie!"

It was a real jolt looking at the Coopers as he materialized. For a split second their eyes were still focused on where Holly's eyes had been—which was somewhere on Steve's chest. And while Mr. Cooper was still taller than Steve, the black eyes that rose in shock to meet his were very close to his own level, while Mrs. Cooper looked up from what felt like a very *long* way down.

"You . . . this is your *real* shape? You're really . . . this is *you*?"

Unsurprisingly, David Cooper was having some trouble forming coherent sentences. Steve didn't smile; there was nothing actually funny in this situation. "Well . . . no and yes, sir. I was *born* like this. Well, not grown up. But I was born Stephen Russ. Holly Owen's just as real and—right now—she's more *real me* than this is. This feels like I'm wearing a huge fat suit."

The Coopers didn't say anything immediately, so he went on. "But . . . I guess I'd end up feeling like this was normal again if I went back to it for a few months. The magic *does* make it feel more natural to be Holly or Holy Aura, though. There's . . . traces, I guess, of the prior Holy Auras, and they help the new one learn the ropes faster. Which really freaked me out even while it was helping me."

They were silent for a moment, and then Mr. Cooper said, "All right. Steve—I can call you Steve, right?"

Tone's awfully calm. "When I'm like this—which I probably won't be very often—sure."

"Steve, would you come out back? I'd like to talk to you in private." He glanced meaningfully at Trayne, who hesitated, then sat down.

"No problem."

"Dad—"

"Stay *put*, Seika."

"Do as your father says," Lynn said.

Steve preceded Mr. Cooper through the door into the darkened backyard. The air was cool but not cold, and there were only a few clouds blocking out stars above; the moon was nearly new and had gone down pretty much with the sun.

"Is that story the *whole* truth, Steve?" David Cooper's voice was hard and level. "Or is it that maybe you're not sacrificing as much as . . . Trayne thinks you are?"

Even being *prepared* for the question and insinuation didn't keep a spark of anger from flaring up. Steve damped it down *hard*. If Mr. Cooper *hadn't* had this reaction, or some form of it, he'd have been irresponsible or clueless or both. *At least it didn't start out with a punch.*

"You mean, am I actually a peeping tom or pedophile who hit some kind of magical jackpot?" Steve said. *Technically*, the geeky part of his brain noted, *it'd be ephebophile*. "No. I can't *prove* that to you, of course. But if you believe anything at all that we've told you . . . choosing someone like *that* would be completely against everything Silvertail's trying to accomplish. It would make Holy Aura *weaker* than she's ever been, and who knows, might do worse. Corrupt her. Maybe make it possible for this Azathoth of the Nine Arms to use her rather than fight her, I dunno."

"You've spent . . . a *lot* of time alone with my little girl," Dave said. "How do I know—"

"You don't." He sighed, sat down on the steps of the deck, looking around. A high fence surrounded the backyard, which was large—most of an acre, he guessed. The Coopers had a nice setup. "Dave, it was *my* idea that we tell you guys everything. The . . . well, the memes that run this whole magical girl thing usually assume it's kept secret from everyone but the girls and maybe a couple close friends. But that was *wrong*, and Silvertail's whole *reason* for choosing *me* instead of some girl like Seika was to do the *right* thing, pick someone who, like you said, was sacrificing a *lot* for this, and who really understood *what* Silvertail was asking."

He held up his hand, looking at the huge, broad expanse of the palm, the thick, powerful fingers, and found himself shuddering. *Holy crap, in only a few months I've gotten myself an* incredible *case of body dysphoria*. "Something else Silvertail didn't detail is that this whole thing is . . . well, temporary."

"What do you mean?" The voice hadn't . . . changed, exactly, but the question showed that Mr. Cooper wasn't just stewing in anger and building up to a punchfest.

"If we win—if we get all the Apocalypse Maidens together and beat Azathoth, seal the gateway or whatever again—the whole period of time when magic and monsters were rampaging through the world gets . . . run back, erased, like rewinding a tape. I won't remember, you won't, no one will."

"Really?"

"Silvertail says so, and given that everything else he's told me has checked out, I'm not going to doubt him on *that*. But it's not like we risk this for no reward; he says that if we succeed, we get, well, *blessed*. Things will work out really good for all of us in the regular timeline, no matter how bad they were or might have gotten before. *As long as*," he said, emphasizing the words, "as long as we're still *alive* at the end. Because anyone who gets killed by our enemies will be dead in the new timeline, they'll just be recorded as dying of some mundane cause."

A long silence. Steve didn't move or say anything more for a while, just stared up at the stars and remembered the vision he'd seen as Holy Aura of the cosmos and how it all connected.

"What do you want us to do?" David Cooper said finally.

"Just . . . know, for the most part. Realize that sometimes we'll have to run off to do the superhero thing, and help cover for us. Otherwise just let us keep going as we were, perfectly normal."

"Including my daughter spending time at your house?"

Steve sighed. He was *so* tempted to just turn back to Holly—he *wanted* to go back to being Holly to a frightening degree—but if he did that *now* it'd look like he was trying to manipulate Mr. Cooper. "We . . . Holly and Seika . . . are friends. That's not a lie and it's not a trick. So yes, I'd like that. She would too. She's already learned the truth, we've gone over it, she's accepted that that's Holly's past. And she knows that if I *did* try anything on her as Steve, she could *kick my ass* as Radiance Blaze."

A blink, barely visible in the gloom. "She . . . she could?"

Steve gave a genuine laugh. "You still don't quite get it, do you? That wasn't just a light show in there, Dave. Your daughter's a genuine, bona fide, one hundred percent superhero as Radiance Blaze, and as Steve

Leon County
Public Library System
www.leoncountylibrary.org
Find us on Facebook
fb.com/LeonCountyLibrary

Russ, I'm just a big ordinary guy. I can't do anything superhuman in this shape. Radiance Blaze could probably lift your *house* off its foundations with her bare hands." He recalled the various feats of speed and strength he'd done as Holy Aura, remembered the lightning-fast speed and power of Radiance Blaze. "She might be stronger than Holy Aura, though not more powerful overall."

"Damnation." Cooper was silent for a moment. "Don't suppose I could get her to help me rebuild that stone fence next week."

The sheer relief made the feeble joke a hundred times funnier than it really was, and Steve found himself laughing until his sides hurt; Dave chuckled alongside him.

"Can I change back, Dave? To Holly?"

"I . . . guess. Now."

Being back in Holly's body flooded him with energy, a *young* energy that was an astounding reminder of the difference. She felt so light and *right* again. *Holy Jebus, I really am separating from my past.* "You mean now that you don't think you have to punch Steve's lights out?"

"Don't suppose I'd have been able to anyway; could've just turned into that Holy Aura and whipped me, right?"

"I *could*, but I wouldn't. If you wanted to punch out me-as-Steve just on general principles I'd already decided I'd just stand there and take it. I wasn't going to fight my best friend's dad."

"You mean that? The 'best friend' part."

"So much it scares the hell out of the part of me that's Steve. Yeah. The worst part of that attack on the school was knowing Seika was in danger . . . and realizing that if she became one of the Maidens she'd *always* be in danger. If there was some way for me to do this alone, I would. If there was a way for me to take that power away so that she'd be out of the firing line, I would, too. Though she'd probably hate me for it." She looked up at the same stars Steve had, and realized she could see them twice as bright, twice as clear. "But at the same time I was so *happy* that I'd be able to finally share the secret with someone I cared about."

"I guess your . . . old life had to be left behind."

"Yeah. No more job at the bagel shop, no more of my bachelor pad nights. Just early bedtimes and homework."

Cooper shook his head. "Well . . . Holly, this is going to take a *lot* of getting used to . . . but you're going to be Holly, right?" He started back toward the house.

"Except when I have to do explanations like this, or if some emergency happened that required me to change, yes, sir. I'm Holly pretty much for good now, until we win this war."

The living room seemed almost to have been in a time stop while they were gone; Seika, Trayne, and Lynn were in the same positions, sitting tense and silent, as they had been when the two left. Seika jumped to her feet. "Dad . . . ?"

"It's all right," David Cooper said, speaking more to his wife than Seika.

"Are you sure, Dave?"

"Pretty sure. We'll talk on it tonight. Maybe tomorrow, too. But . . . I think it's okay."

Trayne stood. "Then I thank you for your patience and understanding, Mr. . . . no, David, Lynn. We will leave you to your own discussions, then. Of course, if you have any other questions I will be more than happy to answer them to the best of my ability."

"Just tell me—to my face—that my daughter's safe with . . . Holly. And you know exactly what I mean."

Trayne's face grew solemn. "Mr. Cooper, your daughter is *safer* with Holly, and myself, than almost anywhere else on Earth. In *all* ways, save only one: that she has the responsibilities of an Apocalypse Maiden, and that risk, alas, none can shield her from."

"All right, then. We'll call you if we have any questions."

Holly and Trayne walked out the front door with normal, if slightly stilted, goodbyes from the family. Getting into the car, Holly let her breath out with a *whoosh*. "OhGodOhGodOhGod I was so *terrified* they'd freak out!"

"That did, indeed, go . . . excellently well," Silvertail said. "Possibly the magic works for us in the sense that the Maidens *must* remain able to work together, and thus there cannot be too many internal forces working against us." He put the car in gear. "But that is only the first."

"Yeah," Holly said as the car rumbled its way down the street. "One down, three to go."

✴ Chapter 25 ✴

"I can't *believe* it's this cold!" Holly said, shivering even within the thick, puffy blue coat she was wearing. "It was *seventy* three days ago!"

"Welcome to New York," Tierra said with a smirk, shoving the door open ahead of her and holding it to let the others pass. A tall blonde girl zipped in between Holly and Seika, muttering a quick "'Scuse me!" and then sprinted down the hallway, causing one of the guards to call ineffectually after her, "No *running*!"

"What was *her* rush?" Nikki demanded.

"Dunno," Seika said, puzzled. "That was Cordy Ingemar, she's second on the cheerleading squad. Maybe she's late for a practice."

But if that's the case she's going the long way around, Holly thought, but then shrugged. The bell *had* rung and they didn't have long to get to homeroom.

The usual stream of announcements was interrupted by Principal Robinson. "I am sorry to announce that one of our students, Glynnis Van Buren, has passed away due to a fatal accident late last night. We will have a moment of silence to respect her memory."

The shock of the announcement itself was enough to enforce the moment of silence; people were still absorbing it by the time the principal's somewhat gravelly voice spoke again. "The Counselling Office will be open to anyone affected by this event."

Holly was sure no one else heard any other announcements; she certainly didn't. "Who was she? I don't think I knew her," she whispered to Seika.

"Wasn't she a sophomore?"

"Yeah," said Tom Pratt from the next row over. "New on the cheerleading squad."

"God, how terrible," another girl—*Dylan*, Holly thought. *Name I always associate with guys, but hey, things change.*

The whispered conversations were still subdued; mortality had brushed close by. *And a lot worse is going to happen to a lot more people if I screw all this up.* Large high schools usually lost a person or two across four years; as Steve, Holly could remember one of his classmates not showing up to school and finding out that he'd had an accident with a thresher.

But it won't be accidents this year, not once our enemies get moving.

With an effort she shoved the issue out of her mind. World-saving heroine or not, she still had schoolwork to do, and until the next manifestation, she might as well do as well as she could.

Now that she was adjusting, she *could* apply a lot of Steve's experience. Yes, some of the methods for classroom teaching had drastically changed, but it sure didn't hurt to have those twenty extra years of knowledge. She still had to do the work, but boy did it go *faster*.

That *did* make her feel a little guilty, looking over at Seika. Holly was staying neck-and-neck with Seika in all the classes, but Seika didn't have Steve in the back of her head; she was doing it with inherent brilliance and focused determination.

Eh, it won't matter. She won't be competing with me when the real timeline comes around.

Of course, that would mean that she wouldn't be Holly's friend any more, and the thought *hurt*. That was another feeling to shove away, though. *Neither of us will remember it. It won't matter.*

But somehow, that made this friendship all the more important.

Mrs. Rizzo greeted them with a pop quiz, plopping sheets of paper facedown on their desks. "Keep them facedown until I finish explaining. *I see you trying to peek, Gerald!* There are five questions on this sheet. You will choose *three* and answer them. They are essay questions"—a weak groan rose from the class—"but not *long* essays. One or two paragraphs should be enough. You will mark the chosen questions by *circling* the number. If you have time and want to try, you may select one of the other two questions for extra credit; mark that one with a *square*. And don't forget to fill in name, grade, and class at the top or I'll dock you ten points for laziness! You have thirty minutes. Now . . . begin!"

Biology questions were easy, and Holly finished the selected three in fifteen minutes, picked a fourth, and finished that well before time was up. She put down her pencil at about the same time Seika did.

"Did you do an extra credit? Which one?" Seika asked as they left the class.

"Sure, number four. Right after I finished the one about the Coelenterata."

"You mean the Cnidaria," Seika corrected her.

"Aaaaaugh!" Holly smacked her forehead. "Damn my . . ."—she barely caught herself in time—"my dad's old-fashioned books! Rizzo *hates* people getting the names wrong!"

Seika's smile was at least somewhat sympathetic. "I know, but what can you do? At least you can afford to lose a few points, right?"

Holly rolled her eyes. "I guess, but still . . . *ugh*! What a stupid mistake!"

The mood around the school was still subdued by the time lunch rolled around, but sitting with their little group lightened things. "Meeting still on for tonight?" Tierra asked.

"Far as I know. Nikki? Didn't you say something about having to cut out early?"

Nikki tossed back her now-violet-dyed hair and shook her head. "My parents were going to go out which would've stuck me with Jill and Aaron, but the people they were going with called this morning and said they were sick, so no, I'm good!"

Caitlin reached out and snagged the pickle spear off of Seika's plate.

"Hey!"

"Oh hey, what? You never eat your pickles!"

"You could *ask*!"

"Too late, I'm already eating it." Caitlin made a big show of stuffing the whole spear in her mouth, making all of them break up.

Of course, right now either Seika or me could blow them away in the eating department. The worst trial school currently presented was that they *couldn't* eat as much as they wanted to without making spectacles of themselves. Seika had discovered that the day after her first transformation. She didn't *quite* keep up with Holly in the eating department, but she was now eating more than anyone else in her house, easily.

"Um . . . excuse me?"

The voice was as completely familiar as it was unexpected, so Holly jumped a little in her seat. Luckily so did the others.

Richard Dexter Armitage stood there, a few feet away, looking uncertain and nervous. His eyes flicked toward Holly then looked around at the others, then down at his feet.

"What is it?" Tierra asked. "Who're you? No, wait . . . you're in junior year, right?"

"Yeah. Dex, Dex Armitage. Sorry to bother you, but, um . . ."

"Well, go *on*," Nikki said. Holly was still trying to figure out how to react. *His* nervousness was making *Holly* nervous. *What's wrong with me?*

"Well,"—Dex took a deep breath—"I, um, heard you guys talking a couple times and then saw you'd started a new club and it was about Steampunk Adventure, and it's role-playing and I really like gaming and my old group broke up and I was wondering if I could join yours, but I mean it's okay if I can't, because I don't want to push, you know, and maybe you just wanted it for your own group so maybe this was a bad idea, you know, maybe I should just forget it, sorry, um . . ." The whole huge unfinished sentence exploded out of him like foam from a shaken soda bottle, and the blond-haired skinny form was already partly turning away.

Caitlin blinked and Nikki giggled—not unkindly, but Dex's cheeks went visibly pink. *Jesus, I'd forgotten how utterly* terrible *Dex was with people he didn't know. Once he* knows *you he's sometimes* too *loud and sure of himself, but before?*

Holly held up her hand. "Hey, don't run off yet, we didn't even say yes, no, or maybe. Give us a chance before you decide for us, huh?"

"Oh. Uh, yeah, sorry." He went even pinker and winced. "Sorry. Sorry, I'm really, you know, bad at this."

"Dork," muttered Tierra, but her tone was more sympathetic than the word would imply.

"So you're asking if you could join the game, right?"

"Right." Dex straightened the slightest bit, and caught himself before he apologized again.

"You game already?" Seika asked. "We're using the *Spirit of the Century* rules with some mods, you know it?"

"Oh, yeah, cool system," Dex said, some animation entering his voice. "Like the character generation, the way it links characters together."

Holly could see Seika relax a little. *That was the right reaction, Dex; showed you're 'one of us,' and did it by mentioning one of the parts of the system that* isn't *about kicking people's asses.*

"I dunno," Tierra said. "We've got a lot of players already . . ."

"But you've got a couple NPCs you're always relying on," Holly pointed out. "If Dex could play someone that'd take their place—"

"That's mostly a support role, though," Nikki mused. "Don't know if—"

"Hey, I'll try anything," Dex said, then winced again. "Sorry, didn't meant to interrupt."

"At least you *recognized* it before I kicked you."

"Sor—"

"You can't join if every third word out of your mouth is 'sorry,' though," said Seika emphatically.

"Sor—" Dex broke off and then burst out laughing.

Never noticed he has such a bright *smile before. It lights a room.*

"Okay," Dex said. "I, um, *apologize* for interrupting your lunch, but does this mean . . ."

Holly looked around. "Well . . . all in favor of giving Dex a chance?"

Seika and Nikki's hands went up immediately; after a moment, the other two joined. Holly raised hers. "It's unanimous, you can join. Provisional member. We'll see how it works out. Okay?"

"Great! I mean, I'll try *really* hard." He ran his fingers distractedly through the long golden hair. "Guess a support role's a good idea. My . . . old GM, he told me I needed to learn to not be a star all the time. Bet he was right. Usually was."

The sadness in his voice made Holly's gut tighten. *Wow, I'm haunting myself while I'm still here, even.*

"Okay, then we'll see you tonight right after school."

"Great! I mean, really! I've got my books in my locker, I'll bring 'em!" Dex practically *skipped* away, clearly buoyed by relief that he hadn't completely messed things up.

"This'll be okay, right?" Caitlin asked, looking a bit uncertain.

"Dex? I think he's fairly harmless," Tierra said. "Plus they've got the guards staying after now for all activities, after the freakshow last month."

"We'll see. If he doesn't work out, he goes. No problem," Holly said.

They had to finish eating a little faster to make up for the conversation, and then there were the afternoon classes. In the middle of English, Holly found herself unable to wait; nature was calling with an urgency she didn't recall from Steve's prior life. Dr. Beardsley granted her a grudging pass to go to the bathroom.

As she put her hand on the handle, Holly became aware of someone speaking inside the bathroom; it would've been completely inaudible during a change of classes, and even now it was faint. Whoever it was, they were speaking in very low, urgent tones.

". . . *that* way!" the other girl said. A pause. "I know I did, but the last time was different!" Another pause. "No. Why can't you *fix* it?"

Talking on a cell phone?

"No," the voice said, and the girl sounded *horrified*. "Go away."

Holly gripped the door handle again. Somehow she had a feeling she should enter. *"Go away"? Is that something you say to someone on a phone?*

"No, I mean it! Go! Don't come back! I never want to speak to you again!"

There was a rushing sound of footsteps and Holly barely stepped back in time to avoid the door as it whipped open and Cordy Ingemar ran out. She was already turning to run down the hallway and didn't even notice Holly standing there, but even from the side Holly could see glittering tracks of tears on her face.

Cordy also wasn't carrying a cell phone.

Holly went inside cautiously, the hair on the nape of her neck stirring, goosebumps rising on her arms. On the counter was a small purse, with a smartphone's shape visible—a phone sealed inside a zipped inner pocket. *Cordy wouldn't have had nearly enough time to put that there.*

She looked around, tense, listening, watching. All was silent. The broad mirrors reflected the empty stalls.

There was no one there at all.

✳ Chapter 26 ✳

"Okay, I like that," Nikki said with a grin.

Tierra looked confused. "Is there a joke in Dex's character's name? I don't get it."

"Seriously?" Holly said. "Geraldine 'Geri' Rigger? Never heard the term 'jerry-rig' or 'jury-rig'?"

"Nope."

"Basically," Dex began, then stopped as he realized Holly and Seika had already started speaking—both of whom stopped at the same time. After a couple of "oh, wait, sorry" moments, they let Seika explain.

"It means to put something together in an emergency using stuff that wasn't really meant for the purpose. I think it came from old navy stuff."

"Okay, I get it. Sorry, I'm so thick sometimes," Tierra said.

"Oh, bah," Dex said. "Not knowing stuff doesn't make you *thick*. You know *tons* of stuff I don't. Like how to make art. I suck at that. I don't even know the terms for whatever it is you do to make some of these things." He gestured at the intricate steampunk jewelry and symbols Tierra had made over the weeks. "So anyway, yeah, Geri's a researcher with a focus on archives and gadgets. One of her key aspects and catchphrases is 'I can rig something up.' Holly said you guys needed someone who could help you find out key information and maybe do quick fixes in the field if you dragged her along."

Since Dex was new, this session had to be spent on character creation—which was just as well, since the weird encounter with

Cordy had Holly tense. She glanced over, saw the hint of white that told her that Silvertail was once more watching them. *Me and Seika need to talk with him afterward.*

Dex was now concentrating on figuring out details for the character and starting to investigate good connections for his character to the others. "So, Dex," Holly said, not without some trepidation, "what *did* happen to your other group?"

The blond-haired boy didn't look up, but his shoulders hunched the tiniest bit as he answered. "The GM, Steve . . . he had to move. Finally got a decent job, which he really deserved, but it wasn't near here. I couldn't walk to any of the other guys' houses, though, not in reasonable time, and I'm not old enough to drive after dark. Well, I *could* walk to Anne's house, but they have cats and I'm allergic to 'em, so that was out. That plus the fact that none of the others wanted to GM, well, it just faded away."

Crap, now I feel terrible about that *too.*

"So you *didn't* just choose our group 'cause it's all girls," Caitlin said.

His head came up just a little, and while there *was* a darker shade to his cheeks he was smiling a tiny bit. *He must have expected that question to come up.* "Um, well, I won't pretend I didn't *notice*, but no, gaming's like the only thing I've done *with* other people, so it's important to me. I've never put *myself* in a group that way, though, so I was pretty scared coming up and asking. Wait, I guess I should say I've never *physically* come up and asked. I met Steve through online RPG stuff and that was how I got into that group to start with."

"Boy, you *are* a total geek," Tierra said, but she *did* smile at him.

"Yes, I *am*," he said. "And my old group said that I sometimes get too loud and pushy so if I do here, I want you guys to *tell* me right away."

"Don't worry," Holly said. "If none of the others do, *I* will lay the smackdown on you."

The rest of the meeting proceeded smoothly; during one point when the others were talking with Dex, Holly texted "need 2 meet" to Seika; the other girl just glanced up with eyebrows raised; Holly nodded emphatically.

As Holly boarded her bus, Seika jumped up behind her. "Hi, you can drop me off with Holly."

Tillie, the driver, nodded and waved her back. "Your dad already texted me to let me know. Everyone sit down!"

The bus ride seemed longer, somehow; they both talked about school stuff on the way, but neither of them was really thinking about what they said, but about what might be said later. *And Seika doesn't even know what's up yet.*

Finally, however, the bus halted, the doors opened, and the two of them bounded down the steps and ran up the driveway. "We're here, Dad!" she called.

Silvertail, in his human guise, stepped out of the kitchen. "Just getting dinner ready. It will be a few minutes. Hello, Seika. Your father texted me to let me know you were on your way." His expression shifted. "Am I to assume there's Maiden business involved in this sudden change of plans?"

"Yes," Holly said. "By the way, how the heck do you get here so fast?"

"I *drive*, Holly. I put my car in various nearby locations so I can reach it easily, and leave as soon as it's clear you're on your way out. With of course wards on my car to make it less easily noticed wherever it is parked."

"Oh. Duh." She saw Trayne pull out his own phone and text something quickly as he went to check on dinner. "Who're you texting?"

"Seika's father, of course; he had asked if this was . . . business, so I am letting him know."

Naturally he'll want to know that. Things had gone mostly back to normal between Holly and Seika's parents in the last couple of weeks; they had apparently questioned Seika *extensively* and made her promise to speak about *anything* that made her uncomfortable—which was all exactly as it should be—but they were adapting with startling speed. *Maybe Silvertail was right; the magic knows we* have *to stay together, so it makes it easier for parents to accept us if we force the issue.*

"All right, girls," Trayne said a few minutes later, putting helpings of a chicken casserole in front of them, "What's our situation?"

Holly described her strange encounter with Cordy Ingemar. "I took her purse to the office to make sure she got it back," she finished, "but I'm sure she didn't have a *chance* to put her phone away, with the timing and all, and if she *had*, well, she'd have had her purse in her hand, so why would it be on the counter?"

Trayne looked pensive. "I wish you could have notified me of this earlier, Holly—"

"Your phone *disappears* when you turn into a rat, Dad. I can't text you, and I'm not going to talk to you in person, or next thing you know they'll call me the Rat Whisperer."

He rolled his eyes. "As I was *saying*, I wish you could but I understand that it was not feasible. Still, I will have to go back there tonight and see if there are traces of mystical powers in the area."

"Mirrors," said Seika positively. "Check the mirrors."

"Why . . . ohhhhh, yeah," Holly said. A number of films and animations ran through her head, along with urban myths such as "Bloody Mary." "If she *wasn't* talking on the phone, the mirror's a meme-riffic candidate as an alternative."

"And one that goes back *centuries*, yes," Trayne said. "With some exceedingly dangerous beings that have made use of mirrors, reflecting pools, scrying crystals . . . yes, I believe you have hit upon a very likely source." He ate a few bites thoughtfully. "Do you agree with my interpretation of the dialogue you quoted? She had arranged for something, or asked for something—"

"—and the result wasn't what she wanted. Sounds like a classic 'Jerkass Genie' to me," Holly said.

"A . . . colorful description, but a well-known phenomenon. Unfortunately there are a *number* of beings that can offer such bargains, and each of them will be somewhat different in terms of how they are to be dealt with. And several, I am afraid, that could potentially be using mirrors."

Seika looked thoughtful. "But these things aren't just going to be randomly popping up in mirrors, right? I mean, if they did, the chances they'll just freak people out is *huge*, and that doesn't get them anywhere."

"An excellent point. If we are correct, your Cordy must have had some *reason* to expect to communicate with something through a mirror or similar means. She would have *invoked* the being. Now unless her family has some extremely old and esoteric traditions, this would mean she heard about it from someone else."

"Got it. You're saying our enemies would've introduced it as some kind of rumor and Cordy must've given it a try. Must have scared her half to death when it worked."

"Yes. But once invoked, such beings *already* have some small hold upon you. It is not easy to simply turn away and leave them, or to avoid summoning them again." He frowned. "And for many of them, a true attempt to reject them once a pact has been made is very dangerous."

"Crap. So *Cordy* is in danger—"

"Or others may be, if Cordy is persuaded to continue to work with this being."

In danger. The words nagged at her, and suddenly she remembered the announcement. "Oh my *God.*"

"What is it, Holly?"

"Dad—Silvertail—these things, can they *kill* people?"

"Some of them certainly can, if that is the request made."

"Someone at our school just died. They announced it this morning."

He leaned forward. "What? Give me the details."

"Don't have many details, but . . ." She thought back and quoted the announcement as best she remembered it. Seika corrected her phrasing slightly.

Trayne Owen looked very grave now. "That fits with Cordy's reaction, and with several possible causes. Holly, you and Seika stay here. I must go examine that bathroom immediately, and I have a far better chance of doing that unobserved than either or both of you."

"But what if something *does* see you?"

"I have become *extremely* good at escaping over the millennia, Holly. Had I not, this war would have come to a very bad end a long, long time ago." He strode to the door. "I assume I will know more this evening once I return, but in any case, you *must* discover how Cordy heard of this phenomenon, and if possible find a way to talk to her, to keep an eye on her. For almost all of these beings will try to increase their hold upon their victim . . . and expend their victim's own soul and will in the process."

As the door closed, Holly and Seika exchanged glances, and she knew what the other was thinking. *The last attack was obvious.*

But now our enemy's getting smarter.

✳ Chapter 27 ✳

Silvertail wriggled harder, and managed to get his furry shoulders through the small hole near the foundation of the school. That accomplished, he could easily drag the rest of himself through. *It is fortunate that rats can fit through any hole their heads can go through.*

He had parked the car at a nearby restaurant. Making his way to the school from there, mostly in rat form, was the real challenge. Proportionately, rats were faster than humans—but proportional speed meant nothing when you were up against absolutes like the land velocity of a car or truck. It had taken him almost ten minutes to find an appropriate window of time to cross in.

I could *have found a different parking spot that wouldn't require me to cross* here, he mused as he made his way through the damaged insulation and into the school's interior, *but unfortunately that would involve more streets, though smaller ones, or going through yards with alert dogs.* Which, while not a danger to him, would potentially attract attention. Naturally he also *could* have used a subtle spell to ensure a gap that would be sufficient . . . but given the errand he was on, using *any* magic at all would be foolish, unless he was already discovered.

Of course, if he was discovered, it might well be far too late already.

From a rat's-eye view, the hallway was a shadowed cavern to equal fictional Khazad-Dûm from Tolkien's *Lord of the Rings*; immense stretches of glossy, dim-lit passageways suited for giants, cyclopean doors—some closed, others yawning half-open with nothing but eerie shadows hinting at mysteries within. It was so silent that even the faint,

faint sounds of his passage echoed, sent a scratching whisper of sound out into the unfathomable distance, to return as an echo of sibilance.

Let's see. The bathroom she mentioned would be in this *direction; second floor, B-Wing.*

As he began to negotiate the stairs, a rumbling, muttering sound reached his ears, and then rose with startling swiftness to a low, resonant roar. Silvertail froze. *What in the name of Lemuria . . .*

A thread of warm air coursed from a grate set near the stairs, and Silvertail chided himself for overreacting. *Just the sound of the heating system activating. I* must *keep a clear and level head. I must react only to real threats, not perceived ones.*

Each step was seven inches high, not much less than his whole body length, so climbing the staircase was something like an adult man having to climb up a succession of twenty separate five-foot-high walls. In *this* case proportionality worked in his favor; he was proportionately *much* stronger than a human for his size, so he didn't simply collapse in exhaustion at the top. *Still, I would much rather* not *have to do that very often.*

He kept to one side of the hallway as he continued the seemingly miles-long trek; as a rat or a human, the comfort of a solid wall on at least *one* side was not to be ignored. At last he thought he was approaching his destination; he smelled a faint odor of other rodents, wood shavings, possibly a touch of formaldehyde. *She said it was across from the upstairs biology lab.*

The bathroom door loomed before him; shut, of course. However, there was a large gap at the bottom—large for a rat, anyway—sealed only by some rubbery weatherstripping. It was the work of a few minutes with the sharp, chisel-shaped teeth to cut away enough to allow him to squeeze inside.

Windowless, the bathroom was as dark as a cave; motion-cued lighting did not notice something the size of a rat. Even if Silvertail hadn't been a very unusual rat, this wouldn't have been a terrible handicap; rats normally have poor vision by human standards, but make up for it with excellent hearing, smell, and touch senses, using the vibrissae, or "whiskers," to touch and evaluate objects around them. But he had at least been allowed to retain his enhanced wizard's sight when he was transformed, so to him the bathroom was clearly visible. He tried to ignore the smells; it wasn't *bad* by the standards of other public bathrooms, but it was of course nowhere near his own standards of cleanliness.

It took only moments to climb up to the countertop; finally he had reached his destination.

The mirrors showed the usual reflections, seeming to be mere low chrome barriers between this and another, identical bathroom—one with another white rat peering in at him. Faint smears on the glass showed that this, at least, was not the case. Attuning himself to the faintest magical traces, Silvertail reached out and touched the surface of the nearest mirror.

The flare of lingering malevolence and hunger *stung*, burned like placing an unwary hand on a cooling ingot of metal, and Silvertail's squeak of pain echoed two or three times around the empty room. *Oh, no doubt of it at all.* A powerful *manifestation happened here,* very *powerful, much more so than I had expected.*

Worse, he thought he recognized the signature. *A Reflecter of Desire, a* tyrpiglynt *in the old tongue. This Cordy must have been strong-willed indeed to reject it after having partially accepted it before. But this manifestation . . . there is something—*

It was only the gut-level instinct of one who had survived millennia that saved him. Without an instant's thought he found himself diving off the counter, falling to the floor and pressing himself up against the floor ducts. Though the mirror remained unmarred, there was a green-blue flash and a ringing hiss, and a thousand shards of glass *exploded* outward, ripping through the air he had just occupied.

"Still you have the speed of light itself, Varatraine Aylnell," came a voice with the deceptive, toxic warmth of a poisoned cookie straight from the oven.

"Queen Nyarla," he said, bowing his head the smallest fraction of an inch. "I see you expected me to visit."

Queen Nyarla stepped from the darkness at the far end of the room. Her form was still veiled in shadow even to his sight, and what could be seen of her was nearly as dark as the pitch-black room itself; only the faintest, eerie phosphorescence outlined her form, but gave away no details that would allow Silvertail to recognize her current human guise. "*Expected* might be too strong a word, sweet sorcerer. *Hoped* would be a better one. It has been so long since we have spoken, Varatraine; can you blame me for such a hope?"

"It is even longer since we had any words for each other that were not mere cloaks for the duel to come," Silvertail replied. He judged the distance to the door, the angle he would have to take.

He was under no illusions; this was a very, *very* bad situation. Nyarla might not choose to kill him—no one, not even he, knew what might happen to the binding enchantment then—but if she captured him, or even badly wounded him, the consequences could be immense.

Worse, he dared not take on human form. They *must not* figure out who he was in the mortal world. While his magical powers were considerably greater in rat form, not being able to assume human form drastically limited his physical options.

"You could still reconsider, old friend," she said quietly. "Your knowledge and skill at *our* disposal? She of the Nine Arms would reward you beyond the dreams of mortals. And"—another smile, this one private, warm—"you would no longer need walk alone in eternity, Varatraine."

Silvertail slowly kept backing toward the door, one tiny rat step at a time, trying to keep her words and voice from distracting him. "You could do the same, Nyarla. You need not serve Azathoth Nine-Armed. Remember who you truly are, who you claimed once to be, and admit to yourself the truth of Her drive to conquer this place: she *fears* us . . . Halei."

Was there a flicker, a shadow of memory, a hint of regret, a softness that momentarily veiled the contemptuous manipulator? He could not be sure; perhaps it was only that he hoped and desired to *see* it so much. But it was gone even as he wondered, and she threw back her head and laughed. "*Fear* you? Oh, Varatraine, you *silly* man. There is no fear, save for those in the lower orders. You cannot destroy us—one of your precious Holy Auras tried, you remember? The seal didn't last *nearly* so long that time, did it? But *you* can be destroyed, and all that need happen, as I told my servants but a short time agone, is that we win *once*."

"Yet *you* are now the second in command. Whence the others, Nyarla? How many of her powerful servants have not yet returned from the shadows of the Beyond?" He bared his front teeth in a rodent grin. "You were supposed to remain at her side, yet here you are, trying to open the way instead of watching from safety. Either you're not in true favor any more, and need to prove yourself . . . or she's running out of those who can be Openers of the Way."

The smile faded for an instant—but it definitely faded. *I'm right! We* have *been wearing them down over the centuries!*

Then her smile returned. "Perhaps, my sweet sorcerer . . . but in *this* cycle, Yog-Sothoth will bear a new brood. I will have new sisters to train and to take up the cause. How many more sorcerers of Lemuria have *you* trained lately, Varatraine?"

He felt his tail touching the door, moved the pink appendage until he could feel exactly where the hole was.

Either Nyarla finally noticed something, or she was simply finished with taunting him. "But enough; you won't take our offer, so . . . I think it's time you were removed from play. Let your little girls try to finish this task *without* you!"

She pointed at the darkest corner of the room, high above the floor, and voiced an eerie, inhuman call.

And distant, reverberating howls answered her.

Silvertail spun and squirmed desperately through the hole under the door, and gestured upward as he did so. He heard the lock bolt slide out and engage with a metallic sound. *That might slow* Nyarla *up if she maintains her current form . . . but . . .*

But the Hounds were coming, and no place of corners or angles was safe within the range of the Calling.

He popped out into the corridor, but despair was already close on him. The eldritch howls were closer now, and echoing from every facet and angled join of the walls. *I must get out of this building! In outdoor settings I have the sky to call upon, but within a building, all right angles? This is* their *territory, this is the center of the Call.*

But they would be *here* in minutes, perhaps less; already he thought he saw dark wisps of smoke and vapor beginning to emanate from the corners of the hallway, felt the cold miasma of the Hounds' approach. *I cannot outrun them. I cannot transform to human, either; Nyarla may still be watching, scrying through their monstrous eyes.*

Even less-sensitive creatures could tell something was terribly wrong; he could hear scuttlings and squeaking panic in the biology lab . . .

Hamsters.

A desperate hope galvanized him into motion, loping at top speed across the floor; the lab door was closed, but unlike the bathroom it had no weatherstripping to speak of, so Silvertail squeezed under with barely a pause. Looking up, he saw several cages, sensed the motions of trapped fear—and watched the smoke beginning to flicker, show signs of the flames that always accompanied the dreaded monsters.

But he *also* saw, gleaming faintly in the light from the windows, a curved shape of promise.

Silvertail lunged up, caught a drawer handle, pulled himself up, even as hungry, alien growls grew more distinct, more *real*, with every passing second. *Another handle above me. A third. The ledge of the lab counter—must it* jut out *so? Surely a mere inch would have been sufficient! This polished granite is almost impossible to grip!*

As he gained the counter, a bubbling, moist-warm growl shook the room, and he saw one of the Hounds of Tindalos.

Just *seeing* one of the Hounds was perilous; his eyes and brain, steeped as they were in sorceries and rituals of a hundred civilizations, refused to accept what they saw, for it was something not merely monstrous, not merely alien, but *impossible*. It had a head, emerging from the coiling darkness and green-hot flame . . . but what was it *like*? There was no *dimension* or *shape* to it, nor did it lack those qualities—it had a clear *structure* yet not one Silvertail could grasp, or ever *wanted* to grasp, and yet he could see it, all of it, inside and out, front and back, all at the same instantaneous moment; there were jagged, angular teeth and twitching rectangular eyes and a long, grasping, zigzag *tongue* with a rectangular, sucking, hooked orifice . . . but even that was only what it *looked* like for this moment, not what it *was*.

Silvertail gave a squeak of horror and denial and tore his gaze from the emerging abomination, scrabbling across the black granite and leaping the last foot and a half as something massive and repellent landed on the counter, stinking worse than the grave or the infernal realms.

But Silvertail had reached his goal and dove through the circular opening, casting a sealing spell even as he did so; the hamster ball closed itself instantly, a perfect, polished sphere of plastic that shimmered to absolute, sealed perfection a moment later; even the air holes were gone.

Not much time, but there's air enough in here for a few minutes.

The Hounds instantly stopped, and their not-heads tilted, very doglike, in puzzlement.

Angles. They can only manifest from angles. They cannot manifest—nor even truly perceive—curves.

And a sphere is nothing but pure curvature.

He began moving forward, and the ball moved with him. Despite his effective undetectability, he was far from safe. They *would* feel it if he bumped any of them, and there were now four, five, six of the unspeakable *things* in this room alone. And of course he had to get out of here *fast*, before he ran out of air—or risk making holes that might have enough of an edge to see.

But I am on the second floor, and any of the doors is many, many yards of corridor away. More of the Hounds will be stalking the hallways until I am far away from the place of Calling.

He had to get out, and get out fast. And his magical power was starting to feel its limits. He had one or two more decent spells left in him . . . but after that, there would be nothing.

Silvertail sighed. "This . . . may hurt."

Then he turned around and started running as fast as he could.

The ball began a cheerful, speedy roll down the dark-granite countertop. The first Hound crouched—or was it standing tall?—on the counter, but it was *big*, and with a leap and a turn Silvertail sent the sphere careening *between* the bent, angled legs with the raggedly-bent claws, past it—

An instant too late, Silvertail saw the spike-furred tail twitching, and the hamster ball brushed against it.

Immediately the Hound whirled, snarling, puzzled, trying to understand what had touched it. It made a swipe through empty air that missed the ball by the width of one of Silvertail's hairs.

But ahead was the glow of streetlights, and Silvertail called out one more invocation. Every window in the laboratory flew open as one, and as the Hounds rushed toward the various windows, the plastic ball shot outward, straight through the window, and plummeted to the ground below.

The Hounds *tried* to follow, but they could not *see* the ball. Even though the air inside was beginning to grow foul, Silvertail laughed squeakily. *Survived! I have survived!*

But as the ball kept rolling farther and farther from the school (and thus closer to safety), the elation began to fade.

Nyarla herself has greeted me, and there is a tyrpiglynt loose upon the world.

The war is joined in earnest.

✳ Chapter 28 ✳

"A . . . tyrpiglynt?" Holly repeated. The word sounded somehow creepy in and of itself. "What is that, exactly?"

"A Reflecter of Desire," Silvertail said wearily. "Also called a Mirrortaint. A being from far Outside, so far that it has a difficult time manifesting in our ordinary world and can do so—to begin with, at least—only as a projection that echoes an existing projection in this one. A reflection, in short, which is a projection of the features of the world on some surface." He began stuffing chunks of leftover pizza into his mouth, obviously famished.

"There's an *awful* lot of mirrors in the world," Seika pointed out, looking worried. "Why aren't these Reflecters all over the place?"

Silvertail tried to answer, but talking around a mouthful of cheese and sauce produced only incomprehensible mutters. He gave a heroic swallow and spoke again. "Because it is not that simple for them. Leaving aside the fact that they can only reach our world at all when the connection between Earth and the . . . well, underpinnings of reality—magic if you will—strengthens, that is to say, during times such as this . . . they still cannot randomly find their way from mirror to mirror. They must be summoned, *called* to a mirror or other reflective surface, and that mirror becomes their home, their only contact with the world. Only if they make a connection with a native—a human, in general—can they expand their range to include any other mirror into which their connection looks and calls upon them."

He took a few more bites. "Of course, given the fact that the tyrpiglynt generally operates by playing on the secret desires of their victims, said victims often are very careful not to try to summon them unless in privacy."

"What do they want? Or what is it they do? Could this tyrpiglynt have actually killed Glynnis?"

"*Could* it? Certainly, if it were strong enough—if it had gained enough power from its connection or connections to begin to affect the world beyond the reflection. Causing accidents is an energy-efficient way of accomplishing such goals; rather than having to actually put forth the effort necessary to snap a neck itself, the tyrpiglynt simply tugs or trips the victim at the top of the stairs or something of that nature." Silvertail paused in his eating and studied them grimly. "As for what it does . . . it seeks out targets with uncertainty, often those with a veneer of confidence that is itself important to them, the vain (for who else will look in the mirrors frequently) and offers them favors. What the victim does not know, of course, is that accepting a bargain with the Mirrortaint is in effect giving it permission to use their soul, their spirit, as part of the power needed to accomplish their wish."

Holly frowned. Her Steve-memories were ringing bells. "I think I've read some stories like that."

"No doubt. Tyrpiglynts are one of the primary sources of the legends of magic mirrors, genies, and such—especially the tales where things eventually begin going very wrong for the wisher."

Seika toyed with one of her tight ringlets of hair. "You said 'connection or connections.' These things can make bargains with more than one person at a time?"

"They *can*, but of course they will be cautious. Unless and until they become strong enough to physically enter the world, their connection can still be broken, and one way to do that is to shatter every mirror they are connected to. This does not *kill* them, you understand, but does cause a painful backlash and leave them once more Outside until summoned."

Holly thought that over. "When you say *summoned*, is that just as easy as, oh, the Bloody Mary legend? I could go to the bathroom mirror and say 'Tyrpiglynt, tyrpiglynt, tyrpiglynt,' and it'd be summoned?"

Silvertail laughed for the first time since he had staggered in the front door and collapsed back to his default form. "Fortunately it is not *nearly* that easy. The initial summons must be by someone who understands not just how to perform the ritual, but exactly what they summon and for what purpose."

"And that means that people like Cordy are victims, right? She couldn't have summoned it herself?"

"Absolutely not, no. It would require someone on our opposing side. Possibly Lady Nyarla has chosen some operatives of her own and sent them into the school, or has them posing as the sort of people who can enter buildings fairly easily without questions—repair workers, survey takers, salespeople, and so on. Or she performed most of the ritual and allowed the key remaining parts to be known by her target."

"Do they only feed on someone when they, well, make a wish?"

"Say rather they can only do so once their victim or victims have made at least one, but they feed on more than merely the fragment of spirit used to make the wish. After all, they can at the beginning only take very small pieces of someone's spirit and such pieces would ordinarily be mostly or completely expended in granting the desire of the victim. However, the *focus* of the wish is also connected to the tyrpiglynt, and it can take an at least equal amount from the target if it is a living being. Moreover, once it is connected to a mirror, it can feed on the overall destructive impulses of those within its range—hatred, fear, vanity, self-loathing, and so on."

"Oh, *fuck*."

The clearly-enunciated curse made Holly snap around and stare at Seika.

The other girl's eyes were wide and her brown skin had a somehow pale undertone. "We've got to get on the job *fast*, Silvertail."

"I agree, but you seem to have a particular urgency in mind. What—"

"Cordy's brought the thing *into our school.* And if there's any group of people filled with unstable emotions, self-loathing, uncertainty, vanity, envy, fear—that's teenagers."

Silvertail froze, then closed his eyes, giving vent to what must be a Lemurian obscenity. "You are absolutely correct. It is a *public place.* It won't need to make more bargains, just feed off the connection to that location, to all the people who enter that room. It will also of course try to protect that mirror, so it likely will not be so simple as walking into the bathroom between classes and smashing it with a hammer."

"Even then, it's still going to have whatever mirror Cordy first, well, met it through, right?"

"Yes." Silvertail looked pensive. "And, possibly, another mirror that our enemies summoned it to; although it is quite likely they used their own peculiar connections to the Outside to attract the creature's attention and prepare it for Cordy's summons. We *must* discover what mirror that is. Unless it is destroyed, the tyrpiglynt will continue to grow."

"What happens if it keeps getting stronger?" Holly asked. "Other than the obvious 'it'll be harder to fight,' that is. And for that matter, how do you *fight* something like that, other than by just breaking a lot of mirrors?"

Rodent or not, it wasn't hard to recognize that Silvertail's face was grim. "If it becomes sufficiently strong, it will be able to manifest fully—in other words, it will be able to emerge from the mirror and take on full existence in this plane of reality. At that point it will be a *terrifying* enemy indeed, with the ability to affect both matter and minds, difficult to harm even with the powers of the Maidens, and ultimately far, far harder to defeat.

"Even if it does not quite reach that level, it will be difficult to attack. It is, as I said, not fully *here* in any ordinary sense, so any assault will have to take place partially in this world, and partially in that of the mirror."

"Why did I guess a *Through the Looking-Glass* trick was going to come up here? You can't just break all the mirrors?"

"Not nearly so simple, no. That would indeed *weaken* it, but it would still have an anchor—the person or persons who summoned it. The anchor would allow the tyrpiglynt to stay near, in cosmic terms, this reality, and be summoned to other mirrors with no need of special preparations, simply the intent to summon."

"Crap and double-crap. How do we break that anchor, then?"

"The person or persons would have to be cleansed, which amounts to them fully rejecting the Mirrortaint and reclaiming their spirit from the creature . . . or . . ." Silvertail hesitated.

"Or *what*?"

"Or, if they are unable or unwilling to attempt this, forcibly cleansed, by the powers of the Maidens. But that could be . . . well, fatal."

Holly saw that Seika's face was as horrified as she felt. "You mean we might have to *kill* Cordy—or someone else who's bargained with this thing?"

Silvertail raised his eyes and met their gazes steadily. "Yes. We will do everything we can to avoid that eventuality, of course, but it is possible that even the effort *to* cleanse them will kill, for it will depend on their strength of spirit—a spirit which will have been slowly eroded by the tyrpiglynt." At their silent regard, he drew himself up, somehow intimidating despite his diminutive size. "Why do you *think* I wanted at least one of you to be an adult to begin with? These are not decisions to leave in the hands of children."

Holly blinked, and suddenly felt Steve's viewpoint wash to the fore. "Hell no, Silvertail. I did *not* sign on to this to kill children."

"Steve," Silvertail said, iron regret in his voice, "I know this. And know that I will do everything in my power to ensure that it does not come to that. But understand: We *cannot* afford to lose this battle, or any of those that are to come. A tyrpiglynt fully unleashed upon the world? Think of your legends, imagine what a being capable of granting twisted, vicious wishes could do once fully manifest, no longer restricted by the barrier of the dimensions? It is *intelligent*, Steve, Holly, Seika. Intelligent and malevolent, but also more than capable of practicality. If it encounters someone who makes wishes that help its purpose, the Mirrortaint is more than capable of choosing *not* to twist the wish . . . and then they can gain a victim who is also a willing partner and protector, one who can even be a *conduit* for the thing's power, and thus serve as a primary combatant and, in honesty, disposable shield."

"*Fuck*," Seika karkatted. "So you're saying if we don't get a move on we will have a super-powered soul-draining jerkass genie *out* of his mirrored bottle, with some sidekicks he can send the superpowers he got from the souls he siphoned off of everyone else."

Silvertail blinked, then nodded. "In a nutshell . . . yes. And if that happens, it will be almost impossible to stop it, especially if there is a large source of the sort of spiritual power it can live on nearby."

"Almost impossible?" Holly heard the seriousness in Silvertail's voice. "Are you saying that if this thing gets loose, we may have *lost the war*?"

Silvertail hesitated. "Perhaps not entirely *lost*, but if we cannot somehow contrive to defeat it, the tyrpiglynt will wreak havoc until Azathoth of the Nine Arms is confronted and banished—and it will certainly intervene in that battle if it can."

"Jesus. Then we need to find a way to talk to Cordy and get a hold of the mirror she used. Fast." Holly wrinkled her brow. Now that she thought about it, she didn't know anything about Cordy, really. "Seika, you know anything about her? What she likes? Maybe we could connect with her . . ." She trailed off, seeing Seika's cynical grin—an expression that definitely didn't belong on that usually cheerful face. "What?"

"The only thing I know about her," Seika said, "is that she's one of the best cheerleaders we've got."

Holly felt her stomach drop. *Even as Steve I never interacted with the sports-guys much, let alone the cheerleaders.*

But I never had this motivation, either. She forced herself to smile. "Well, in that case, we'd better get our team spirit on!"

✳ Chapter 29 ✳

Holly shivered a little, then pulled her coat tighter. "Jeez, I'd forgotten how *cold* it gets sitting in the bleachers."

"Did you forget how *boring* this is?" Seika muttered to her, barely audible over the cheers and other shouts as Whitney High's White Lions contested with Columbia's Blue Devils.

"You don't know anything about football, do you? This is a pretty good game."

Seika gave her a scandalized look. "You call yourself a geek and you like *football*? You are not one of us!"

Holly blew a raspberry at her friend. "Hey, at least I'm less bored because I know what's going on."

Seika rolled her eyes. "Okay, okay, I'll listen to the explanations a little. But I'm watching down there mostly."

Holly felt the smile fade from her face. "Yeah."

"Down there" was at the sidelines, where the cheering squad was. Even to Holly's untutored eye, there was something subtly off about their routines, and most of the apparent mistimes and bobbles were happening around Cordy Ingemar. "She's missing her cues a lot, isn't she?"

"Looks like it. I mean, I'm not a cheerleader, but it's not hard to see what they're trying to do, and it's not working."

"The half's almost over. Maybe we can work our way down there and see if we can somehow catch her?"

"I *think* the cheerleading squad's supposed to perform at halftime, but maybe they get a break before they come out. I guess we could try."

It wasn't easy to thread their way through the crowd—because it *was* a crowd, despite the chilly late-fall clouds above; the White Tiger/Blue Devil rivalry had been a fixture of Whitney High football since before *Steve* had graduated, she remembered that. But finally they got near enough to see that the squad had in fact gathered together to the side, near the gymnasium entrance that faced the field. The two of them made their way closer, trying to look as though they were just taking advantage of the way the big building cut the wind.

As they approached, it became clear that they needn't have bothered pretending. None of the cheerleading squad or the two coaches were looking at them.

". . . wrong with you, Cordy? You've missed timing on half the routines today!"

Cordelia Ingemar's reply wasn't audible; her tone was half-apologetic and half-apathetic, as though she was sorry to have made people mad but didn't care about the actual subject of the argument.

The older coach—Mrs. Banner—rolled her eyes. "For heaven's sake, Cordy! You don't even seem to be paying *attention* to me! Honestly, after all the complaining you did about poor Glynnis, I would think—"

Holly had winced at the mention of the dead girl's name, but Cordy's reaction was far more violent. She suddenly gave a muffled scream into her hand and then turned, shoving her way blindly through her teammates and running away headlong into the school building.

"Oh, god, I shouldn't—" Mrs. Banner said, a contrite tone in her voice, but Holly didn't bother to listen to the details of the coach's self-recriminations. *Where's she going to go now? Upset, thinking about Glynnis, about her own failure?* The part of her that was still Steve was grimly certain. *Dollars to donuts she's heading for a bathroom.*

A bathroom with a mirror.

Seika followed as Holly ran. The other cheerleaders were hesitating—probably wondering what they should say, or whether they could afford to chase after Cordy when they had to be back on the field in a few minutes. *That gives us a chance to catch up with her alone.* Holly wasn't sure what they could *say* to Cordy, but she figured the first business was to catch up with her and find out if they were right about where she was going.

The first bathroom—part of the locker-rooms off the gym—was

empty. The two of them checked to be sure; there was no one in the stalls, let alone in front of the mirrors.

"Of course," Seika said. "She knows this is where the rest of the team, or the coach, will look for her."

"But then where—" Holly smacked herself in the head. "Second floor!"

"Right. Where she's talked with it before."

It didn't take long to reach that bathroom, though it seemed longer, with their footsteps echoing emptily through the deserted corridors. But finally they saw the door ahead; Holly slowed, gesturing for Seika to do the same. They didn't want to startle Cordy at this point.

The sound of someone—Cordy—sobbing was audible even through the door. Holly reached out, grasped the handle—

And another, different voice spoke. "I am truly sorry, mistress."

It was a pleasant voice. A warm, intimate tenor that sounded like a sympathetic boyfriend. Yet Holly could somehow hear another undertone, something darker and cloying, something that reminded her of the voice of the slasher-monster she and Seika had fought.

"*Sorry?*" Cordy snapped, voice brittle and shaky. "You said you *meant* to kill her! Said you wouldn't even try to bring her back! I never *wanted* her hurt, and you went and *killed* her!"

"Mistress, please! It has been centuries since someone like you called me, let me serve them, found the way to open the door! Back then, if someone wanted a rival removed, they *meant* for me to slay them! I had no idea!"

Seika and Holly exchanged glances. "You're not buying his excuses, are you?" Seika whispered.

"Not for a splintered second, no."

"And it is not that I *won't* bring her back, it is that I *can't*, mistress. I am not nearly so powerful yet. I have tried my best to serve you—were you not pleased by the results of the first wish?" The voice held a strangely compelling property; even though the words were not directed at her, Holly found that it actually took *effort* to disregard what it was saying. *What must it be like for Cordy?* "Did I demand too high a price?"

"I just wanted perfect skin! That's . . . yes, that was nice, thank you and no, just asking to be able to speak to me from other mirrors, that was fine. But . . . but this was—"

"A mistake, a lack of understanding. I will try to understand your world more, if only you will stop rejecting me." The voice dropped lower, and Holly strained to catch the words. "Just turn back, call on me, I will grant you any desire within my power. And that power is growing, Cordelia, has been growing much greater since you brought me here. Perhaps soon I *will* be able to restore the dead."

For a moment Cordy was silent, and Holly began to slowly turn the handle. *We'll have to intervene. Should we change? But if we do that'll alert everyone—*

"N-no." Cordelia Ingemar's voice suddenly firmed. "I . . . I can't trust you, Procelli. I wish you would just go away, leave the mirrors, all of them. All the mirrors I've brought you to, stop appearing to me in them."

"You cannot mean that, Cordelia!" Its voice was sharper. "*That* is your third wish? Truly?"

"Yes! I wish you would get out of this mirror, and never appear to me in this or any other mirror ever again!"

Suddenly Seika gasped, and Holly caught on an instant later. But Procelli was already speaking. "And you will pay the price for this? You *accept* the price for this wish?"

"I cost someone their *life*!"

Holly yanked on the door handle, but the door opened slowly, slowly, the pneumatic system resisting opening almost as much as closing. Even as she began to shout a warning, Cordy said, "Yes! I accept the price, whatever it is!"

"*DONE!*"

The voice shook the room with a triumphant laugh, and light blazed through the doorway. As the door came fully open, Holly could see a tall, slender, dark-haired young man in archaic clothing standing before the mirror, looking at it with a broad grin.

And in the mirror, a stunned Cordy Ingemar stared back, pressing against the other side of the glass.

"A simple and symmetric price, yes? I have left the mirror—*all* mirrors—so in return you are *in* the mirror, all the mirrors I once occupied, and therefore can never see me in this or any other mirror." The voice was wavering, no longer sounding quite so pleasant, the undertone more clear. "And I sense such an assemblage of young and vulnerable people, feel their emotions . . . Thank you . . . *mistress*"—an ironic emphasis on that word—". . . for releasing me so swiftly!"

The form blurred and vanished.

The two girls ran into the bathroom, to stare in horrified shock at the desperate, despairing face of Cordy Ingemar. "Oh my *God*," Holly murmured. "How do we get her *out*?"

"That thing's gone to the crowd outside," Seika said, still staring. "Crowd's signals were so strong the thing didn't even *notice* us. We can't take too long here!"

"It's *out*. Out of the mirror. Dammit, I thought it would take longer—"

Seika shook her head. "You heard it—the first price it required from Cordy was to bring it to other mirrors. It's been here for a while. Lot longer than we thought."

"Well, the feline's escaped containment," Holly said, winning a very faint smile from Seika. "This is a job for the Maidens!"

"What about her?" Seika said, glancing at the mirror.

"She's already involved. I don't think there's much point in hiding anything from her." She raised her arms. "To avert the Apocalypse . . ."

Holly became aware of another sound to her right, just as they completed the invocation, ". . . Mystic Galaxy Defender, Princess Holy Aura!"

And in the detonation of sacred white and fiery red luminance, she saw the astounded face of Tierra MacKintor staring at them from the open bathroom door.

✳ Chapter 30 ✳

Silvertail felt the fur rising on his back even before his more conscious senses recognized the surge in power from within the building that the girls had run into. *Oh, no, Lemuria's* Memory, *no . . .*

It was the merest flicker of motion, a motion only eyes like his own could have seen, but he knew instantly that the worst scenario was now upon them. A Mirrortaint was now free, and in a crowd . . . a crowd whose emotions and lifeforce would not only feed it, but *mask* it.

If only I had been able to follow them, perhaps I would at least be able to recognize *the creature, know the form it has taken.* But that hadn't been possible; as Trayne Owen he had dropped the girls off, and been watching from beneath the bleachers as Silvertail. A white rat could not in any way keep up with sprinting humans, even if it didn't care whether it was seen.

How could it have escaped into the world so soon*?* It must have been active in the school longer than they had thought. *Either Cordelia was making use of its powers much longer, or she brought it to the mirror I saw much earlier, perhaps near the beginning of the school year.*

But analyzing the past would have to wait. The tyrpiglynt was already here, among the people. The creatures were *intelligent*, and capable of subtlety; this thing would not be found so easily as a shoggoth or the stalker-monster. It would wander through this crowd, sensing desires, offering in veiled words to grant those desires that struck its fancy as either corrupt or likely to lead to chaos, looking perhaps for a partner as well as tool. Silvertail scuttled along under the bleachers, sniffing, listening, trying to sense anything that indicated the creature's presence.

Attuned as he was to the particular magical signature, he sensed the Apocalypse Maidens' transformation. *If only I could establish my telepathic link with them!* The link would work at considerable distances *after* it was established, but to make the link to begin with required that he be either very nearby, or within direct sight of the Maiden. At the moment, Silvertail remained on his own.

He scuttled around the bleachers, listening, sniffing, sensing. *It will not have left. There are so many opportunities. It will be looking for the best chance to sow chaos, to encourage dark fantasies, to trigger dangerous events, perhaps to find a person more fit to be an ally than Cordelia.* It was slightly less noisy now, with the cheerleaders performing their halftime routines; there were more conversations but less of the coordinated roars of the crowd during the actual game. Still, he was surrounded by hundreds of people talking loudly on a hundred different subjects. If he didn't get lucky . . .

". . . a wish?"

No human could possibly have heard the words, or distinguished them from the babel of background noises; but rat senses enhanced and filtered by both magic and thousands of years of experience helped. Silvertail froze, then turned his head, letting the highly directional ears focus the sound more clearly.

"Within reason, yes." The voice was unfamiliar, but Silvertail knew by the undertones that this *had* to be the tyrpiglynt. "I—"

The laugh was deep—this was an adult man. A father or possibly one of the teachers, then. "What a bunch of crap." The overtones of the man's voice were amused, yet there was a faint touch of . . . hope? Desire? *The words of a Mirrortaint are very hard to ignore. It speaks with magic that works on the level of your subconscious; hypnotic, suggestive.* "If you're so bright, then I wish . . . you'd grant me what I want right now."

Silvertail couldn't *see* the two yet, but he could easily imagine the smile. "Based on what I see I can *guess* what you want. Do you give me permission to grant that wish?"

"Sure, magic-boy, go for it, then after it doesn't work, go bother someone else."

Now Silvertail felt the magic, activated not ten feet from him. *There! Yes, right there, whoever's seated in the—*

A roar from the crowd, but not like a cheer. Some of it was gasps, others appreciative whistles, others shouts of "Oh my God!" In the distance he thought he heard a commotion on the field, girls Holly's age angered or distressed.

"Holy shit," the unknown man's voice said. "What a show. You *did* that?"

A smug tone. "I did. Was that not what you wished?"

"Sure as hell was."

The noises on the field and from the announcement finally told Silvertail—indirectly—what had happened, made even clearer as several girls were hustled off the field wrapped in coats. *That salacious monster.* But that *was* a Mirrortaint's specialty, working with suppressed or hidden desires, and in this society such desires were terribly dangerous. *And rightly so.*

The tyrpiglynt was focused on its prey—or possible partner—now. Silvertail set his tiny jaw. *I will at least minimize what damage you have done.*

He visualized the entire field, the people, the geometry, and then touched on the hidden geometry of symbols he had been carefully burying about the school for weeks. One set of symbols created a pentagram around the stadium, focusing his power. He laid out the spell's parameters precisely, then cast it outward, speaking the ancient phrases as quietly as he could.

Immediately he heard a momentary catch in the creature's conversation, but he was certain the thing did not know what *direction* the magic it sensed came from; as it resonated and was amplified by the pentacle the real power would seem to come from all directions.

As for the *effect . . .*

"Damn. My camera must've glitched. None of these pics are in focus!"

He allowed himself an instant's satisfied grin. He had been honing his ability to interfere with electronic devices for decades, and specifically to locate and edit particular images from any imaging systems. This was of course mainly to prevent pictures of either himself or the Apocalypse Maidens from being recorded, but it applied to anything he chose to modify. *Your memories I cannot touch, but those girls' privacy will not be violated repeatedly, nor transmitted to the world.*

But now he had to act swiftly. The tyrpiglynt would undoubtedly guess what had happened, and more importantly had found someone very open and amenable to its peculiar talents. It would not be long before it was granting even more dangerous and vile requests . . . and hunting down the source of interference.

With the unexpected events on the field, the halftime had been cut short, and the teams were now returning to the field. *This is no better. With the emotions such a contest engenders, the Mirrortaint will be able to turn a simple sports contest into something more closely resembling the worst gladiatorial arena.*

Princesses Holy Aura and Radiance Blaze had not yet emerged from the school. *Complications must have happened if they have not yet pursued the monster outside. I must go, be ready to advise them.*

As he bounded toward the school, his ears caught another voice, a man's, ahead of him. "Where is she? Why wasn't she on the field?"

"I don't know, Mr. Ingemar," a girl's voice answered. "She was really upset about something, not even into our routines. Last I saw she ran into the school, but that was a while ago."

Silvertail could feel the man's worry, the concern over his daughter, and it echoed, resonated within him as he recalled his terror over what his own Aureline was to face.

And the combination of the Mirrortaint's sudden release with a father's worry suddenly *clicked*, and Silvertail knew what had happened, and—just possibly—how he could fix it.

He transformed to Trayne Owen as he emerged from the shadow of the bleachers, caught up with Mr. Ingemar as he was heading for the school. "Mr. Ingemar, I know where your daughter is . . ."

✴ Chapter 31 ✴

"Holly? *Seika*?" Tierra said after a few frozen moments.

"*Fuck*," Seika said succinctly in the powerful soprano of Radiance Blaze. "But, that's the way the meme rolls, right?"

Holly found she'd covered her face with one of Holy Aura's hands. "Yes. Yes, of *course* it is."

Is Tierra *going to be one of the Maidens? Or one of those ordinary characters that happens to learn the secret?*

If it was the latter, whether Tierra survived the next hour would depend on just *which* memes were in play.

"What the *hell* is going on?" a desperate voice said from in front of them. "I don't understand *any* of this!"

Tierra's gaze shifted and her eyes widened even more, as Holly realized the voice was coming from the mirror. *Cordy! She can talk to us from the mirror?*

Even as she thought the question she wanted to smack herself for it. *Of course she can. The tyrpiglynt could and it swapped places with her; stands to reason she gets to talk like he did, at least for a while before the magic wears off.*

She looked at Radiance Blaze, saw the same "what the hell do we do *now*?" look on her face, then shrugged. "Cordy, Tierra, okay, we don't have much time at all, so I'm going to have to dump a lot of this on you all at once and explain the rest later." She took a deep breath. "That spirit Procelli you were talking to is a monster called a Mirrortaint and he gets more powerful by granting wishes and warping people's personalities, and your last wish got him out of the mirror and into the real world. Seika and I are the Apocalypse Maidens who are—you don't know what *mahou shoujo* or 'magical girl' means, do you?"

At Cordy's confused, stunned headshake, she went on, "Okay, we're like *Supernatural*'s brothers, but with magic powers, we hunt these things, it's more complicated than that but that's the thing right now, we've got to stop this monster as fast as we can, and get you out of there back to the real world."

The two other girls stared blankly at them for a moment. Tierra recovered first, tossing her flame-red hair back and giving a half-disbelieving grin. "Ooooo-KAY. I wouldn't believe *any* of this if I hadn't seen it but I did, so I do." The smile faded as she looked back at the mirror. "How do you get her out?"

I have no idea. Silvertail? I could really *use your help right now.* "Cordy, look around. He switched places. Are you basically just in a mirror version of this bathroom, or is there more to it?"

Cordelia Ingemar blinked, shook herself violently, then stood, still leaning on the glass as though hoping it might somehow open and let her out. Her gaze tracked around, looking around as well as behind her, and she shuddered. "There's . . . at the edge of the bathroom, past wherever you'd be able to see standing anywhere in front? There's like . . . swirling red and black mist. There's the door to the bathroom, too. Don't know where that goes."

"Maybe it goes to other mirrors," Seika said. "How many mirrors did you bring this guy to?"

"Only three," Cordy said after a minute. "My compact mirror, my dresser mirror, and this one. He asked me to bring him to more, but I didn't want just anyone walking in on him everywhere. Even if he *said* he only appeared to me, I'd heard other people talking about the trick to summoning him."

Holly looked around; there was no sign of Cordy's purse. Then she looked up and saw the purse still securely slung from Cordy's shoulder. "Cordy . . . is your compact *in your purse*?"

She looked down and then reached in, pulling out a circular compact. "Yes."

"Can you break that mirror? It's the one you summoned it into first, right?"

Cordelia stood, dropped the mirror on the reflected floor, raised her heel, and stamped hard.

"Ow! That felt like stomping on marble!" She lifted her foot. "Nothing. Even the plastic *backing* didn't crack."

Naturally, Holly thought grimly. *It's infused with magic, inside the Mirrortaint's natural world. The thing wants its mirrors intact. Ordinary force probably can't break it inside the glass; that's why it sent her in there. A perfect way to protect it.*

"Oh, *fuck*," Radiance Blaze/Seika said. "How can we break a mirror that's *in* a mirror?"

"If we can get her *out* of the mirror, that's not going to be a problem, her compact comes with her. And if we *can't* get her out, I don't know if we *can* break this mirror; what'll that do to *Cordy*? She's not some transdimensional super-monster with somewhere else to go."

"So check me on this, guys," Tierra said. "You two are really Holly Owen and Seika Cooper, right?"

"Right," Seika said, still studying the mirror.

"And there's some kind of monster that was in the mirror, and it's somehow switched places with Cordy so she's in there and it's out here."

"You're with us so far."

"And you've got no clue how to get her out."

Holly bit her lip. "Not really. Beating the tyrpiglynt, the Mirrortaint thing, might do it, but I really need to know more. We've got to go find Silvertail. He'll know."

"Silvertail? What, is that the codename for Power Ranger control or something?"

Holly couldn't repress a snort of laughter. "You're closer than you think. Yeah, if *mahou shoujo* means nothing to you, we're sorta the first couple fighters in a *sentai* show like Power Rangers. And we *do* need to find our boss, he'll have ideas."

"Go, Holy Aura. Find Silvertail and see if you can find the tyrpiglynt," said Radiance Blaze.

"Shouldn't we both—"

"No, someone has to watch this area. That thing's still going to have connections to its mirrors, according to what Silvertail said, and we've got two of the three right here."

Holly realized that Seika was right. They needed Silvertail's advice, and they needed to start interfering with the monster's plans right away—before it got new anchors in this world. And they couldn't leave

Cordy or—now that she knew—Tierra alone. "Got it. I'm on my way, I'll be back as soon as I can!"

She sped out the door, charging down the corridor at a speed even a cheetah would have envied, bursting out into the wintry day in mere seconds.

There was a roaring from the crowd that sounded like the game had already started again. *Were we in there for the whole halftime? Didn't seem long enough.* She glanced around, thinking. *Silvertail? Silvertail, answer me, we need your help bad!*

But there was no answer. *Where is he? Somewhere he can't see me, maybe on the other side of the crowd?*

The dull roar rose louder, and it sounded . . . *savage.* The announcer's voice was barely audible: "A *vicious* hit by the Blue Devils' defense! The old rivalry's back in full force, folks, and it looks like . . . yes, Hawn, the White Lions' running back, is down, clutching at his leg. The referee's calling in the stretchers for the second time already in the third quarter, and doesn't the Whitney crowd love it!"

The usual concern for the injured isn't even being expressed, Holly thought with growing horror. *This monster's worse than I thought. It's only had a few* minutes, *maybe ten or fifteen at the outside, to do this work.*

But while she couldn't remember the *math*, she remembered the *concept* of positive feedback. *The tyrpiglynt gets its power from the darker impulses of people, and it can make those impulses worse, grant wishes to make people indulge them. So it gets more powerful, grants more wishes, pushes people more . . . yeah, that's something that doesn't take much time at all to get rolling.*

But she couldn't *locate* the thing. She found she could in some way *sense* its magic, but it lay like a dark miasma over the entire field, a repellent aura permeating everything in its range and growing darker and more powerful by the moment . . . and obscuring any sense of where it truly *originated* from, like a spring of dark water.

Well fine then. I'll have to force it to come out. *And maybe Silvertail will spot me then.*

She meditated for just a moment, preparing herself for battle. *I don't want to be caught unfocused again.* Then in three huge bounds, Princess Holy Aura sprang to the very top of one of the banks of lights that illuminated the field. "*STOP!*" she shouted.

Her clear, high voice cut through the ugly snarl of the crowd, the grunts and shouts on the field, the increasingly enthusiastic narration of the announcer, a ringing cry like a trumpet across a battlefield, and everything paused, held for an instant by the sheer astonishment of that echoing voice.

She raised the Silverlight Bisento and concentrated, let its pure holy argent light shine like a beacon. "Remember yourselves! Is this who you are? Look at what is happening to you!"

As the crowd began to murmur—with a tone shifted, less hostile, less hungry—Holy Aura felt a pressure on her, something trying to dispel her light, to repress her will, and she instead set her feet and lifted the weapon higher. "Those are *children* on that field! Some of them your own children! Do you truly take joy in their pain, in this becoming no game, but a battle?"

Mutters of confusion, of denial, began to rise below her, and *now* that pressure began to have a sense of direction, for the oppressive, mounting corruption was fragmenting, dissipating, and only near its source could it continue. She whipped the blade around and pointed down, as near the center of the remaining shadowy taint of the soul as she could judge. "And I know you are *here*, monster! Tyrpiglynt, Mirrortaint, I call you by your name, Procelli! You have brought harm to the innocent and unleashed the darkest of our natures, and for that, this Apocalypse Maiden says that *you* are going *down*!"

A slender form slowly rose from the bleachers, and the power gathered about it; now that she knew where to look, she could recognize the beautiful young man who had stepped from the mirror. "Oh, brave words, little Maiden, and well spoken!"

Without even a pause, the thing was *there*, not ten feet away on the narrow catwalk atop the light assembly. "But are you not human? Surely there are things *you* desire, Princess. Something I could grant you, even—for I have become strong indeed already, and will become stronger yet."

At close range, directed at her, the words struck with almost physical force. She could *feel* the truth in its speech, that it could grant many, many desires, especially the ones neither Holly nor Steve wished to acknowledge . . . nor could completely deny. And she knew that it would happily *join* power to hers, for she offered it a wellspring of almost unlimited power to draw from; together . . .

"Together," it whispered, as though it could read her thoughts, "together we could transform the world. Perhaps even save it from the Nine Arms, save it for ourselves . . ."

Holy . . . I'm actually considering *it!*

The sheer shock of realization broke the momentary hold, and she whipped the Silverlight Bisento down, pointing directly at Procelli's heart. "I *deny* you, Procelli," she said, hearing her own voice shaking, forcing it to steady as she remembered her friends, her ideals, the *reason* she had become Princess Holy Aura. "Your power has no hold over me and never will. I deny you a second time, and I laugh at the thought that you would ever *dare* oppose the mistress that surely caused you to be summoned! And I deny you a *third* time, and you can see your victims are already leaving, slipping through your fingers!"

It was no longer smiling so broadly, but the smile had become more that of a shark. "Oh, for now, yes. For now. But once I have removed *you*, little Maiden, then they shall return, and more besides. But you *are* right, I would not be fool enough to oppose She of the Nine Arms; instead I will spread darkness over this world and *welcome* her, and be set above all others!"

Only sheer instinct and the speed of Holy Aura saved her; she spun her weapon up and behind her, to catch the impact from the Mirrortaint. *That teleporting trick will get* real *old, like about now!*

The huge lighting fixture shuddered and jangled with the force of the blow, and then rang anew as she and Procelli exchanged multiple strikes, the *bishonen* Mirrortaint's arms flicking in and out like striking snakes, rippling as though boneless, hitting with the force of sledgehammers. Screams echoed from below, and the crowd began to evacuate in earnest. Most were running, but she saw Devika Wetherill and a few others trying to direct the crowd; the tall basketball player looked up, light flashing from the Khanda emblem on her chunni, gave what looked like a quick salute, and then returned to urging the others on.

The momentary encouragement didn't help much, though, as the creature's blows almost made her knees buckle. *It's ridiculously strong! I'm pretty sure I've been getting stronger all along, but this thing's* pushing *me, just like the damn stalker-thing!*

But she'd also made sure she was *focused* when she began her speech. She could feel the power of the stars, of the *universe* surrounding all, and while it was inconceivably outside her ability now to channel anything like all of it, she could call on far more, draw upon the power of the Cosmos that lay behind, above, beyond all things. She *blurred* into motion, matching the Mirrortaint's teleport-trick with a reaction speed that almost *over*matched the thing, and it barely, just barely, parried a lunge by the Silverlight Bisento, parried it with arms that morphed midmotion into dark nightmare blades.

"So eager for the *kill*, are we?" it said tauntingly, though she thought she heard, beneath that sneer, a caution, perhaps fear from the nearness of the strike. "But is there not an innocent trapped? Or is she disposable, do you think?"

"And you'll let her out? I laugh at you, Procelli. Maybe we'll find a way to free her after you're no longer alive to hold her?"

It laughed. "Ha! Oh, foolish girl!" A flurry of whirling blows, and she was forced to leap away, dropping to the fast-emptying stands below, but it was already there, waiting as she fell, and she twisted desperately, feeling one edge scrape across her armor with a blackboard-fingernail screech as the other was caught in the nick of time by the shaft of the *bisento*. "My mirrors are my weakness, as you surely know . . . but you can no longer *reach* one of them, and the one who holds them is powerless to destroy them! Her will must be nearly gone by now!"

Holy Aura felt her forehead crease in thought. *That last speech was true . . . yet not. Cordy was on the edge of* panic, *but hardly without will. I'd be panicked in her situation too.*

They separated in that clash, both jumping back for a new angle, a reevaluation of their opponent. The tyrpiglynt's head tilted, and suddenly it smiled broadly. "Ohh, but what's this? A distressed panic, someone desperate indeed, desperate and faced by the impossible? I sense . . . a *wonderful* opportunity, before I rejoin a *most* promising ally!"

It vanished.

Holly cursed, but concentrated. *I've been* close *to you now, monster. I've fought you one to one. You can't hide from me* that *easily, with the crowd no longer—*

Oh, no.

She ignited in white power and *streaked* across the field, back toward the school. *No, that's bad, if he meant what I think, it's really, really* bad—

The bathroom door was off its hinges, and she could see Seika and Tierra sprawled outside, shaking their heads. *Seika? What happened? Did the thing somehow force her to change? What's going*—

Another voice was speaking from inside the room. "I just wish I could *get* to my little girl!"

CRAP.

She lunged through the door, for the second time that day, seeing Mr. Ingemar standing before the mirror in horrified desperation, and the grin widening across Procelli's face. "*DONE!*" he shouted, even as Holy Aura screamed, "*NO!*"—a cry echoed by Cordelia from the mirror.

Two shouts an instant too late.

Mr. Ingemar vanished. Nausea and rage welling up in her, Holy Aura skidded to a halt, to see the form of Cordy's father falling to his knees . . . within the mirror.

✴ Chapter 32 ✴

Even as that happened, Procelli loomed somehow larger, though his physical form changed not a bit. "Another wish granted," he said with a slasher smile, turning to Holy Aura. She could see Cordy, now in her father's embrace, but her face showed only the shock and anguish and confusion of the impossible; even a father's presence could only do so much.

"You . . . obscene . . . *thing*," she choked out, unable to even form a proper insult. "I hope you're ready for a beating!"

It laughed, and she saw the *shadows* behind it laugh, too, crawling like the memory of the shoggoth in the dark space at the far corners of the room. "Dear, dear little Maiden, I was already matching you, was I not? And now I am stronger! How can you possibly face me alone?"

Holy Aura bared her teeth in a snarling grin; behind her, another voice was speaking: "To avert the Apocalypse, and shield the innocent from evil . . ."

The sneer vanished from the Mirrortaint's face and it lunged forward, obviously trying to prevent Seika from completing her self-summons, but though it vanished and reappeared, arm raised to strike, it found itself forced to dodge with inhuman speed as the Silverlight Bisento cleaved the air where it had been but a millisecond before. "Too obvious, Mirrortaint!"

Fire-bright light erupted throughout the hallway, and once more Princess Radiance Blaze emerged from fire. Even as she materialized, her flaming chains were streaking out, crisscrossing the entire area with purifying heat and light, forcing Procelli to retreat partway down the stairs fifty feet away.

But why did Seika change back*? Why wasn't she Radiance Blaze when I arrived?*

"Back up, Holy Aura," Radiance Blaze said. "He can come at us TWO ways in the hallway."

"So what?" Holly said, turning partway so their backs met. "Now one of us will be facing him no matter where he comes from."

"Where should *I* be going?" demanded Tierra. "This superhero crap's going to get me killed!"

"Get in the classroom over there," she answered. "You'll at least be out of the line of fire." Tierra glanced at Procelli, bit her lip, nodded, and practically *dove* into the biology classroom. Holly felt Seika-Radiance's hand grip hers . . . and something, two somethings, complex and metallic, were pressed into her hand. *What the . . .*

Procelli was surveying them from the stairs, obviously trying to decide how—or if—to continue his attack. Since her body was facing the other way now, Holly risked a glance at whatever it was Seika had slipped to her under cover of the maneuver.

Brooches. Two elaborate brooches of a design she could not mistake.

All of a sudden it made a ridiculous sort of sense, and she resisted the urge to look into the bathroom again. *But without Silvertail, what* use *are these brooches anyway?* She looked back at their enemy.

The Mirrortaint straightened and smiled. "Well, I *really* must deal with you two, I suppose. You'll keep interrupting my fun otherwise. Although,"—he paused, tilting his head, listening—"I *am* able to keep things interesting now."

The roar of chaos outside had grown louder. Police sirens were audible in at least two directions, and it sounded as though much of the crowd had regained its anger. The humanlike creature smiled, and its mouth was filled with razor teeth that had not been there before. "Now I can affect things *around* me. And the more they indulge their dark passions, the stronger I can become."

Crap. We have to take this guy down fast *. . . but Silvertail said once he was out it would be almost impossible . . .*

But on the other hand, would Silvertail have gone and left them without . . .

Of course I wouldn't, came the voice she most wanted to hear. *But the situation is desperate and I admit . . . we are not yet prepared to face him.*

I don't have a choice, *Silvertail.*

The creature began to stalk forward, a slow, measured pace, watching, waiting for one of them to move, obviously looking for an opening. Rather than attacking right away, Radiance Blaze began backing up herself; Holly went along with it. She knew they needed time to figure out a strategy.

A sensation of worry and guilt. *I know you don't. But . . .*

At that moment Tierra MacKintor stepped from the biology lab door to Procelli's left, and unleashed the full force of the lab fire extinguisher directly into his face.

Focused as it had been on the Apocalypse Maidens, the Mirrortaint did not even realize its danger until the fog of chemical dust was already plastering its humanoid face. It staggered back, choking for an instant before it was able to regain control of its body, and in that instant Radiance Blaze's fiery chains hammered it in five places. Clothes on fire, it hurtled like a meteor, spinning slightly sideways, ricocheting off the wall, and then tumbling down the stairs.

Holly had frozen at Tierra's action. *And now I'm sure. Dammit. Another of my friends . . .*

Yes. And it is now your time. You, not I, must do this, for I cannot.

"Sei—er, Radiance Blaze, go, go, keep him busy, I just need a minute!"

The brilliant smile from beneath Radiance Blaze's spectacular head of hair told her the other girl understood. "*Hell* yeah."

With Seika on her way, Holy Aura ran quickly to Tierra, who dropped the extinguisher. "That *worked*?" Tierra said, an uncharacteristic squeak in her voice. "I thought I'd get *killed*."

"It worked. But we'll need a lot more to finish this, Tierra, and you're going to have to be the one to help."

"*Me*? What, I'm nothing like you guys! I can't—"

The redhaired girl's words cut off with a gasp, and Holly could see understanding in her wide-eyed green gaze. "You're kidding."

"I wish I was. This is real, this is dangerous, you could die, Tierra, and I don't have time to explain everything. But once you accept it—once you accept the power—there's no going back."

The entire building shook, and fire and darkness flared from the stairwell.

"That's little *Seika* fighting that . . . thing," Tierra said after a second. "Do it."

For an instant Holly felt panic. *What was it? How did Silvertail do this? I didn't see what—*

Calm yourself, Holy Aura. I am with you, and I assure you, the memory and knowledge of the power lies within you too. Just speak; the words are there.

She swallowed, and the part of her that was Steve closed his eyes. *One more kid drawn into this war. Dammit.* "My name is Princess Holy Aura, and you, Tierra, are one of the Hearts we have Sought, bearer of the Courage that is needed, the Will that is eternal. Take you up the Apocalypse Brooch and become one of the Maidens who will stand against the ending of all things!"

Tierra MacKintor snatched the brooch from her hand, and the gold, silver, and crystal *blazed*. Her eyes widened anew as she realized she was speaking, words she had never been taught flowing from her lips with the irresistible force of an avalanche:

"To avert the Apocalypse, and shield the innocent from evil, and stand against the powers of destruction, I offer myself as wielder and weapon, as symbol and sword!" Tierra's voice, clear and high, still rumbled, shook the ground with the incomprehensible might of an earthquake. "Mistress of the earth, foundation of the world, I am the Apocalypse Maiden, Princess Temblor Brilliance!"

The ground quaked and leaf-green light burst from Tierra MacKintor, levitating her into the air. The luminance burned across her body, erasing her to a sketch done in mist and shadow, and she spun—or the world rotated about her—as a new *self* condensed from the ancient magic, hair waterfalling like crimson flame, boots of dark green crystal solidity, armor of silver and gold and sapphire and topaz. A coronet of blue steel and transparent diamond bound itself across her brow in a flare of Earthlight and a detonation of force that staggered Procelli, who had just regained the top of the stairs.

The tyrpiglynt's mouth fell open. "*Another* one?" He barely dodged Radiance Blaze's fiery kick. "Oh, this is becoming actually *annoying*."

He caught a whipping fiery chain, wincing visibly as he did so, and yanked hard, sending his opponent flying up the stairs and down the hallway, smashing into the wall as she did so. He shook his hand like a man who had grabbed the handle of a pan that was far too hot, but smiled as he glanced back. "But I have my own ally."

A man's voice spoke from lower down the stairwell. "Let's see if I've got this right, Procelli. I wish that I'd be safe coming up there with you."

Procelli grinned broadly, showing sharklike teeth. "As you wish, so let it be."

Holly felt the pulse of power wash around her, as the newcomer advanced up the stairs. *Wait. I know him. Assistant coach on the boys' side, John something.* With the recognition, and Steve's longer experience, she realized that she'd actually seen this guy more than she'd seen any of the other boys' phys-ed teachers. *Oh. So* that's *why.*

Exactly, came Silvertail's equally cold thought. *That was what drew the two of them together.*

John's eyes widened with appreciation as he saw them, and the broad grin that spread across his face made his interest obvious. "Oh, boy. I wish—"

Procelli's hand snapped up. "Wait, my friend. My power cannot directly affect them. Not yet, anyway."

"Well, can I say I wish *you* were stronger?"

Shit.

Procelli's laugh was inhumanly loud. "*DONE!*"

"And I wish those other girls were waiting for me at the exit, know what I mean? 'Cause I'm not much into fighting."

"You *slimebag*!" A flaming chain streaked straight for the assistant coach even in the moment Procelli said "Done!" again; but the chain rebounded from thin air three feet from the startled man's face.

"Stop, Radiance Blaze," Holly said. "Our fight's with that monster. The other guy the cops can handle, if we win."

"But— "

"Are you *sure*?" Procelli's voice said, strangely reasonable, eerily compelling. "Even without me, is your justice so sure, so reliable? How much does it protect you, girls? How many boys get to walk away?"

Tierra/Temblor's teeth were bared in a snarl. "Oh, I just *wish*—"

Both Seika and Holly's hands were across her mouth instantly. "Don't!"

The other girl blanched. "Oh, my god. That's . . . that's how it works."

"It'll grant anyone's wishes," Holly confirmed, seeing Procelli's grin stretching even wider, beyond human limits. "I think it *has* to grant any wishes directed at it, or at least in its presence. But it gets to *choose* how to grant them. For an asshole like Coach John, there, well, his wishes fit with Procelli's goals, but *us*? I don't think we'd like what we got out of *any* wish from him."

"Wisely reasoned, little Maiden. Yet not entirely true. *He* wished for power and for certain pleasures forbidden by your people. But I could just as easily grant *your* desire for justice, for him to be seen as he is. He wished me greater power, and I can now reach farther, much farther, and draw strength from far more people. You do not *need* to be my enemies. Were we *allies*, now, there would be little that could stand against us."

The three Maidens looked at each other. Holly could see her own desperate resistance against that echoing, tempting voice reflected in the eyes of the others. But looking at them also reminded the part of her that was still Steve of *why* he had become Holy Aura . . . and a similar realization sparked to life in the others, snapping them out of an almost entranced state.

"Enough of *that*," Princess Temblor Brilliance snapped, and she leapt forward.

The tyrpiglynt dodged, watching her narrowly—but he was clearly alert for the manifestation of a Maiden's weapon, and so left himself utterly open when the crystal-armored heel of Tierra's right boot smashed into his shin.

Procelli went down, flat on his face on the stairs, and only the preternatural quickness of the creature kept the axe-kick follow up from crushing his skull. Instead the impact blasted a hole in the staircase that broke through to the floor below, leaving twisted rebar rimming a seven-foot hole. "I am gonna *gesso* your canvas right now, creep!"

The creature leapt up and shot a clawed hand toward his opponent, but one of Tierra's long legs came up, blocking it, looping *around* the arm, and then straightening, sending Procelli hurtling into the wall with a shocked expression on his face.

Holly sprang toward the two along with Seika, and for a few moments there was a furious exchange of blows. They were driving the Mirrortaint back, landing punches and slashes and kicks, and

Holly thought momentarily that they might actually be winning—that they could take the monster down here and now.

But as it recovered from the startlement and confusion of dealing with three Apocalypse Maidens, its defense began to harden. Impacts that should have sent it flying were now merely nudging it, and its blows no longer rebounded from the Maiden armor harmlessly; they *hurt*, and Holly staggered, saw a tremendous blow to the face send Tierra reeling, a punch to the solar plexus leave Seika momentarily stunned and retching.

Procelli stepped back, grinning, the scrapes and cuts and bruises they had inflicted fading away like dreams. His next blow created a literal shockwave, a tsunami of pressure that left all three of them sprawled, gasping and pain-wracked, fifty feet down the corridor. "That might have been sufficient when first I emerged, little girls," he said, dusting off his clothing, which also was magically mending itself. "But do you understand the term *exponential growth*? Each increase in my power broadens my range, which allows me to further increase my hold on those within it, which grants me more power to expand my influence. I am already fifty, a *hundred* times, perhaps, more powerful than I was then. You *might* hurt me with your most fearsome attacks, but then, I do not think this building, or many of the innocents in and around it, would survive."

Holly pushed herself to her feet, feeling Tierra grasp her arm and help her up; she gripped Seika's hand and helped her stand as well. "We're . . . getting stronger, too. Can't help it—not when one of us just got born, right?"

"True, true. And who knows which might win given all the time in the world? And so I will wait no longer. All three of you will die, this very mo—"

Without warning, a dark-skinned arm snaked over Procelli's shoulder, around his neck, and clamped *tight* in a classic chokehold.

Whatever powers Procelli had to bend reality, Holly realized, were constrained in the same way as theirs or Silvertail's: Physical law held sway unless and until magic was *deliberately* used to negate them. And Procelli's powers had been focused on protecting him from the Maidens. For a moment, his eyes bugged wide and his mouth gasped, pure shock overriding his prior confidence.

Behind his shoulder, the grim face of Devika Kaur Weatherill tightened, and the taller girl bent Procelli backward, leverage lifting his feet from the ground and preventing the Mirrortaint from bringing its own strength to bear against the girl.

But this *was* a being of nigh-unlimited power, and only the momentary surprise of yet another entry into the combat had given Devika a chance. With a voiceless snarl Procelli shifted his hands into clawed talons and sank the black claws deep into the arm holding him. Devika screamed in pain and shock; despite an astonishing attempt to maintain her hold even with five claws embedded in her arm, Procelli tore free and hurled the basketball player over his head; only Seika's quick reactions kept Devika's head from smashing hard on the polished stone floor.

Shit. But once more I've got no choice, do I? "Temblor Brilliance, Radiance Blaze, take him—there's a combo you should be able to do!"

Holly hoped Seika would understand, both what she meant by "combo" and why she needed the two of them to attack Procelli. She bent over Devika, who was sitting up, cradling an arm now bleeding dangerously, spilling red all over her clothes and starting to pool on the floor.

"Devika, that was awesome. But you'll need a lot more strength to fight that . . . thing." She ripped a strip from the ribbony decorations on her skirt and started tying it tight. *A tourniquet, something to slow the bleeding I hope . . .*

Devika's mouth was half open, yet the ebony eyes were more alert, less stunned, than Holly had expected. "I . . . see that. Sure."

Seika and Tierra had driven Procelli back with a double strike; now, as he reeled, the two linked hands. "*Volcanic Eruption!*"

A seething mass of liquid stone, glowing a brilliant orange-white, spewed forth from the Apocalypse Maidens' joined hands and caught a furious, shocked Procelli squarely. *You got it, Seika! Please let that be enough to keep him slowed down.*

"You can be one of us," Holly said quickly. "One of the Apocalypse Maidens, fighting monsters like that—you saw what it was doing outside. But if you say yes, there's no going back. You're one of us forever. And I can't explain all the—"

Devika cut her off with a raised hand—the injured hand, still covered with blood, and even Steve Russ doubted that he could have forced himself to move his arm that badly hurt. "Is this a *Dharam Yudh*?" At Holly's blank expression, she said, "A righteous war?"

"Um . . . I think so. We're fighting things that will destroy the world." Procelli tore himself from the hardening stone, and his form was no longer human; it was skeletal, fanged and clawed, trying desperately to rebuild itself from its encounter with incendiary rock. "But . . . we could fail."

Devika looked at her as though she was an idiot. "It doesn't matter if you fail. What matters is that we fight for the *right* reasons." She nodded. "Do . . . whatever you must."

Jesus, I want to cry. Don't think I've seen this kind of bravery from adult men I've known, and here I'm seeing it in people not old enough to vote.

But she shoved that to the back of her mind and took out the other brooch. "My name is Princess Holy Aura, and you, Devika, are one of the Hearts we have sought . . ."

As she completed the invocation, Devika took the brooch and her own words echoed out, humming with power and touched with the scent of ozone, familiar, yet changing at the end to define the Maiden she would become: ". . . Mistress of the storm, ruler of the winds, the very air eternal, I am the Apocalypse Maiden, Princess Tempest Corona!"

A sphere of lightning burst outward, enveloping and transforming Devika Weatherill, the crackling lambent purple outline lengthening, black hair stretching out like a cloak, as armor of lightning white and corona indigo and incandescent orange, crystal and cloth, coalesced from pure energy to clothe her. Her crown brought with it a streaming cover of deep-blue silk, a *chunni* that covered the cloak of hair without concealing its magnificent length, and in her hands materialized a great double-edged sword.

Procelli froze, mouth dropping open. "Oh, come *on*!"

Holly laughed, not merely at his stunned expression but at seeing the transformed Devika whole, uninjured, and feeling a renewed surge of power through her own body. *Every time one of the Maidens is born, all of us get stronger!*

With a dramatic, gymnastic whirl of steel and cloth Tempest Corona entered the fray. Procelli snarled in frustration but met her halfway, a blackened plate of bone forming on his arm to parry the blow as he struck back. "This will only *delay* the end, Maidens!"

And despite the surge of strength, Holly felt a creeping conviction that Procelli might be right; he was still strengthening, and if they couldn't take him down soon . . .

The bathroom, Maidens. Bring him back here. Drive him in, by whatever means you can.

What? Silvertail, I sure hope you know what you're doing.

Vision of a furry-faced smile. *Trust me, Holly, Seika, and our new friends Tierra and Devika. I know this monster is fearful, but you must hold out only for a few minutes longer!*

Devika's voice answered. *I have* no *idea who you are. But . . . I see Holy Aura does. So yes, I will trust you.* A flash of a mental smile. *Then trust* me.

Suddenly they saw the battlefield through Devika's eyes, and a strategy in motion. *I get it. It's like a passing strategy in sports, to move Procelli like the ball on the court. Do it, people!*

"On it!" Seika sang out aloud, and leapt over Procelli's head. Tierra matched her and the two landed on the stairs just behind the Mirrortaint; but he was so fast that by the time they landed he was already facing them, claws lengthening, and Holly knew there was no time—

Procelli *staggered*, clutching his head as though a knife had been rammed straight through his ears, his scream of shock and rage echoing through the hall. Holly had no idea what had happened, but for the moment the tyrpiglynt was entirely gripped by the pain that had assailed him.

And that left him wide open.

Another channeled-lava strike sent Procelli straight toward Devika-Tempest Corona. She whipped her blade around like a baseball bat, the flat of the blade smashing into the monster and sending him hurtling farther up the corridor, directly toward the Silverlight Bisento. Holly spun the huge ball at the end around and with a tremendous impact Procelli streaked through the air, through the bathroom door, and hit the far wall so hard that he went halfway through *it* as well. The creature shuddered, momentarily stunned, giving all four of the Maidens the chance to follow. Tierra kicked him away from the wall, through a stall, and into the center of the room; the four of them now faced him in a ring, even as Procelli slowly, waveringly rose to his feet.

"What . . . *how* . . . one of my mirrors is *broken*!"

Holy Aura glanced, puzzled, at the mirror. It was pristine, untouched.

Tell him it is time for him to be banished hence, to return from the world from whence he came.

Holly raised the *bisento*, guarding herself from any strike. "Procelli, it is time for you to return to the place that was yours, to leave this world and be banished from it forever."

Shocked though he must have been, Procelli managed another laugh. "Banished? Little girls, you have not a prayer. You need a full pentacle to do that, and the point must lie in my own world!"

And then he froze as he heard, from the mirror itself, Cordelia's voice speaking, filled with anger, with the roar of the sea behind it. "To avert the Apocalypse, and shield the innocent from evil, and stand against the powers of destruction, I offer myself as wielder and weapon, as symbol and sword!" Cordy said, and her voice was the thunder of wave and cataract. "Mistress of the seven seas, ruler of rivers, the water of life itself, I am the Apocalypse Maiden, Princess Tsunami Reflection!"

✳ Chapter 33 ✳

Silvertail felt a cold, cold smile crossing his tiny face as he saw the Mirrortaint stagger back in disbelief. "But . . . *how* . . ."

Seika's face was radiant with understanding. "It was *you*, not Cordelia's father! But he *sensed* the distress—"

Silvertail locked gazes with Procelli, and he could see fear in the defiant Mirrortaint's eyes. "I merely allowed myself to remember the day I gave my daughter to this fate . . . and let my fear for all of you drive it. I have had *millennia* to learn the guidance of my fears. They were real. They were pure. And you fell for that trap, tyrpiglynt." He thought the next lines to the Maidens. *Extend your arms toward each other. Form the pentacle.*

Procelli recovered, realizing his danger—but a minuscule fraction of a second too late. The girls' arms extended, and from each—now that all five Maidens were at last incarnate—streamed the power that was their heritage and their destiny. He rebounded from the field; though it wavered, it held, and the furious glares of the Apocalypse Maidens seemed almost powerful enough themselves to hold him locked within that seal. "I will break—"

"Given time, perhaps. If the wills of the Maidens were insufficient, or your power allowed to grow long enough. But with the breaking of one of your three mirrors, your anchor to this world has been weakened, and I shall give you no more time." He turned to Holly. "I give you the words; speak, and focus your will on banishing this monster from the world."

"Oh, that's my *total* focus," Seika said, not removing her gaze from Procelli.

He thought the words, clearly and carefully, and saw each stand a little taller as they spoke. "By the Earth, the world on which we stand—"

"—by the Water that cradles all that lives—"

"—by the Air, that gives us breath and life—"

The pentagonal seal's colors were brightening, making the light seem solid, glowing glass binding the five Maidens together, even through the boundary of the mirror itself.

"By the Fire that burns within, that warms us in the night—"

"And by the power of the Spirit, the foundation of all," Holly said, and her voice echoed through the walls and floor; Silvertail thought he could even hear a deeper note, the voice of the soul that had chosen to be Holy Aura.

"By all the Powers we banish thee, we abolish thee, we drive you hence from all Time and Space!" they said together, and Silvertail felt himself straighten, felt the pride that even though three of the five had been forced to themselves in but moments, that all five were already united, had at least for this moment recognized that there were evils to be fought without doubt or restraint. "Procelli, Mirrortaint, tyrpiglynt, your summoner denies you, her heart rejects you!"

Cordy spoke then, and the voice of Tsunami Reflection was the crushing cold of an iceberg. "I deny you from within your own mirror, Procelli, and I reject the gifts you offered. Take all your lies and your twisted truths and begone to the void that reflects nothing!"

Procelli screamed, a sound of agony and denial and fury and desperation. His form twisted, became something inhuman and impossible to describe, with bends and twists and folds that the eye could not follow, with claws and mouths and eyes, distorted hands that gripped the stone in a vain effort to retain a hold in a world that rejected it.

With a soundless shock, Procelli vanished.

In the same instant, Princess Tsunami Reflection appeared, now standing *before* the mirror she had just been within, and in the center of the pentacle Silvertail sat, holding Cordy's purse in his paws.

They turned and regarded the mirror. Procelli stared, shocked and unbelieving, from its surface.

And then Cordy raised her now-armored fist and *smashed* the mirror.

It shattered as though a bomb had detonated within it, sending sparkling dust and shards spattering throughout the room; only the buff-colored backing, severely dented in the center now, remained, with a few broken pieces still adhering to the edges.

She reached down and picked up the purse; Silvertail relinquished it willingly. Cordy, still as Princess Tsunami Reflection with her rippling golden hair touched with crystal blue, withdrew her compact and opened it.

Staring out from the tiny mirror was Procelli. His voice came thinly, carrying only a minuscule fraction of its former power: "Please, no, Princess! I will never attempt to trick you again! I understand you, I know what you want, know how—"

"You," she said in a voice low and filled with trembling fury and revulsion, "know *nothing*."

Her hand spasmed shut, and with the splintering, cracking noise of the compact shattering came a sudden feeling of lightness, as though a weight had lifted from the world, a weight they had barely felt before.

"Well *done*, Maidens," Silvertail said, after a few moments of silence. "Well done indeed."

"Silvertail," Holly said, "what about all the people—"

"Yes, that is a problem. But for the most part not utterly insoluble. I will need to borrow your powers, now assembled, but I can undo the worst of what that monster has wrought and prevent innocents from suffering long-lasting consequences."

"Can you make sure that slimy coach *does* suffer long-lasting consequences?"

He smiled. "I think that, too, can be arranged."

Once more, foresight paid off well. The same sigils and talismans buried about the area allowed him to invoke the powers across much of the town. It would not, alas, encompass the fringes of the tyrpiglynt's former influence, but there was only so much one could do.

He *could* make sure that not only were certain images on Coach John's phone now clear, they were also impossible for him to *erase*. And a much more mundane phone call would be all that was needed for the rest. *He already had other . . . images present. This was not just a matter of the tyrpiglynt bringing hidden impulses to the fore; this man had already been indulging those impulses when he could get away with it.*

Silvertail collapsed back against Holly's hand. "I . . . believe I am done."

The new Maidens stared at the other two and Silvertail. "Um . . ." said Tierra.

"Yeah. We'll have to all get together and talk," Holly said immediately. "Tomorrow? I'll talk to everyone and figure out a time. But there's a *lot* to tell you guys."

"There *must* be a lot," Devika said after a moment. "But I'll be there. Um, Mr. Rat—"

"Silvertail Heartseeker is my name."

"Mr. Heartseeker, how do I change *back*?"

Seika laughed. "Just *think* hard about it. Will it, real hard, and it'll happen. With all your clothes intact."

Remembering the sequence of events as he had sensed it through the others, Silvertail forced himself to rise again. "Which means I need do at least one more thing."

Devika emerged from the light of Tempest Corona; while her arm was still healed, her clothes were rent and covered with blood. Another spell, drawn from his rapidly dwindling reserves of strength, removed the grim stains and restored the clothing to completeness. "There. Now let us all separate swiftly, that you are not all seen together or all in the Raiment of the Maidens."

"Wait!" Cordy said. "You . . . you were my dad. Then you weren't. But you knew what he sounded like, you *sounded* like him, so where—"

"Where do you think?" Silvertail asked with another smile. "Who else could have reached your house, so nearby yet so private, and entered it, and destroyed the mirror?"

"But my dad would *never* believe any of this stuff, at least not right away! How could you possibly convince him to break one of my mirrors that *fast*?"

"You may somewhat underestimate your father. He *knew* something was terribly wrong, though I do not believe he could articulate it or, perhaps, even consciously accept that it lay beyond the mere physical. But I had a far better way to convince him, or most people." He saw their confused expressions and allowed himself another laugh. "Two thousand dollars to break the mirror, and two thousand more when the job was done."

The girls suddenly joined him in laughing. Cordy was almost crying as she did—not surprising, when laughter and tears and fear were so near. "Well, that's . . . he better give me some of that for a better dresser!"

"I will so advise him. And as soon as I can resume my more normal human form, I'll have to arrange the second payment—with a bonus, I believe. He could not have timed his action more perfectly had he been *watching*." He heard movement farther down the stairway. "And we must part *now*."

After hasty goodbyes, the group split up; Silvertail rode on Princess Holy Aura's shoulder as she bounced to the rooftop to survey the area. "Crap. There's still a *lot* of damage."

"I was focused mainly on removing *personal* penalties—fading memories of evil done, reduction of arrests and such, and so on. Restoring physical structures that were grossly damaged . . . lies beyond my current power."

"Jebus. I don't know if the school will be open any time soon. We *trashed* B-Wing's second floor. Including the stairs."

"We'll worry about that tomorrow. For now, I think we'd best go home. We don't—*look out*!"

The attacks came from two directions at once, and Silvertail knew he had no chance to dodge; quick though his reactions were, he was just too *small* to cover enough distance to evade the nets that were spreading to enclose them.

But Princess Holy Aura was a different matter.

Holly had reacted as soon as he shouted—possibly had even seen a flicker of motion from the corner of her own eye—and leapt *upward* in a tremendous bound, forty feet in an instant. The nets crashed together, entangling each other directly below, but four *more* were fired almost instantly. *Coordinated action. These people* expected *her to jump up!*

She tried to evade this volley, but though she was able—to some extent—to maneuver even in midair, it was not enough. The wide-flung nets entangled her, dragged her back down toward the roof. A series of hollow *thumps* sent a cloud of white mist around them.

Crap! Gas! came Holy Aura's thoughts. *Am I immune to gas? I'm holding my breath!*

Resistant though not immune. You have but to call on the power of Holy Aura and it will neutralize any such toxins—mundane ones easily, others slowly. I am relatively immune to all such, one benefit I have gained over the millennia.

She wavered slightly even as a white glow shimmered about her body. *It's not mundane, not completely. I can finish fighting it off, though. Should I pretend to fall? What's the game plan?*

Yes, let us at least give them enough confidence to reveal something of themselves without us frightening them immediately. Fight it but fall.

Holy Aura struggled violently with the nets, breaking a few of the strands; Silvertail himself fell off her shoulder and let himself lie immobile near her feet. Holy Aura wobbled, her efforts becoming more sluggish and ill-directed, and then slowly sank down to her knees and then slid limply to lie face-first on the asphalt-covered roof. *Fine playacting there, Steve. For that* must *be you, Steve.*

Heh. It does *come from those memories, but . . . shit, it's actually starting to sound really strange to be* called *Steve. Wonder if I'll have dreams of being Holly after this is all over? That'll kinda mess with me.*

Perhaps a few vague ones. But nothing to disrupt your old life as it becomes your new life. Now pay attention to what happens.

Several minutes passed. *These people are professionals. They're not going to charge forward right away.*

His sensitive ears picked up whispered conversation.

"Should we tranq her directly, ma'am?"

"Orders are to obtain *alive*, so I'd rather not. She's not very big and we just hit her with enough CM-112 to knock down a bull elephant. And she fell faster than said elephant would. What's her respiration?"

"Slow and even according to the remote acoustic."

"Could she be playing possum?"

"She *could*, ma'am, but like you say, she took a *hellish* dose of one-twelve. If she's faking it, the nonlethals probably aren't gonna cut it."

"What about the animal?"

Well, they were *paying attention. Good for them, perhaps less so for me.*

"It fell off her almost right away. If it's still alive, it's definitely in dreamland for a while."

A low, almost inaudible chuckle. "Operative, if you live long enough, you'll know better than to say *anything* like 'definitely' about an OSC target in the field. All right, she's either playing us or she's down. Either way, time to secure. I'm moving in. Operative One and Three with me, Two and Four cover us. That means, One and Three, you *keep your line* and leave a clear field of fire for Two and Four, you got me?"

"Yes, ma'am."

And now I know who they are. Well, I suspected as much. Holly, if you had to move fast, could you?

Think so. That whole struggle business was show. I could've ripped those nets like they were that cheap netting they use for oranges in the store, easy. Why?

Because we'll have to get out of the central line of fire once we show we're awake. These people are careful and smart. I think we already met their leader.

A flash of understanding. *Got you. If they go to tie me up, I'm moving. Okay with you?*

I concur. Their bindings will likely be far stronger than this net.

The dark-clad figures were nearly invisible in the late-evening gloom, and with the noise and light below it was likely they could have had a full-scale gun battle on the roof and no one would notice. They approached cautiously but with a relaxed professionalism that Silvertail recognized all too well.

The taller figure made a quick gesture to the other two, who both pulled out something that appeared to be restraints.

Instantly Princess Holy Aura moved; the pearl-bright light flared about her and she tore her way free and streaked to one side, so swiftly that the shots from operatives Two and Four passed through empty air. At the same time, she threw the nets up and over the three around her. A streak of silver-white then shot to the other two corners, and the ones called Two and Four were suddenly tumbling into the other three as they tried to free themselves from the entangling nets.

Holy Aura stepped up to the group and dropped the rifles—which she had literally tied together in a knot. "OSC, I presume?" she said, picking up Silvertail and placing him on her shoulder again. "My . . . advisors mentioned your group, among others. This feels like your kind of work. Am I right?"

The leader finished pulling the net off and studied Holy Aura for a moment. "And what if we are?"

"Back the *hell* off, that's what. I don't want to fight you. I don't want to hurt anyone that isn't a bad guy. But if you people get in our way you'll be putting a lot of *other* people in danger. Don't make me be sorry I let you go."

For several moments the OSC operative studied her. "I think you *mean* that." The operative pulled off her hood, revealing the red hair Silvertail had expected. "Do you have *any* idea of who we are, really?"

"Eh, I guess. Super-spy organization trying to protect the world from the scum of the universe. Which is great, if you understand what's going on and you've got the power to do the job, but I don't think you do, and you don't."

"Really?" Agent Kisaragi raised an eyebrow. "Well, you certainly aren't the usual sort of monstrosity we collect, I'll admit. Still, I can't just ignore the fact that disastrous manifestations have been happening here *very* frequently of late, and on an unprecedented scale."

"Hey, I *fight* them, I'm not *causing* them. And I don't think you could've stopped most of them. Maybe the dhole."

"You may be right. But we have . . . resources that might surprise you. Still . . ." She shrugged. "Obviously we're not taking you in tonight, and I admit to being doubtful that our snipers would succeed in dropping you."

Silvertail admired the way Holly didn't react to the word at all. For *his* part he felt suddenly woefully overexposed on top of an almost empty roof. "They wouldn't," Holly said calmly. "I've been hit by lots worse."

"All right. For now. But we'll be watching . . . Princess Holy Aura, yes?" She didn't smile as she said it.

"That's my name."

The agent reached into her pocket, pulled out a card. "If you ever *do* think you need our help . . . or think that things are going to go out of your control . . . please call me."

Holy Aura took the card. "Agent Dana Kisaragi, huh? Okay, I'll keep that in mind." She tucked the card inside her skirt. "Now, can I leave, or will someone try to drug me or net me or use a telepathic mind-bolt or something?"

That got a small chuckle. "You're free to go. Back off, operatives. We're aborting this mission."

"Then . . . see you around, Agent!"

Holy Aura bounded away across rooftops, and then through the small park nearby, at lightning speed.

What's the hurry, Holly?

Not taking chances, that's the hurry. She bounded over a small stream and Silvertail saw the card drop into the swirling water. *Can I somehow burn off anything that might be on me?*

Comprehension burst in on him. *Oh, very clever. Yes, they* could *be using a chemical or even radioactive or magical tracer on us. If I can borrow a bit of your power, I can cleanse any such material from us; it wasn't embedded, so it will be a matter of causing it to separate from us.*

Her fear proved well-founded; Silvertail felt a small but significant resistance as he performed the short ritual. *A chemical tracer with mystical elements. Complex, very difficult to detect; most people would be unable to do so.* He allowed himself a bit of pride. *Of course, they have no way of knowing they were attempting to trick the last living Lemurian.*

Of course not, Virgil, she replied with a mental grin. *Now we can actually, finally, go home!*

Yes, we can. As she bounded toward their home, he continued, *But . . . why did you call me Virgil?*

Another laugh was his only answer.

✴ Chapter 34 ✴

"Arlaung! Welcome back." Queen Nyarla waved casually from her high seat, where she was drinking something black from a tall glass.

He bowed low, feeling tension within slowly being released. The Queen's words were spoken with a lightness, a cheer, that told him that his lateness did not matter . . . this time. "My apologies for the delay, my Queen; I felt it best to be circuitous in my return."

"No apology needed; your judgment was sound. I was returning directly, thus it would be unwise for both of us to draw attention to this, our stronghold." She surveyed him and he straightened. "You have improved your hold on shape and seeming, Arlaung. Well done. This was a trying time, yet your human disguise remained flawless."

He judged that this was the best chance he would ever have to question her. "Might I . . . speak plainly of what weighs upon my mind, great Queen Nyarla?"

The eyes narrowed slightly, but her head nodded. "If you have concerns, Arlaung, then speak. I promise to hold nothing said now against you, unless it be open rebellion."

"Never!" he said, the words torn from within. The very *thought* of rebellion made his skin itch as though he had been a thousand years away from the open sea. "It is . . . the tyrpiglynt. I am *concerned*, my Queen. You allowed, even *encouraged*, one such as Procelli to manifest and find his freedom. His power was growing at a pace to make those beneath the sea quail. Was there not great risk in this? I have heard it whispered, in ancient tales, and written in *De Vermis*

Mysteriis, that a tyrpiglynt could grow beyond any bounds given time and freedom."

The narrowed eyes widened, and she laughed, the lilting sound that a human would have found unaccountably menacing. "Why, Arlaung, you *are* worried for me. Or is it just for our mission, and your destiny beneath the waves?"

"For both, Majesty," he answered honestly.

"It was a *calculated* risk, Arlaung, one hinted at in the Trapezohedron and whispered to me by the Nine-Armed Herself. If the Mirrortaint succeeded in destroying even one of the Maidens—or even poor Varatraine—it would have sealed the fate of this world and we could have brought our great Ruler through far more swiftly." She smiled, and there was a chill menace to the smile that Arlaung found comforting. "And Procelli would not have become *that* great, not so swiftly, that he would dare move against Queen Azathoth of the Nine Arms. He would have been disposed of if he tried."

Arlaung frowned, then nodded slowly. "Then there was much more to your plan. You expected that even the tyrpiglynt would fail, would be destroyed by the Maidens." It was a statement, not a question.

"Correct. The power of the Cycle those accursed Lemurian wizards began is great, and changing more than minor details is something we have, thus far, failed to do. Thus it was almost certain, to my mind, that fate would ensure that there were sufficient Maidens to win the day. If what we sensed is true, at least three Maidens more were present—making four at least, and I suspect all five of the Maidens must have been present to remove him from this world."

"And this is good? Pardon my tone, but—"

"But of *course* it is, dear Arlaung. With all five Apocalypse Maidens now assembled, the pattern is complete for them. They cannot expect sudden reinforcements to simply appear on the battlefield—or at least none of nearly their own power; I am not so foolish as to ignore the possibility one of the other native defenders of this speck of a world might have already awakened." She shrugged. "The point, however, is that it is *now* possible to break the pattern. It was necessary that all five be *born*; the force of their destiny protected them, to a great extent, from anything we might do—although, of course, we would still try. But now that protection no longer holds, and we need only cripple, turn, or kill *one* to assure the victory of our Nine-Armed Queen."

Arlaung considered. "I understand, Majesty. Yet it seems little enough, this acceleration of the timetable, to justify unleashing a being that could rival or surpass you."

She rose, placing the now empty glass on a side table, and strode toward the room of the Trapezohedron. "You *do* surprise me, Arlaung. When first I chose you, I expected . . . oh, a strong arm, *muscle* as they say, and little else. Your distant lineage of the line of Dagon seems far stronger than I had thought.

"You are correct, indeed. If that were all, it were nowhere near a justification for such risk. But as you show a surprising penetration of truths, I ask you, Arlaung: What was the *effect* of the tyrpiglynt's emergence, and what would that mean for *us*?"

Arlaung thought back, remembering the wave of power that had emanated from the escaped creature of the Outer Void. He recalled the way the behavior of the crowd had changed, the shift from their stilted and dull sport to amusements of far greater interest . . . and he thought, suddenly, he understood. "You were interested in the *crowd*."

"In what his *power* did to the individuals of the crowd, yes, my dear Arlaung. Their actions, their choices in the midst of chaos, their *feelings* were unguarded. I could watch them through the lens of my power, illuminated by Procelli's power, and see who they truly *were*, unless they were cloaked or protected by some other power."

He leaned forward, suddenly eager. "So you know them! Know the Maidens' mortal identities!"

She shook her head. "They were protected. Oh, had I the time to watch, to memorize and cross-check and index, I could easily have discovered which girls did *not* appear before my mind's eye, and from that deduce that they were the Maidens. But that was not my interest nor my goal, not this time."

"Then what . . . Ah."

"Precisely, Arlaung. The Maidens are all Chosen now . . . and I have found my Knights. The conditions were perfect to find me five flawed hearts hidden within cloaks of light. And more." Her smile was sharp-fanged and not quite human. "I have found the perfect vessel, Arlaung! The perfect host through which She will be born into the world."

"A heart of true darkness, then," Arlaung said. "One utterly without what they call humanity."

She shook her head, disappointment writ large on her face. "Not at *all*, Arlaung. Just as our Nine-Armed Queen enters the world through a portal that is but a speck compared to the world, her vessel must also be only *slightly* flawed, an otherwise worthy soul with *just* enough potential for corruption to be ensnared by themselves."

She threw open a cabinet and with a swift murmur of invocations and a casual channeling of power that made Arlaung gasp with envy and awe, five quivering, noisome masses of gelatinous ectoplasm materialized. The masses pulsed and glowed with eldritch power and a vile, innate malevolence that appealed to Arlaung, sang to his heart so loudly that he nearly took a step toward them.

Nyarla must have sensed that impulse, for she flung out one clawed hand, interposing it between Arlaung and the pulsing objects. "Do not touch them, Arlaung; they are made for others than your kind, and would destroy you in an instant."

The glutinous, transparent things shuddered, and began to shrink, dwindling, condensing under Queen Nyarla's continuing invocations. Slowly they took on a hardness, a shining crystal solidity, a shimmering beauty that only those with the right senses could tell was but a mask for something indescribably *alien* to this world. Five rings lay quiescent on the table before him.

"They are summoned and complete," she said in satisfaction. "*Now* you may take them, Arlaung. They are harmless to you. Lock them in the cabinet in the parlor. Then you will find the five I have chosen," a series of images and sensations suddenly filled his mind, leaving behind the sure knowledge of the individuals he sought, "and bring them here."

"And the One? The one to give birth to the Nine-Armed?"

"That, Arlaung, is my task, and mine alone. I must proceed with care; all must be done in absolute perfection when it comes to Her vessel. Go, find the Knights, and I shall require no more of you for some time."

He bowed, and turned away, cold blood warming itself with anticipation. *Soon. The time will be soon.*

✳ Chapter 35 ✳

“Hi, Tierra, come on in,” Holly said, trying not to yawn. “Hi, Ms. MacKintor.”

“So you’re Holly! Tierra’s said a lot about you.” Marli MacKintor gave a quick smile that momentarily eased visible lines in her face.

“Only good things, I hope,” Trayne Owen said. “Would you like to come in . . . Marli, is it? Have a cup of coffee?”

“Oh, God, I’d love to, but I barely have time to get to work as it is. I can’t say how grateful I am that you’re letting Tierra come over here this early.” Holly noted that while Marli had the same brilliant red hair of her daughter, Marli’s was streaked with gray and she had the pinched look of someone under constant worry.

“Well, we were all caught off guard, to say the least, by what happened at the school. As Holly was going to have her friends over anyway, it’s no problem at all. But if you can’t come in and sit down, I insist you at least take one of these muffins; when I knew you’d be coming this early I baked some—”

The part of Holly that was Steve recognized the almost *too* intense longing in both Marli and Tierra’s face at the sight of the home-baked goods. “Well, I suppose I could take one—”

“Take two, here, I have a bag.”

“Well . . . thank you very much, Trayne.” Marli’s flash of a smile was very like Tierra’s. “Tierra, you behave yourself—”

“*Mooommmm,* I’m not five years old anymore!”

“All the more reason to behave yourself,” Marli said, then gave her obviously slightly embarrassed daughter a hug. “I’ll pick her up—”

"No need, I'll bring her home. If they don't decide to all sleep over and make it impossible for *me* to sleep. I understand the school's closed for an entire week, so it's an unexpected vacation."

"Well . . . I'll call you later." She glanced at her phone. "God, I have to go. Bye!"

Once her car had departed the driveway, Holly saw Tierra sink slowly down into one of the chairs, eyes scanning the room. She knew *that* look, too.

"Your mom's kinda run ragged, isn't she?"

"Two jobs, sometimes three," Tierra said, with that expression of defiant embarrassment that showed a past filled with both sneers and oppressive, useless sympathy.

And I've never heard her mention—

"And . . . no other parent?" Silvertail asked gently.

Tierra grimaced. "Well . . . um, can I have one of those—"

"Of course. I made them for everyone."

Tierra took one of the muffins and bit into it. "Orrmgrrrd, thss's gud," she mumbled ecstatically through her second huge mouthful, then swallowed. "Yeah, well, like I was saying, I *have* a father. Biologically. Other than that, he's an asshole. Sorry."

"No need to apologize. So your mother takes care of you by herself and cannot afford to miss work because school schedules change. Don't worry; we'll handle that part for her during the time school is unexpectedly out. You're always welcome here."

"It'll mean a *lot* to her."

In the back of her mind, Holly/Steve had already decided that they'd do more than just play babysitter occasionally. *I know* exactly *what it's like to live that way.*

Trayne Owen picked up a muffin himself. "Well, it will be no trouble at all. Now, the others won't be here for quite a while, but I suppose it's unreasonable to expect you to wait to ask questions. . . ?"

"Can I . . . transform again? I mean, like now?"

Holly giggled at Silvertail/Trayne's expression. "I . . . yes, this place is protected, our enemies will not detect it. But I admit that was *not* the first question I expected."

Even before he finished the sentence, Tierra had leapt to her feet and begun the invocation, concluding with ". . . Princess Temblor Brilliance!"

In the mundane setting of the kitchen the transformation was even more stunning than in the midst of a battle; Holly found her own mouth open again in awe, staring at the six-foot-tall flame-haired warrior in crystal and gossamer armor before her.

"*Wow*," Temblor Brilliance murmured, staring at her hands and the costume she could see. "It's *real*. I . . . like, yeah, it was real, the school's *closed* because it was real, but still, it wasn't like *real*. Does that make sense?"

"Every bit," Holly said. She was forcing herself to stay relaxed; they'd gotten through one of these meetings before, and she had to have faith that they'd get through the big meeting too. "Like I said, even now that I've been Holy Aura for months it's still hard to really *accept*."

She looked at Trayne. "And you *really are* a magic white rat?"

For answer he disappeared in a flash of light and appeared on the table, leaning against his muffin.

Tierra gave a simultaneous smile and wince. "*That*'s kinda tough for me. I hate rats."

"If it helps at all, I was not *born* a rat, this is just the form I am . . . well, reduced to. And whatever your prior experiences with rats might be, I am at least rather more civilized and articulate, I think."

Tierra/Temblor giggled. "Yeah, that's true. Maybe if I paint you I can detach myself from the image, or accept the image as art, or something like that."

"A portrait? I have no objection." He resumed the Mr. Owen form. "Holly showed me some of your work for the game; you are quite talented, Tierra, leaving aside your newfound role."

"Thanks, Mr. Owen!" Tierra said. Without a pause, she went on, "I wonder if I'm strong enough to lift the fridge," looking at the large stainless-steel appliance.

"Please do not try, there are water hookups you would break. We have an entire practice room set up for superhuman young women to exercise and show off."

"What? A secret training area! Totally awesome!"

Trayne gave a resigned sigh. "Holly, why don't you and Tierra go down and look around what you called our 'cut-rate Danger Room' for a while?"

Holly laughed. "Okay, Dad!"

That turned out to be a very good idea, Holly mused a bit later.

Finding out that she really *was* superhuman as Temblor Brilliance kept Tierra distracted, gave plenty of time to talk about the less-sensitive areas of being an Apocalypse Maiden, and helped the time go by.

It was almost lunchtime when the door buzzer alerted them to come out. Ascending the stairs they could hear the voices of the other girls already in the dining room. "Hey, everyone!" Holly said as she came in.

Seika waved cheerfully; Devika and Cordy looked, naturally, less relaxed but did manage a "Hi" each. *At least Tierra knew both of us before.*

"I've gotten an assortment of food," Trayne said. "I didn't know if any of you had dietary restrictions, so this covers all the common bases."

"Holy sheep, Dad, we'll be eating the leftovers from this for like a week and a half!" There must have been samples of half a dozen cuisines on the table.

"Perhaps some of your friends will take some home with them," he answered with a quick smile. "Besides, unless I miss my guess, your friends have already discovered their appetites are . . . considerably larger than they were earlier."

Tierra looked up, startled. "You're right. I woke up this morning and I found I ate an entire *box* of cereal without even thinking about it. That's *normal*?"

"For an Apocalypse Maiden? Yes, and I will explain why shortly. Please, choose whatever you like. We'll talk once everyone's ready."

Holly looked over at Cordy as they got their food. "So, Cordy—can I call you that?"

The blonde nodded. "It's what most people call me. *Cordelia* is usually what Mom or Dad use when I'm in real trouble."

"I get the three-name address," Seika said. "*Seika Lynn Cooper*, you get your *ass* in here!"

Devika cracked a smile. "It's just the *tone* in my house. My mother can say *Devika* so quiet it's like she whispers, and I *still* know I'm in *so* much trouble."

Holly grinned at that. "Anyway, Cordy, was there any, um, trouble over your mirror?"

Cordy shook her head, managing a tiny laugh. "No, I got home and Dad mentioned he'd had an accident and broke the mirror, and I said

'Thank you, Daddy' and really confused him. Promised I'd explain later. If I could. Can I?" she asked, looking at Trayne.

"That is the plan, yes," Mr. Owen answered. "While those of you familiar with the concepts of the magical girl or similar, er, super-teams might be also wondering if they must keep their identities secret, we do not intend to conceal such vital information from your parents. We *did* want to discuss the more . . . delicate aspects of the situation with you *before* such a, shall we say, parent-superhero conference, however."

Devika looked *supremely* relieved, and both Cordy and Tierra smiled, looking somewhat surprised. "I did *not* want to hide anything from my parents. Especially not something like this," Devika said. "You have already made me feel a little better about being an . . . Apocalypse Maiden."

"That *is* an awfully corny name," Cordy said. "And it was *really* creepy how I just *knew* what to say—"

"I know, right? It was like I was a preprogrammed robot or something!" Tierra said with a shiver.

"Hey, wait until you get to face the bad guys at the right dramatic moment," Seika said. "Then you get to do the pre-ass-kicking speech that's programmed in, too. Rest of it isn't as automatic, but you *do* get a gut feeling of what you can do and how."

"Which was a damn good thing," Holly said. "Given three of you had to come into the fight without even any warning. Anyway, let's listen to Silvertail as he gives us the rundown on what we've gotten you into."

Having heard the lectures twice now, Holly could focus on watching the reactions of their three new members. She could see that Seika was doing the same. *She probably* memorized *everything Silvertail said the first time. She's incredibly bright.*

The others listened and asked a few questions, but for the most part they accepted what they were told. *Like Silvertail said, the magic probably helps there.*

"Do we know when this Azathoth of the Nine Arms will be brought through?" Devika asked.

"Not yet," answered Silvertail. "I incline now to believe it will be likely around March, possibly as late as June. We are doing things somewhat differently, and so are our adversaries, and this undoubtedly changes the timetable."

"That Mirrortaint-thing was getting more powerful every second, right?" Cordy said thoughtfully. "Sounds like something *I* wouldn't want out there if I was a bad guy. Monsters like that would rather *they* be the big bad wolf, right?"

Silvertail, now in his default furry form, nodded. "A wise observation. There was undoubtedly more purpose behind that assault than met the eye. With the chaos and emotions unleashed, Nyarla might have been inserting more agents—physical and otherwise—into the school, or examining the spirits she could see to determine if they were suitable vessels, or attempting to locate the Maidens herself."

"Vessels? For what?" Seika asked.

"Our adversaries, like the Mirrortaint, often reflect us. The reflections of the Apocalypse Maidens are the Cataclysm Knights."

Holly gave him a narrow look. "I don't remember you mentioning that we'd have counterparts on the bad guy side!"

He shrugged, a small movement beneath his white fur. "Until this point, it did not matter much; the Knights do not ever show themselves until all five Maidens are incarnate."

"And these guys—they *are* guys, right?" Seika asked; seeing Silvertail nod, she went on, "These guys will have powers that are like reflections or distortions of ours, right? So they'll have all the elemental powers plus, what, influence over something like a sin or corruption opposite to what we represent."

"Precisely. Corruption, distortion, perversion of nature, these are their signatures. Like you, they will also vary the *details* of their behavior and so on, so I will not be able to tell you ahead of time what to expect from them except in general terms."

The Steve within Holly felt another nasty shock. "And these guys . . . they're like us. Teenagers, I mean, students."

"In all great likelihood, yes. They reflect the Maidens deliberately."

Son of a bitch. *More kids drawn into this mess.*

"But if they're on *that* side, then they're bad guys, right?" Tierra asked hopefully.

Silvertail's expression was not comforting. "Ultimately? If they triumph? Yes. But they need only start with a sufficiently human set of flaws that the Queen and her people can *corrupt* them. Which is, alas, most people. Even you girls—and I, myself—have such flaws. We may be fortunate enough to resist them, overcome them, but all of us have them. Most will be . . . less pleasant, perhaps, than the five of you, but they will not *begin* as monsters but merely young men who are tempted, and almost certainly misled, onto a path that will *transform* them into monsters. The same, and worse, is true of the one who will be chosen as Azathoth's vessel."

"Vessel? Whoa, hold on," said Seika. "I thought you said they had to open up some *gateway* to let this bad girl through. What's this vessel stuff?"

"In the finale of our battle against the tyrpiglynt," Silvertail answered, "you saw that to return Procelli to his own realm required that you have someone—an anchor, so to speak—in that realm, a focal point as it were that allowed you to translate your power directly from *here* to *there*.

"The same is true for Queen Azathoth Nine-Armed; she requires a focal point native to this world that is connected to her, and in her case, it must be a living inhabitant of the world, through which she will be born into this universe when the stars are right and the gateway is opened."

Cordy was looking at him wide-eyed. "So . . . what, this Azathoth-thing is going to burst out of someone like that *Alien* movie?"

There was no mistaking the grimness on the tiny furry face. "Oh, far worse, Cordy. They must remain *intact* as an anchor until the world *itself* has been completely enveloped and subsumed by the gateway—until this world *is* the realm of Azathoth of the Nine Arms. Until that has occurred, the victim and vessel will remain *alive and conscious* within Azathoth as her form coalesces and solidifies about them, and then they will, slowly but surely, be absorbed into the Nine-Armed's being." He shook his tiny head. "I do not think there are words for the horror that the one chosen as a vessel will suffer."

They were all silent for a moment. Holly thought now that one of the keys of being *worthy* to be a Maiden had to be empathy, sympathy with other living beings and the ability to envision themselves in those other beings' places, and that meant that all of them now were imagining that hideous possibility.

Finally Devika rose. "That's enough of that. Silvertail, you said there was another issue we needed to be aware of. Let's get this over with. I want to focus on our job, what we will need to know to defend our world and save our families, not waste time on what will happen if we *lose*."

The others nodded, a couple smiling faintly. *Well, she's straightforward, that's for sure.*

"As you will, then." Silvertail launched into the preamble that inevitably ended up with the reveal that Holly Owen had not started life with that name *or* appearance.

And . . . it's bothering me more and more that that's true. Stephen Russ's *memories* and to some extent personality were still part of Holly, but the parts tied to the *body* that had been Stephen Russ were more and more . . . well, *repellent* to Holly. Sure, there were things about the teenage body she'd been handed that weren't all that much fun, but overall . . . this, Holly Owen, this was who she *was* now.

Jesus, I'm so *fucked up. It's a good thing this all gets erased later, because if I had to go back to my old self* with *these memories? I'd be a basket case.*

Even *thinking* about them as separate wasn't accurate; Holly Owen had a convenient, and very clear, set of demarcations that showed when she was . . . born, so to speak, but her background memories, the only memories of *childhood* she had, were Steve's. She *was* Steve, and Steve was her. And Steve/Holly *liked being Holly better than Steve.*

But ultimately it *was* still true. He had been born Stephen J. Russ, and if the magic were banished from the world, he would be Stephen again.

And so once more, now in front of three astounded and wary girls, Holly stood up, gathering her courage to reveal that ugly truth. "And so, well . . ."

Another hand gripped hers. She looked over, to see Seika standing next to her. Seika smiled. "I'm not scared of you. Not you-Holly, and not you-Steve. And I'm with you one hundred and ten percent."

Feeling a great weight lifting from her heart, Holly Owen released the magic. And despite the weight that descended upon her, she still felt light as a feather.

✴ Chapter 36 ✴

"Well, um, Trayne—we're all here," Henry Weatherill said, looking a bit nervously around at the group assembled in the Owens' large living room. He didn't *look* the part of a man who was often nervous; he had the broad build, and generous dirty-blond beard streaked with gray, of a veteran biker, something the brilliant blue turban resonated with in some odd fashion.

"Yes, we are. Or I presume we are?" asked Ashley Ingemar; her poise and face echoed that of her daughter, twenty years farther down the line, although it was her husband Matt's hair and build that had been passed down to Cordelia. "I wasn't clear on how many of us were supposed to be here."

Marli MacKintor was quiet, almost hiding in a corner; Holly could tell how ill at ease she was. *She's giving up her only free evening in two weeks for this.*

"My apologies for the mystery," Trayne Owen said. "I think you will understand better once we have had the discussion."

"Mystery is right," Henry said with a chuckle. "Almost feels like one of those shows where the detective calls in all the suspects so he can grill them, or watch how they react to each other. Right?" he finished, turning to his wife Satjit.

She gave a slight eye roll but smiled, gripped his hand, and said, "I suppose." Holly wasn't sure *where* Devika's height came from. Henry Weatherill wasn't short and he was solid, but neither of them were giants, and Devika *towered* over everyone in the room except for Trayne and Dave Cooper—and was close to looking them in the eye.

"In any event, please, everyone get anything you like to drink, take anything from the trays—I've tried to make sure there's something for everyone—and get comfortable. Then I'll explain." Holly could sense that Silvertail had enhanced his natural persuasiveness *just* a hair. Mind control they weren't going to do, but enhancing the mood was excusable. She didn't *like* it, and neither did Silvertail, really, but they hadn't planned on having to have all three remaining families briefed in one shot, but there really wasn't much choice.

As the others got their refreshments, natural habits of introduction asserted themselves, so that by the time they were all seated the parents had all exchanged names and the atmosphere was, if not cordial, at least a bit less tense and confused than it had been.

"All right, Trayne, we're ready. I came because you said it had to do with what happened over at the school, that . . . riot," Matt Ingemar said. He *looked* like a parent at a conference, dressed in business casual, his still-bright golden hair brushed just so, his expression curious and sharp. "That what he told the rest of you?"

Most of the others nodded. Dave Cooper glanced at Trayne, and said, "Well, me and my wife already know what the deal is, but we'll let Mr. Owen handle it for now."

Holly watched as her father moved with his accustomed precision to the front of the room. *My father. Holy crap, that thought's become absolutely* real *to me. My real dad . . . Steve's dad . . . I* remember *him but I have to* focus *to feel that he's actually* my *father and not someone else's.* She shuddered, trying to hide it but she could feel Seika's sudden concern. *Got to get over this. I knew sacrifice would be part of the deal. This is part of that. If we win it'll all go back to normal and I'll never have had this problem.*

But the *real* problem was that a large part of her . . . didn't *want* to "go back" at all.

"First, thank you all for coming; I know that this sudden, and admittedly mysterious, request must have been difficult to agree to. I hope you will see that it was absolutely necessary, once we are done."

As before, he set the stage by establishing that this was connected to the frightening and bizarre events of the past months. "The 'riot,' of course, was another of these events, although the most extreme and supernatural parts of that evening have been either erased or at least dimmed in the minds of the vast majority of participants. Even so, anyone reading the account of the events can see there was *something* most peculiar going on—"

"Hold on, you're saying . . . what, there was something *magic* about that mirror? The one you had me break?"

"You broke Cordy's mirror on *purpose*?" demanded Ashley of her husband; Matt winced.

"Well, yeah. He paid me two grand to break it and promised two more if I actually did it. I kinda thought this might be a *Candid Camera* kind of stunt, actually, but two grand by itself was more'n enough to buy a better mirror, so I thought 'why not?'" Matt Ingemar spoke lightly, but there was a nervousness behind his words that made them ring false.

Holly thought everyone could hear it, but it was his wife that called him out on it. "Matthew Donald Ingemar, that is the worst excuse you have ever given me, and you've given me some *horrible* excuses! You knew there was something wrong with Cordy, but you ran home in the middle of it to break a mirror?"

His gaze dropped, then rose to look at Trayne. "I . . ."

"You *felt* it, did you not?" Trayne said quietly. "You could *feel* there was something wrong, something tugging at your emotions. You noticed, in the grip of your pure and unselfish concern for your daughter, that *other* impulses were rising unnaturally to the surface. You could *see* what the crowd was doing, that it made no *sense*."

The others were all staring at Matthew Ingemar now, and his face had gone steadily paler as Trayne talked. "Yes," he said after a long, silent pause, and his voice was a whisper. "I felt it. Something so *wrong* that I was *terrified* for Cordy. I just knew, somehow, that she was in terrible, terrible danger, and I didn't even know from *what*." He focused abruptly on Trayne, a startled expression on his face. "And . . . just as sure. . . I knew that *you* were trying to help."

Trayne smiled. "That, Mr. Ingemar . . . Matt . . . is because you truly are sensitive, behind your controlled exterior. I suspect that is something you do not show often, and I am grateful you trusted your instincts then. It is not an exaggeration to say that without you, we might not be here to have this conversation."

Marli was staring at them both, then at her daughter. Slowly she turned, looking in turn at each set of parents. "How are our daughters involved?"

"She's *sharp*," Seika whispered to Tierra.

The redhaired girl looked proud. "Mom's not stupid at *all*."

Trayne shrugged, smiled again. "You are correct. This does concern all of your daughters—which is why they, too, are here. Obviously two of these events have already occurred at their school, but there is more to it than that. And rather than waste time in circumlocution . . ." He nodded to them.

Holly stood, Seika beside her, and the other three rose as well. "To avert the Apocalypse, and shield the innocent from evil . . ."

The detonation of light—pure white, blazing red, chill blue, crackling violet, forest green—was a nigh-physical force. Some of their parents cried out, others merely gasped, but all stepped or shrank back for an instant . . . and then stared in awe, confusion, fear perhaps, as their vision cleared and they could see the five Maidens standing before them.

Matthew was the first to speak. "Oh my *God*, my daughter's *Sailor Moon*!" There was actual *excitement* in the voice, so startlingly at odds with his prior reserved demeanor that everyone in the room stared at him, and brilliant red embarrassment flamed in his cheeks.

Before anyone could speak, the red drained out, turned to white, and he repeated, in an entirely different, horrified tone, "Oh my God. *My daughter* is Sailor Moon."

Henry Weatherill had slowly risen, but his expression was compounded equally of a father's fear and pride. "Devika . . . is that really *you*?"

Lynn Cooper smiled faintly. "We asked the same thing when Seika showed us."

Tempest Corona nodded, and those who knew her could see Devika's face and expressions beneath the young warrior goddess that had replaced her. "Yes, Dad. It's me. I'm here. I'm just . . . different."

"Why?" Ashley Ingemar demanded, voice shaky. "Why them? Why are they . . . changed? What does this *mean*?"

Trayne's smile was sympathetic. "I can see that your husband has already recognized something of what it means. As for why they appear so different, there are two reasons. The first and most consistent is that our enemies will of course seek to destroy the Maidens, and if they looked obviously the same as their counterparts, they would be easily tracked and their families endangered." He studied Tempest Corona and shook his head. "In some ways the change is not sufficient; it seems that your daughter, Henry, Satjit, had a powerful core of your faith, and that has affected her manifestation in a way that may well make it easier to connect her to her mortal form."

He shrugged. "The second reason is that the transformation is an *idealization*. It is symbolic both of the power the Maiden wields and the expectation of . . . call it the collective consciousness of the society. In other times, other places, they would have looked . . . quite different to your eyes, but in all such places their appearance would have reflected what the ideal of their society was, moderated of course by their personalities, preferences, and inherent spirituality."

Matthew suddenly rounded on Trayne. "Take it back. This . . . Apocalypse Maiden thing, now, take it back, give it to someone else!"

Silvertail/Trayne shook his head. "I cannot. Once done, it—"

"*Bullshit!*" The shout was filled with the fury and panic of a man defending his children, and he had slammed Trayne Owen up against the wall before anyone could react. "I know what this kind of thing means, I'm not stupid! You're the guy in charge, there's got to be a way, some . . . some ritual, something—"

Holly grabbed him, yanked him away. "Get your hands off my father!"

Cordelia shoved *her* back. "You keep off *my* dad!"

"Enough, both of you!" Trayne's voice was suddenly deafening, and everyone in the room froze. "I appreciate your protectiveness, Holly, but Matt's reaction is not terribly surprising. And Cordelia, Holly would not have harmed him, and I am sure you know it."

Cordy, still in the guise of Tsunami Reflection, looked both sheepish and uncertain. Holly swallowed her anger. *That was stupid of me. Silvertail can take care of himself.* "Sorry, Cordy. Sorry, Mr. Ingemar."

Matt Ingemar had fallen half-over on one of the couches from the push Holly had given him. Now he rose and shook his head. "No. All right, I am sorry, Holly, I shouldn't . . . but do you understand? Holly . . . Princess Holy Aura. . . you've already *done* this, you have to know—"

"Daddy, if they *hadn't* . . . if *I* hadn't . . . I wouldn't *be* here," Cordy said after a moment.

"So you *can't* undo this?" Ashley said, unnaturally quiet.

"No. Once a Maiden is chosen, there is no power that can undo that choice—not mine, not the Maidens', not even that of our adversaries."

"Then we move, Matt," she said. "I'm sure you could get a transfer, they were hinting you could get a promotion if we went to the West Coast, and then—"

"No, Mom," Cordy said, even though her voice shook.

"That won't work either," Seika said, and Devika and Tierra nodded.

"The things we're going to fight want to destroy the *world*," Devika said earnestly to the Ingemars.

"And boy, would they just *love* to have us all separated so they could pick us off one at a time," Seika added. "They'll *chase* you."

Before anyone could say anything else, Marli MacKintor suddenly burst into loud, uncontrolled sobs. Holly saw that no one was more shocked by this than Tierra, who changed back without so much as a thought and ran to her mother. "Mom? Mom, what's wrong? Mommy, stop!"

But Marli's sobs continued unabated, and aside from "I can't take it," her words in reply were disjointed, nonsensical.

Most of the others, Silvertail included, were obviously at a loss. As Trayne, he moved tentatively toward her. "Marli, I—"

"*Get away from me! From my little girl!*" The words were savage, tearful, fearful, and Trayne backed away; Holly could sense he did not know what to say or how it might be said.

But I think I get it.

She changed back to Holly Owen and walked slowly over. "Ms. MacKintor, please, please listen to me, okay? I know it's just too much. You're living in a tiny apartment, working two, three jobs to keep Tierra safe, to make sure she's okay, spending your *life* on her to give her a better one. You don't have anything *left*. You wake up in the morning after only half the sleep you need and you think *maybe I should stop, I should call in*, because you hurt all over and your body's telling you you're not twenty any more, but you can't, because you need the forty, fifty dollars you'll get after taxes to buy the gas to get to the *other* job tonight, so *that* forty, fifty dollars will buy a few groceries and part of the rent and maybe let you catch up on the power bill.

"And you've read half a book and maybe seen one movie in three years, your best entertainment is getting that one day when you can sleep *in*. And you think of all the things you wanted to do when *you* were a kid, and all the jobs and dreams you could have had, and you know you can't ever have them, because you can't go to school, can't take even the few weeks or months to get training to start *climbing* that ladder because you haven't got the money to live that long away from work or the time left in the evenings to do it in."

Marli's head had slowly lifted, the sobs slowed, and she was staring at Holly as though this was the first time she had seen her. Holly's own voice was thick with Steve's remembered pain and fear and frustration. "And so you're afraid of that one disaster every day, the car breaking down when you don't have the money to fix it, you falling and breaking an arm and losing your job, just maybe getting sick and not able to get to work . . . or worse, Tierra getting sick, and wondering if there's any way you can *not* take her to the ER because you can't afford it even if you *had* insurance."

She looked up and met Marli's gaze. "And then we dump *this* on you and you suddenly know that everything you've done can't keep her safe and there's nothing you can do about it. And I'm sorry. We're sorry."

Marli MacKintor swallowed, then scrubbed the tears away from her face, yanked a wipe from her worn purse and tried to dry her face, even while another sniffle escaped—the movements of someone who was used to being badly judged for any lapse in control or capability. She stared again at Holly. "You . . . you're right. How you know that, how you can *feel* that so well at your age, I don't understand, but you're right." Her voice trembled despite obvious effort to stop it. "I just . . . I don't know how to *think* about this. I try and all the other things just mash up together and I want to scream—"

"I understand as well, Marli," Trayne said. "I have not always been in as . . . posh, shall we say, circumstances as you see here. I have—literally—eaten what others have thrown out, on occasion. Not, I will admit, for the same reasons, entirely, but I have seen and understand your own circumstances. And I am very, *very* sorry to have added this to your burdens . . . but we will try our best to help."

"Why did you *choose* her for this?" There was still a trace of anger, but it was more existential—anger at the way the world worked, rather than at the man in front of her.

"That *is* the question," Satjit said, and the other parents nodded. "Why our daughters? Why *children*, in the name of God?"

Trayne sighed, and explained the nature of the Apocalypse Maidens, and the reason for their existence—and the specific reason for their age. And from that he proceeded to explain the nature and goals of their enemies.

Not entirely to Holly's surprise, Devika's parents accepted it with the greatest equanimity. Devika's reactions when she first became Tempest Corona echoed her parents' attitudes: maybe they'd rather this destiny hadn't come to her, but the thought of their daughter taking a stand, personally and deliberately, against evil *worked* for them, and though they were clearly worried they didn't seem inclined to argue about it at all.

Marli MacKintor was still drained from her breakdown; she didn't argue, nor did she seem happy about the situation—and why would she be?

The Ingemars were the hardest sells. They regarded, at least to begin with, everything that Trayne said as suspect, and tried to appeal to the others that this was in one way or another crazy—although it was clear to Holly that the worst thing for them was that in their hearts they both knew that it *wasn't* crazy, and that meant their daughter would be one of five warriors standing between the world and total annihilation.

It was the Coopers who turned the tide. "Ashley, Matt, I get it. Really, we both do," Dave said. "We thought about packing up and getting out of Dodge too. But what's the *point*? You just saw our girls turn into some kind of superheroes, none of us are stupid enough to pretend that there aren't going to be supervillains to match. Trayne's been straight with us and from what Seika's told us, they *need* all five to make sure we've all got a world to live in."

Lynn Cooper nodded to her husband. "Dave and I would like nothing better than to keep our little girl safe, but . . . that's not how it's working out. It's *them* that's going to keep *us* safe. And they've got to be together to do that."

Ashley finally collapsed into her seat. "All right. All right, you're right."

Matt nodded. "As long as Cordy's all right with it."

Cordelia—who was still in Tsunami Reflection guise—sighed with relief. "Yes, Dad, I'm okay. It was my fault I got stuck with this anyway, and they saved me—and I guess everyone else."

"Don't downplay your own courage and dedication, Cordelia," Trayne said. "The Mirrortaint may have initially used you, yes, but it was your strength of will and focus that allowed it to be defeated at all."

Cordy grinned. "Okay, I'm a superstar, Mom, Dad." She looked over to Holly. "We've got one other . . . thing to tell you."

Matt looked puzzled, but it was Satjit whose eyes suddenly narrowed. "Yes. Mr. Owen, you said you could *choose* the first Maiden, but I cannot believe a man with your history—one who already sent his first daughter on this mission—could bring himself to do that again."

Marli raised her head. "And Holly . . . you don't always *talk* like a teenager."

"No," Holly said. "Dad . . . could you . . . ?"

Once more, Trayne Owen emphasized the requirement of sacrifice—the source of the Maidens' greatest powers—and his own determination to do things *right* this time. Holly saw Dave casually position himself in a way that he could interpose himself between Holly and anyone who might have a violent reaction to the revelation; she caught his eye and mouthed 'Thank you.' He grinned and nodded.

She could also see a few gazes narrowing as part of the truth dawned. "And since some of you've probably already guessed," she said, "yeah. I wasn't born Holly Owen. Holly Owen *is* who I am now—she's as real as who I was when I was born—but you still deserve to know the truth."

With a flash, Stephen Russ stood before them.

It turned out to be a good thing that Dave Cooper—all six feet three inches of him—was nearby and watching, because after the initial shock, Matthew Ingemar launched himself at Steve, who closed his eyes and braced for the impact, bringing his arms up to shield his head if necessary.

Instead, Dave Cooper caught Matthew and stopped him. "Whoa, hold on, Matt."

"Hold *on*?" Matthew's expression was incredulous and filled with rage and revulsion. "This guy's walking around disguised as a girl with *our daughters* and you're—"

Cordelia stepped up. "Daddy, *stop*."

That got both his attention, and the white-faced gaze of her mother, focused on her. "Cordy? But—"

"They already showed us the truth the time we all came over here. Aside from now and then, Holly's always been Holly."

"This is like the fourth time I've been Steve in the past . . . god, what, six months?" he confirmed, a bit startled to realize it. *And Jesus do I want to change back as soon as I can.*

"And we've known about it for quite a while," Dave said, letting go as Matt backed slowly away. "This's only the second time I've seen Steve, but me and him had a pretty straight heart-to-heart when they told me. I can't *prove* it, but I believe he's not some perv after our daughters. He didn't get chosen for this job at random either; Trayne knew what he was looking for, and a guy like that wouldn't have been on his list."

Marli MacKintor was staring at him with revelation on her face. "*That*'s how you knew."

"Yeah. I could've been that guy living upstairs from you. Lived in a place like that on Green Street. Had neighbors living like you."

Matt still didn't look entirely convinced. "Cordy . . . are you *sure*—"

"Mr. Ingemar," Seika said with a grin, "when he's in *that* shape, he's just some guy. Looks big and strong, but . . ."

She stepped to the side, still as Princess Radiance Blaze, and grabbed up a weight bar they'd left lying there deliberately. ". . . but if he tried anything on any of us . . ."

Her delicate-looking hands closed on the steel bar and without so much as a pause she bent the metal shaft into a pretzel shape. "We could *break* him. Or fry him, shock him, drown him, whatever. And if we win, like Mr. Owen says, everything goes back to normal. Steve's himself, he's never met us, we've never done any of this. That kinda disappoints me . . . but that means that if you think he's some kind of supernatural peeper, he's not even going to remember what he saw after we save the world."

Matt was goggling at the metal bar. He picked it up with an effort and tried to straighten it—discovering that it wouldn't move. Temblor Brilliance took the bar and tried to straighten it; it broke in half halfway through. "Oops."

He stared anew at that, then transferred his gaze to Steve. "And you . . ."

". . . could probably hold my own against you, and maybe against Dave, though he's in a lot better shape than I am," Steve said bluntly. "But the *Maidens*? They'd bat me around like a Ping-Pong ball. And sure, I could change, but that's just diamond-cut-diamond. I'd never beat two of them, let alone all four. My word might be worthless, but I give it to you anyway that I would *die* before I let anyone, especially me, hurt any of them."

Matt looked around at the others, and then especially at his wife. "Ash?"

She swallowed hard. "You'll pardon me, and Matt, for being doubtful. I had some . . . experiences when I was younger, a little younger than Cordy . . ."

Steve nodded. "I get you. And I wish there was a way to prove it's safe. I know what that kind of thing does to trust."

"It's . . . hard. But if my little girl can defend herself, and knows she *should*—"

"Mom! Of course I do!"

"Then . . ."—she drew a deep breath—"then I think we have to accept this, Matt. They say it's the whole world at stake and I . . ."—she gave a shaken smile—"I wish I didn't believe them, but you know, I do."

"Yeah." Matt stared at Cordelia, then straightened. "Yeah, so do I. Ever since they changed."

Steve gave an explosive sigh of relief and collapsed into Holly instantly. "Oh, thank *God*."

And as a ripple of laughter went around the room, Holly felt the fear of rejection, of the possible fracturing of this still-fragile alliance, run out of her.

Yet, somehow, that didn't make her feel better. Everything was still wrong. Unbalanced. Her legs felt wobbly and her stomach churned like a washer on agitate. Everything—the tension of arranging the meeting, the shock and arguments of the adults, trying to get through to Marli, revealing Steve . . . having to *be* Steve, having to confront the parents' fears, even the relief, all of it was just too much.

She closed her eyes, biting her lips, trying to keep control. *I've fought monsters! I've lived on my own for years! I've had arguments, I've done all sorts of things, I can handle . . . I can . . .*

Holly tried, but without even understanding *why* she turned away and ran, ran out of the living room, hearing her own gasped, indistinct "I'm sorry!" over the startled gasps and someone's—several someones'—cries of "Holly?" She didn't even know where she was going until she found herself in the bathroom, locking the door, sliding down to the floor and sobbing, crying uncontrollably, *bawling* like a child, dammit, stop, what's *wrong* with me?

The self-targeted anger didn't help; it made it *worse,* filled her with self-loathing at her inability to deal with simple emotions, knowing someone that *weak* couldn't possibly lead anyone, let alone warriors against monsters. She heard her sobs, sharp, piercing and vibrating with confusion and denial and a loss she couldn't even *describe.* It mixed with that alien aversion to her old form, the fear of loss to come, made her *sick*, so sick she dragged herself to the toilet and hung her head over it, just before her stomach emptied its entire contents into the bowl.

"Holly? Holly, what's *wrong*?" Seika's voice was half-panicked, hearing her friend's pain and having no idea what to *do*. Holly knew how much that would hurt *Seika*, the girl who loved to have the answers, and that just made her cry *harder*, the guilt over inflicting a pain she didn't even grasp *herself* that much stronger.

"Hey, it's okay, Holly." Cordy's voice was quieter, lower, not desperate. "I understand. I know where you're coming from. All the shit's coming down at once and it's all swirling around in your head and you can't even *catch* it."

The tone somehow penetrated. It sounded like Cordelia actually *did* understand. Holly's sobs caught, and she grasped desperately, gratefully for any hint of control, of *stopping*.

"She okay?" That was Devika's voice, whispering, but still audible. Holly heard another sound, the adults following.

"Shh! No, Mr. Owen, out, everyone else back!" Tierra hissed.

"Come on, Holly, just open the door," Cordy went on. "I . . . I know we don't get *everything* you've got in your head, but we *all* know what it's like to have *too much* in your head, right?"

Holly finally felt the emotions . . . not *recede*, but pause, give her a moment to stop. Her chest hurt, her mouth was burning; the awareness of the sharp stench of vomit almost made her throw up again, *did* get her to reach up and pull the lever, flush the toilet. Her shaking hand managed to reach the paper, get some to wipe her face. "C-Cordy? You do this . . . after?"

"After I got home that day? I locked myself in the shower and screamed into my hands for half an *hour*," Cordelia answered. "And . . . well, cheerleading and sports has a lot of pressure. Seen this kind of thing before." She hesitated.

"We're all here, Holly," Seika said.

Holly took a breath. "Some . . . some of you don't really *know* me. I . . . I'm not even sure *I* know me. I *hate* Steve!" she said, even though that itself wasn't entirely true, tears starting from her eyes again, and she hated *that*, too. "And dragging you guys into this . . . and seeing your parents wonder, they're *afraid* of me, maybe of *you*, and . . . and . . ."

"Open the damn *door*!" Cordy said sharply. "*We* aren't afraid of you, Holly, but we're afraid *for* you right now!"

Where did she learn that *tone? Did her teammates depend on her, even though she was just a sophomore? No wonder they were so confused and angry by her failing.*

With a tremendous effort, Holly forced herself to stand, feeling the room tilting around her; she gripped the countertop until the dizziness subsided, then bent down, rinsed her mouth. Only then did she feel she could move, reach out, pull the latch free.

The door popped open instantly, the other girls almost falling into the room with the sudden release of pressure. Seika was first, wrapping her arms around Holly fiercely. "It's okay, we're here, really!"

"I feel . . . I shouldn't be putting this on you, I don't even know what *this* is," she answered, hugging back and feeling the tears trying to start again.

Cordelia hesitated, then took Holly's hand, squeezed it. "Holly, you're the *first*. And you . . . well, you took a bigger step than *any* of us to start with. You haven't had this kind of breakdown before? Haven't lost it like this?"

She shook her head.

Devika gave a quick, short laugh, even as Tierra came around and joined Seika in hugging her friend. "You are the *leader*. And a lot harder to lead than a sports team."

"You feel *responsible* for us. Like our parents. For them too, I bet," Cordy said. "I know. I've felt that way too . . . when my parents argued, sometimes, I thought maybe it was my fault, maybe something *I* should be fixing."

Tierra gave her a sharp, surprised glance, and nodded. Cordy went on. "But it's *our* choice. Right?"

The tidal wave of a hundred emotions was finally receding, and Holly swallowed, nodded. "Yeah. Your choice. But it wasn't a *fair* choice."

"Wasn't *fair* for the world that it's being invaded by alien Lovecraft-meme-monsters, either," Seika said, still hugging her tight. "Or for you to get dragged into it by Silvertail. But you took it. And so did we. And we're *okay* with it."

"Took me . . . a little bit," Cordy said, her smile tremulous all of a sudden, "but . . . yeah. Things like Procelli need to be fought, and I'm really totally okay with helping."

Holly looked at Seika, then at the rest of them, feeling her own body still shaking with reaction, aching with the aftereffects of that body-wracking outburst. "And you . . . you guys aren't afraid of me? Of . . . well, that I'm not really—"

"Stop that!" Tierra kicked her shin—gently. "You're just what you are, Holly. And I'm never going to be afraid of Holly Owen, or anything about her."

"Me too," Seika said emphatically.

Cordelia did not let go; she squeezed Holly's hand tighter. "Not afraid of you. Or Steve."

Finally Devika stepped forward, and her arms were long enough to enclose the whole group. "We're *together*. Warriors . . . and I think we can be friends, too. And I'm not afraid of you."

The tears came again, but this time they were tears of relief, washing away the doubts, the tension, the self-destructive hatred, the recriminations and even the resentment she had hidden away against Silvertail for starting the whole cycle. She sagged limply in her friends' embrace, and despite the tears, she smiled.

Part III: PRINCESS OF DARKNESS AND LIGHT

✳ Chapter 37 ✳

"No, I mean it absolutely," Trayne Owen said, looking sympathetically at Marli. She was holding a muffin and staring at him disbelievingly in the early-morning light, having once more come to drop Tierra off.

"But . . . I can't just take charity."

"It is *not* charity," he said. "If you need this put in cold, rational terms rather than those of someone who sees another in distress and wants to help, very well. Princess Temblor Brilliance will *never* be at her best if she is worrying about her mother, about her next meal, about all the little things that the other, more fortunate, families in our little group *do not* worry about. I want—the world *needs*—the Apocalypse Maidens to be one hundred percent focused and, as they say, 'together.' Making sure that all of them are safe, comfortable, and happy in the times they are not risking their lives? That is part of my *job*. You heard what Steve's living conditions were; I have changed that for him, for the duration of this cycle. I will do so for you, as well."

She shook her head, though he could see, and sense, the terrible longing—and the terrible fear of loss—within her. "Even if I did . . . what if someone starts asking where my money comes from?"

"It is true that banks sometimes send up . . . alerts to certain law-enforcement agencies these days," Silvertail conceded. "But I have a simple solution. I could make it known that I hired you to help care for my house and my daughter, along with your own. A nanny position, perhaps. In that situation I am, of course, able to set whatever pay or duty requirements I wish, and there will be little the law is likely to make of it even if they care to look into the matter. I am known to be very well-off and can certainly afford to pay a nanny a handsome salary, and the fact that your daughter is a friend of my own makes for an obvious and rational connection leading to your hiring."

The incredulous hope that lit up Marli MacKintor's face momentarily erased the lines and tightness of her life, and Silvertail could see more clearly from where Tierra got her laughing, fiery beauty. "You would . . . you *could* do that for me."

"For you, for your daughter, for my own, for myself and the world, yes, I could and would." A sudden flash of insight. "You haven't dared quit any job, no matter what, since Tierra's father left."

"No," she said in a near whisper. "No matter what."

He sighed. "Marli, I *could* go even farther, though it would take a bit of arranging, and make you as independently wealthy as you like. You would not need to work for me, or anyone. You would never be beholden to anyone else, and I would never demand anything of you for it."

A sudden flash of humor despite her incredulous stare. "*That* would be charity."

"That it would, though—as I explained—still self-serving charity."

"How could you *afford* this?"

He bit into his own muffin, aware of the distant sounds of Holly and Tierra arguing good-naturedly about what they were going to do today. "As I explained to Steve, I have had, literally, thousands of years to collect resources. While I must draw upon them only rarely, I have found it useful to be financially prepared." He felt the cynical twist of his own smile. "I have yet to see the society where being wealthy is not more useful than being poor."

"Universal truth," Marli said emphatically. She was silent for a few minutes, eating her muffin, occasionally stealing a glance at Trayne as though to assure herself he was still really there.

Finally she glanced at her watch and a heartbreakingly sad smile crossed her face. "I . . . may have already decided. Should have left twenty minutes ago, and they *really* don't like lateness at Ancho's Mexican." She looked up again, that terrible uncertainty still there. "You really *mean* this offer?"

He reached out and took her hand. "Marli, I promise you I mean it *absolutely*."

Marli MacKintor swallowed, then gripped his hand for just an instant before standing. "All right. God, I feel *terrified,* but I'll do it. Right now, before I lose my nerve." She walked out of the kitchen into the outdoor winter sunshine. He busied himself with cleaning the dishes and straightening up the kitchen for the day.

The door opened and a swift wash of chill air accompanied Marli as she returned and dropped, shaking, into a chair. "It's done. God, I hope I did the right—"

"Then you begin your *new* job today," he said with a smile.

A little while later, he entered the underground training area. He could feel vibrations under his feet just before he opened the door and saw the two Apocalypse Maidens sparring with each other; Holy Aura had evidently been flung full length on the ground and was just rolling aside from a kick that shook the floor again. "I see that I might have to consider the possibility our adversaries will locate us through seismology," he said dryly.

Holly grinned and Tierra laughed loudly. "Especially with Princess Temblor Brilliance on the job!"

"You also are making *holes* in the floor, Tierra," Holly said.

"Yeah, sorry about that. I keep forgetting how strong I am. Think I'm stronger than you?"

"Sure of it."

"In general, she who represents the power of Earth is extremely strong, yes," Silvertail said, popping into his normal furry form. "Physical strength is the forte of Earth and Fire and Water, somewhat less so for Air and Spirit—although it seems rather clear to me that our own Princess Tempest Corona may be an exception to that rule."

"So I'm the weak and fragile flower here?" Holly said, grinning as she stood up and surveyed the damage they'd already done.

"In sheer physical strength? Most likely. In overall *power*, of course, you outstrip them all. Holy Aura is the core and key to the entirety of the Apocalypse Maidens, and ultimately can surpass them. You can also draw upon their power, something we will have to discuss later."

"But our powers can be used for other, good things, right, not just smashing the crap out of monsters?" Tierra asked.

"Of course. You represent the power of Earth, but also its solidity, its materials and elements for building, the basic foundations of life in its minerals. The same is true for each of the others; if, indeed, you listen to each of your invocations, you will hear hints of this."

"So if I try . . ." Tierra bent down, touching the crumpled concrete.

In a few moments, a leaf-green glow began to emanate from her hand. Gradually, like a video run in reverse, the bottom of the hole began to rise, the fragments to trickle into the hole, settling into their places, the dust to coalesce back into the concrete. Within a minute or two, the floor was as smooth and unblemished as it had been before their training. "Oh, *wow*. That's *awesome*."

"Creation is, indeed, a wonderful feeling, and one that reminds us that we are not warriors alone," Silvertail agreed. "You should all practice this, especially as in battle you may need to repair both buildings and bodies."

"So," Holly asked, glancing upward, "has Tierra's mom gone to work?"

He gave his best rodent grin. "She has gone to deal with some issues she had left unattended to, before she begins her *new* work."

Tierra blinked. "*New* work?"

Holly laughed. "What Silvertail means is that your mom's not going to be working two stupid jobs anymore because she'll be working for *him*—taking care of the house for a hell of a lot more than she ever made."

Tierra stared. "Mom *hates* charity, though!"

"I convinced her that this was not mere charity. Had I merely wished to do charity, I could have done far more than give her a job." He reflected inwardly that he could, and now that he thought of it, would extend that charity outward. As long as he was in a position to assist the less fortunate in society, he might as well avail himself of the opportunity.

Tierra's eyes filled with sudden tears. "You mean Mom will be able to *rest* for once?"

The tone of joy at the prospect of something so . . . ordinary stung Silvertail's eyes, and he saw Holly blinking back tears as well. "Tierra, I will *insist* on it. And more. Her daughter will be risking her life; the least I can do is ensure, as I told her, that she will have a home that is safe and happy to return to."

Tierra looked down and suddenly scooped him up, hugging with a force that almost choked him. "I . . . I think I'm not afraid of rats any more."

"I . . . wish I could say . . . the same about rats not being afraid . . . of you. Ease up, please?"

"Oh, sorry, sorry!" she dropped him.

He drew in a breath, then chuckled. "No real harm done. And the sentiment is highly appreciated."

Tierra looked at Holly. "I guess you really know what that means."

"As Steve, yeah." Holly was clearly uncomfortable with the thought. "Right now I'd rather just be Holly."

"Okay," Tierra said.

Silvertail shook his head inwardly. *And so Holly has become the . . . true persona, and Steve the secondary, despite what he was before. A strange journey, and a difficult one. But if we win, the pain will not be remembered.*

"So, Silvertail," Holly said, clearly looking for another subject, "we just beat down that tyrpiglynt. How long have we got before our next problem, you think?"

"Not long, I am afraid."

"Why?" Tierra asked. "From what you said, you've only had four things in the last like six months—the earth-worm thing, that shoggoth in the mall, axe murderer at the school, and then the mirror monster. Shouldn't we have at least a month?"

"Now that all five Maidens are manifest? No. They will now begin trying more methods to lure you out, to trace you, and ultimately to destroy you, in one manner or another." He nodded at their now-serious faces. "And they will be drawing those methods from those things that terrify both the young and old. Your true training and preparation begins tonight . . . for it may only be a few more days before the next assault on our reality begins."

✳ Chapter 38 ✳

"*Tsunami CATARACT!*"

Blue-green water fountained at hurricane speeds, catching the white-clad girl full-on despite her desperate attempt to dodge, sent her skidding and ricocheting back and forth between the tables of the deserted restaurant. Distantly the sound of alarms rang, and Holly knew the police would be here soon. *And Gulliver's Skating and Entertainment Center's gonna be* really *pissed at the damage.*

The black figure rose slowly, dripping, her white dress hanging limply from her thin figure. Her head came up and the matted, bedraggled black hair parted to show the chalk-white, distorted, furious features. "You can't kill me," she whispered. "You've *seen*. You *watched*. You can only live if you *give*."

By its rules, it is correct, Silvertail's voice echoed in their heads grimly. *It is, like the urban myth of earworms, only escapable by passing on, creating a new copy of her file and causing another to view it.*

"But we're not playing by *her* rules, are we?" Tsunami Reflection asked uncertainly. "Because right now we're kind of stuck with only one of us fighting her."

That much was true, and Holly *hated* it. The creature, which Silvertail called a *samias* or thought-eater, didn't just attack with its slow-ticking death sentence; once driven out of its electronic refuge, it had manifested terrifying electrical powers that could hurt most of them badly. Devika's Tempest Corona wasn't vulnerable to that, but neither did her powers work against the spirit-girl; only running water was able to both ground her powers and strike back.

Alas, as with the tyrpiglynt, we must. Oh, her death sentence possibly *will not affect you, as your absolute power exceeds her own, but it will . . . not be pleasant, and if you cannot defeat her directly, she will still be free to kill again.*

A sudden sensation of a smile. *Guys, keep Goth-Girl there busy for just a few and I think I've got her!* Seika's mind-voice was filled with an unholy glee.

The other four glanced at each other; Devika and Cordy in their Maiden forms looked momentarily uncertain, but seeing both Holy Aura and Temblor Brilliance grinning like sharks, nodded. *Let's do it.*

The floor rippled, unbalancing the girl momentarily, and wind tore at her dress, making her back up; she screwed up her twisted face even more against a blaze of holy light. "Your powers are useless," she hissed.

"It's not the powers, it's the *performance* that matters, loser," answered the voice of Tsunami Reflection. "Try breaking out of *this*! *Maelstrom Ring!*"

Water swirled up and around the deceptively tiny figure, sending sparks cascading from the floor lights as it streamed over and around them. The samias tried to leap over the ring but the Maelstrom rose higher, a spinning wall touching the ceiling, curving inward, becoming a spiraling emerald sphere completely enclosing the now staggering figure within.

The drowned-looking girl hurled bolt after bolt of lightning at the rippling wall, but it had no more effect than the fury of a storm trying to change the sea. It merely rippled then returned. Tsunami Reflection held it that way, increasing strain showing on her face, but her determination unwavering.

All right, guys, the next part won't be fun; you've got to grab her and hold her still, facing this way. Tsunami, especially, keep her head up.

"Do it!" Holy Aura shouted, already guessing what Seika was up to.

The four Apocalypse Maidens leapt forward, even as Tsunami Reflection let the sphere of water collapse. Holy Aura grabbed the soaking-wet body with both hands, holding the girl-thing's legs so they could not move. Electrical fire coursed through her but Holly/Holy Aura refused the pain, hung on doggedly. Tsunami had the thing's head in a deathgrip, and the others had grabbed an arm each. It was frozen for a moment, unable to move, glaring forward with helpless hatred. "You cannot hold me forever!"

"How about for *three seconds*?" Radiance Blaze shouted, and with easy strength ripped a widescreen TV monitor from the wall, trailing cables that led back to the computer Radiance Blaze had been at.

The screen was already lit, and the eerie rippling water effects washed across it. A bluish, eldritch-lit beach and something . . . something moved within the surf.

The samias screamed. "NO! NO!"

"*Yes*! I made a *copy* of your stupid file and now I'm showing it to someone who's never seen it—the person *in the file*, the one who's never watched from the *outside*!" In the shadows behind the screen Holly could see the beautiful, older face—that was, somehow, still so very much Seika's—dark and triumphant. "And like the rest of your victims, now that you've seen it start, you *must* watch it! To the *end*!"

Through their link, Seika's mind-voice said, *Devika—that big boom trick we talked about? Do it* right *after this ends.*

Understood.

"I . . . cannot destroy myself!"

"If you're *solid* you can. And right now, you *are*!"

Holly let go of the girl-spirit and backed off; the others did the same. As predicted, she could not run. She could not flee. She had to watch the short, horrific video to its conclusion. The samias walked slowly forward, as though drawn by the screen toward its own ironic doom.

Behind her, Holly saw Princess Tempest Corona raising both hands. Air swirled inward, lightning crackling between her hands, focusing, funneling into a coruscating mass of energy that was growing ever stronger, a rippling globe of electrical power that filled the room with the smell of ozone. Metallic objects nearby began to glow, edged in faint purple, and some stirred, debris rattling around the Apocalypse Maiden's feet.

The video came to an end; the thought-eater suddenly gave a hideous smile. "All I need to do . . . is make a *copy*!"

She lunged toward the computer.

"*TEMPEST BLACKOUT!*"

The seething sphere of concentrated power exploded in a flickering ripple that sent sparks dancing from every metallic surface throughout the skating and amusement arena, brilliant blue discharges from the chrome edging everything in the faux-fifties restaurant, caused explosions of light and smoke from the arcade games, and—

Plunged the entire building into darkness. The only light now came from the Apocalypse Maidens themselves, glowing with their native power. The alarms had gone silent; even the streetlights outside had gone dark, although some light was visible from the city in the distance.

The samias froze, hands touching nothing but dead metal and plastic. "Wh . . .what . . . ?"

"Electromagnetic pulse," Holly said in realization. "Shut down *everything* electronic in the area. There's nowhere for you to go. Nowhere to transfer into. No phone, no power line, no cable, no video games or computers. And you're under your own death sentence." She let the power build within her. "And that means *you are vulnerable.*"

Even that distorted hateful face, it seemed, could register the simple expression "Oh, *crap*."

"*Ginhikari no Bisento—Solar LANCE!*"

The purifying holy power of Princess Holy Aura was driven *through* the girl-monster in her moment of paralyzed shock, driven straight into and through by the Silverlight Bisento's blade. The samias screamed as the light burned *outward*, erasing her from existence beginning with the core of darkness within, and ending with the last twining strands of bedraggled hair.

Silence filled the room, along with the stench of burned electronics and the drifting miasma of smoke.

"Is it over?"

"Pretty sure," Holly said after a moment. "Seika, you've got to . . ."

". . . make sure the live copy's not on the drives. At least we got them here. No one infected decided to be so much of an asshole as to upload the thing to YouTube and kill thousands at a time. Devika?"

The electricity of Tempest Corona didn't just erase the hard drives and memory drives: it *vaporized* them. "There, copy *that*!"

"Well done, Maidens. You are really working well together." Silvertail crawled out from a hole in the wall where he had sheltered during the conflict.

"Yeah, well, we've had some practice now," Cordy said, still warily looking around in case the samias wasn't actually finished. "This one was a lot easier than that Jack Great-Pumpkinhead thing on Halloween."

"Or the Phantom Clown," said Tierra with a shudder. "*God*, I had nightmares about that three days running. And still have 'em once in a while."

"Ugh. Can't blame you," Holly said. "Never understood why clowns were supposed to be funny, they always creeped me out. But one of my friends absolutely *loved* 'em, so it takes all kinds."

"Still . . . with Video-girl there, that makes three of these things in a month," Seika said. As they quickly made their way out the back door, sirens now whining again in the distance and getting closer, Seika went on, "You sure weren't *kidding* about Nine Arms' people stepping up the attack."

"And they are refining their methods," Silvertail said. "Manipulating people from a distance, influencing others to spread the corruption, making it very difficult for us to find and trace them directly even with our powers." They got into Trayne Owen's minivan and he started the engine, pulled out of the parking lot, and turned down the main road. A mass of flashing red and blue lights was headed toward them.

Holly heard Silvertail mutter and gesture; as Holy Aura, she was able to *sense* the tiny ripple of magic that flew outward and enclosed the van. The squadron of police cars flew by, oblivious to the passage of a vehicle that had obviously just left the scene to which the alarm had summoned them.

Devika shook her head. "That is . . . a convenient trick. Although I don't like fooling the police like that, much."

"In honesty? No more do I. But it is a far, far better thing for them to simply try to sift the ashes of the conflict than to be drawn into the war."

"I didn't mean it was *wrong*. I suppose. I don't know."

"It is wrong, in a way. We all make choices that are a mixture of right and wrong; it is our duty to make it as much right, and as little wrong, as possible." In the flickering lights of passing streetlamps, Trayne Owen's expression was bleak. "After all, the very *mission* of you Maidens is such a choice, and I am always aware of how very wrong it could be—"

"Oh, God, Silvertail, don't go all wangsty on us!" Tierra said. "You're not emo goth enough anyway. We'd all say yes again, right?" She glanced around, seeing nods from the others. "So forget it. You needed us as soldiers, you've got us, we're cool."

The older man's smile was rueful. "I suppose I may sometimes sound a bit maudlin in my maunderings, yes. My apologies."

They drove in silence for a few moments, Holly just luxuriating in the opportunity to *relax*. If the bad guys kept up this pace, chances to slack off were going to be few and far between. "Crap, it's only two weeks to *Christmas*." She glanced over at Devika. "You guys don't do Christmas, or do you?"

Devika, who was rearranging her hair under her *chunni* after changing back to her mortal form, grinned, an expression that made her look slightly less imposing than usual. "Technically no, since we're not Christian, but many Sikhs have no problem at all with a celebration of lights and gift giving. Plus Dad converted to Sikhism from, well, agnostic Americanism? He never had a faith before, but his family celebrated Christmas. So yes, my family does."

"We've got to get together during the holidays—for like *not* Maiden business."

"Oh, my house coming up," Cordy said, now her normal self. "Yes, everyone let me know when you're free and I'll coordinate, okay?"

"Great, I'm terrible at scheduling," Holly said promptly. The rest also agreed to let Cordy match schedules up. The minivan came to a halt and Cordy got out, waving to the others.

Trayne watched her pensively as she went to the door, and pulled away once the door opened. "What is it, Mr. Owen?" Seika asked.

"After each battle, I always wonder . . . as you mentioned, Tierra . . . what new nightmares you must go home with." He shrugged it off visibly. "But once the task is done, you will no longer have those memories, so I suppose it truly is worrying about nothing."

They dropped off the others in quick succession, finally leaving Holly alone with Trayne as they headed back to the house. "Dad . . ." she said slowly.

"Yes, Holly?"

"Isn't . . . isn't there *any* way for us to keep some of the memories?"

He was silent for long minutes; as they pulled into the driveway, Holly thought he might have decided to simply not answer the question. But finally, as they entered the house and closed the door, he sighed. "The *memories* . . . no. I do not think so. It is a closed time loop, one which literally resets the world to the state it was in before the beginning of the cycle, minus those spirits or souls which met with unfortunate ends during that time. But . . . *feelings*, certain links between the souls of those who were close . . . those might be able to be at least partially retained." A quick smiling flash in the dimness of the hallway. "The artist and the computer nerd may well find themselves oddly in tune with the cheerleader and the basketball player, for instance."

She tried to smile, but that didn't work. "But probably the big guy selling bagels down the street better not find *out* if he's oddly in tune with that group."

Trayne wrapped her in a hug, and she gripped her father's chest tightly, aware of how utterly strange it was that the feeling was so *right*, so *comforting*, when this man wasn't truly her father, had been born before her *country* existed . . . and yet *was* her father so much that her heart *ached* with the thought that one day she would not know him. "I am sorry, Holly. More than you could imagine."

She took a breath, let her shaking subside before she let go. "No. I'm not. I told you . . . I'm *happy*. Let that much be . . . remembered, let that much be *true*, and I guess Steve'd say we're even."

Trayne's face was not dry. "That much I will promise."

"Then . . . I guess I'd better go get ready for bed," she said, trying to smile, and succeeding this time. "And we've got shopping to do this weekend!"

"The mall . . . at *Christmastime*." Trayne gave an exaggerated shudder. "I think I would prefer another eldritch horror!"

She did laugh, then, and while the melancholy was not gone, it was replaced with an acceptance. *Maybe this won't last forever . . . so I'll just have to hold on to all the time I* have.

✳ Chapter 39 ✳

Holly sat quietly and as still as she could on the floor, legs crossed under her. *Boy, Steve wouldn't have been able to do this for long. For this body, it's* easy.

Then with difficulty she corrected herself. *I* *couldn't have done this for long.* It was sometimes painful to force herself to remember that there was no separate being called *Stephen Russ*. She *was* Stephen Russ. It was just that Stephen really, really preferred Holly's life. Or maybe simply had hated his own life in ways he preferred not to think about.

Stop it. You're distracting yourself. Listen to the service, to the chant.

The rhythmic singing chant swayed like a great tree in a wind. Unlike Devika, she didn't *understand* everything that was being said and done, but the Weatherills had made clear that she just had to look respectful and relaxed. *Especially relaxed. Devika goes to temple services regularly, she wouldn't be tense.*

To her astonishment, the Weatherills had told Devika's brother and sister about the entire Apocalypse Maiden situation. Both were admittedly older than Devika, but still, Holly knew that she—or Steve—would have been very hesitant about telling anyone else about this if she could avoid it.

But Ajit, the brother, who was now seated to Holly's right, and Vidia, a diminutive girl who was nonetheless the oldest of the siblings, had both accepted—after a quick demonstration by their sister—what they were told and were vocal in their pride that Devika had taken up this life.

Which really helps right now.

That was because Devika wasn't present; anyone *watching*, however, would see the unmistakable, tremendously tall figure of Devika Kaur Weatherill sitting between her brother and sister.

Looking relaxed was *not* easy. Not only was this a completely different worship service compared to anything Holly or Steve had ever seen; she also had to evade any significant conversation with people who might know Devika while staying visible here and on the way back from the service.

Far worse, though, was the fact that somewhere out there, in the snowstorm turning the city into a gray-white blur, the real Devika, Seika, and Cordy might already be in a battle for their lives.

Holly shoved that out of her mind as best she could, though the thought that they could be hurt . . . or even killed . . . without her there was horrifying. *Focus on the ceremony. It's a lovely service and I wish I* did *understand it better. And I* have *to convince anyone watching that I'm really Devika.*

Silvertail had assured her that the illusion would hold regardless of almost any event. "I cannot make it *act*, only you can, but the combination of my skill and drawing upon Holy Aura's power should make this guise—and the other two layers of the illusion—nigh impenetrable. Yes, if Queen Nyarla herself were to attempt to pierce it, she would quickly realize that you were not Devika, and shortly after would recognize you for who you were, but aside from anything so drastic, you should be safe from discovery . . . if you can manage this performance adequately and then, with the other two layers, make your way home unmarked and undetected by our enemies."

She had nodded. "Okay. And I know this is vital—we *have* to make our enemies certain that Devika *can't* be Princess Tempest Corona. So I'll do my best." She'd studied the white rat narrowly. "But you know, you haven't ever given us the whole story on this Nyarla. She showed up and sicced the Hounds on you when you checked out the school for the tyrpiglynt, but I don't remember you saying anything else about her."

She remembered the expression on the white-furred face—one of pain, sadness, and ancient, burned-out anger, maybe more. "No, I have not. But . . . yes, that too you should know. After this is done."

Holly shoved herself out of her reverie. *Good thing my job during this part of the service is to just sit still.* She caught her hand moving up, and with a minor spurt of panic dropped it back down. The *chunni* on her head still felt odd, and she had to work to keep herself from trying to adjust it; indoors, her instinct was to push things *off* her head, like taking off a hood, and there would be no worse way to screw this up than violating one of the most fundamental rules of Sikh respect in the middle of a service.

Seeing the *karah prasad* being handed out, Holly realized the service was almost over. She received the sweet like the others, in her cupped hands. *Tastier than Communion wafers, I have to admit.* The Weatherills had assured her that there was nothing wrong with her either receiving it or eating it, especially given the reason she was here in the first place. *Still feel a little funny doing it, but that's my problem, nothing to do with the faith.*

The *Guru Granth Sahib*, the huge book of the Gurus' teachings, was finally raised up and carried out; everyone stood and some, including the Weatherills, bowed as it passed.

Ajit turned and whispered quietly, "We'll go into the Langar, but Dad's planning on leaving pretty quick; the storm gives us a great excuse."

"Remember to get some rice pudding," Vidia said from the other side. "Devika *never* passes up rice pudding. It's one of her favorites."

Ugh. One of my least *favorite desserts. Well, get into the* role, *Holly, you're a role-player, Steve was, just remember you* love *the stuff and play it that way.*

Vidia stayed with her as they entered the Langar for the communal meal served after the service. Passing through the line didn't take long, and she made sure to get the rice pudding. *And smile while I'm eating it.* The glutinous texture was something Holly *really* didn't like, but it was only a few minutes, a couple dozen bites. *I can do this and do it right, darn it! Not like someone's trying to kill me!*

"Good to see you, Devika! How's the season going?"

The speaker was a young man, maybe a year older than her, wearing a bright blue turban and with a beard that was just starting to grow in earnest.

"Oh, hi, Naman," Vidia said smoothly. "Let her swallow first, would you?"

Oh, thank *you for that perfect save, Vidia!* "Just barely started,

Naman," she answered. Given that they had to be aware of each other's schedules, she *could* at least remember that much of the sports calendar—and she remembered something Devika had said about the first official game that month. "Tori made the final score this game."

"Tori? Wasn't she on the volleyball team?"

"Sure, but volleyball season ends about when basketball season tryouts start, so Tori made the team this year."

"Devika! Vidia! Let's go, I want to get home before this weather gets any worse!" called Henry Singh Weatherill.

"Coming, Dad!" She got up and put her and Vidia's plates with the other dirty dishes, gave a quick wave to Naman, and followed the family out to the entrance where they could put their shoes back on.

The wind was whipping briskly through the parking lot and the hard pellets of sleet mixed with snow stung Holly's cheeks. Still, she felt a rising sense of elation. *Almost done. I* think *this might work out!*

"You did pretty well, Holly," Vidia said as they buckled into their seats in the Weatherill van. "Maybe you shouldn't have waved at Naman, because Dev thinks he's kind of a nuisance, but it's no big thing."

"I'm most concerned with how you're getting home, Holly," Satjit said. "Are you *sure* we can't drive you—"

"Absolutely not. For this performance we've got to minimize connections as much as possible, so you can't drive me to my house and Dad can't pick me up here."

"But walking in this weather—"

"Won't be fun," she agreed. "Still, it's supposed to taper off by late afternoon."

Henry and Satjit studied her with concern, but then shrugged. "You must do what you must do, Holly. Just promise us to be careful."

"I will. Promise."

While the Weatherill household was comfortable, and there were books and games and of course the ubiquitous television, the hours dragged on as though mired in quicksand. Holly had to force herself to *not* look at the clocks, because sometimes she swore they were running *backward.*

Finally, later afternoon *did* arrive, and with it a paradoxical lightening of the windows. "Wow, the storm *did* let up."

Henry stuck his head out the door and looked up and around. "It certainly has. Makes me feel a little easier about you going home. But how are you going to be able to *leave* without people seeing you?"

She grinned. "Second layer of the illusion is a 'don't notice me' charm. That'll last for a while, maybe about a quarter of the way there, then the last layer will make me look like some other girl about my age, but not Holly or Devika or anyone else we know."

"All right. You're going now?"

"I'd better, while there's still *some* light out." She saw the rest of the family watching her and another spurt of guilt wracked her. "I hope to God Devika and the others are all right, I'll never forgive myself for doing this playacting here if—"

"Holly—Holy Aura," Satjit said, quietly but so firmly it cut Holly off as though it had been a shout, "stop, please. You did this to protect *us*, as well as my Devika, and Devika does what *she* is doing to protect everyone."

"Listen to Satjit. Don't worry about what *could* go wrong, just about what you have to do *now*. Which is get home across half the city, and that's enough to worry about, as far as I'm concerned."

She closed her eyes, swallowed, and nodded. "Okay. You're right. And I've got to have faith that no matter what kind of a monster they've found out there in the storm, they'd beat it, with or without me."

"*That* is the way to believe, yes. Now go, go. Let's see this through."

A few minutes later, she stepped out the back door and made her way across two other yards, wading heavily through the snow. As far as she could tell, no one even looked into the yards while she was doing this, and the wind was already starting to erase her trail as she stepped out onto the road and started walking. Most of the sidewalks, of course, hadn't been shoveled off yet, but the plows had been out since midmorning and instead of a foot and a half of snow there were generally only a few inches of slush on the roads.

About three miles to go, maybe three and a half. If it was good weather I could do that in an hour, easy. Probably take me two in this crap. But hey, I'm in really good shape and my coat's warm and I've got good boots.

She had to suddenly jump to the side as brilliant lights shone out behind her and a massive plow rumbled through the area she'd just been walking in, throwing accumulated slush and snow like a fountain around and over her. "God*dammit*, why the hell wasn't he watching where . . ."

Oh.

A spell that said "ignore me," it suddenly occurred to her, was a two-edged blade. Yeah, no one would see her even leaving the area . . . but drivers wouldn't take her into account when driving, either. They'd ignore her, and that could get her killed. *Have to think like I'm invisible in* every *way, or I'm going to be someone's hood ornament.*

Somewhere along around three-quarters of a mile she felt a faint tingling, and sensed that the third and final layer of the illusion was active. *Okay, regular girl who's not me, let's finish this!*

The wind was dying down, but even with the plowed road and more assurance that any other drivers would probably see her now, the going wasn't easy. Her boots slid and slipped, and the layer of snow caught and dragged whenever it was more than an inch or so. Her coat *was* doing its job, but that meant that Holly was actually getting *hot*; she pulled back the hood and let the breeze stream past her face. *That's better.*

There weren't many other people out now, especially since the sun had gone down and it was getting dark. Even with the streetlights now shedding their sodium-yellow light everywhere, she could only make out three other pedestrians right now, one down the side street she was crossing, one about a hundred yards ahead of her, trudging along with head bent down, and another a hundred yards back, in a similar pose.

Yeah, I'd forgotten how cruddy this neighborhood is. Tierra's mom hadn't lived far from here. It wasn't much, if any, better than the place Steve had lived in. In the yellow-lit twilight, the buildings looked black and forbidding; some had more cheerful bright lights blinking in defiant cheer around them, celebrating Christmas despite circumstances, but others were completely dark, boarded-up husks that were either empty, or hiding those you didn't want to intrude upon.

Holly felt herself shiver slightly. For the first time, she felt isolated and vulnerable, as though she were a child trying to venture into the darkened basement without her parents around. *Stop that!* she scolded herself. *You've walked these streets* hundreds *of times before. At night, too. Nothing's ever bothered you before. When Steve worked at Fralla's, he had to walk right down that street up there every day.*

That lifted some of the foreboding and she continued on, a bit faster even though her legs were starting to really ache. The person ahead of her had vanished inside of one of the buildings; glancing around, she saw she was alone except for the person behind her, maybe seventy-five yards away.

Let's see, if I follow the main drag I'd go up here another several blocks, then cut down Route 6. But that's kinda the long way around. I wonder if they've plowed Hogan Street? Check it when I get there.

Sure enough, Hogan—a narrow two-lane between brick and concrete industrial buildings a few stories high—had been plowed. *Must be at least one or two of the businesses still operating, then.* Most of them hadn't been for at least a few years, and while this was a good shortcut to where she wanted to go, it sure wasn't the scenic route.

She was a few hundred yards along Hogan when a casual glance showed her that the other pedestrian, too, had turned down the same street and was now less than fifty yards away.

A sudden trickle of apprehension began to work through her. She was abruptly aware of her *size*, of the shortness of her steps, the ache in her calves and thighs, of the fact that her memory of Hogan Street didn't have it looking so *high*, so *long*, so . . . menacing.

She sped up her steps, pushing past the more insistent throbbing in her legs. *It's nothing. I chose Hogan as a shortcut, why shouldn't this guy?*

But "this guy" was a lot taller than Holly, and probably twice her weight, and she could hear his steps now, longer than hers, less hurried yet covering at least as much distance.

I can't transform to Holy Aura. Out here that could be a signal our enemies could read. And if they realize I was here, for no good reason . . .

That could, of course, make the entire maneuver pointless. But worse, even if she *could* . . . she wasn't sure if the power was *meant* for use against the mundane.

And really, why am I so scared? He's just walking.

She looked over her shoulder, quickly, trying *not* to look nervous, but this time she could see a glitter of eyes, a sudden smile, and she remembered all the stares in the malls, the people watching her that would sometimes turn away, and those that wouldn't. She *knew* that look.

It was the look of a predator, and Holly felt a stunning, cold, queasy realization that she was entirely vulnerable here, isolated between buildings whose broken windows yawned wide, jagged black uncaring eyes staring sightlessly down at the girl and the pursuer now perhaps sixty or seventy feet behind.

She suddenly remembered all the times she—Steve—had heard her friends, her girl friends, talk about watching where they went, about never going alone, about always fearing the isolated figure near them when in a parking lot, and the empathy he had felt then flared into *understanding*. She *knew* what that horrid, helpless feeling was, the anger and worry and bone-deep caution and mistrust that until now she had never felt . . . because she had not been born and raised to learn it.

A furious, sick rage burned up within her at that understanding, and without warning she burst into a sprint, dashing around the corner ahead into a narrow alleyway that turned and twisted. She thought she heard a low laugh behind, but she didn't care. *Okay, then . . .*

The pursuer sped up, footsteps thudding on the snow-covered pavement, slipping a bit, but gaining all the same. But for a few moments he couldn't *see* her . . .

And when he came around the corner he suddenly backpedaled, skidding to a halt, staring with ludicrous disbelief at the massive figure that was already lunging for him. "Holy *shit*—"

Steve Russ caught the other man—two inches shorter and a hundred pounds lighter than he—and yanked him to his feet; the man's hood fell back, showing a narrow, shocked face, pale in the reflected sky glow, uneven teeth revealed in a snarl of shock. "Chasing little girls your idea of fun, *asshole*?" Steve growled, and despite the repulsive heaviness of the form he now wore felt the paradoxical *safety* of that form. "Who's gonna do the chasing *now*?"

The man scrabbled inside his coat, and Steve had seen enough in his years to recognize someone going for a weapon; before the hand came out, Steve Russ slammed his opponent into the brick wall as hard as he could, three hundred pounds and more of mass hammering the other into unyielding hard stone with such force that the air left his opponent's lungs with a *whoosh* and he went momentarily limp; a wickedly curved karambit folding knife dropped to the ground.

Inside, Holly felt a slight bit of vindication through the fog of frightened fury. *That's not something a harmless pedestrian hides in his coat, I don't think.* Steve stamped on the knife and kicked it behind him, then threw the other man down. "Get the *fuck* out of my sight, and pray to *God* I don't ever, ever see you again!"

"Sure, right, going, fuck, yeah!" The pale-faced would-be mugger scrambled to his feet and fled around the corner.

Steve sank back, shaking, feeling the chill of winter suddenly piercing through the summer clothes he'd appeared in. *I think I'm going to be sick.*

His stomach agreed with him, and he barely scrambled up in time to make sure that the vomit sprayed only into the dirty snow of the alleyway and not all over his T-shirt. With a panicked sort of detachment he wondered if someone analyzing it would find the remains of *Holly's* last meal, or whatever it was *Steve* had last eaten, months ago.

Steve leaned against the wall, shaking, waiting to see if he was going to have to puke again. Finally the nausea receded enough that he felt ready to straighten up; looking around, he found a ledge that had accumulated the snowfall, scraped the top inch or so off just in case, and used the rest of the pristine white to scrub off his face and help rinse the sour, sharp taste from his mouth. By the time he was done, he was shivering, but he knew he couldn't do much about that. *I've got to get away from this area, a long way away, before I can change back to Holly. Illusion's broken, and I* can't *let anyone connect Holly with this.*

With a deep breath, Stephen Russ turned and strode up the alleyway, sneakers already becoming cold and sodden in the snow, and began to make his way home.

✳ Chapter 40 ✳

"Are you *really* all right?" Cordy asked tensely.

Holly opened her mouth to answer, closed it. "I . . . don't know." She looked at the blonde with new understanding. "You've . . . done this before."

Cordy looked away for a moment; Devika's face was shadowed for a moment, and both Seika and Tierra gripped Holly's shoulders tighter, reinforcing their presence.

"Cheerleaders get a lot of attention, let's put it that way," Cordy said finally.

Holly felt a cold, visceral understanding of what she meant. "I'll be okay. Maybe I'm not quite okay *now*, but I will be. I mean . . . I got out of it fine. Won't be in that situation again, right?"

It was Silvertail, in his furry white form, who answered. "That *precise* situation, no. But the danger, small though it should be, is not zero. And you were quite right that it would be extremely unwise to unleash the powers of Holy Aura against a mundane threat, however repulsive and deserving."

"She still *transformed*, Silvertail. Won't that have alerted our enemies?" Devika was clearly trying to focus on the practical aspects, and Holly preferred that. *Let's not dwell on what happened. That was two days ago, anyway. I'm fine. Or I will be.*

"Fortunately, no," Silvertail said after an instant's pause. "The shift from Holly to Steve is . . . a *lateral* move, shall we say, rather than a sudden ascension to a vastly greater power. Yes, if one of our adversaries was *very* nearby they might have been apprised of the situation, but that is extremely unlikely."

"Okay, then," Holly said, standing. "Let's get to business now that we're all here."

Seika and Tierra exchanged glances and looked at Holly in a way that made her certain there was more to come from them, then nodded. "Right," said Seika. "So what's up?"

"Two things—Silvertail mentioned that there's more to the connection between us and our powers that he's got to instruct us in, and I also told him he needs to tell *us* about this Queen Nyarla character."

Despite his bewhiskered inhuman face, Silvertail's discomfiture was plain. "Er . . . yes. Which shall we address first, then?"

"Queen Nyarla," Devika said with iron emphasis. "She's the first one of our adversaries you've given a *name*, except for the Big Bad. And the others say you knew her?"

The rat's form shimmered, and Trayne Owen rose and paced to the far side of the living room, looking out at the snow-covered landscape beyond the window. "Yes. I knew her all too well."

"She was your wife, wasn't she?" Holly asked.

A faint chuckle. "It is not *quite* that hackneyed nor that simple, Holly. But . . . we were close, yes."

He turned slowly, looked about the room as though for some form of comfort, finally sank into one of the high-backed chairs. "It was—as you undoubtedly all have guessed—in Lemuria itself that I first met Haleisinia Zithalan."

He glanced at each girl in turn. "She was—then—only a bit older than you girls, seventeen. She was a student of mine at . . . well, the name would mean nothing to you; call it the Institute of Transphysical Studies, which dealt with all forms of what today would be called magic, psychic powers, and other phenomena ordinary science does not cover. I was already a senior instructor, though I was only thirty-five at the time."

"She got a crush on you. A *yandere* crush," Seika guessed.

There was no chuckle this time. "I see I need not go into some details. Yes. I must emphasize that I did *not* encourage this. In fact, I was utterly unaware of her thoughts for *years*. She was a brilliant student and I became her advisor in advanced studies.

"It was during this time that Azathoth of the Nine Arms first discovered our world and began her attempts to enter it. Halei was one of those who first *recognized* the apparently scattered events for what they were, brought it to my attention, and together we were able to convince the entire . . . call it the Oversight, the council of people who shared rulership of Lemuria . . . the entire Oversight of the threat."

Trayne's cheeks were a shade darker. "It was that night—after the Oversight acknowledged we were right and pledged their full support in our quest to fight the then-unknown enemy—that I discovered Halei's . . . mistaken views of my regard for her."

Tierra was looking at him with intense suspicion. "You didn't . . . do anything with her?"

"Most certainly *not*!" The anger in the retort was as clearly genuine as his sudden chagrin. "My apologies. That was of course a reasonable question. Understand, while Lemuria's religious and social structure was broad and complex, I personally belonged to a group that included very strong belief in a monogamous, permanent pairing, and I had no thought of breaking my bond with Ryumi, even leaving aside our children and the importance of a stable household for them. I tried to, as the saying goes, let her down gently, pointing out my beliefs made any relationship beyond professional friendship impossible, and that our professional past also made it ethically questionable for me and could cause us both trouble."

"And she didn't take it well."

Trayne's laugh was hollow. "She *seemed* to take it as well as I could have expected. Hardly *happy* about it, and for a few weeks she did not speak to me outside of necessary professional interactions, but we continued our work together and as some time passed she became more her old self.

"Then the solution—the concept of the Apocalypse Maidens—was envisioned. And at a family dinner, Aureline stood up and said she would be one of the Maidens—even before we had begun the search."

The expression on Trayne's face was heartbreaking, gazing into the past at an ancient loss that had still not lost its power to inflict pain. "Ryumi . . . did not accept that choice. She had *seen* some of our enemies, fought some herself, for she was . . . call it a captain, in our small military forces. The idea of sending any of our children against those monsters horrified her, and even worse the thought that our daughter would be one of only five facing Azathoth of the Nine Arms."

He swallowed and bent his head. "I lost my love that night, though she still lived. I would not—*could not*—abandon the one project that I believed offered a chance of stopping these invaders from the infinite beyond, and Ryumi would not and, in truth, *could* not accept the requirements of that plan."

There was a momentary pause. "I can't blame her," Cordy said finally. "It *is* a horrible plan. And I'm part of it so I think I can say that."

Trayne did not look up. "Do you think I disagree? I *agreed* with her. To place children between ourselves and destruction? In any ordinary sense this would be the work of a cowardly monster. I could not argue against her heart, for mine was also breaking at the thought . . . and that Aureline insisted she be a Maiden both broke my heart anew, and made me more proud than . . ." His voice broke and Holly could see the glitter of tears on his cheeks.

"So Ryumi left me," he said finally. "And tried to take the children—Aureline, Varalynde, Mindalen, Kantri—with her. Aureline refused, and by our laws she had the right to choose which parent to stay with—or to reject them in exchange for another caretaker, for that matter. Ryumi stated that she would find another way, that she refused to allow her children, and the children of others, to be her own shields."

Holly swallowed. Knowing the ultimate result, she could envision a few possible paths from that point . . . and none of them were good. "What happened?"

"Nothing immediately. I thought . . . thought she might have realized in her heart that I was right, just could not bring herself to give her blessing to such a horrific enterprise." He tried to smile, and it was one of the most painful expressions Holly had ever seen. "Halei . . . tried to comfort me. To her credit, not in an obviously predatory fashion. She undoubtedly saw me vulnerable, in a position to accept her, but she was far, far too intelligent to be obvious about it. And I needed the support—by the Five Jewels, I needed it then. So she was often with me."

"You mean with you, or, like, *with* you?" Seika asked.

Another humorless laugh. "As a friend. Never as a lover. Without knowing what I was doing, in effect I rejected her a second time. Looking back afterward, it was obvious what she intended, but I was, literally, oblivious to her motives or her actions. The loss of my family—except for Aureline—and my need to now prove that this loss was not in vain? I am afraid that subtlety was utterly lost on me, and a direct approach—as she knew—would have backfired utterly.

"And then . . ." He hesitated, took a breath and continued, a man diving headlong into an abyss. "Then word came that the Oversight had chosen a different way to address the invasion, to launch a direct counteroffensive into our enemies' realm and force their withdrawal."

Devika closed her eyes. "And your wife . . ."

". . . was leading the assault, yes." Trayne looked again out at the windswept snow. "I tried to convince the Oversight that this was a terrible mistake, that we had neither sufficient forces nor knowledge of that alien realm for us to effectively counterstrike, but I was overruled; the Oversight had listened to Ryumi's commanders and—understandably—preferred almost any alternative to the one I had proposed. We had also our weapons of mass destruction, physical and mystical, and it was the Oversight's belief that a sufficiently swift and powerful counterstrike would convince these beings to leave our world alone. They also did not accept some of our findings about the connection between our world and that of Azathoth—that our worlds were intimately connected on the fundamental level of the powers of creation itself, and that it was thus not so simple as merely convincing them to . . . stay put, so to speak."

"And she died."

"Ryumi and the entire task force—five thousand soldiers and equipment, servitor constructs, weapons, armor—entered that . . . place and were never seen again. If they had any effect at all, we never saw it. The encroachments against our world increased, and they gained a foothold on Earth soon after.

"That was what finally convinced Oversight that they had no choice but to accept the Apocalypse Maiden approach. At last, any of us could *see* what lay in wait for mankind."

"So wait, this is going to be just a story about a woman getting pissed because she couldn't get a guy? That's *stupid*," Seika said.

Trayne looked at her in startlement, and suddenly broke into laughter that somehow sat on the ragged edge of tears. "I suppose many things are stupid viewed in that light. But no, it was not *quite* that simple. Although yes, it seemed that way at the time. For Halei had one more attempt to make. She tried to volunteer in Aureline's place, justifying it both as trying to follow through on our work and as trying to protect Aureline.

"Of course, that wasn't possible; you all know now why girls of your ages are chosen, and Halei was by then in her early twenties, far too old to serve the purpose. So . . . once more . . . I rejected her."

He turned from the window and finally took a seat. "What I—what none of us—knew was that Halei had already been contacted by our enemies. Yes, a large part of what made her vulnerable to them was her unfortunate fixation upon me, but you have experienced the tyrpiglynt's effect; it plays upon your every vulnerability, your desires—the more easily debased the better.

"It was not a tyrpiglynt that she met, but something like it—something much more powerful, something that saw in her a chance to create an agent for their side. Our studies made this a risk—we *had* to investigate our adversaries with a closeness that could easily become contact. I do not know precisely when Halei was suborned, but I believe it started long before that point, perhaps when she appeared to have accepted that we could only be friends and colleagues."

He shrugged. "It could just as easily have been me, you know—they could have played upon my feelings of abandonment, of frustration, of fear for my people. By the end we discovered that they had done so not just to Halei, but to hundreds of others."

Trayne's eyes grew distant again. "I only learned of it the night before the ritual. She came to me again, as I lay awake knowing that not only might my daughter and her friends die, but that I, too, would almost surely perish before even learning whether my sacrifice, and Aureline's, had been worthwhile. She told me it didn't have to be that way, that we could live—I, and her, and Aureline, and our friends. That all we had to do was *step aside*, and we would be spared, most of our people would be spared, that Azathoth only sought the Oversight and those that might threaten them."

"That was bullshit, right?"

The smile was weak but genuine, this time. "Almost completely, yes. Oh, technically I might have been spared destruction, along with those I cared for, but the world that would have resulted would . . . not have been suitable for ordinary human life. Still,"—his face grew grave—"I . . . almost yielded. Not for myself, but for Aureline and her four friends. But in my preparations for the morrow I had already begun to focus myself, and for a moment I *sensed* the being behind her, Nyarlathotep, and I knew that what looked at me through poor Halei's eyes was utterly and completely inimical to every form of life that belonged on this earth."

Another chuckle. "The resulting conflict rather stepped up the timetable; I and the others barely drove Halei—now openly calling herself Lady Nyarla—from the Oversight Fortress, and most of the Institute's other magicians found themselves desperately trying to hold shut a dozen gateways that our enemies summoned. We called the Five Chosen from their sleep, rushed to the rooftop array, and . . . well, the rest you know."

The others were quiet for a few moments. Finally Holly nodded. "Thanks, Silvertail. So 'Nyarla' really is short for Nyarlathotep?"

"Yes. She is . . . not precisely *possessed* by that creature, but she is its agent. You may encounter it more directly soon, as it is one of Azathoth's most useful and powerful generals." He frowned. "I am . . . concerned by the fact that we have yet to encounter any of the Cataclysm Knights."

"Our opposite numbers? Isn't it good that they're not showing?" asked Tierra.

"I do not think so. It indicates a . . . deviation from the pattern, and there is never any deviation without a purpose. It certainly makes some of your missions *easier*, but the Cataclysm Knights have always been formidable adversaries and at least once succeeded in killing one of the Maidens. The seal was successfully made, but much weaker, and the cycle repeated in only a few decades instead of centuries. If they had managed to slay two or more Maidens, all would have been lost."

Holly understood his concern, but from her point of view, this was a better setup. The less their enemies could neutralize them point for point, the more chance they had of winning. "So, how about the second question? Connections between us and the powers we haven't discussed yet?"

"Ah, indeed!" He dismissed his human guise and the white rat replaced him, looking at them with a professorial gaze. "When each of you first transformed, you likely recall the instant when your headdresses—coronet, crown, whatever you like to call it—materialized?"

Holly recalled that instant, twin arcs of flame, ice, and lightning binding themselves to her temples in a flash of ecstatic pain, and nodded. She saw the other four do the same. "Yeah, it stood out even during that whole transformation thing."

"That is because the coronets are your Apocalypse Seals. The Seal helps channel your power, and also helps *control* it. Understand that the Maidens are connected directly to the symbolic, fundamental forces of the universe, powers that lie beyond any easy description. The human form is not *intended* to channel such power directly, and the Apocalypse Seal ensures that only a small proportion of that power is made available at any given time."

"But we can take these Seals off and kick more ass for a little bit, right?"

"In essence, yes, Holly."

Tierra blinked. "But that doesn't—"

Silvertail raised a tiny furry brow. "Doesn't what?"

"Well, I changed a couple of times—to get used to it," Tierra said, explaining quickly as though she'd been caught doing something wrong, "and I took off parts of the costume including that coronet thing, and I didn't feel like I was suddenly more powerful or anything."

"Ahh," Silvertail said. "It is not a matter of simply physically removing them—you can remove the entire costume if you wish and dress in other outfits, and may do so for some missions, I suppose. You must formally, and mystically, *release* the Seal. It will reestablish itself if you will it, or if you shift out of Maiden form or are rendered unconscious."

"And how do we do this formal release?" Devika inquired.

"You call upon your symbolic element—much as you did when you banished Procelli, and as you will when sealing away Azathoth Nine-Armed—and command the release."

"So," Tierra said, "Something like 'By the Earth, the world on which we stand—RELEASE'?"

"Exactly so, yes." The others nodded their understanding. "Now, Princess Holy Aura, as the representative of Spirit and the first and central Maiden, can become the channel for *all* of your powers, for all the elements unite within the Spirit. She can thus also command the release of your powers for that purpose."

"Whoa, wait, won't that like leave us helpless? That'd be a pretty desperate move!" Cordelia said, looking uncertain.

"It *is* a desperate move, but it does not leave you helpless. It *does* weaken the Maidens somewhat, although as the powers you tap are nigh limitless it does not reduce you to anything like mortal levels, and it naturally means that you cannot yourselves call upon the power of the Release as long as she does. The advantage is that she can draw upon not merely the power, but the *aspect*, of each of you, under those conditions."

"Oh!" Holly thought she understood. "So like if we were fighting something vulnerable to fire but Radiance Blaze couldn't quite *beat* it, I could Release all the others but channel that power into pure fire?"

"You have the essence of it, yes. As the nexus of the Maidens you have many potential additional capabilities." Silvertail's whiskers quivered pensively, but he still smiled. "Of course, you will not have the time to explore most of them; we made the most flexible and complex of mystical weapons in the Maidens, but ironically their very effectiveness and the overall shortness of their missions means that they have never truly explored the limits and intricacies of their powers. That would take years indeed of experience and action against many adversaries of varied capabilities."

"Hey, I'll be perfectly happy if this only lasts a few more months," Cordelia said. "If that means I don't learn all the ways I can 'waterbend,' I'm okay with it." She looked at the others. "I mean, we don't really want to spend our lives doing this, right?"

Tierra hesitated, as did Seika and Holly. Devika raised her eyebrow and looked down at Cordy. "As long as there is evil *worth* fighting? It sounds like *exactly* what I'd like to do!" At Cordy's stare, she grinned. "I *like* playing basketball and all, but that's not going to make a difference in the world. I could work like my mother does for elections and fair voting and everything, but this? This *really* makes a difference in the world and it's something no one but us can *do*. So if it's only lasting a few months and I won't remember, that's the will of God. But if it was longer? That's something *really* worth doing."

Cordy looked at the others, sighed. "Well . . . okay, yeah, it's important, but am I really the only one who'd be relieved it was over, if we got to remember it?"

"Yes and no," Holly said after a glance at Seika. "I've *always* wanted to be, well, a superhero. But if *not* being one meant that the world would 'stay saved,' like Mr. Incredible says, I'd be happy with it."

"And all that matters," Silvertail said, "is that you all *have* accepted it for now, for what has to be done. You don't have to *want* to do it for its own sake, Cordy; the fact that you will do it for the sake of others, despite your own feelings, is in its own way a sacrifice that strengthens you all that much more."

He sniffed at the air, then suddenly transformed back to Trayne Owen. "And with that, who would like some pie and ice cream?"

✳ Chapter 41 ✳

"Oh. My. God," Holly breathed, staring at the screen.

"I'm standing in front of Whitney High School," the reporter, Geri Anderson, was saying. The brown-haired woman gestured at the brick-faced building with its unmistakable watchtower. "While these . . . mysterious events have occurred in several places around the metro district, Whitney's been particularly hard hit, with the authorities confirming that two separate events here have been linked to these new phenomena."

"Geri, that includes the one previously reported as a violent intruder, correct?"

"Yes, David, it does. Detective Dana Kisaragi of the State Police has told News 13 On-Time that they had hoped the event was an isolated one, and the investigation was still ongoing, so they had withheld that information until now."

Holly continued to stare, mesmerized, as the special report went on. *Wow, they have actual clips from the security cameras in the mall.* Seeing herself fighting the shoggoth made her wince with the memory. More startling was a clip of footage from inside the school, the stalker-monster striding slowly and implacably up the hallway. "Holy crap, they've actually got stuff on video."

Seika nodded, trying to wrap a present while still watching the TV. "Look, there's the worm. Outside security cams?"

"Bank's, maybe. No, wait, that's too high. Must've been one of the other stores."

There were others, too; night-camera footage of the jack-o'-lantern-headed demon, stalking its way through the Halloween decorations as Devika prepared to fend it off, a momentary glimpse of a hideously smiling clown (Holly remembered the immense satisfaction of wiping that grin off the thing's face), a short snippet of Princess Holy Aura standing atop the lights of Whitney's bleachers. "Authorities are still very closemouthed on the subject, David, but no one can deny something . . . bizarre is happening in our region."

The older show host nodded and the screen focused on him. "Multiple witness reports and captured footage show an assortment of . . . monsters. Monsters which seem always to be faced and defeated by young women." A closeup of a slightly-blurred Holy Aura showed onscreen. "This was the first of the girl heroes seen, calling herself Princess Holy Aura. Others have been seen of recent."

"Hey, Silvertail, have you *seen* this?" Holly shouted down the stairs.

"Seen what? Holly, I've got some actual work to do that . . ." Silvertail, in his Trayne Owen form, trailed off as he saw the images on the screen. "Ah. I suppose this was inevitable. We saw prior incident reports but now that it has become obvious that these events were not singular mysteries but ongoing problems, people are forced to grapple with the concept of the supernatural in a way they never truly have before."

Agent Kisaragi—once more obviously in her identity as a State Police officer—was on screen now. ". . . just fighting these monsters we would have less of a concern about them," she was saying. "But they are not confining themselves to that."

Holly half rose, staring at the screen. *What the hell is she talking about*?

As if reading her mind, the reporter Geri said, "What Officer Kisaragi is referring to is the recent set of at least three incidents in which one of these girls intervened in criminal activities."

A dim security camera image showed two men exiting a gas-station convenience store, one pointing a gun at the door to forestall pursuit. As the two sprinted for their car, the view suddenly shuddered; when it steadied again, the two men were on the ground; a blurred figure whipped into sight and out again, and the men's weapons were gone. Their car was now also tipped entirely on its side.

Holly didn't hear any more of the special; she was staring at the frozen frame of video. The features were impossible to make out, but the length and hints of curl in the hair and the way the entire scene had shuddered told her everything she didn't want to know.

"Tierra," Seika said after a moment.

"Tierra," agreed Holly. "Playing the Goddam Batman."

"We must call a meeting immediately," Silvertail said.

"We've got one tomorrow, so—"

"I would *much* prefer it be sooner." His voice was hard and cold.

"Not if you're using *that* tone of voice, Silvertail. I don't know why you're *that* mad—"

"Because she has not the *faintest* idea of the risks she is taking, and those risks endanger us all!" he snapped.

"Calm down and *talk* to us, Mr. Owen," said Seika, wide-eyed at the sudden shout. "You *know* Tierra, she's not going to respond well to yelling."

Trayne Owen clenched his fingers tight, then took a huge breath and nodded. "You . . . are right, as usual, Seika. So many things I take for granted that you have never learned, and *could* not learn, here."

Holly nodded. "Bet I can guess part of it; by doing this she's made herself a big fat target for our enemies, and since she was doing this on the sly we don't have a chance to watch out for her and be ready if they make a move."

"Indeed that is one aspect, and not one to be passed over lightly. Worse, however, is that your powers are meant for use against truly malevolent adversaries of humanity. You are not *meant* to be judges of men and women, and your powers are at least partially *constrained* by the purity of your mission and motives—constrained and dependent upon them."

"You mean if she screws up one of these vigilante things, she could *weaken* us?"

"I mean *exactly* that." Trayne Owen sank into a chair, visibly calming himself. "It is all too easy to make a mistake in such judgment. Comic books—or movies—have the advantage of ensuring that what *looks* like a robbery *is* a robbery, that the one the hero thinks is the villain truly *is* a villain. Real life . . . is rather less accommodating, and given Tierra's difficult background she may or may not be capable of proper judgment in these situations."

"Okay, that's a lot more reasonable, you're not ready to blow your top." Holly pulled out her cell. "I'll text her to get here ASAP."

There was no answer to the text after several minutes. "Huh. She's usually got it on her all the time." A chill went down her back. "Oh, crap, you don't think—"

Trayne looked out the window at the already deep twilight of winter afternoon. "It is entirely possible. Let me call Marli; she was at home today, preparing for the holiday."

Trayne picked up the phone, dialed, waited. "Marli? Yes, it is. Holly was wondering if Tierra could come over this evening . . . Ah, all right, I see. Yes, I'll tell her. And you as well. We'll see you on Christmas Day. Good-bye!"

The lightness in his voice vanished as soon as he hung up the phone. "According to Marli, Tierra's doing a sleepover with your friend Caitlin."

"Caitlin? Well, maybe . . ." She opened her favorites menu on the phone and selected Caitlin's number.

"Hey, Holly! We still on for a game on New Year's?"

"As far as I know, yeah. What's up with you tonight?"

"Oh, not much. Mom's got me studying, actually, since they say they're opening the school again after the break. Maybe I'll do a little raid in Warquest later—you can join in if you want."

"Maybe—I'll see what Dad thinks. Thanks, I'll let you get back to studying."

She hung up and nodded. "Yeah, she's not there."

With a flicker, there was just a white rat sitting on the chair. "Then we can waste no time."

The two girls transformed immediately; Silvertail had impressed upon them all that when possible they should do that within their homes, as the homes were now all shielded against detection by their enemies. "I get that we can't wait, Silvertail," Princess Radiance Blaze said, "but there's an awful lot of city out there. How are we going to find her?"

"The same way our adversaries will, Princess," he said, leaping to Holy Aura's shoulder. "Through sensing her power and unique mystical nature. We of course have an advantage in that you five are all attuned, linked to each other—and most strongly to the first of you. Holy Aura, if you will but concentrate on Princess Temblor Brilliance and, as well, the spirit of your friend Tierra? Remember the sense you had of each other in combat. Think back to the battles you have now shared."

Holly closed her eyes, concentrated, focusing first on her coronet, what she now knew was the Apocalypse Seal—and one that connected her directly to the other four. *Tierra, Temblor, come* on, *where are you?*

A momentary sense of presence, then gone. "I'm not getting her!"

Despite being a diminutive animal, the deep breath Silvertail took and exhaled was audible. "Calm yourself, Holy Aura—Holly. Yes, this is a grave situation, but your worry and fear disrupt your focus. You are trying to *force* the connection, but rather than think of it as reaching out or trying to grasp something, imagine it as trying to thread a needle."

Holly bit her lip—noting the slightly different sensation with the body of Holy Aura rather than Holly Owen—and nodded. "Right. Like threading a needle. You know, most kids today have never *threaded* a needle?"

A squeaking chuckle. "You might be surprised. But of course *I* know that Stephen Russ learned to patch his own clothes of necessity."

Holly smiled at that. It was true; Steve *had* gained a lot of tiny little life skills and experiences that helped Holly understand more of the world than she might have. "Okay, threading a needle. Got it. Needs concentration and focus, and more force doesn't work at all."

Princess Radiance Blaze was clearly barely restraining herself, but Holy Aura met her gaze, and found she could *sense* Seika's worry and impatience . . . and somehow, that calmed her, showed her why her own panic had been disrupting her focus. *It's okay, Seika,* she thought through that connection. *Just hold on a moment. I'll get this.*

"Okay," Radiance said, with Seika's cadence and tone if not voice. "I guess I don't have to say we need to hurry. You know that already."

"We both do. Why don't you call Cordy and Devika? If things go bad—"

"Right! *Baka,* why didn't I think of that before?" She grabbed up the portable phone in the room (her regular cell phone having vanished along with Seika's mundane outfit) and started dialing.

Now . . . thread that needle. She pictured Tierra, rolling her dice and then returning to the sketch she was making; her awed acceptance and transformation to Temblor Brilliance. *Tierra, where* are *you?*

A faint sense of presence; this time, Holly forced herself to relax more, to build on that sensation of the girl she'd come to know. Memory of that tremendous kick to Procelli; the redheaded

Apocalypse Maiden holding the Great Jack-o'-Lantern demon at bay, blocking with the same legs that lashed out and hammered the flaming pumpkinhead between the glowing eyes; Tierra looking with tearful gratitude at Trayne for finally letting her mother find safety.

And suddenly the presence was strong; almost Holly could *see* her, could hear the wind nearby, sense the pavement and snow drifting.

"I've got her," she said, and pointed.

"That way."

✳ Chapter 42 ✳

Silvertail clung desperately to Holy Aura's shoulder. "Are you all right, Silvertail?" she asked, even as she made another bound.

"Barely," the white rat answered with only a trace of his usual humor. "Despite the natural protective power that emanates from you, and my own personal supernatural strength, it is nigh impossible to—*oof!*—hold on!"

Another rooftop, another leap. "Do you want us to slow down—"

"No! I will manage somehow. We *must* reach her quickly!"

Holy Aura glanced at him but nodded. Focused on the chase, she bounded from rooftop to rooftop with a speed and agility that easily outraced the cars on the streets below. Radiance Blaze matched her leap for leap, following that sense of presence, of Tierra's spirit, guiding them toward the center of the city, where larger buildings rose against the clear dark sky and erased the stars with their own light.

A sense of power, a flicker of darkness. "Princess—" A small cry, almost whipped away by the wind.

"I sense it, Silvertail. Something else is out there."

And then they no longer needed special senses; half a mile ahead, something shot *through* the roof of a building as though fired upward by a cannon, a slender figure curving in limp flight, then stirring as it began a plummet toward the ground far below.

"T. . . Temblor Brilliance!" Princess Radiance Blaze blurred forward and Holy Aura matched her in that impossible speed, but even so she could see they would be too late—

The earth quaked beneath the buildings, shaking dust from the windowframes and making the tallest sway the tiniest bit, and a column of gray-brown stone reared up, spread like a flower; Temblor Brilliance landed perfectly in the center and struck a pose, one leg lifted to strike, one supporting her, the arms flung wide for balance as well as drama, as five armored figures rose up before her.

Oh, shit. Silvertail—

"Yes," he said quietly. "The Cataclysm Knights have arrived."

Riding on a swirling green-black storm cloud that somehow supported them, the five figures were clearly boys or young men, slim waisted, broad shouldered, with armor of crystal and black metal and hints of silver, the colors warped reflections of the Maidens' own.

In the center was the tallest, matching even Devika's transformed height, with armor of smoky quartz; black touched with sparks of cold white swirled about him, a dark nebula to the divine starlight that surrounded Holy Aura, and he leaned on the haft of an axe nearly as tall as he. On one side of him, long straight black hair and armor of poison-green malachite, a rippling of deadly emerald flickering along the edges of the jagged blade he held. To the other side, the shortest of the group, diminutive, his colors glacier blue and storm-cloud gray, and wind and lightning swirled about him; it was he, clearly, who controlled the cloud on which the Cataclysm Knights rode, and he held a longbow sighted on Princess Temblor Brilliance.

The last two, on either end of the line, were of only slightly greater than average height, and both broader than the others—though still slender by ordinary standards. *My god, they're an entire* bishonen *squad!* On the left-hand side a young man with short curly hair and armor that was solid black, crisscrossed with cracks that glowed with dull crimson threat, blood and fire mixed. Smoke and sparks flowed up and around the scythe that was his chosen weapon. The last had hair of a dull green, and his armor too was muted greens and browns and grays. Dust continually shed from the immense hammer he had slung over his shoulder.

Before any of them could act, Holy Aura and Radiance Blaze landed, flanking their friend, weapons drawn and ready; Silvertail bailed out on the arc of their last leap and landed on a nearby rooftop, cushioned by his own magic. The guilty start Temblor Brilliance gave at their arrival clashed with the usual serene confidence of an Apocalypse Maiden.

Yes, you are *in trouble, Tierra, but we'll talk about that later,* Holly thought.

But . . . yeah, okay. A sense of embarrassment and shame. *I . . . guess I knew I shouldn't do it.*

Indeed, Silvertail's mind-voice said dryly. *Else you would hardly have concealed it from us. Now focus!*

The five newcomers had recovered from the momentary surprise of having two new adversaries arrive. The one in the center—as obviously the leader of his group as Holy Aura was of hers—lifted his axe and twirled it in a salute that showed off his strength far too clearly. "Wow! This party's getting *fun* now." He made a point of surveying all three of them from top to bottom. "*Lots* of fun."

"No party without introductions, bro," said the hammer-wielding one.

"Sure," said the black-and-red armored one, "but we can do the intros while we *dance*!"

He lunged forward as he said it, and the other four were but a split second behind him.

Instinctively the three leapt aside; even as she did it, Holly realized it was the wrong choice. *Crap. Back-to-back badasses was the right tactic there. Now they've separated us!*

She found herself confronting not one, not two, but *three* of the group, and suddenly she realized that *they* had thought through this entire conflict. The leader's lips curled in a smile as he saw her understanding. "Knight Eclipse Umbra's your first partner, babe!"

She parried the axe with the massive ball of the Silverlight Bisento, felt a wave of heaviness and cold radiating from the weapon, even as she twisted the blade around to catch a blow from the red-glowing scythe. The curly haired boy made a kissing noise and winked. "Knight Infernal Pall is the hottest of the group!"

Oh, please, she thought. *Getting powers didn't give you guys any skills in superhero banter, did it? And what's with your* names?

Like yours, Silvertail commented, *fairly literally translated, and of a similar pattern—a word related to the relevant sphere of operation, and one denoting in this case a form of darkness rather than light.*

Her third adversary she could not quite parry, and the immense hammer caught her chestplate and sent her tumbling away like a toy, as the wielder said cheerfully, "But it's Avalanche Oblivion that hits on you!"

Holy Aura forced herself to stand, but the breath hadn't just been knocked from her. *Feels . . . like my chest . . . just hit with acid or something! Can't breathe right!*

Corruption of Earth, of life—you've been struck by the Hammer of Decay, Princess!

She staggered backward, but even without looking she could *hear* the swift, confident footsteps circling her. *Three to one. Even if these guys aren't actually our equals, they're close enough that* one *of them will keep the others busy for a few minutes . . . long enough for them to take me down.*

She reached for that well of star-sprinkled power, called on the energies that infused her very soul; the power of Holy Aura began to drive back the creeping destruction of the Hammer, even as she twisted her body to evade a strike of the axe, then smacked the Hammer of Decay aside—

And could not restrain a scream as the burning Scythe cut across her back. Only her armor kept the Cataclysm Knight from carving her spine in two, and she could tell it had been a near thing. *I'm in* trouble, *Silvertail!*

But she knew there was nothing he could do. Devika and Cordy might be coming, but if they were even a few *minutes* behind, they might as well be an hour back. Holly tumbled between Eclipse and Avalanche and tried to think of the right phrase. *I think I need that Release thing, right now!*

But Tierra was backing up, blocking furiously against the barrage of black-crystal arrows her opponent was raining down upon her, and the entire roof was shaking as venom-emerald water contested with brilliant orange flame in a straight-up battle of will and power that could only end with one of the two utterly annihilated. *I have to release myself only—*

The thought was never completed.

Holy Aura rolled to her feet, but in the same instant the axe came down with such force that even her parry failed; the black-glowing blade sank into her shoulder, a fang of absolute-zero ice seemingly driving straight to her heart. She fell back, horror rising, as she realized that she could barely raise one arm, and the other two were closing on her—

A streak of wavering light cut across the space between her and the Knights, striking their weapons aside. "Three against one? And fie, on you who would call yourselves Knights!"

The battle froze, all the combatants whipping about to stare upward.

Standing on a circle of auroral luminance was another young man, a cascade of straight moon-gold hair falling from beneath a broad-brimmed, plumed hat. The light of the moon flared argent from the silver rapier held in one long-fingered hand, and a cloak of tarnished silver flowed behind the impeccable costume of a bygone era.

As they looked, he dropped from the sky to the ground, landing with perfect precision at Holy Aura's side. He flashed a smile at her and bowed, though his attention remained on the enemy. "Canst thou stand, Princess?"

Holly's brain simply froze, as though its gears had seized. She was staring at the handsome face, outlined in shadow beneath the hat, and she felt somehow dizzy, embarrassed and elated and relieved and eager in a mix that made no sense.

But the pause *had* given her power a chance to rise to her defense; her arm's numbness was beginning to recede and the Hammer's blow no longer held her breath hostage. "I . . . I think so."

She rose, and the Cataclysm Knights raised their weapons—but more cautiously. "Who the *hell* are you?"

"Prince Twilight Dawn—the light that comes at the darkest hour," he answered with a laugh.

Eclipse Umbra wasn't apparently impressed. "Infernal, go barbeque Twilight Dork there; me and Avalanche will finish Holy Aura."

But the pause had been just long enough. "In the name of those who were lost, by the power of the spirit and the imperishable light of the stars themselves—RELEASE!"

Pearl-white light *fountained* up around her and the shockwave of her Release staggered everyone on the rooftop. The concentrated power was burning agony and concentrated ecstasy, an echo and reification of her first transformation. It wiped away the wounds of the battle as though they had been mere dust and grime to be washed away in a torrent of pure water, lifted her up, the power steadying her legs and bringing a surge of certainty to counterbalance the earlier fear and trepidation.

"Oh, yeah, come finish me," she said, grinning. "Let's try this again."

A tremendous *thud* shook the roof, announcing the arrival of Devika—in the form of Tempest Corona—and almost immediately after, a roaring sound of unending water, rising up to show Princess Tsunami Reflection standing atop a controlled waterspout.

Another laugh from Twilight Dawn. "And the tables are turned, are they not? Good hunting, Maidens!"

The mysterious newcomer leapt away into the night, even as the Cataclysm Knights wavered, evaluating their chances.

Whoever Knight Eclipse Umbra was, he wasn't slow or stupid. "Knights, this just went all wrong. Retreat!"

"But Mi . . . Eclipse, I—"

"Shut *up*, Abyssal Night! Move it!"

The five retreated—some leaping off the building, others into the air. Holy Aura began to pursue, gesturing to the others to follow, but Silvertail's mental voice cut sharply across their minds. *Do not follow! It may be a trap, or not, but if they have a stronghold of any sort, we are woefully unprepared to deal with them in such circumstances.*

Reluctantly, Holly let herself settle back to the roof . . . and restored her Apocalypse Seal. The burning power receded. "Tierra, you okay?"

"I'm . . . fine. Stupid, but fine."

"Seika?"

"A couple bruises. He never landed anything serious on me, though. We never finished that power duel."

"Then I think we'd better go back home." She looked straight at Tierra. "We've got *serious* talking to do. With everyone."

The other girl looked down.

"And . . ." Holly glanced up and out into the starry night, and felt a familiar presence climbing to her shoulder. "Silvertail, who and what the *hell* is Prince Twilight Dawn?"

The white-furred face showed utter bewilderment. "Maidens . . . I must confess that I have not the *faintest* idea."

✳ Chapter 43 ✳

"Who the *fuck* is this Twilight Dawn asshole?" demanded Eclipse Umbra. "We *had* those girls. Without him getting in the way, we'd've finished Holy Aura before the other two *got* there!"

Arlaung, from his position near the door of the huge shadowed room, clenched his fists, feeling the rage near to overcoming his control of the human seeming he wore. *How* dare *he speak so to the Queen?*

To his surprise, Queen Nyarla did not immediately chastise the mortal. "My sympathies, Eclipse Umbra. It is always distressing when a plan is disrupted by events beyond one's control." She bowed—something which distracted the young man due to the construction of her current outfit. "The fact remains that you successfully ambushed them and were able to demonstrate that your drills and tactics were effective—as you had told me they would be."

Why is she so tolerant? Arlaung knew she was not always so. She had been kind to Arlaung himself, true, but there were bones buried in the cellar below which were the remains of others who had met with a very different reception. And Arlaung was, and had always been, extremely respectful; it made sense she would tolerate minor missteps. But this foul-mouthed, disrespectful brat, now ogling the Queen as though she were just some mortal display piece? Why?

Her words *had* changed the tone of the conversation, however. Eclipse stood straighter and his voice had less of a demanding, petulant ring. "Well, yeah, you're right, and thanks. But that's also a problem, if I assume this Silvertail guy you've mentioned isn't stupid."

A tiny quirk of the mouth. "I assure you, Silvertail Heartseeker is very, very far from stupid. What problem, then?"

"Well, he'll have seen how close his girl squad came to being shut down. So he'll start training them how to deal with groups."

"Right," Tornadic said. "They've been fighting boss fights most of the time, see, with maybe a couple of mooks thrown in to start, but mostly just all of them on a big enemy. Their tactics *sucked* for fighting a group like us."

"So what?" Avalanche said contemptuously. "They're *girls*. We were kicking their asses. No way some girl's going to match—"

Arlaung was immensely satisfied to see the fool's breath catch as he realized his mistake. Smiling sweetly, Queen Nyarla stepped forward and backhanded the offending mortal so hard that he bowled over two of his companions in his trajectory across the entire room, to fetch up with a loud crash against the stone wall.

Even before Avalanche Oblivion could recover, the Queen was there, lifting him easily by the front of his earth-colored armor. "Those *girls* are empowered by the greatest enchantment ever forged by mortal minds, you simpleton," she said, still smiling as though sitting at table for tea. "They are *more* powerful, individually, than any of you. And it is a '*girl*' who has given you your powers, Knights. You had best remember that, little *boy*." She tossed him aside as casually as if he had been an empty soda can. "If you *were* 'kicking their asses,' as you say, it was *only* because of the element of surprise, and Eclipse and Tornadic's tactics."

The other four were staring at her now with far more respect—and possibly a little fear. Arlaung allowed himself a broad grin, with inhumanly sharp teeth in evidence.

Avalanche rose slowly, muttered an apology, and slunk back to the others. Eclipse waited until she looked at him again. "Understood . . . your Majesty. That's the right term, right?"

"It is certainly one of the acceptable ways to address me, my Knight. I hope we will not require any additional reminders?"

Eclipse looked around at his companions. "We damn well better not. Got that, guys?"

Arlaung noticed that the two who had not yet spoken—Infernal Pall and Abyssal Night—nodded, but looked resentful. *There will be trouble from those two. I am still unclear as to the Queen's plans.*

"Now, pray continue, Eclipse Umbra."

"Um . . . yeah, where was I? Yeah, so, this Silvertail guy, and maybe the real tall one, Tempest Corona? They'll be drilling the Maidens in many-many tactics now. No way they'll make noob mistakes like they did this time. Sure, if they *were* just ordinary girls maybe they'd panic, but if they were going to lose their heads, they've already gone through that in the fights they've had. Right? I mean, right, Your Majesty?"

Her smile acknowledged his effort. "I agree entirely. Whatever immediate weaknesses they may have had, they have had time and more to address them. You must assume they are as competent as you in controlling their actions. But I am curious—why do you single out Tempest Corona?"

The leader of the Knights exchanged glances with Tornadic Gloom, who had evidently become his second. "Because I'm *sure* she's Devika Weatherill. There's a reason she's captain of the basketball team when she's only a sophomore, and it's not just because she's such a huge freak of nature. She's *good* at team strategy and tactics. And she wears that hijab, and Tempest Corona's got that huge hijab-headdress going on too, like none of the others."

Arlaung saw Tornadic roll his eyes. "It's a *chunni*, not a hijab. She's a Sikh. Which just makes the case stronger, 'cause that sword Corona uses is a straight-up *khanda*, one of the traditional Sikh weapons."

"We *investigated* that, Knights," Arlaung said, "and though we believed that as well, it is an unsupportable idea. While Tempest Corona and two others of the Maidens fought and defeated yet another adversary, one of my agents observed Devika Weatherill at a public Sikh service. She then went home and remained there for the day. No other people were seen to go in or out."

"Oh, come *on*," Infernal Pall said. "I'll bet *you* could figure out how to use an illusion or something to make that work. You saying these guys couldn't? Um, Your Majesty?" he added, glancing with concern at Queen Nyarla.

Arlaung said nothing; he and the Queen had already discussed this part of the conversation, and it was up to her to decide how to respond.

Nyarla nodded her head. "It is *possible* that—despite our careful observation, which you should realize was not merely surface but mystical—we could have been deceived. Our adversary does not, however, have the broad base of resources to draw upon that I do. His agents—the Maidens—are vastly powerful, but he himself is very limited in what he can do. But let us say you are correct. Do you have any thoughts as to who the *other* Maidens might be?"

Eclipse scratched his head. "Um . . . sorta, Your Majesty. But I'd like to check a few things out first? If that's okay?"

"I would encourage you to do so, Eclipse," she answered. "And I agree that your adversaries will be preparing to confront you more effectively. This is why—at least for now—I do not intend to put you in the field as a group. I have other assignments for you that should improve our position."

"Awww, come on . . ." Avalanche began, but then winced. "Er . . . I just mean, Your Majesty, I would really like to get another shot at them. Without being interrupted."

"Your enthusiasm is noted, Avalanche . . . as is your attempt to learn to curb your tongue. I agree with it . . . to an extent. But that 'interruption' will warrant its own investigation. You know nothing of this Prince Twilight Dawn, save the rather disturbing fact that neither side expected him, and yet *he* clearly knew of, and was prepared in some fashion for, both sides. I do not believe he can have power to match you, but he *is* an unknown factor and one to be considered well before you venture out again. Do you not agree?"

Avalanche grimaced, but nodded after a moment. Eclipse and the others did the same. "You have any ideas, Majesty?"

"A few. But I have my own . . . things to check out, as you say . . . before I speak on this subject." She seated herself in her high-backed chair. "For now, Knights, dismissed. And I remind you to also be circumspect in the use of your particular gifts in the mortal world. It is not yet time for us to rule openly, and there are mortal forces whose attention we do not yet wish upon us."

The Knights bowed—more respectfully than they had when first they had entered—and left, Eclipse leading the way.

Once the door had closed, Nyarla leaned back in her chair and laughed long and loud.

"What amuses you, my Queen?"

"Those children, Arlaung. They are so sure in their power, and then so quick to be chastised. Hardly the example of human warriorhood."

"Meaning no disrespect, my Queen, but . . . I had thought you would select more . . . interesting tools. That was my reading from the past cycles. Was I wrong?"

"Not at all, sweet Arlaung. Yet that subtlety, of choosing flawed heroes to corrupt? Has it ever succeeded? No." She studied him for a long moment. "Come forward and sit before me, Arlaung. You have shown far more promise than ever I had expected. I think it is time to tell you the truth."

His heart beat faster, his cold blood warming at praise and in the anticipation of finally—*finally!*—being brought fully into her counsel. "The truth, my Queen?"

"You are aware, I think, that I am as human as our Knights, or I was, yes?"

"It is not something spoken of, my Queen, but yes, Father Dagon so informed me." He dropped his gaze, then raised it. *If she wishes to trust me, I must trust her.* "He instructed me that he did not believe you were to be relied upon, and that the Nine-Armed was making a mistake in choosing you as her emissary. I was to watch and report to him any . . . questionable actions. I find I do not agree with him."

The eerie, monstrous undertones to her laugh simply emphasized its delighted sound. "Why *Arlaung*! So you are throwing in your lot with me, even against Dagon Itself?"

"I am," he said, keeping his gaze steady.

"Then surely I will tell you all now, Arlaung. The Cataclysm Knights have never succeeded in their true purpose. At best they have, once or twice, slain one of the Maidens. A good thing, yes, and if they could succeed in slaying Holy Aura it might be sufficient. Yet *this* set of Maidens . . ." she shook her head, and her smile faded, became a pensive look. "They are *strong*, Arlaung. Much, *much* stronger than at least the last three or four incarnations, possibly the strongest I have heard of. Why, in her first appearance Holy Aura *broke* a dhole by main force of arms, without even invoking her true power. That's quite astonishing."

"And this newcomer? I have never seen a reference to Prince Twilight Dawn before."

She nodded. "No more have I . . . before." Arlaung noted the secretive smile and thought he was beginning to understand. "But—and I have no doubt our opposite numbers know this as well—there are and have been other powers in the world, and they may be attempting, this time, to assist in the defense of the unending cycle."

He thought about that, and other things, and what she was not saying began to come clear. "So . . . the Knights . . . they are not even a major part of your plan?"

"*Very* good, Arlaung. They are . . . how do I put it . . . a stalking horse. A distraction. A set of useful tools that will be most useful when disposed of. While I certainly wish you, and all five of them, to continue to search for the most potent adversaries and plans to pit against those little girls, I expect the day to be won only on the same day that the stars are right. And you and I, dear Arlaung, will be standing before Queen Azathoth of the Nine Arms in the very moment of our triumph."

She leaned forward and began to explain.

✳ Chapter 44 ✳

"Okay, people," Holly said, leaning back in the chair until it almost tipped over, "after-action briefing."

The other four, plus Silvertail, looked at her quietly; Tierra looked more nervous than the others. *I guess I really* am *the leader*, Holly thought. *Well, then, I have to lead.*

That included dealing with the less-pleasant parts of the job. She looked directly at Tierra. "You nearly got yourself killed out there. Nearly got *three* of us killed out there, really."

Tierra scrunched her face up, not crying but not far from it. "I know! I already *said*—"

"Tierra, it's not just that," she said, hating the fact that she had to keep her voice level and focused. "It's that you *hid* this from us. That means you *knew*, like Silvertail said, that this wasn't a good idea. And because you hid it, you *really* endangered us, more than you know. Silvertail?"

In his white rat form, Silvertail hopped to the center of the table. "Tierra . . . I want you to know I *understand* the desire to make use of your powers to fight other evils in the world. That, by itself, is not at all a bad impulse. However,"—he looked around the little circle—"the symbolic nature of the Maidens is, in a way, very fragile. If you *ever* were to make a mistake of judgment—attack what you thought was a mugger when they were actually the one being attacked, for example—you could severely weaken, even *corrupt*, the operation of the enchantment on you, and possibly even on the rest of the Maidens."

Tierra's eyes widened. "Oh, God. It could *spread*? Not just hurt me, but—"

"Exactly. You have already sensed the connection between you in multiple ways; it extends to the mystical foundations of your powers. Misuse of the power—evil or selfish exploitation of those abilities—can and will rebound upon the user and, quite possibly, all those connected with them."

Holly noticed Seika wince. *She hesitated and felt a little nervous when we first had this discussion.* Holly renewed her resolve and looked at her best friend. "You have something to tell us, Seika?"

The way the smaller girl's shoulders hunched gave the answer. "I . . . Look, I didn't go out and play hero. But . . . a couple of times I just went out, you know, as Radiance Blaze. Not in the armor, though, just in regular clothes. To see what being older and, well, tall and really beautiful was like. In the regular world."

Silvertail sighed. "It seems no harm has been done in either case, Seika, but that, too, was risky. Not only because it was a selfish action, even if minimally so, but because it was concealed, revealing that you, like Tierra, knew in your heart that this was not what the power was intended for. But now that you all understand the implications, we should not need to worry about it anymore, correct?"

All five of them nodded emphatically. "Good. Then I think we can leave this subject, Holly."

"Okay, moving on, then. Our cataclysmic friends—any ideas on them?"

Devika nodded. "One began to speak a regular name, which I would guess to be 'Mike' or 'Michael.' The co-captain of the football team is Michael Collins, and if I assume the transformations of the Knights are similar to our own, I think Eclipse Umbra has at least as much similarity in voice and general appearance to Mike Collins as the Maidens do to us."

Cordy's eyes narrowed. "Yeah, now that you mention it. Yes, I think you're right, that was Collins."

"With that as a hint," Silvertail said, "have you any thoughts on the other four?"

"Maybe they're all football players?" Seika asked. "I mean, football players are used to charging at people and hitting them so they're used to violence, right?"

"Oh, for *God's* sake let's not be Nerds Versus Jocks Classic, okay?" Cordy said. Holly felt a little guilty, as her thoughts had started down that path too. "There's a *lot* of difference between tackling a guy on the field, when you're playing a game and you've got all the protective gear on, and trying to kill someone. Most sports players are perfectly decent people." She frowned. "But there *are* assholes in every sport, and a lot of them know each other. Collins isn't an out-and-out bastard, though. There's worse."

"Lance," Devika said slowly. "Bob Lance. I will *bet* that he is Tornadic Gloom."

Tierra looked up. "That fits. He's on the wrestling team in one of the smaller weight classes, and he was *also* head of the Archery Club last year." She paused. "You know . . . there was a guy in one of the art clubs last year—a real creeper. Obvious he was in the club because it was mostly girls. He made bad, stupid puns like that Avalanche guy, and something about that voice was similar. What was his name . . . Corbin, that's it, Corbin Freeman."

Silvertail raised a tiny brow ridge. "Not bad. We have tentatively identified three of the five. I suppose it's too much to ask that you have guesses for the others?"

The five looked at each other, but nothing seemed to occur to the others. For Holly's part, she wasn't as familiar with the school and students as the others were, so she hadn't expected much. Finally they shook their heads. "They're *probably* connected to one of the sports programs," Devika said after a moment. "But that's just a guess."

"Ah, well, it is still a fine start."

"Which leaves us with Prince Twilight Dawn," Holly said. "Silvertail, you said you had no idea where—"

"—and I still do not," the white rat said emphatically. "He has never been seen in any of the prior cycles—having been present at all of them, I can say this quite categorically. At the same time, he is clearly fighting on our side—had he any particularly hostile intent he had excellent opportunities to finish off one or more of you."

"I like the idea of having more allies," Tierra said, "Especially now that we've got more enemies. Why are you worried? Because I can tell you are, your whiskers are twitching more than usual."

"Really? I had no idea I had so obvious a . . . what is the term . . . *tell*, that is it, in my behavior." Silvertail scuttled back and forth on the table in what was his equivalent of pacing. "I am concerned primarily because he represents an unknown quantity. *On the surface* he certainly appears benevolent, but I cannot discount the possibility of some more subtle plans which would require this Twilight Dawn to play the hero for a considerable time before revealing his true nature."

Holly could *sense* the concern from her mentor. "There's more to it than that, too, isn't there?"

He sighed. "You are quite perceptive tonight, Holly. Yes, there is. As you know, the Maidens are the most powerful force ever created by mortal magic—and, in fact, one of the most powerful of any sort of magic, or their power would avail little against Azathoth Nine-Armed. This Prince clearly draws somehow on very similar magical elements to mine, but is not actually *of* that enchantment. He *must* be considerably weaker than any of you, and thus I must be concerned for his safety. He may not, technically, be my responsibility, but if he has assisted us, we owe him a debt—and the way the enchantment works, that obligation is not merely an empty phrase."

Holly smiled sympathetically, saw similar expressions on the others. "And so that means you're going to *worry* about him along with us, huh?"

His own laugh was subdued. "You see through me too easily, girls. Yes. I have chosen this path. Someone else has chosen to place yet another young person on a similar path, one that is obviously based on and following my own . . . and one which places Prince Twilight Dawn on a direct collision course with the most powerful and hostile forces the world has ever seen. It is my *duty* to prevent his death . . . if I can."

Holly shook her head. "Jesus, Silvertail, you can't take responsibility for people you don't . . ." She trailed off. "Ugh. I guess we already are."

A faint rodent smile. "If we are prepared to protect the world in general, can we help but be concerned for those we meet in specific? He protected you; I cannot help but feel we must also protect him."

"Of course we must," Devika said firmly. "He came of his own will and joined our war—on the righteous side."

Holly grinned at that—in some ways, Devika *was* the warrior the rest of them were just playing at, and Holly was damned glad Devika was with them. "And if he's playing us, we'll deal with that later." She straightened up. "We haven't seen the last of him—the *mahou shoujo* memes will see to that—and for now, I'm just grateful he showed up when he did."

She looked over to Devika. "Aaaand that brings us to the future. Dev, Cordy, we need some *serious* training."

"Training and tactics," Devika agreed. "We need to be able to deal with groups as well as individual threats, and make *use* of the connection we share."

"And *that* means drill, drill, drill," Cordy said cheerfully. "Devika and I have already started working out the program, and it's going to be *packed*."

Great, Holly thought with a rueful smile that she saw mirrored on the faces of Seika and Tierra. *We're the superheroes out to save the world . . . and now we're getting homework from our teammates!*

✶ Chapter 45 ✶

". . . and as the Time-Tower collapses, you see the gigantic minute hand come loose and plunge straight down on top of Doctor Tempus!"

"Ouch," said Dex in the slightly higher-pitched, Bronx-like accent he used for Geri Rigger. "I guess his time was up."

The whole group turned to stare at him. "You beat me to that line!" Seika said, enviously.

He shrugged, grinning. "Good . . . timing?"

Everyone around the table laughed. Holly shook her head. "Okay, Dex, for an absolutely perfect scene and adventure ending quote, I'll have to figure out an appropriate reward. Not sure it warrants anything major, but you'll get some kind of bonus for that."

"Sweet!"

Glancing at the real clock on the wall, she continued, "And since they're actually planning on opening the school tomorrow, we'll have to stop there." She couldn't mention that she, Seika, and Tierra were all also sore from the earlier training that Devika and to a lesser extent Cordy and Silvertail had been putting them through, and so they *really* needed to get some rest.

The others began to pack up. She saw Dex, looking suddenly stiff and nervous, bend over and get something—several somethings—out of his pack. "Hey, um, guys," he said.

As Caitlin, Tierra, Nikki, and Seika turned back, Dex swallowed, but then put down a set of brightly wrapped small boxes. "I, um, well, didn't get to see you guys closer to Christmas, and things were busy, and anyway, these are for you."

Tierra blinked. "Presents for us? Jeez, I didn't get you one, now I feel terrible!"

"Don't!" He looked half panic stricken. "I didn't do this to make you feel bad or like you had to give me anything! You've been great friends, letting me into the group, and I just wanted to, you know, say thanks."

Caitlin had opened hers already, finding a small white box. Inside, there was an elaborate, Gothic-script *C* cast of what Holly was sure was pewter, holding a clear glittering stone inside its curve. As the others opened theirs, it became clear the gifts were all similar—shining metal initials ornamented with a crystal.

Tierra looked at hers closely. "Dex . . . you *made* these, didn't you?"

"Well, um, yeah, it was for that shop class I was taking, you know, my parents thought taking a practical class was good and they had this sand-casting option and I saw there were molds for the letters and I thought it'd be kind of neat—"

"Stop the nervous narration, Dex, no one's *mad* at you!" Nikki said, and leaned over impulsively and hugged him. "Thanks so much, they're beautiful!"

"This isn't glass," Seika said. "Quartz?"

"Herkimer diamonds, yeah," Dex said, looking startled but gratified after Nikki's warm thanks. "When I was a kid we lived near Herkimer and my dad used to take us mining every summer."

"Well, thank you *very* much, Dex!" The others, including Holly, repeated the sentiment. *Dex must have spent a lot of hours working on these. This isn't just a quick "glue them in" trick.*

"Everyone getting ready to leave?" Trayne Owen asked. "I'll go get the car warmed up."

The others trooped out to get their coats, as Holly started packing away her own books and notes. She was suddenly aware that Dex was still there. "You okay, Dex? That was really nice of you."

"Sure, um. I'm fine. I am. Look, about everything . . . I mean, you guys letting me in the group on probation—"

"Is *that* still worrying you?" She laughed. "You've been great, Dex. Even when I have to sometimes smack you down for hogging the spotlight, you don't make a fuss about it and I can tell you're *trying* not to. I think probation's way over."

He *was* turning red! "Um . . . maybe not. You might put me back on. Or kick me out."

She stared at him, confused. "Why would we do that? You haven't done anything—"

"Well, not yet, but I am going to. I mean . . ." As she continued to look at him, he took a breath and let it out, then reached out and took her hand. "I . . . just wanted to know, I mean, if maybe, you'd go to a movie or something like that with me."

A bomb exploding under her chair couldn't have stunned Holly more. She found herself blinking stupidly at Dex, unable to speak.

He turned redder, then pale as she was silent. He let go her hand and looked down. "Um, sorry. Sorry. Forget I said that, I was really, really stupid to ask, I know, I guess I'd better get going." His voice was wavering; he clamped his mouth shut and grabbed up his backpack.

As he got to the doorway, Holly finally overcame her paralysis. "Dex, *wait*!"

He stopped, looking back with an expression of guilt and hope mixed.

"Sorry, Dex, I . . . you just caught me totally off guard, I didn't expect this." *Maybe I should. Holy shit, what the hell,* Dex *just asked* me *out on a* date? The part of her that was Steve was running around in circles trying to deal with it, and not succeeding, and the regular Holly part was just about the same way, though not entirely for the same reasons. She felt a terrible, wonderful excitement at the thought and just as suddenly a wrenching fear. *Crap, I'd forgotten what first date thoughts are* like. "I . . . I'd love to go out with you," she heard herself say, and felt as though she were listening to someone else. *What? I just said I wanted to go out with Dex? Yes, I do. But . . . oh my* GOD *this is so messed up.*

"You . . . you *would*?"

Dex's face suddenly went from tense and embarrassed to filled with utter, surprised joy that transfigured him. Suddenly he was *beautiful*, his long blonde hair framing a face that wore the most incredibly happy smile she had ever seen. "Um . . . holy shit, um, I didn't think . . . you *would*? Oh wow, look, I hadn't even picked out the day, because I didn't think there'd be one, so I'll like have to look up the movies and all, but—" He got a hold of himself with what appeared to be heroic difficulty. "Thanks. Holly, I . . . Thanks. I'll call you tomorrow? Talk times and stuff?"

"Sure, that'll be great!" her voice replied, as the rest of her looked on amazed. "And don't be so *nervous*, okay?"

He blushed again momentarily, but his head came up with some of his usual humor. "Can't promise *that*. It'll be my first date." He stopped, and repeated, with audible wonder, "I'll be on a date. You know how that *sounds* to me?"

"About like it does to me?"

"What? I kinda thought you'd—"

"When did I have the *time*?"

"I meant before you came here."

Holly paused. "Oh. Well, okay, but no. So don't be nervous, or you'll make *me* nervous."

"I'll . . . try. Um . . . okay, see you later, bye!" He literally *skipped* out the door, and Holly understood what books meant when they said someone was walking on air. It looked like Dex's feet weren't even touching the ground.

Trayne poked his head into the room a few moments later. "Holly? Aren't you going to say goodbye to your friends before I drive them home?"

"Um . . . sure! Sorry!"

She wasn't quite sure what she said, or how she said it, but she *did* know that Seika was looking at her funny before the door closed.

Alone in the house, she stumbled up to her room, and sank into a chair, shaking. "Oh my *god*, what have I just done?"

They'd be going on a date. A movie? *My dating days were like twenty years ago as Steve, what's things like now?* He said a movie. She imagined sitting next to Dex in a dim theater, watching some SF film—of course it'd be an SF film, neither of them would choose anything else, right? *Oh my god, will he put his arm around me?* Of course he would, if he thought it was a date. *Not* thought, *it* is *a date. Right?*

Her cell phone rang, making her jump. She fumbled it out of her nearby purse and turned it on. "Hello?"

"Okay, talk, what was freaking you out before we left?" Seika's voice was filled with concern.

"Seika? Jeez, my dad isn't even back—"

"He dropped me off second, so he's still got three more to go. So what's up?"

"Dex asked me to go out with him."

There was dead silence on the other end for a few moments. Then, "Oh. My. God. What did you *say*?"

"I said yes."

"You said *what*?"

"Yes, I said yes, I said I'd love to go out with him, I'm *totally* freaking out about that, Seika, I mean, I never thought about dating him, more like dating you or Tierra, but—"

She froze, realizing what had just slipped out, something she'd never even allowed herself to acknowledge before.

Seika was silent again. "Oh, shit. Seika, I'm . . . I'm sorry, I never meant to say—"

"Me? You wanted to date *me*?"

"God, I just said I'm sorry, I didn't mean to—"

"Jesus, Holly, don't *apologize,* there's nothing wrong with that. Being gay. Or bi, or . . . what would it be?"

She giggled, not an entirely under-control sound. "I haven't the *faintest*. I don't know how I'd even figure it out. Maybe I'm straight, just two parallel lines of straight? Or I'm twin railroad tracks of gay?"

Seika burst out laughing. "Twin railroad tracks of gay! I love that! I want that to be a *meme!*"

"Stop laughing, I don't know if it *is* funny!"

The voice on the other end was suddenly serious. "Holly, it's *funny*, but that doesn't mean I'm making *fun* of you. I can't imagine how messed up it must be in your head over this, with Steve and his age difference and your age as Holly and all that."

"I don't know if this makes me some kind of a real sicko or—"

"Holly, shut *up*. There's nothing wrong with you that isn't Silvertail's fault. You don't want to hurt me, you don't want to hurt Dex, and *you aren't going to*, understand me? I trust you, and I *believe* in you. Got that?"

The absolute certainty in Seika Cooper's voice steadied Holly, and she finally found herself relaxing. If Seika believed in her that much . . . "I . . . Okay. I got that."

"You've said yes to Dex. Did you say it because you were *sorry* for him?"

"No! Why would you think—"

"Well, that'd be the only halfway good reason to say yes if you didn't actually mean *yes*. So I guess you *do* mean yes."

She thought back to the first day of school, when she'd almost gone into a complete nervous breakdown thinking that Dex might learn her secrets, and her other reactions around him. "Crap. You're right."

"Okay, good. Glad we got that clear. You just keep me *informed*, right? When you guys set the schedule?"

"I . . . okay. Yes, of course I will."

"Good."

She felt rather than heard the *thud* of the door closing downstairs. "Dad's here."

"Good. Talk to *him* about this."

"Yeah, I'd already figured I had to do that." She managed a more natural grin. "After all, it's going to be either him or Dex's parents driving us to the movies!"

✳ Chapter 46 ✳

"Holly, that is the *seventh* time you've come downstairs to check the clock. Which is a ridiculous thing for you to be doing, given that you have a clock in your phone, a clock in your tablet, one on your bedside table, and one on your computer desktop."

"I'm just so *nervous*!" she said, realizing that it was also probably the seventh, or seventieth, time she'd said *that*. "How do I—"

"Beautiful, naturally, and do you expect your father to say anything else? Take a deep breath. We'll be leaving in ten more minutes. I'll drive you both to Palonia Mall and drop you off. You'll have plenty of time for dinner before the movie, it's a perfectly safe location—"

Despite her nervousness she snorted. "I'm not worried about *safe*, Dad! If Dex suddenly turns into a psycho asshole, *either* of my other forms could break him like a twig, not that Steve would have to; I already went through that in the blizzard, remember? And if you're talking about Maiden business, isn't pretty much *everywhere* not safe?"

He smiled faintly, the movement echoed by his mustache and short pointed beard. "Aside from your homes, yes, I suppose you are correct."

She nodded, then stopped, a terrible thought suddenly rising from the depths of her subconscious. "Oh no. Silvertail, our homes are *protected*, right? Shielded, so activity in them can't be sensed, and something to keep Queen Nyarla's monsters from just waltzing in through the front door?"

"Correct. What is wrong?"

"Well *Jesus,* Silvertail, isn't that like a *dead giveaway* of our identities? All they have to do is look for the houses that are protected, and then . . ." she trailed off as she saw the sometimes annoyingly superior smile appearing.

"Firstly, Holly, they would have to approach the house in question *quite* closely in order to make the assessment. And if they did not have a good idea which house or houses to test in the first place, the chances are that it would take them considerable dedicated effort to find them. However, it is true that they might well *make* that effort; there are only a few hundred candidate homes, after all, that would have young women of the appropriate ages in Whitney High."

The smile broadened to a grin. "Which is why—in the months you were accustoming yourself to being Holly, and in those following—I have been very systematically laying protective wards and preparatory magical elements throughout the area. Not just around the school, though that obviously proved highly useful during the tyrpiglynt incident, but in the relevant neighborhoods. By now, over fifty percent of the candidate households are warded."

She stared at him, then burst out laughing. "You *have* been doing this a long time!"

"Long enough to cover my bases, as they say, from the start. My personal powers are far less than my opponents' . . . but with the right preparation, the right symbols and magical circles and figures in place, I will prove more formidable than they believe . . . and of course I can use these tactics to sow confusion and obscure the truth." A more serious look descended upon his face. "And in no way is it a bad thing that many houses are protected, at least to some extent, from such monsters. I wish I could protect them all."

Holly hugged him impulsively. "Well, that's what we're doing, isn't it?"

He hugged her back quickly. "Yes. Yes, we are." He looked at the clock. "And we have at last reached the time of departure."

"Oh my god!" A fresh wave of near panic assailed her, while in the mental distance Steve was searching for a metaphorical bomb shelter to hide in.

"Deep breaths. You have faced deadly peril, a date should not be any worse than the Mirrortaint."

"Easy for *you* to say," she muttered as she followed him out. The latest dusting of snow crunched under her feet, squeaking in the way that emphasized the cold. Vaguely she recalled Steve's father mentioning that it only made that sound when the temperature was at or below zero. The way the still air nonetheless prickled her nose confirmed it. "*Cold* tonight."

"It is that," Trayne Owen agreed as they got into the minivan. "But a lovely clear night. The stars are bright, and—at least for the moment—I sense no shadows waiting about us."

"Yeah, don't get too relaxed. You know *this* meme, don't you?"

"Eh?" As he pulled the car out of the driveway and turned down the street, she saw him grimace. "Ah, yes, of course. The heroine on a date must be interrupted by duty, leading to some form of romantic miscommunications."

"Fuck that noise, I've said before I am *not* playing lead in a stupid romantic comedy. But yeah, if the meme gets *any* play at all, something might go wrong tonight."

"Which is why after I drop you off I will park the car and remain nearby."

"Dad, you are *not* spying on my date!"

"How else will I be able to—"

"I have a *cell phone!* If you or any of the others *has* to reach me, there you go! And I can call *you* if something happens here!"

"You . . . have a point. Such has not been an option through the prior cycles, but yes, today you have such communications. Very well."

She glanced at him with some suspicion. Not only had *she* come to accept that she *did* think of Trayne Owen as her father, she could tell that *he* thought of her as his real daughter most of the time. Which must pose something of a temptation when you were also a stealthy shape-shifting wizard and your daughter was going on her first date.

Still . . . if something bad *did* happen, it might be really, really good to have Silvertail Heartseeker mere seconds, not minutes, away. She decided to act as though he wasn't going to be there, even if he was.

Not like we were going anywhere private, right? This is just hanging out with a friend, really. I shouldn't be nervous. Holly's known Dex quite a while now, and as Steve I knew him a lot longer. Wait, though, can't think about that, not only will me-as-Steve freak out even more if I keep doing that, but also I'll be more likely to screw up and mention something that Holly Owen would never know about.

"God, maybe this was a bad idea. What am I doing? I could mess everything up—for what, just to pretend I'm a normal teenager?"

She'd been muttering to herself, but Trayne Owen still had supernaturally good hearing, as she should have remembered. "Is that really why? Are you doing this to *prove* something, Holly?"

She swallowed but found she didn't have immediate words to answer with.

"Is that why you said yes? Or did you really *want* to say yes? I seem to recall having this discussion the night Dex asked you."

"Yeah," she finally said in a small, frightened voice. "I . . . I did want to. I really . . . really *like* Dex Armitage."

"Then *stop* second-guessing your choice, Holly. The only acceptable reason to cancel so late would be if you truly did not want to go, or if there were some *concrete* reason that it would be a bad idea."

She nodded, then sat quietly, waiting, her foot absently moving nervously back and forth like a metronome with tense energy.

They pulled up in front of a brown-and-white house with a brick walkway—one Steve had been to a few times. *Boy, looks a lot bigger when you're not six foot three.*

The door opened as she and Trayne reached it, and Dex's father Rich—short for Richard Leonard Armitage, she remembered—waved them in. "Come in, Mr. Owen. This must be Holly?"

"Indeed it is. Please call me Trayne, however."

"Then you call me Rich. Welcome, Holly." Rich Armitage's smile was welcoming from beneath a light-brown beard and mustache streaked with gray. He raised his voice. "Dex! Your date is here!"

There was the sound of a door opening upstairs and quick footsteps. Then the rhythmic thump-thump-thump of someone coming down the stairs was broken by an abrupt, quick thudding. Dex skidded into view, barely catching hold of the banister to keep himself from crashing into the wall of the landing. He straightened slowly, face now flaming red with embarrassment.

His father chuckled. "Take it easy, Dex. I'm sure we all want you in one piece."

Holly found herself staring. Dex never dressed up, and in fact usually followed the same pattern of clothes year-round. Today, he was wearing black slacks, a matching sport jacket, a very nice bright-blue button-up shirt, and black shoes polished to a mirror shine. His hair had obviously just been trimmed and had the sleek, fluffy look of hair that had been brushed or combed many, many times. What trace of incipient mustache and beard he had had was gone, shaved to complete smoothness.

He looked . . . very nice.

Holly realized that Dex hadn't yet finished coming down the staircase; he was frozen in the act of straightening, staring at her, and she felt her own face heating up. *Why is he* staring *so much? I don't look* that *different!*

She'd spent probably an hour, or more, dithering over what to wear and tried everything from ultra-casual T-shirt and jeans to a formal, a slip dress, and a sheath before she'd settled on a flared black dress with sapphire accents, trimmed with lace to around ankle-length, with black knee-high stockings and polished semiformal chopped-out ballet flats. She had a few silver bracelets for accessories, and a pair of silver and sapphire-blue combs holding her hair back from falling in her face, and she'd put everything that her friends had taught her about makeup to use.

With the cold weather she'd started to think she'd made the wrong choice, but Dex didn't take his eyes off her as he finally came down the stairs. "Holly, you . . . you look . . ."—he blushed again—"*amazing*."

That helped her find her own voice, as well as made her feel that the cold outside wouldn't matter much. "You look great too, Dex. Thanks."

Both parents chuckled, and a third, higher-pitched laugh joined in. Dex's mother was standing in the doorway that Holly knew led to the kitchen, wearing a heavy winter coat. "You behave yourself, Dex," she said.

"*Mom!*"

"Where are you going, Katie?" asked Rich.

"We're out of garlic, which I can't do without. Trayne, I'm Katie Armitage. Holly, glad to meet you; Dex talks about you a lot."

At this time-honored "parent line," Dex looked acutely embarrassed.

"Only saying good things, I hope," Trayne said.

"She's apparently a paragon of all things geeky, so yes," Rich answered with a laugh. "Now I can see they're impatient to get away from the usual predate parent talk, so why don't we let them get going?"

Thank goodness.

"Certainly. Holly has my number, of course, but let me give it to both of you just in case," said Trayne.

A few minutes, and a repetition of the night's general schedule, later and Holly found herself sitting in the back seat next to Dex. *Ohmygod, I'm actually on a date now.*

"I'll drop the two of you off—it will be about seven-thirty when we get there. That should give you plenty of time to get dinner before your movie."

"Sounds fine, Mr. Owen," Dex said, his voice so tense that she heard it on the edge of cracking. Somehow, that managed to help her relax. *C'mon, this really* is *Dex's first date. At least I've gone through it on his side before. I know what's going on in his head, I think.*

The two of them sat in nervous near silence for most of the trip; it was clear that Dex wasn't sure how to talk about a date in front of her dad, but didn't know what to say to her dad either, and she had to admit that the stress of trying to be casual made *her* want to be quiet, too.

Finally the car pulled up before the glass-and-steel entrance. "All right, kids. Have fun. Holly, call me as soon as you need to be picked up. Dex, you have my number as well, yes?"

"Yes, sir. In my phone. Holly's got my parents' number too, just in case."

"Excellent. Well, have a good time and I hope you enjoy the show too."

Trayne Owen closed the van's window, and with a low rumble of its engine the vehicle—and her father—disappeared into the night.

Leaving her alone with Dexter Armitage.

✳ Chapter 47 ✳

The two of them were left standing on the sidewalk as the car vanished into darkness. Holly let out a nervous, relieved breath just as she heard an explosive sigh from Dex.

They looked at each other and burst out laughing. "Is it crazy that I'm simultaneously relieved he's finally gone and totally terrified I'm going to screw this up?" Dex said after a moment.

"No, that's, like, me too."

"*You* are worried *you* will screw this up?"

"Yeah. Can't I be nervous too?"

"Sure. I guess. I just figured . . . you always look so much more in control."

The mall didn't *look* much different, aside from the decorations that hadn't all been taken down yet. The shoggoth hadn't done that much damage compared to what it probably could have managed, but it had still taken a month before the mall reopened. *Probably part of that was the OSC's trying to go over everything with a fine-toothed comb.*

"So, where do you want to eat?"

At this point, *eating* was one of the farthest things from Holly's mind; but she knew that'd change eventually, and this was at least something to talk about. "Well . . . not at Hearty's." She suspected she'd never be able to sit in that restaurant again without keeping an eye on the bathroom door.

He made a face. "Of course not! I was planning on something better than *that*."

"You don't have to spend a lot of money on me. Heck, I can pay—"

"It's *me* taking *you* out, so I pay." He managed a grin. "If I don't mess everything up tonight, you can always ask *me* out next time. Okay?"

She smiled back. "Deal." A tiny relaxation of the knot in her gut. "Well, then, um, let's look at what our choices are."

Only a few yards away was the usual tall illuminated square sign showing the layout of the mall and a list of shops; the two of them read over the selection. "You have a budget I can't break?"

"You eat that much?"

Danger, Will Robinson! But on reflection, there wasn't going to be much she could do to hide her appetite, unless she wanted to basically starve herself through the evening and then binge-snack as soon as she got home. "Probably a lot more than you do."

His eyebrows raised. "I dunno, I eat an awful lot. But hey, fine, I still don't think you can break my budget."

"Okay, then how about Sakura Sushi and Hibachi?"

"Works for me."

He walked next to her as they headed for the escalator. Then his hand very tentatively touched hers.

Wow. You really can *get tingles from someone touching your hand.* Without even thinking about it, her hand reached out and gripped his.

They didn't let go until they reached the restaurant.

This stuttering silence is bullshit, she thought, as she stared at Dex across the dimly lit table in Sakura. "Look, did your dad give you any advice?" she asked.

"Advice?" he said, puzzled. "About what?"

"This date."

"Oh. Uh, nothing except the one you always hear, 'be yourself.' But being myself usually gets me in trouble."

Boy, do I know what that *can be like. But . . .* She suddenly laughed. He looked uncertain, as though he wasn't sure if she was laughing at him or not. "Dex, you're sitting there thinking something like 'what do I say,' right? Well, do you have any trouble saying things at the game meetings?"

"No, but that's not a—"

"Why did you *want* to ask me out? Just because I'm pretty?" *At least I don't have much of the internal conflict about whether I'm pretty or not. One advantage of starting with Steve's perspective.*

"No! I mean, you *are* beautiful." He stopped and swallowed. "I . . . can't pretend I don't see that. Right? But no, it's . . . you're . . . you're *fun*. You know how to run a game—way better than me. You know how to make people *happy*, I guess? How to see what's going to work for me, and for Caitlin, and Nikki and all, and make it all work *together*."

And there's a compliment I could love in either of my lives. She finally felt a relaxed, genuine smile spreading across her face. "And you think you don't know what to say?"

His answering smile was tentative. "Well . . . maybe. Sometimes."

"Dex, don't pretend I'm not a geek because I've dressed up. I mean, don't psych yourself out. And I shouldn't either. Because I was."

Their waiter placed the first appetizers—*gyoza*, the thin-skinned Japanese dumplings—in front of them as Dex bit his lip and then laughed. "Right. My dad said you date friends, and you're saying . . . well . . ."

". . . we're both trying to act *different* because it's a date, instead of just trying to enjoy what we *like* about each other."

"Duh. But . . . it *is* different."

She couldn't deny it. "Because we're alone, I guess. Because we *wanted* to be alone. Together."

Despite the dimness of the room, she could see his cheeks darken again. "Yeah. But . . ." He squared his shoulders, then leaned forward. "Okay, I was thinking that maybe we could alternate games. I'm not as good as you . . . you're like as good as Steve was, and believe me, that's a *big* compliment I'm giving you."

Well, I'd better be as good as Steve was, but I know what you're saying. She ignored the sudden re-realization of the situation by the part of her that *was* Steve and tried to concentrate on Dex.

"So since you're doing a steampunk-adventure type game, I've been working on a star travel game. I don't know if all the others would want to play, though."

She grabbed a dumpling, dipped it, and bit it in half. "Well, Tierra's not really a gamer as much as the rest of us. But if you give her some inspiring visuals, something to grab her artistic mind, she'll probably play, and maybe help you bring the whole thing to life."

The talk of the games—of design not just of a world but of the interaction of the people who would play it—made the tension disappear. It was something they shared, and understood, and they *clicked*. Dex's lightning-fast comprehension of rules and strategies and his ability to create designs for even fictional universes that made *sense* complemented her understanding of the interaction of the *people* in the games, the deeper strategy of long-term plots that took into account both drama and emotional requirements, and so on.

They continued talking their role-playing concepts, as the dishes arrived, were cleaned off, and more arrived to replace those. Dex, somewhat to her surprise, was matching her bite-for-bite. *Well, I guess all those jokes about teenage guys had to come from somewhere.*

". . . so why not, it's been done before; I think I even saw an old supplement of a space game with a Roman Empire–based civilization I could steal the whole thing from." Dex had his tablet out and had been taking notes while they ate.

"I think it'll work. You've got a broad base for your universe, adding that in as a sort of side area will produce some interesting interactions, and I know that Tierra loves the Greco-Roman art styles. She'll probably enjoy the idea of trying to build on that. Nikki'll be cool with the straight-up space-marine-type character, I think."

She noticed that the waiter was hovering near their table again. "Would either of you like a dessert?" His glance was half-hopeful, half-disbelieving.

Wow, did we finish our whole dinner? Or maybe dinners? She glanced at the top of her phone. "Oh my god, Dex, the movie'll be starting in like ten minutes!"

"What? Wow. We were here *that* long?" He shook his head at the waiter. "No, um, we've gotta get moving. *Doomfarers* starts at nine-fifteen!"

As they hurried down the mall toward the theater, she saw Dex glance to the side. There was a clearly different-looking section of railing there.

"Must be where they fixed it after . . . the black-ooze monster. Right?"

She remembered that particular section of railing well, as it was the one she'd stood on to challenge the shoggoth. "I guess so," she said.

"Monsters. Never thought I'd be talking about them outside of the games, though."

"Me neither," he said, and she saw him give a tiny shiver. "I mean, I kinda believed in Bigfoot—there's just too much independent evidence for me to ignore—but not . . . well, rock-worms and slime-monsters straight out of Lovecraft and whatever the hell happened at our school and stuff like that."

"But here we are going to a movie like everything's normal." It was funny how conversations like this mirrored what was going on in her head.

He was silent for a moment, but then Dex gave a shrug. "No other choice, is there?" he asked. "I mean, what're we going to do? Barricade our houses and stay inside them?" He shook his head. "Well, I guess some people are moving away. They figure things are going to stay focused around the Tri-Cities area. I dunno if they're right. But . . ." He suddenly grinned. "We also got *superheroes* in the bargain, so I'm not so worried."

Argh. I'm going to have to be talking enthusiastically about myself and my friends as though I've never met them. Because, honestly, if I didn't *know them I'd be super excited about the whole thing, so I can't act like I don't care.* "I know, right? It's like *Demon Nemesis Mystic Nanako* come to life!"

"You watched that one too?" He laughed as they stepped onto the escalator that led to the theater. "Of course you did. Sometimes it's scary how many things we've got in common." She realized they'd been holding hands all this time and it had been so *natural* that she'd hardly given it a thought, but now he squeezed her hand gently. "Even the older stuff. 'Course once you told me about the homeschooling and I saw your dad's collection I understood where *that* came from."

His face shifted to a pensive expression. "Damn, but sometimes you almost remind me of Steve."

Crap. How do I divert that *train of—*

The blue eyes widened and he winced. "I mean, just the fan stuff! Er, that is, I don't want to—"

She managed what she *hoped* was a natural-sounding laugh. "It's okay, Dex. You meant that in a good way. That I reminded you of this guy who was obviously really important to you, because we shared a lot of the same likes. Nothing wrong with that." *Whew.* "Don't be so nervous." *Sure, follow your own advice, Holly!*

"Sorry." They had reached the ticket kiosk; Dex had bought the tickets online so he just had to run his bank card through the machine and the tickets popped out. "Want a snack?"

The line was short, so they were able to snag popcorn and a couple boxes of candy, plus a bottle of water, just in time to get into the theater as the previews started. She let Dex choose the seats—about midway down. As *Doomfarers* was in its fourth week of release, there were actually a lot of empty seats, so the two of them were fairly far away from anyone else. *Is that good? Do I want to be really alone with him?*

She finally identified part of the tension, as they sat down, as excitement, anticipation that had nothing to do with the movie, and Holly had to really face the fact that she was *happy* to be here on a date. *Holy shit, I really am.*

The lights went fully down as the previews played. About the middle of the third preview—advertising some forthcoming superhero film—she sensed, rather than saw, Dex move. His arm rose up and came to rest on the seat back behind her. With exquisite, hesitant gentleness that sent a tingle down her back, he let his arm drop the tiniest bit to rest—just barely—on her shoulders.

Somewhere inside, Steve was doing the mental equivalent of closing his eyes, plugging his ears, and shouting loudly LA LA LA LA I CAN'T HEAR THIS. But that was a very, very distant protest, just one small element of a greater tension. She swallowed but did not move, holding herself as still as possible, afraid that he'd jump away if she moved at all.

Slowly . . . *very* slowly . . . he relaxed, allowing some of the weight of his arm to rest warmly across her shoulders and back, his long fingers resting on her upper arm. Holly felt her heart *bounding* within her chest, hammering so hard she was sure it must be vibrating the seats around her. She felt dizzy and her mouth was so dry she felt as though she hadn't had a drop of anything in a week. With a sensation as though it was really someone *else* doing it, she leaned toward Dex the smallest bit.

Through the thundering bass of the trailer she still heard or felt the catch of his own breathing, and as her head came gently against his shoulder, she felt the vibration of his own pulse. *He's as scared and excited as I am. Holy . . . everything, Silvertail, what the* hell *have you got me into?*

A scattering of cheers echoed around the theater at the end of the trailer, and Holly realized that she had literally no idea of what the trailer had been about. *I'd better focus! What's the point of a movie date if you never see the movie?*

She remembered a few friends—of Steve's, anyway—who would've said something like "Those are the *best* kind of movie dates," but she'd actually really been looking forward to seeing if this adaptation of one of her favorite books was any good.

Dex must have been of a similar mind, because while he kept his arm around her, his head stayed mostly turned to the screen and he grinned broadly as the scene faded from the Prince's victorious duel in the rain to a more modern combat setting. "Looks good so far," he murmured to her.

"We'll see. But yeah, it does!"

She had no intention of ever moving, but by the time modern weaponry had prevailed over a raging dragon, she couldn't sit still any longer. "Dex, I have to go."

"Go?" Then he caught on. "Oh, the bathroom. Okay, but try not to take too long or you'll miss something good!"

"I know!"

Holly carefully edged out past the seats and the one young man seated on the end of the aisle, then walked quickly toward the bathrooms. *I always need to go more often when I'm nervous anyway.*

After she finished, she went to check her makeup and hair. On impulse she pulled out her phone and dialed Seika's number.

It rang about half a ring before she heard Seika's voice: "Well? How's it going?"

She tried to keep from sounding, well, like a stereotype, but her voice insisted on answering in a whisper that rose to an undeniably girlish squeal: "It's fine and dinner was great and then he put his *arm* around me in the theater and my *God* I'm so nervous!"

Seika laughed. "So it's all cool there?"

"Yeah, I've got to get back, anyway. Probably won't be home before midnight, though, so I'll have to tell you about it tomorrow."

"You *better!* But I'll let you—"

Even through the phone, the distant scream was piercing. The spurt of fear came with the recognition of the voice. "That's—"

"*VAN!*" Seika and, more distantly, her parents called out. The sound of running footsteps, as Seika dashed to her brother's room.

Holly gritted her teeth and tried not to demand to know what was going on. It'd do them no good to try to talk on the phone while dealing with Van.

But the fragments she heard made her blood run cold. ". . . at my window . . . black claws . . . standing outside . . ."

Finally she couldn't wait any longer. "Seika! Seika, what's *happening*?"

Seika's voice was grim. "Holly, I really, really hate to do this . . . but I think this is Maiden business.

"Van said he heard a noise outside his window, turned, and saw something reaching out—a hand or claw that he says was almost as wide as the window. He was frozen, couldn't move, and then he saw a figure, a silhouette just outside of the window, looking in."

"Looking in *Van's* window? But that's—"

"—fifteen, twenty feet up. Yeah. And . . . I've got a real bad feeling, like the room's even colder than it should be."

She looked around the women's room; it seemed to be deserted. "Silvertail, we've got trouble," she announced to the room at large.

"I heard," Silvertail answered, his voice faint but clear. "Tell her to call the others immediately. You will have to disengage yourself from young Armitage."

Damn this goddamn meme to hell. I knew *something like this would happen. But I can't ignore it. If something happened to any of Seika's family . . .*

"On it. Seika, can I use you as an excuse?"

"Sure, just let me know what story you gave so I can match it. We might be taking Van to the hospital—he's really freaky and seems kinda sick."

Silvertail appeared on the counter next to her. "Sick? Weak and pale?"

"Yeah, he looks almost grayish."

"That *could* be simple emotional shock . . . or something worse. Yes, get him to the hospital . . . Saint Michael's, not Bellview. I haven't warded Bellview."

Seika's fear was palpable in her voice. "Oh god, you think Van's in danger?"

"I think it's best to assume the worst rather than ignore the possibility."

"Mom, Dad, Silvertail says take Van to Saint Michael's *now*!"

"I'll catch up with you as soon as I can," Holly said. "Call the others!"

"I will. Holly—hurry. I'm . . . scared now."

"Fast as I can."

Crap.

She looked down and sighed. "I guess you'd better go get the car."

✳ Chapter 48 ✳

"What was Van doing before he saw the . . . being?" Trayne asked Seika. "Did he say? Did you notice anything?"

Seika glanced around, but Holly noticed that despite being in the hospital lounge, no one was paying attention to them.

Trayne noticed the direction of their gazes. "A minor and subtle enchantment; nothing we say in this room will be noticed or remembered by anyone not involved."

Seika nodded. "I don't know. His computer was on, but . . . well, I was *worried*! I didn't check it out, I was too busy trying to see if there was anything out there."

"How'd it *get* to Van at all, though? You said our houses were warded, Dad!"

"*That* is precisely my concern. It could not have affected Van unless something he did weakened the defenses, at least with respect to Van himself."

"Is that . . . possible?"

Trayne's lips tightened to a thin line. "Very. For example, the connection that Cordy had to the tyrpiglynt would have allowed it to affect her even if all its mirrors were removed from the house."

Cordelia shuddered. "So what you're saying is that if Van had somehow been, well . . . *touched* by this thing . . . ?"

". . . it would at least be able to manifest near the house and touch it, without being destroyed, and produce this . . . exhaustion, enervation, that is currently affecting him." He looked back to Seika, who was sitting between Holly and Devika. "Did any of you turn his computer *off*?"

Seika thought for a moment. "No. No, I'm sure no one did. I was on the phone with Holly when it happened, so it wasn't more than a few minutes before you told us we had to go to the hospital. Mom and Dad just grabbed what we needed for a hospital trip and wait in the ER and ran."

He nodded. "Then in all likelihood anything he was looking at should still be there. Had Van been acting any differently? Anything unusual?"

Seika scrunched up her face. "Not . . . really. Honestly, I know this will sound so stupid, but he's just my little brother. He plays and talks with his friends and I don't notice much of it. I think I *would* have noticed if he really went through a big change, but . . . I guess he's been more interested in monsters and such, but that's no surprise."

"No, I'm afraid not." He sighed. "I see no other choice but that I must go examine his room, and swiftly."

"Not by yourself," Holly and Devika said simultaneously. Holly blinked, grinned, and nodded to Devika, who went on, "You were ambushed once already. Two of us should go with you, at least, and the rest of us will stay in case Van's actually a target."

Trayne spread his hands in acceptance. "I cannot argue your logic. Then Seika and Holly are the obvious choices."

Holly stood. "All right, then we'd better get a move on."

"Tell my parents where we've gone," Seika said, to which the other three nodded. "And we'll make sure they're all safe," added Tierra. "You have your phones, right?"

"Yeah. See you."

"Creepypasta," Seika said. She managed to make the word sound like both a vindication and a curse.

"Well, if he was into monsters and stuff, that makes sense."

"Yeah, but that site has stuff that's *really* over the top for someone that young! He shouldn't be on it!"

"Let us focus more on what the young man was actually interested in, rather than what he *should* have been looking at," Silvertail said. He was sniffing around the monitor and the window.

"You sense anything?"

"Something *very* alien and hostile was here, and not long ago. And there is a sense that something penetrated the ward, at least to a small degree—and the state of the ward tells me that this had to have been caused from within."

Holly found herself staring with horror at Silvertail; Seika's expression echoed her feelings. "Silvertail, are you saying he deliberately *called* . . . whatever it was?"

"Not necessarily," Silvertail answered after a pause, the words coming with careful deliberation. "Simply *thinking* of certain things can draw their attention, if your thoughts happen to be clear and focused enough. Can you determine precisely what interested him?"

Replaying the video that had been on the page, and backing through Van's browser history, answered that quickly enough. "Slendy. The Slender Man."

Holly remembered reading about that. "Ugh. That fits too well."

"Describe this 'Slender Man' to me. I need to get a sense of what kind of being would be likely to be embodied in the meme—that is, what of the many beings that exist would have been drawn to this concept and made it real."

Holly pursed her lips. "Well, I went through some of this a while back—you even did a quick look-through with me." As she talked, she skimmed various articles to refresh her memory. "He's usually described as an excessively tall manlike being who's very thin—thus the 'slender' bit—with arms and legs even longer in proportion to his body than they should be. A lot of images and stories give him tentacles that come from his back, but he can apparently hide them. He's always dressed in a black suit. His face . . . isn't, mostly, sort of like a regular head wrapped in bandages. There's usually hints of features but he doesn't actually *have* eyes or a working nose or mouth."

Silvertail's rodent features were already set in a grim expression—the ears tense, the whiskers twitching. "Associations? Goals or actions? Other powers?"

"Forests," Seika said; she was now paging through information on her laptop. "He appears in forests a lot. Lures children into them. There's argument over what his real interest in children is—does he just want to terrify them, kill them, control them, whatever. He can just appear and disappear, maybe from shadows. Hides his appearance, does what the game *Vampire* calls 'obfuscate'—he can be seen walking through a crowd by children but adults won't notice anything strange. Cameras aren't fooled, though."

Silvertail cursed in what had to be Lemurian. "That is all too accurate. People, and even animals, can be misled by illusions, seemings, and compulsions, but if it has no mind or spirit, it cannot be so affected. Is this Slender Man a popular, er, 'creepypasta'?"

"Probably *the* most popular. There's a few others that got some traction, but none of them would compare to Slendy," Holly said. "And a lot of the stories say that the more you *learn* about him, the more you *think* about him, the closer he gets, the more power over you he has."

A high-pitched hiss emerged from Silvertail's mouth.

Seika looked narrowly at the little rat. "You've figured it out already."

"I am afraid so. There is, I suppose, good news and bad news here. Which would you like first?"

"Ummm . . . Gimme the bad news first?" Holly said after a moment. "That way I've got an antidote ready."

"Perhaps not. The impeccably dressed monster, one who is powerful, who hides in the shadows, who corrupts, controls, or destroys those who learn of him, whose face is never seen—I believe this is the avatar, the embodiment of the emissary of the Nine-Armed, her herald and executioner, Nyarlathotep itself."

Something about the way Silvertail pronounced the name made Holly shiver. "And because Van was interested in him, reading about him . . . ?"

". . . because of that, yes, he established a link with the concept and thus the being which allowed it to find him even through the wards. The power of this meme is clearly great enough; Nyarlathotep must make an appearance in any event, as he or it is also the patron and empowerment of Queen Nyarla."

"Well, that's pretty damn bad news. What's the *good* news?"

Silvertail's furry smile was coldly uncomforting. "Unfortunately it is only good in the sense that we are coming to the end of our road. The confrontation with the Crawling Chaos, the Herald Who Opens the Way, means that the stars are very nearly right. We have weeks only, at most."

Holly felt a slow, creeping chill moving from her very *ankles* upward, and it had nothing to do with knowing how close the final confrontation was; if anything, that *was* good news, the knowledge that there weren't months of monsters still waiting for them.

No. It had to do with her finally understanding something she had always wondered vaguely about, but never quite gotten around to asking. "Silvertail," she said slowly, carefully, "by thinking about him, by *knowing* about him, we've made him . . . real, incarnate. We've called him to us. And because so many people have thought about this form of Nyarlathotep, he's that much stronger—he's connected to *all* of those people."

He nodded.

"Oh, *fuck*," Seika breathed. "And that's true for *all* of these monsters, isn't it?"

"Yes."

"Jesus, Thor, and Isis," Holly muttered, wondering if she should have worked Olorun, Izanagi, and a few others into that list. "*That's* why those bastards are unleashing all the monsters, one after the other. That's why *Nyarla* is hiding, but her *servants* are all about smashing malls and chopping kids down on Halloween. They're not trying to kill the *Maidens*—though they'd love it. They're making people *think* about them. Making people *fear* them." Her eyes met Seika's, wide with the same terrible understanding. "Making people *believe in them*."

Silvertail closed his eyes in assent.

"We're *calling* them," Seika finished in a horrified whisper. "It's the *human race* that's going to 'make the stars right' and let Nyarla open the Gateway for Azathoth Nine-Armed!"

✳ Chapter 49 ✳

Silvertail looked at the fearful faces of the two girls and sighed. "Yes. And now you understand all the rest: why I could not predict with accuracy *when* the time would come, why our enemies prefer to use such . . . spectacular means to draw you out, why I have avoided giving you details on the various and sundry *possible* foes you may face . . . and why the cycle can never be ended. Humanity is its own beacon in the darkness, and the brightness of our lives is also what draws the alien and monstrous to us—to consume, to enslave, or to destroy."

"We can't . . . hide ourselves?" Seika asked.

Silvertail laughed, hearing the bitterness in his own voice. "Had we of Lemuria fully understood our peril and our enemies in the earliest days? Perhaps. After all had fallen, and the cycle ongoing had shown me the truth . . . I tried. There was one cycle I tried. I traveled the world, engraving symbols into earth and stone, at the tops of mountains, in the depths of the sea, sent aloft to bind themselves at the boundaries of space and sky, whispered by the calls of beast and bird. But it failed. Oh, the cycle began far later that time, and so I knew it was *possible*. But not with one weakened practitioner of the art, not with so little power remaining on the world except at the time of our enemies' greatest strength."

He pushed the bitterness and grim memory and fear from his heart. "But even if I could . . . now, I would not. It would be a barrier saying that we dare not step beyond our world, beyond that which these monsters would allow. It would be an admission of cowardice. And

I—like you, Holly—believe they also fear us, as you saw when you looked *Beyond* and realized the truth of your power. We cannot, and shall not, cower behind a wall hoping the monsters will ignore us. We will meet them, and throw them back, a thousand thousand times if we must."

Holly's head came up, and Seika took a breath and raised hers as well. "Right."

"But . . ." Holly looked out into the night. "Doesn't that mean that now *we* might be . . . well, connected to it as well?"

"I am afraid so. I, of course, have had literal millennia to perfect my own personal defenses, else I would long since have been sought out and destroyed, but while the *power* of the Maidens is eternal, the rebirth in each era means that you begin with no more spiritual defenses than anyone else. And, unfortunately, defenses against that subtle spiritual connection are *very* hard to create."

Seika's face had acquired an uncharacteristically hard edge. "Fine with me. I *want* to meet this asshole. He's put my baby brother in a *hospital*."

"Not by *ourselves* we don't want to meet him," Holly said. "If he's the right tentacle of the Big Bad, he's going to be rougher than anything else we've fought, except maybe Procelli." Her face tightened as a new thought struck her. "And Van's probably not the only one. That meme's been around for a few *years* now. That guy, um, Knudsen? Yeah, Eric Knudsen, he invented the Slender Man like in 2009. So if that's what Nyarlathotep hooked himself to . . ."

All too likely. Silvertail tapdanced over the keys of the computer, looked at the results of his search, refined it . . . "Yes. There has been a *definite* upswing in sightings, and reports of illnesses, madness, and even deaths, since this began. It is clear he has been gathering his strength all along."

Holly looked at him. "Can we tell if he's *out* there?"

Silvertail shrugged, stretching out his perceptions, but felt nothing. "The wards attenuate my exterior senses, and Nyarlathotep is very adept both at hiding his presence from other spirits, and at traveling through space and shadow."

"Shadow? Fudge. That's going to be a *pain*."

"Yes. Shadows—of the metaphorical *and* physical reality—are one of his primary powers."

Seika snorted and pushed past them, running down the stairs. "Come *on*."

Silvertail allowed Holly to pick him up as she followed; from her expression, she was just as puzzled as he was by Seika's action. The puzzlement evaporated when he saw Seika stop before an inconspicuous monitor set into the wall. "You said he can't fool cameras, right?"

Well thought, Seika. "Indeed. His image cannot be hidden from that which does not think, and within the wards—even with whatever connection you may now have—he will be unable to distract you from the image."

Seika activated the security monitors and started clicking through the camera views. "Nothing in front of the house. Nothing in the garage. Side toward the Hansens . . . nothing. Rear of the house—" She gave a sudden gasp.

Towering up above the rear deck—standing at least ten feet high—was a freakishly attenuated figure, a stretched-out man with pipe-thin arms and legs, dressed in an impeccably clean and neat black suit. His arms ended in hideously long, curled fingers tipped with edged, curved, glittering claws like polished onyx daggers; from their vantage point, Silvertail couldn't see his feet. In the glow of the deck lights—a glow that was somehow weaker and less certain—something moved and squirmed and shifted and waved behind the figure, tendrils of living darkness barely visible against the gloom of night.

But the head was the worst.

It was an elongated ellipse, pallid and somehow fungoid in texture, without eyes or nose or mouth; there were no ears, no hair, just spongy almost-smoothness over *hints*, eerie and unsettling *hints* of features—faint hollows where eyes should have been, a suggestion of a rise in the center of the face, just the slightest indication of a crease below the not-nose.

And that hint of a mouth turned upward, became the spectre of a smile. The huge, skeletal figure bent in a terrible mockery of a courteous bow, and swept its hand in an unmistakable gesture:

Come out.

"He somehow *knows* we are watching," said Silvertail, and despite his best efforts heard a trace of fear in his voice. "How? Did the camera move?"

"No. These are fixed cameras, not PTZ," Seika said, her voice almost a whisper.

"Well, screw him, I'm not coming out yet." Holly pulled out her phone. "There's other guests to invite, after all."

As Holly did that, Seika touched another control on the security system, setting it to a regular scan of the perimeter. At his questioning glance, she said, "Just making sure he doesn't move—or didn't bring any friends that might surround the house or something."

"Good thinking, Seika."

Devika picked up on the other end of Holly's phone before the first ring was complete; Silvertail could hear her speak. "Yes?"

"We've got our new friend waiting for us outside."

There was a burst of interference, but the connection didn't drop . . . yet. *He may sense she is trying to contact the others; Nyarlathotep* was *associated with science and learning as well as other, less savory pursuits.* "—eed us?"

"Do we need you? Yeah. Silvertail says this guy's one of the worst."

Another snarl of static. "Y . . . break . . . up. On our way. Let—"

The connection went dead.

"Crap. Cut off. Seika?"

Seika pulled out her phone. "I'm not even getting bars. Guess he decided we shouldn't call our friends."

Holly grinned. "Well, too late for that. Devika says they're on their way."

"Then we'd better dress for the occasion!"

Just watching the two girls transform lifted Silvertail's spirits. Nyarlathotep was hellishly dangerous, yes . . . but he had been beaten many times before, and *these* Maidens were *special.*

Of course, he reminded himself, the Crawling Chaos might well have become stronger too. The power of such a meme, spread across the world, concentrated in the minds of so many . . . no, it would not do to be overconfident.

But the very presence of the light buoyed his spirit, and he saw in their smiles and stances that it did the same for them.

"We going out?" Holly asked.

"No way," Seika said, even before Silvertail could answer. "He can't get in here—or he'd have done it. We wait until *all* of us are here, and *then* we go lay the smackdown on him."

"Makes sense. Just hope it doesn't take them too long."

Silvertail gave a smile that made his whiskers tilt up in front of his eyes. "Remember your own swiftness over the rooftops, Holy Aura; they will be here in a few minutes, I think."

They were quiet for a minute, then Seika said, "Hey, since we're waiting—Holly, what *did* you say to Dex?"

Holy Aura didn't look happy, but she managed a tiny grin. "The truth. Mostly."

"The *truth*?"

"Well, not about *us*, duh, but about your baby brother getting sick and you being all upset and wanting me there."

"So what'd he say?"

"He wasn't *happy* about it, but he didn't argue. Said of course I had to go."

Seika looked narrowly at her. "You *did* make sure he didn't think you *wanted* to bail on him, right? 'Cause it'd be easy for Dex, nervous as he is, to have decided that he'd done something to creep you out."

"I did what I could to alleviate that myself," Silvertail interjected. "I asked Holly which hospital we were going to when I picked the two of them up. That should have made it clear to young Dexter that there was no subterfuge involved."

"Plus I told him I'd call him tomorrow or the day after to set up another—look!"

A flicker of movement—two—three, all in front of Seika's house. Even in the gray-toned image of the security camera, the three Apocalypse Maidens glowed with power and purpose. The camera view switched to the rear, and Nyarlathotep was straightening, the featureless face rising as though realizing something had arrived.

But Seika had already opened the front door. "Get inside, quick!"

Even with the speed of the Apocalypse Maidens, they were nearly too slow; as the door closed, a lash of solidified darkness whipped out, but only brushed the heel of Tsunami Reflection's boot as Seika yanked the door shut. "*Damn* he's fast!"

"Who's fast? And why are we in here? I thought we were coming here to kick ass!" Tierra demanded.

Devika gave her one of her patented "you're not *thinking*" looks. "*Obviously* because they've got something to *tell* us about our enemy before we go charging in and get *our* asses kicked. My lessons, remember them!"

"Ha! Infected you are by the memes, speak like Yoda you will!" Seika said. "But yes, we've got intel on our enemy, and it's *not* fun-time stuff."

At her nod, Silvertail briefed the others on what they knew about their adversary. Devika and Cordy exchanged glances, while Tierra looked more serious and then looked to Devika and Holly.

"So," Devika said, glancing at the screen which showed the attenuated figure calmly waiting outside, "probably as powerful as the tyrpiglynt, controls shadows, mind influencing, can add in tentacles as needed. That a good summary?"

"Reasonably so, yes."

Devika frowned, but then her face cleared. "I think I've got some tactics that could work." She outlined several approaches—modified by occasional interjections by the other girls—and Silvertail nodded his approval. *She has excellent instincts in this. Holly is the leader, but Devika's tactics will make them more formidable still, and Cordelia's insight into how to encourage and motivate them helps tie the group together—and restrains both Holly and Tierra from their more impulsive actions.*

"Now, remember, we escalate *in order*. If we don't *have* to turn it to eleven, let's not give them a look at what's past the max on the dial," Devika said.

Tierra wrinkled her face as though smelling something bad. "Isn't that like, what'd you call it . . . making us *re*active instead of active? I thought that was bad."

Holly shook her head. "No, we're going to *act*. We're going to try to control this battle, at least some. What she's saying is we're trying to keep a *reserve*, so our enemies don't know *everything* we can do. Remember, if Silvertail's right, we might be more badass than the prior incarnations, and wouldn't it be great if we can *hide* some of that until we finally get to give the Big Bad the beatdown?"

Tierra nodded after a moment. "Okay, I got it."

Silvertail's moment of optimism began to fade, replaced by the old, familiar, yet never blunted edge of worry and fear for these children he was forced to hide behind. The five girls stepped toward the sliding door to the patio . . . and out.

The cadaverous figure unbent, rising to its full height as they did so, and the sensation of a smile emanated from it. Nyarlathotep bowed deeply and then spread its arms, and even without speech somehow its meaning was clear: *Welcome, Maidens. I have been waiting for you.*

"That's right, we were waiting to meet you too," Radiance Blaze said, and there was no smile on *her* face. She raised her arm, and the other four raised theirs. "You have spread terror in the shadows of the world, and used the tools of knowledge for the creation of fear and corruption!" Seika's voice took on an edge of personal fury. "You have wounded the souls of children and left them to die and worse, and for that"—the other Maidens' voices joined in, in perfect synchrony—"the Apocalypse Maidens say that *you*"—all fingers pointed, and then thumbs raised and thrust toward the earth—"are going *down*!"

The towering, gaunt figure tilted its head. The impression was of a sardonic smile. It beckoned once, twice, and then vanished into the shadows of Seika's large, partially wooded back yard.

The preparation of the Maidens showed; though Seika obviously wanted to simply unleash fire upon their adversary, the five advanced carefully, fanning out in an arc. Holly spun the Silverlight Bisento and then stabbed upward. "Silverlight *Beacon*!"

A spark of pure white light streaked from the blade, shot upward, and detonated, becoming a hovering, shimmering sphere of luminance that banished the gloom below and lit up the yard.

Instantly the black-clad skeletal shape was visible, standing at the edge of the sparse woods. Its arms were upraised, and one moved slightly, as though to shield its nonexistent face from the holy light. But there was still the impression of a smile, and then they saw it.

Movement.

Movement beneath the trees. Movement *throughout* the scattered trees. Something—*many* somethings—approaching, emerging from the shadowed dimness. And as the figures became clearer, Silvertail heard himself give vent to a Lemurian oath.

Blank-eyed, implacable in their motion, faces contorted in fear or hatred or loathing, streaming out of the woods on either side of the Crawling Chaos they came. Not nightgaunts, or zombies, or monsters, but something far more terrible, far more difficult to oppose, and the Maidens shrank back, horror eloquent in their poses.

Children.

✳ Chapter 50 ✳

"Oh, *fuck*," Radiance Blaze breathed, equal parts shock and anger mingled in her voice.

Holly gripped the *bisento* tighter. *Devika, this wasn't in the script!*

An impression of a humorless smile from the towering Sikh girl, even taller in her form as Tempest Corona. *"No battle plan survives contact with the enemy," some German guy once said. But this isn't a showstopper.*

Tierra and Cordy stared at her. "You're kidding!"

The children were closing in, and Holly found herself taking a step backward; her friends followed suit, their motions unsure in the flare-light and shifting shadow.

But Devika *was* smiling. *They're* children. *Not monsters. Remember how fast we are? How carefully we've trained? Trust me.* Flickering impressions, mental gestures, tracing angles and directions. *We take* him *out, I don't think the children will be a problem. Except maybe figuring out how to get them home.*

"Then let's *go*!" Tsunami Reflection leapt forward, bounding over the heads of the nearest children. The other four sprang after her, following the converging directions Devika had laid out to take them to Nyarlathotep.

Tsunami landed in a momentarily clear spot—and fell flat on her face with a bone-jarring *thud*. "What—" Holy Aura began, as she also landed.

Her attempt to continue her bounding progress came to a stunning halt, as her foot *refused* to leave the snow-powdered ground; her body continued its forward momentum, and she smashed down, only her right arm and the shaft of the Silverlight Bisento to reduce the impact. To her left and right she heard a swift sequence of matching, crashing sounds; all five of the Apocalypse Maidens had fallen.

And now they were in the middle of the mob of children.

The glaze-eyed girls and boys turned with a dreamlike slowness. Holly tried to rise but now her hand and arm were stuck, the *bisento* shifting a hair but mostly immobile, like something held down by a dozen ties. But there was nothing *there*, just the sliding, eye-baffling motion of shadow and light.

She jerked her body sideways, *hard*, evading a slow lunge by the first nearby child, and managed to yank her arm free, the weapon coming up as well. But her legs were firmly held, and she had nowhere to go. Around her, she heard sounds telling her the others were in trouble as well. *What is it? How are we—*

As she brought the Silverlight Bisento around, ball-end first, in a slow but firm motion that shoved back and knocked over the nearest children, understanding struck her. *Shadows.*

Fuck fuck fucking fucker's really fucked us with this, Radiance Blaze's thought confirmed. Now that she understood, Holly could *see*, could recognize that the shadows were *twining* around her, not merely shifting with the movement but solidifying, becoming translucent bonds that hugged the ground and pulled anything they wanted into an almost unbreakable contact with the earth.

Two children landed on her back, gripping hard to her shoulders, one around her neck. She reached up, disengaged one with care, but that took *time*, another was now holding her right arm, two more on the *bisento*, the mob closing in. *Silvertail! Silvertail, I know what to do, but I can't get free!*

But Silvertail did not respond; all she could sense from him was a horrific paralysis, not physical but spiritual, and she understood all too well. His knowledge and training told him that a few children were a small price to pay to save the world . . . but he was utterly incapable of giving such an order.

And . . . I wouldn't want him to be, she thought, even while her sight was darkened by another child, a little girl, grabbing her head and hair and holding on like grim death itself. Holy Aura had the first child off, and a second, but for every one she removed two more were there, grabbing hold with silent desperation, a grim and macabre implacability of purpose in the motion even if awareness itself was absent from the fear-filled, blank gazes. *Seika! Cordy! Tierra! Devika! Can't* any *of you move?*

But she could feel the same desperate immobility from all of them, the recognition that they *could* break free . . . if only they could accept injury or death to some of their tiny assailants.

And none of them could.

A wave of cold amusement struck them, a nigh-palpable force of frozen mirth and contempt. She heard, through the now almost suffocating layer of children blanketing her, the faint crunch of snow as Nyarlathotep approached.

Failure was always your destiny, came the thought, a thought that was not words, but the entire *concept* of failure, a leaden weight of despair in the gut, a sodden and chilling blanket of certain defeat. The cold of the air was now nothing to the freezing ache spreading through her soul. *Even hope was the snare, the delusion to draw you to this ending.*

Despite her will fighting against it, despite her *knowledge* of what the ancient Thing was doing to her, the utter weight of loss, of the wretched ending of all things, pressed in upon her. Even the Maidens were but five tiny people; they might blaze as brightly as a star, but they were on a world that spun endlessly through inconceivable gulfs of absolute night, where even the true stars were dwarfed by the imperative of blackness, of the dominance of shadows deeper than black. She heard a faint gasp of hopeless defiance escape her, felt the weak, futile struggles of the others through the bond that, itself, was fading like the last traces of hope, and sagged farther, her face brushing the chill snow whose cold now radiated up to embrace her.

And then a cheerful, sunny laugh cut through the winter of loss. There was the whistling shriek of a blade cutting the air, and a flash of deep blue-violet light that she somehow saw even through all obstructions, light that passed in an instant across all her nonexistent field of view. A momentary wave of delicious heaviness rolled over her, the feeling of being in bed, about to roll over for another two hours of wonderful sleep.

In that moment, as her eyelids became so heavy that she could barely keep them open, the children suddenly slumped, sliding almost bonelessly to the ground. Their eyes were no longer blank, but falling closed, and they lay in the positions they fell, unmoving. At the same time her own feeling of sleepiness passed and Holly found she could rise, but the immobility of the children sent a pang of fear through her heart. "What happened? Are they—"

She saw Nyarlathotep, the hint of a smile gone, the towering scarecrow figure glaring sightlessly upward, and turned.

The figure standing on ethereal light smiled and laughed again. "Nay, fair Princess Holy Aura; they are but resting. For is it not in the very twilight before the dawn that dreams lie most heavily upon us?" He spun his silvery rapier and then pointed it at the monster. "Now let us see what manner of vile coward it is who hides behind children!"

Prince Twilight Dawn darted down to engage Nyarlathotep himself.

How powerful is *this guy?*

He cannot be that *powerful,* Silvertail said, absolute certainty in his thoughts. *I have had knowledge of all powers of the past and present, and there are limits to any powers that are not the Maidens or their adversaries.*

The others had risen, shaking off the pile of sleeping children. Even as they gathered themselves, Prince Twilight Dawn dodged a slashing blow from the cadaverous figure, passing between two broad, dark trees—

—and slammed to a halt, caught like an insect in a web of shadow, traceries of darkness adhering to him as tightly as shadows trace the contours of the ground.

"Oh *no* you don't!" Tierra said sharply, seeing the clawed hand drawn back for a blow at the helpless young man, and brought her heel down in a tremendous axe kick.

The earth split in a straight line between Nyarlathotep and Twilight Dawn, razor-edged shards of stone *fountaining* from the rift, and the skeletal shape disappeared momentarily into the darkness beneath the trees rather than face the impact of those projectiles.

And rose out of the shadow stretching *behind* Tierra.

A warning thought from Holy Aura and the others was the only thing that saved Tierra; she fell flat, the air screaming around the talons that carved the space she had been an instant before.

Crap and double-crap! Shadow teleport? That's one of the really broken *powers! Who rolled this guy up?*

GM's pet NPC, obviously, Tierra thought back as she somersaulted away. Nyarlathotep faded back into the darkness and the five Maidens stared around, searching, while still trying to keep an eye on the dim forms of their friends.

Wait a minute, Holly thought. *They shouldn't be dim . . .*

She snapped her gaze skyward, saw that the Silverlight Beacon's light, moments ago brilliant, clear, pure, was dimming, fading. It was no longer a shining white sphere but a dim, gray circle, shedding barely any light.

Silvertail! Why is the Beacon going out?

It is not, he replied, his mental tone grim and fearful.

Even as he said it, she understood. Shadows were gathering, *rising* around them, smoke-glass murkiness reducing all shapes within to the merest adumbration of their true sharpness and hue. The shade-mist *clung*, not merely obscuring but impeding, and the gray-white oval of the Elder Thing's not-face faded in and out, now near Tsunami, now looking over Radiance Blaze's shoulder, again but a pace from Tempest Corona, then towering above Holly herself, and the impression of a cruel and covetous smile was even stronger.

"Twilight Dawn! Can you free yourself?" she called out.

"Alas . . . fair Princesses, I am well and truly ensnared," Prince Twilight Dawn replied; his voice sounded as though it was a mile away, and receding. "I must beg succor from all of you, when I had thought to be the rescuer!"

Movement in the tenebrous dimness and she lashed out with the *bisento*, its light faded but not wholly erased as it cut through air as dark as ocean depths. But she cut nothing but air, the figure fading to her left. *Dammit! But maybe if I keep it up . . .*

But no; she heard similar attempts by the others, the rattle-whip-sizzle of Radiance Blaze's chains, the shockwave impact of Temblor Brilliance's heels hammering the ground, the keening whine of Tsunami Reflection's twin swords and the deeper sighing moan as Tempest Corona's huge blade ripped the air, Nyarlathotep or perhaps illusions of him taunting them all.

And then she realized she did not know where she was.

Crap. I've gotten turned around, moved, lunged after him once too many times. I can't see anything past my feet! Silvertail!

But there was no answer. Even the sense of the others was muffled, almost inaudible in her mind, and the feel of their enemy was all around her.

But we need not be enemies, she heard—or merely felt?—from the darkness.

"Oh, come *on*. Like that's going to work. Procelli—"

Procelli? A child of great power, without the wisdom to understand. The merest hint of a pitying smile. *But you are not truly* happy *to be in this war, are you? Of course not. You understand* duty, *you understand* necessity, *but these are not your* goals. *What do you* want?

"Never ask that question," she muttered, but the voice that was not a voice was *in* her head, pushing at her mind, confusing her. And then she saw another shape in the darkness . . . a shape that became clearer and clearer.

Her own shape. Her face, her hair, her armor, but all touched with onyx and obsidian where silver and light might have been, and with darkness and fear written across the face in its paleness and the lines etched at forehead, eyes, mouth.

Uncertainty, fear, doubt; you throw yourself at powers ancient before your species was more than a possibility, and for nothing. If your powers fail, you will be crushed.

"And if I don't fight, I'll be crushed too. And my whole world turned to a living hell—"

The soundless laugh cut her off. *Of course that is what the sorcerer has told you. But surely you do not believe that. Why expend the effort to conquer a world that is not even what we* want, *and then the effort to* transform *it? All we wish is the end of this cycle, this weapon, and the sorcerer himself—who forged this weapon, you Maidens, to seek our destruction.*

"Oh, *please*," she said, trying to shake the doubts that the dizzying, directionless nonwords were planting within her. "Like I haven't heard *this* speech in a dozen different books." She tried to keep her voice light, her words easy and dismissive, but despite her resolve she found herself questioning, once more, Silvertail's true nature, his ultimate goals. *Dammit! It's . . . shadows. Playing with shadows metaphorically as well as literally. Shadows of doubt, shades of possibility and meaning. That's Nyarlathotep's* power.

It paused, but the impression was of a raised eyebrow and another smile, a pitying shake of the head. *Believe as you will, Maiden, but if you were to lay down your weapons, fight not against us, you will not be destroyed. You will be* protected, *and you will be free to return to . . .*

A sudden flash of stunned amazement, followed almost instantaneously by a soundless laugh. *Ahhh, so* that *is the source of your unprecedented power!* Eagerness and emphasis. *Then know that you may return to yourself, unmolested, unopposed, and we shall reward you. The sorcerer alone is our true target, and if he and his enchantment are broken, you and yours need fear nothing more from us.*

And suddenly Holy Aura laughed. It was no touch of bravado, no act, she suddenly found herself laughing with such pure amusement that Nyarlathotep recoiled from her, the very shadows drew back for the barest moment at her response. "Go *back*? That's the biggest joke of all. After all this . . . *I don't want to go back!*"

She clenched her hands and concentrated on her *self*, on who she had *become* ever since Silvertail Heartseeker had found Stephen Russ and, and the tiniest glow appeared, a shimmer of silver. "And you? You use children as chew toys and soldiers. I don't care if you'd leave us alone or not—we've already told you, you are going *down*!"

Holly leapt back as huge taloned hands cut through the darkness, felt the shadows trying to slow her down, and called out, focusing as hard as she could through the Coronet. *Maidens! All of you—it's time! Devika's second-to-last option!*

And—very faintly—she heard their assent, at first distant, with echoes of the fear and uncertainty that the alien creature had been directing at them as well, and then strengthening, becoming more clear and strong, as they realized that all of them had managed, once more, to stay true to themselves.

With a spin of the *bisento*, Princess Holy Aura cut through the shadow of herself, dispersing it to noisome-smelling vapor. She parried another strike, then felt the resistance fade. She tried to spin, but the immense hands were now wrapped around her arms, claws digging in, trying to pierce her Maiden's armor.

Got you.

She dropped the *bisento* and whipped her own hands up, clamping down in a viselike grip one of the fingers holding each arm. She sensed its startlement and sudden understanding—with a firm grip on it, her hands shimmering slightly with power, Nyarlathotep could not *escape* her, not unless and until it could break that grip.

Which it would do in moments, of course—the creature's strength was immense—but moments were all she needed. "In the name of those you have taken, for the sake of faith in a friend," she began, and felt the power rising, sensed her bond with the others echoing her words, and reverberating with other words in turn, "by the power of the spirit and the imperishable light of the stars themselves—"

And together five voices shouted out as one, "RELEASE!"

Light *exploded* from her body, dispelling the shadows like mists before a hurricane at dawn, ripping Nyarlathotep free of her grasp and casting the stick-figure monster away, a leaf in a gale. The power screamed and sang, a torment of joy and pain that she could barely contain. Surrounded by silver-bright radiance, she lifted her head to see four other lights—fiery crimson, shimmering blue, emerald-leaf green, and crackling violet, and at the center of each a Maiden so dazzlingly perilous and beautiful that her own breath caught in her throat.

"You have woven your web of darkness and whispered your lies and half-truths, monster," Princess Tempest Corona said in a ringing voice, "but we know our own, and have faith in friends and the Light within us all, and you have no power over us!"

It rose to its full height and glared sightlessly upon them. *Yet it is still night, and filled with shadow, and that is my power.*

But the soundless words had barely been spoken when fiery chains hammered into the tall figure—from *behind*. It had turned, it had *seen* . . . and yet this time, it did not fade away, did not escape. Instead, the scarecrow shape buckled at the waist and tumbled back, rolling once, twice, three times before finally recovering and rising to its feet.

To find itself in the center of the circle formed by the five Apocalypse Maidens; and for the first time it looked uncertain.

"Take a look around, shadowboy," Radiance-Seika said. "We *are* light. We don't *have* shadows for you to play with any more."

"And with all of us shedding light from all directions around you," Tsunami-Cordy continued, with a tight grin, "even *you* don't have a shadow here!"

Even as that horrid realization struck Nyarlathotep, the girls were extending their arms in the same way Silvertail had shown them on the first day they had all met. A star of multicolored fire blazed into existence, and in the center of the pentacle Nyarlathotep rebounded from an immaterial wall.

"Silvertail!" the five Maidens called at once.

The tiny white shape of the last wizard of Lemuria appeared now near the northern point of the confining mystical shape. "Make the true Sign, Maidens. For only the Sign can truly banish him."

True Sign . . . ?

And then she remembered the brooch. *Broken-pointed . . .*

Across the brilliantly shining lines, she saw startled understanding in each of the other's eyes.

The power of the pentagram's lines *burned* within her, flowing around the five-pointed perimeter like a cataract of sunfire and lightning, reinforcing and amplifying the tearing ecstasy of the Released power within. She could see the same transported strain on the others' faces, but focused inward. Each of her arms pointed out at an angle before her, following precisely one line of her point of the star.

She began to stretch her arms out and back.

It was like trying to pull against flaming elastic bands—bands that could hold cars. *I can* move *cars. I can* throw *them if I have to. This can't stop me.*

The being within the pentagram went berserk. No longer a humanoid figure, it became something monstrous, a ragged winged cloak of darkness with a three-lobed *Eye* of flame and shadow, and hammered against the immaterial walls that surrounded it with fire twined with night.

The impacts echoed through Holy Aura, striking her across the body like branches coated in ice, but she refused to allow it to distract or move her. *This monster was taking* children. The rage burned hot within her, and it was both her own and that of Stephen Russ, the anger and determination to protect the innocent focusing her as nothing else could have.

The tension on her arms increased as she moved them back, farther back. Now they were almost straight out to her sides, making her point flat, cut off. *But not broken. I have to go . . . farther . . .*

Aching, deep-muscle fatigue began to scream at her from her arms, her shoulders, her back, but she refused to pay it any heed. *Back. Another inch. A half inch. As far back as I can . . .*

The Crawling Chaos was a blur of panicked motion, darkness and green embers and glint of yellow, terrified eyes spinning and clawing above, below, to every side. It returned to the towering scarecrow and its huge, clawed hands ripped across every face of the pentagram. Tiny cuts on her face and body mirrored the vicious strikes, caused her friends' faces to begin to trickle with blood . . . but none of them moved, save only to bend their arms back, back . . .

And now her arms stretched *behind* her, like a pair of wings. The fire of the star rippled along her arms, out, and around, a jagged shape, twin points with another small shape between. The others, too, had managed it at the same time.

And the broken-pointed star—the Elder Sign—was complete.

Without warning the star flared to pure whiteness and Holly felt power draining from her at an incredible rate. But Silvertail was shouting now, thundering out a final ritual in an ancient language that nonetheless she could understand: "You are bound and sealed, Herald and Servitor, and your power severed from this world! Your hold is broken, your time is done! Go now, back to the void that spawned you, and trouble this world no more!"

The unvoiced scream of fury and denial was a curse, an imprecation of such hideous and incomprehensible vileness that Holy Aura felt nausea ripple through her at the mere *perception* of those thoughts, intentions of a being so absolutely opposed to everything normal and sane in her world.

At the same moment, however, Nyarlathotep screamed and *stretched,* his angular form extending, elongating as though an unseen giant were pulling him apart. The pale head became a distorted ellipse, a line, and then it shot skyward, followed by streaks of lines that had been arms and legs, and vanished into a shimmer of shadow and distortion that finally flickered and disappeared completely.

Holly released the power and collapsed to her knees, then to hands and knees, trying to keep from simply falling on the grass and lying there, maybe forever.

And in that instant, the web of darkness between trees vanished, and Prince Twilight Dawn plummeted unceremoniously to the ground, to land with a *thud* flat on his back.

✳ Chapter 51 ✳

To her surprise, Holly was the first to reach the young man. *I was on the far side of the circle from him. Why didn't Tierra or Cordy get here first?*

Even beneath his mask, Twilight Dawn's grimace of pain was clear. "Are you all right?" she asked, wondering if she dared help him up or whether he might be more seriously injured.

His breath was short, but a wan smile replaced the wince for a moment. "I . . . do not believe I am sorely injured; yet truly it was something of an impact, as I fell twenty feet and there appears to have been a root directly below me."

He half sat up but gasped and fell back; she caught his head, keeping it from smacking against the ground once more. The others had gathered around by now. "Don't move; give yourself a minute, at least," Holly said, hearing surprisingly intense concern in her own voice.

"Yes," Devika said. "The danger's past, at least for now. Tsunami Reflection, can you tell us if he is badly hurt?"

"*Tell* you? Ha!" Cordy's transformed face grinned. "Who's the top-ranked healer in the Maiden team?" Tsunami Reflection's brow furrowed the smallest bit, and blue-green light momentarily bathed the Prince. His eyes widened, and they saw the tension of pain flow out of him.

"And so 'tis true, I am surrounded by angels," he said, then laughed and rose in a single swift motion. "Truly, the pain has been erased as the shadows before the dawn."

"Least we could do," Radiance Blaze said with an answering grin. "You saved our *asses* there."

"Indeed," Silvertail's voice said from the snowy ground. "And we owe you a debt. But I still would know, Prince, from whom you have gained this power; for enemies have been known to come cloaked as friends."

Twilight Dawn's masked face registered his surprise as he recognized that the question was coming from the white rat, nearly invisible against the starlit snow. "What the . . ." he said, and for that moment Holly thought that his voice sounded . . . different. Not truly changed in timbre and pitch, perhaps, but more natural, less affected, without the hint of accent that Prince Twilight Dawn had been using . . . and it was almost *familiar*.

But if so, it was only for those two words. A smile burst out across his face and he laughed again. "And so, of course, the spiritual advisor! Pardon my startlement, sir. Might I first be introduced to you before I reply?"

"I am Silvertail Heartseeker."

"Then Sir Heartseeker, first I say that you owe me nothing; it is naught but truth that I rescued the Maidens from a dire situation, but they in turn prevented that foul beast from rending me limb from limb. The scales are more than balanced."

He studied Silvertail more seriously. "To answer your question, my power and my mission are laid upon me by one named Queen Lucent."

"Queen . . . *Lucent*?" Holly could see Silvertail's eyes narrow. "Prince, the one whose name might translate to this language as 'Queen Lucent' has been dead for dozens of centuries, one of the victims of the invasion in the days of my youth."

"Of *your* youth, you say?" Prince Twilight Dawn drew back, momentary surprise clear in his stance. "Then . . . I ask you, sir, what was the name you bore in those days?"

"Names have power, Prince," Silvertail said, as Holly picked him up and placed him on her shoulder.

"And time's passing fast," Seika said. "Now that his magic's off them, those kids aren't going to be doing too well in this cold."

"Address that issue, at least, Radiance Blaze," Silvertail said, not taking his eyes from the mysterious Prince. "This must be resolved."

Twilight Dawn folded his arms, drumming his fingers absently on his upper arm. "Very well. I believe I know it already, however. Spell it, or halve it?"

"Halve it. Speak the first half, and I shall give you the second, if you have the first right."

"So. I believe the first name is *Varatraine*."

Silvertail's whiskers twitched, registering his astonishment. "Varatraine Aylnell, yes."

The young Prince laughed softly, shaking his head. "So it *is* true, though she did not say to me you had assumed such a different form. So be it. My Queen had given me instructions for this, to prove her existence. Let us hope I can do this properly." He paused, obviously concentrating. "*Nyalena hintalatan min daliwe sen vo challa ton vies, Sendan, Gyllis, Ovithalen, Mintakas. Tala ken mos, Varatraine.* Does that mean anything to you, sir?"

Silvertail was silent for long seconds, and Holly could feel his body was tense, vibrating. "Yes," he said finally, so quietly it was almost inaudible. "Yes," he said again, more firmly. "Allowing for your accent in a language you have never spoken . . . yes." A sigh that was almost a squeak. "Only the true Queen Lucent—*Ruloa* in Lemurian—would have known that."

"What did he say?" Holly asked.

"Not to detail things . . . it tells me who was present at the last audience with her before she died. Five of us. It was a private audience, a meeting arranged through many layers of intermediaries. No one, not even her closest servitors or ours, would have known or even been able to reasonably guess who all five of us were." He looked back to the Prince. "Will we be able to meet with her? An ally of her strength would be . . . invaluable."

"I will ask," Twilight Dawn said, as he bent over to retrieve his sword from where it had fallen. "She has hidden herself—as you yourself have—to ensure our enemies do not find her. But I am certain she will be glad of your survival. Still, time passes. I must bid you farewell, for now!"

He bowed to them all and a second time to Holy Aura—with a wink that somehow sent a warm, shivery feeling through her—before bounding into the sky and vanishing.

"Such a *poser*," Tempest Corona said, looking after him.

"But that poser saved our asses, so he can be as melodramatic as he *wants*," Tierra said, as Cordy flicked swift sapphire healing across them all, closing cuts, wiping away bruising. "Now what the *hell* do we do about these kids? There's *dozens* of them here!"

Jesus, this is bad. Holly looked over the literal mounds of sleeping children—kept warm, at least, by a soft flickering-fire glow from Radiance Blaze—and tried to think. "Where'd he *get* them all? Silvertail, could he have just drawn in all the kids from some radius around us?"

The white rat shook his head. "No. The level of control he had over them argues for considerable exposure, perhaps even direct contact, stretching over days or more, and that many disappearances would have been front-page news. His power over shadows would allow him to draw in all his controlled servitors from any distance."

"Well, now that he's gone, they'll be okay, right?" Tierra asked uncertainly.

"I wish it were so. But this is not just a matter of a spell cast over them to control them; it is long term exposure to something alien and monstrous that has insinuated itself into their minds and souls. Banishing him is certainly good—it will make it possible to try to assist them. But . . . it will not be easy."

Devika muttered something in Hindi that Holly was pretty sure meant roughly *Oh God* or *God help us*. "We will have to find somewhere to bring all these children. And figure out *how*." She looked around, and even those broad shoulders under the Maiden armor sagged as she took in the enormity of the task. "There's, I don't know, fifty, maybe a *hundred* of them or more? We'd need a fleet of ambulances! And calling them all *here*, to Seika's property? Are they going to suspect Mr. Cooper of kidnapping all of them?"

"Fuck that!" Seika snapped.

"What do we *do*, then?" Cordy asked, her voice so deliberately calm and steady that Holly knew she must be making an incredible effort not to scream. "We can't leave the kids here." She looked over at Silvertail with sudden hope. "Silvertail, can't you just, I don't know, fly or teleport or something them over to a hospital or—"

Silvertail's laugh was bitter. "In my youth, yes, but as I am now? With magic at its current level? I can do subtle things, but there is no trickery that will negate the sheer power needed to move dozens of living beings from one point to another safely." He sighed audibly. "I could remove the traces, cover up the fact that they were *here*, but not move them myself."

It was the term *cover up* that triggered the thought. "Hey . . . Silvertail, do you think there would be any way to contact the OSC?"

"What?" Seika looked at her as though she'd grown a second head. "Are you *nuts*? I mean, *fucking* nuts? Why would you want those spooks—"

"Yes, I could," Silvertail said slowly. "And that might be an excellent idea, Holy Aura."

"No offense, Silvertail," Cordy said, "but I'm more on the *fucking nuts* side of this. Didn't these people try to *kidnap* Holly once already?"

"Yes, they did. And possibly would again, if they thought it was within their ability to do so. But you must understand, their basic *mission* is still benign, even if they often will take . . . drastic measures to carry it out. The important point is that as a government organization they have *vast* resources to respond, and as one with knowledge of the shadowy edges of reality they have certain capabilities which would be of great assistance to us in this situation."

Devika frowned. "But it's a very large risk."

"Certainly. They may suspect Seika is one of the Maidens based on the location, or may not—but anything that gives them more data on us does, to an extent, increase our risk. But . . ." he gestured with a tiny paw. "We have what I see as another risk, and not just for ourselves."

Silvertail looked around their little group, and despite his size Holly knew they all felt the weight of his regard. "In truth, I would be more reluctant to think of such a step if it were not for the fact that we know now that the ending of this Cycle is close upon us." Holly shuddered, trying to push into the back of her mind what that meant for her. "But the ending comes soon, and we risk little for ourselves compared to these children."

The Maidens looked at each other, then finally Holly found them all staring at her. *Crap. That's the problem with being the leader.*

Really, though, there wasn't any choice. She looked down at the tousled head of a boy no older than seven or eight and felt her hands clench into fists. "Right. Then let's do it. Call them, Silvertail."

"I believe *you* should make the call, Holy Aura," he said. "They do not know of me. And while they know of the existence of the others, only you would be expected to know how to contact them."

Duh. As far as they know, Silvertail's just a white rat. They might guess he's more, but no reason to give them that info, or tell them we've got some older guy as an advisor. "Guess I'll change back—"

"No. Use a disposable phone." He reached into the same apparent emptiness from which he had produced their brooches, and handed her a phone.

"Wow. Wish *I* could do that."

"If you studied Lemurian magic for, oh, twenty or thirty years, I have no doubt that you could. Now, pay attention. Here is the number."

She took the phone and moved away from the others; no point in giving them even useful background noise to work with. Then she punched in the number Silvertail had memorized.

The phone on the other end only rang twice before she heard a voice on the other end. "Kisaragi," said the familiar voice of the redheaded OSC agent.

"Agent Kisaragi, this is Princess Holy Aura."

There was a tiny pause, a faint hint of indrawn breath. Then a low chuckle. "You have my attention, Princess. I admit I didn't expect you to call us, especially after ditching our card."

"If your card hadn't also been a trick to track me, I'd have kept it. But I like to think we're still *basically* on the same side, and I've got a problem that I hope you can help with."

"Hmph. An interesting notion, but the OSC is not generally in the habit of *helping* anomalies that are not under control."

"I get that. But your *primary* mission is to protect the world from 'anomalies,' and that includes trying to cover them up or minimize their impact, right?"

"To an extent."

"Well, I've got something like fifty to a hundred children who were under the control of one of our enemies, probably from all over the country, and they're probably pretty messed up. We can sort of help them physically, but . . ."

There was a pause, then a throaty laugh came from the other side. ". . . but the Maidens can't transport so many, or find their homes, and so on and so forth. Of course. And that *is* part of our responsibility. I presume these children are traumatized?"

"I . . . expect so. They're sleeping right now, but no telling what they'll be like when they wake up."

"And can you tell me anything about the . . . entity that had them?"

"How well do you know your Lovecraft?"

Silence. "Understood. Where are the children?"

"In light woods behind one of those semirural houses at the edge of town . . . hold on, let me check the address. . ." She bounded to the front of the yard and to the door and nearby road intersection. *Yes, I actually know Seika's address, but* they *don't know that, and might be physically tracing this phone.* She could hear sirens in the distance. *Light show in the back yard might have triggered calls.* "9 Flower Hill Drive."

"Understood. What about the occupants of that house?"

Careful. "There wasn't anyone here when we arrived. I don't know why. As far as I know there's no connection between this place and the monsters."

"We'll look into it." Her voice became slightly dimmer but Holly could tell she was shouting. "*Gilbert! Hughes!* Call out teams One through Ten, we've got a large-scale incident!" Her voice sharpened. "I presume you won't be there."

"No. But we'll make sure they're safe for the next, what, half hour until you get here."

Agent Kisaragi's voice was amused. "Don't underestimate us. Ten minutes."

Probably meaning five *if I guess right.* "Thank you, Agent."

She crushed the phone in her hand. "Okay, people, we've got to bail *now*!"

✴ Chapter 52 ✴

"What *is* it, Holly?" Seika asked.

They were all together, sitting against the cushioned walls of the training room. Devika and Cordy looked at each other and Cordy said "Yes, Holly, what's wrong? You've been . . . distant the last couple of days, even when we were together. Something's bothering you."

I guess I couldn't hide it from them. "*Lots* of stuff," Holly said after a long moment.

"Well, do the King of Hearts thing," Tierra said.

"Didn't know you read *Alice in Wonderland*," Holly said with faint surprise.

"After I saw the Disney movie when I was a kid. You're stalling."

"Ugh. Um. Okay, the simple one first. I think our Prince is Dex Armitage."

The others stared at her with such comical disbelief for a moment that she almost burst out laughing. But almost instantly, Seika grimaced and smacked herself in the head, mirrored by Tierra. "*DUH!* That's *just* the way he'd talk if he was playing a character like that!"

"And that's why he's not nervous and stuttering," Holly agreed. "He's playing a character. He's decided how to play Prince Twilight Dawn and so it's not *him*."

"Not saying you're wrong, or that it's not a good guess," Devika said, "but why?"

"First," Seika said, "because it's so meme-riffic. I know, some of you guys never saw a *mahou shoujo* series, but it's not all that different from other stuff. Isn't it like *always* the way that the mysterious new superguy is someone the main heroes know, especially if it's a repeating hero? Anyway, it's like *ten times* that likely in this kind of thing. If Dex didn't always act so dorky outside of the games we might've figured it out after the first time."

"Right," said Holly, "and there's more. The change makes us all super-perfect and all, but if you know what you're looking for, you can see that it's us. I mean, my hair's changed color when I'm Holy Aura, but the dark hair, the face, all that, there's a similarity. Seika might end up with hair that makes a blaxploitation Afro look puny, but it still *does* kinda look like her hair, and so on. Dex's long blond hair and Twilight Dawn's white gold, pretty similar, same with the way he's built, right?"

Cordy nodded thoughtfully. "It could work."

"But the clincher for me was when Silvertail spoke up. He was startled and when he exclaimed, it wasn't in that semi-English accent. It was straight Middle America, just like Dex. Who else is going to transform and then start *acting* after they transform like that, complete with fake accent?"

"We will take it as a working assumption, then," Devika said. "But I don't think that's really what was bothering you."

"Well, not by itself. I'm kinda peeved that I *think* he's hitting on Holy Aura, when he was asking *me* out on a date."

"Oh, yeah. I didn't think he was that kind of a dick, but sure, he was *definitely* checking you out."

"Maybe he is and isn't," Tierra said after a moment. "He's 'in the role' for Twilight Dawn, right? And he knows the memes. No, wait, more than that. The memes drive this kind of stuff from the background, too. So the character *would* be attracted to the leader of the Maidens, and the meme's going to be pushing that on him, too."

That *fit* for Holly, and she felt one small part of the knot in her gut easing. "I think you've got it." She felt herself blushing. "And, um, I have to be honest, I was kinda checking him out too. Felt something between us."

"Meme push on *both* sides," Seika agreed.

"No more stalling, what's the *big* problem, Holly?"

"Jeez, Devika, you don't give *up*, do you?"

"Never. Especially when it's hurting a friend and going to hurt our team. So talk."

Devika was, of course, right. Holly couldn't argue that. "Nyarlathotep. Worked out well, but there were things said . . ."

"He was mindgaming all of us. No biggie," Cordy said. "You obviously didn't fall for it, so—"

"Worse than that," Holly broke in. "No, he didn't get to me, but it's *why* he didn't that's really bothering me. I mean . . . it doesn't bother me, but it does. *Shit*. This is messing with my head just trying to talk about it."

Seika put a hand on her shoulder; the other girls moved closer. "We're *here* for you, Holly. You're the leader, and we're here to keep you going, 'cause you've kept us going. Right?"

The others nodded.

That makes it . . . harder, Holly thought, and felt a sting of tears that was nigh impossible to hold back. "Guys . . . that's . . . well, part of it. He tried the old 'your master's really just using you' bit, and then figured out what my secret was and told me if we just stopped fighting them I could go back to my old life forever."

She tried to take a breath, but it caught on the way in and turned to a sob. The tears overflowed, but she refused to let that stop her. "And so I . . . heh . . . I busted out laughing, because . . . because . . ."

Seika had never been slow. "Oh . . . God, Holly."

". . . because I don't *want* to go back." Her tone sharpened. "I don't *ever* want to go back, because I love all of you, dammit, I love being *Holly Owen,* I love Trayne-Silvertail as my dad, I'm even fucking liking being back in *high school* for chrissake, and I *hate* the idea that I'm going to lose it all, lose all of *you*, and there's no way I'm giving up even one second of it to go back to being fucking Stephen Russ."

Her old name broke the rest of the floodgates open and she couldn't speak any more. Part of her hated this. *Not the first time I've broken down in front of them. Some leader. Some tough badass Maiden I am. Loser.*

And it was *self* hatred in both directions, she had to acknowledge. Steve Russ wasn't some other person. She *was* Steve. She had his memories, his *life*, as her background. It wasn't some other girl, Holly Owen, not wanting to be turned *into* Steve; it was, in truth, Steve *himself*. Because they were, in the end, the same *person* even with the changes they had undergone. *Well, okay, Holly's also infused with the, well, essence of the prior Holy Auras . . . but still, I can't say I'm not him.*

But none of her friends moved away. She felt a tentative touch on her other side, sensed the circle closed around her, and finally forced herself to look up.

To see tears on every face—a practical *flood* from Seika and Tierra, but even Devika's usually stern, controlled face glittered with sadness.

"We don't want to lose *you* either, Holly," Seika said in a choked whisper. "Don't want to forget being the Maidens. Don't want to go back to being . . . what I was."

"What? There was . . ." Holly sniffled. "There was nothing wrong with *you*."

"Oh, fucking *bull* fucking *shit* on that!" Even her *Homestuck* troll voice sounded thick and sad. "I wasn't just a geek, I was a geek without any *friends*. And when this is over, that's what I go back to?"

Tierra nodded. "Not so bad for me . . . but neither of us will know what friends Cordy and Devika could be."

"You guys saved *my* life, and I'm going to forget *that*?" Cordy said.

"Well, it *does* mean you don't remember getting totally suckered by Procelli," Devika pointed out, trying to put a smile on her face and failing. "Sorry. And I'll forget being *given* this chance to make so much of a difference."

Seika hugged Holly. "But I know, that's nothing compared to what you're going through."

Holly shook her head hard. "No. No, it's just as bad. We're *all* friends. We'll *all* be losing. And I'd do anything to change that."

"But we can't."

Holly swallowed hard, feeling prickles of pain and tightness that always came after crying so hard. "No. Not if we care about the world."

"And we do."

She was silent a moment, then managed the tiniest of smiles. "Yeah. Because all of you are in it. And Dex. And all the others."

"Silvertail says our lives . . . will be good after, right?" Cordy asked.

"That we'll be lucky as hell and things will go our way. Yeah."

"Do you believe him?"

Holly thought about that now, with everything that had happened, and nodded.

"And . . ."—Tierra hesitated, and then pushed forward—"will it *really* be so bad, then, to be Steve?"

She hated thinking of that. The old, big, clumsy body, the constrained life . . .

But then, the life wouldn't be so constrained.

"I . . . dunno."

"I do," Seika said firmly. "Dex thinks Steve Russ was like the best thing ever. So it can't be *that* bad to have been him. Or be him, if he's not going to have to keep living his life eating ramen."

Holly let herself really *think* about that. Let *Steve* come to the fore, so she could *look* at him, really look at who she had been.

And in her imagination, his face was filled with sympathy. *I'd go away for you, if I could. You know that. You're me . . . and not me. I'm a lot happier like you are now.* An internal chuckle. *Language really isn't made for this, is it?*

No. Guess not. It wasn't so much talking to another person . . . but arguing with herself about something that conflicted within her.

As Steve, she thought, *Maybe, though, I'll be happy afterward. And our friends will still be alive. So'll the world. We're cool with that.*

A smile to herself. *Yeah. We are. I am.*

Then we've got a job to do.

She pulled away from Seika and the others, stood up, scrubbed the tears from her face. "He says . . . *I* say . . . we've got a job to do. And we do, don't we?"

The other four rose up around her and nodded. Tears still showed, but their faces—*oh, god, so young,* echoed one of Steve's thoughts from deep within her—showed the same resolve that was crystallizing within her.

"Then we're going to save the goddamn world and we'll be *happy* about that," she said.

"Right." "Yeah." "Yes." "Definitely." Her four friends didn't hesitate.

A flicker of white motion caught her eye. She looked over at Silvertail. "You heard all that."

He sat up on his haunches, nodded. "I did. I am truly sorry for what I have done. Even though I felt it was necessary."

"'Salright," she said, making sure she wouldn't get all teary again. "But I want you to do one thing for me. Make one promise."

"What is it?"

"You . . . remember, don't you? Every cycle?"

He looked down. His voice was a sad whisper, a hint of a voice that she strained to hear. "Yes."

"Then promise me *this*: you'll make sure that my friends find each other again. Dreams, hints, whatever. I know Steve can't be part of that, but they can."

"Holly . . . after the cycle ends, I am much diminished for—"

"*Promise me!*"

He looked back up, his ruby eyes gazing unwinkingly into hers. Finally he gave the softest of chuckles. "As you wish. I shall do it, regardless of the cost. I will, after all, have time."

Her heart relaxed within her for the first time in days. It wasn't a perfect answer . . . but it was an answer. "Okay. Then we'd better get back to practice."

"Yes," Silvertail said. "For the last confrontation will not be long in coming."

✳ Chapter 53 ✳

"That was totally awesome!" Dex said, waving his arms so wildly they almost hit two people on either side of him.

"Watch it, Dex! But yeah, it *was*. I can't believe they got it all so close!"

They continued talking about the movie—reviewing the best parts, quoting lines, with Dex bouncing around and reenacting combats and making sound effects to go along with them.

"And this time we got to finish seeing it, too," Holly noted.

"Well, yeah, that's cool. Glad that Van's all right. Did they ever figure out what was wrong?"

Sure, he was touched by the essence of a Lovecraftian monster. Which, if I'm right, you know or guess, but then, you don't know that I *know.* "No. He went into some kind of shock, but what caused it they don't know. Doctors want him to take a battery of tests, but if it doesn't happen again, they probably won't learn much."

"Then I hope they don't learn much. That must've been scary. I have a little brother too."

"Yeah, you mentioned him. David, right?"

They headed to Cakes 'N' Shakes, one of the places still open to cater to the after-movie crowd. "Yep. He's in his last year of junior high now. Van's younger though, right?"

"Quite a bit. He's still in elementary school."

"Anyway, at least it's over and everything's cool now. But *man* that movie's got me pumped for epic fantasy now."

She laughed. "I can't blame you. You think I should change over? Or you do it, instead of the space travel one?"

He grimaced. "I dunno if I want to dump all the work we've been putting into planning that one. But yours *is* getting to a break point, if I read your plot right."

"I think you're close, anyway." They got their sundaes and sat in a corner; while there was a fairly brisk business, most of the people were grabbing stuff to go, not sitting down, so there was plenty of space. "I guess I could start working on an epic fantasy setting while you run your space game."

"Could work. Maybe we start alternating once you're ready?" Dex took a huge bite of his sundae.

She started thinking about how she might build a new world. Of course she knew all Steve's old campaign, but she couldn't use *that.* But she could steal bits and pieces from that and a lot of other things. "I guess. You thinking on the grittier, shinier, or weirder side?"

"How about crossing the straight-up epic with the *anime* side?"

"Take your epic and crank the dramatics up to eleven, got it." That could work. Mix in a bunch of the series they knew with a few other sources . . .

"Yeah, then I might be able to use one of my favorite characters, Francisco d'Artanian!" he said with a reminiscent grin.

"Too showboaty, Dex, he'd be wayyy too much a spotlight stealer, unless we redesigned him a lot, and the sword would have to come *way* down," she answered absently.

Almost instantly she realized her mistake. She tried not to show her reaction. *Maybe he won't catch it.*

But he was staring at her, blinking in confusion. "I . . . I didn't ever *tell* you about d'Artanian."

Quick, think quick! "Sure you did, after one of the games, a couple months back!"

His eyebrows came together and she had a sinking feeling in the pit of her stomach. Dex was the kind of geek who could damn near replay entire game sessions in his head word for word. Trying to convince him he'd described an old character in detail, when he hadn't? Not a good bet.

"No . . . no, I didn't," he said, slowly, but becoming more certain with each word, staring at her now with those crystal-blue eyes sharp and calculating.

"Well, you *must* have told me sometime!" she insisted.

That *did* set him back. "Well . . . yeah, I guess. I mean, you moved here this summer, you couldn't have—"

Dex froze, staring at her with eyes growing wider and wider until she wondered if they could *literally* fall out of his head. "Oh my *God.*"

She found herself frozen. *What do I do? What do I say?*

"Oh my *God,*" he whispered again. "I thought that weapon collection just had a lot of *similarities* . . . but . . . but those *are* Steve's. Aren't they?"

She sat, rigidly unmoving, unable to speak. Finally she forced her mouth to move. "What are you talking about?"

Then he shook his head. "But no, that doesn't make sense. Your dad's nothing like Steve, except for the hair. But he wouldn't have sold the collection. Even if he had, why would *you* know anything about *our* games, it isn't as though you were . . ."

She'd thought his eyes were wide before, but that was nothing now—as his face also went stark pale. "No."

Holly tried to say something, but her voice caught in her throat. She couldn't imagine what she *could* say that would matter.

Dex leaned forward, staring incredulously. Finally, the faintest, strained whisper escaped his lips: "*Steve?*"

She closed her eyes. *Crap.*

"It *is* you. Oh my *God* of course, that's why it was as though we'd been playing for years, as though you *knew*, and I guess I can see why you'd say you'd moved, but I don't get it, how, how's this possi—"

And once more he froze. "Holy shit." Dex looked down, started ticking things off on his fingers. "Timing . . . first appearance less than a week before Steve left. Then a couple months . . . almost like someone training? Seika's *brother*, yes, of course, and you've been seen hanging with Cordy and Devika . . . starting right after the thing at the game, oh my *God* . . ."

Holly took a deep breath. "You've pretty much got it down now . . . Prince."

Dex jerked, and then started to laugh. It wasn't entirely a *happy* laugh, not even a very controlled or comforting laugh. "Whoaaaa, ha, ha ha ha, you guessed *my* secret, but it's like only a *tiny* secret compared to . . . ha, ha, HA HA, yeah, I'm on a date with, ohhh, shit, with—"

She grabbed his hand and squeezed tightly, *willing* him to look at her, to listen. "Dex, *please*, focus, get a grip!"

With an effort so extreme she could *see* the strain in his face, in the corded tension of his neck, he stopped, still staring at her.

"Yes, you've figured it out, but *this* is who I am. Really, truly who I am now. Somewhere along the line I stopped *being* Steve Russ playing a part. I'm Holly Owen, and that's—"

"Jebus. *Holly Owen*? That's like the least subtle alias *ever*!"

"You didn't notice it until now!" she said defensively. "Besides, that was Silvertail's choice."

"Silvertail. Well *crikey* as they say, I didn't even make the connection with Steve's new rat. I think he even *said* his name once, just didn't stick much. He . . ." Dex suddenly snorted with laughter so hard he started coughing. "Ugh . . . my *God*, Holly, your *Dad* is a *rat*!"

"It sounds bad when you say it that way. And . . . it's complicated."

Dex finally gained some control over himself; he looked around, but it didn't seem that anyone was paying much attention to them. "I got the rest, right? Seika, Tierra, Cordy, Devika?"

"Yes." There wasn't much point in denying it, especially when Dex wasn't likely to believe any denial. With that hint, he could easily match up the fantasy-girl appearance with their real-girl counterparts anyway. "You know how dangerous that is."

"I won't tell anyone. Even Queen Lucent. Promise."

She looked up, surprised. She'd expected an argument on that point.

He grinned, though the expression still looked tense and shaky. "I've read enough and watched enough to know the shtick. I tell *anyone*, it'll somehow get back to the bad guys." He looked down at his hand in hers; she felt his grip quiver. "Um . . . Holly . . ."

"It's *me*," she answered quietly. One advantage of having *been* a guy was knowing what someone like Dex was thinking. "Holly, not Steve. Steve *liked* you, loved you like a brother even, but not . . . any more than that. Holly, well . . . maybe more." She felt her cheeks growing hot.

He still had a shellshocked look in his eyes. "Seriously? I mean . . . *seriously*?"

As quickly as she could—and with a dreamlike slowness that made the motion seem to take forever—she stood half up, leaned over, and kissed Dex straight on the lips.

The simple, warm contact felt like a bolt of warm, tingling lightning shooting straight from her own mouth through her body. She felt his lips stiffen for an instant, then relax, respond, kiss back, and that sent another thrill of excitement and confusion through Holly, even as she was already breaking the kiss, sitting back down.

Dex's hand came up to touch his lips and he was staring at her as though he had seen a revelation. For long seconds he didn't move.

At last, his hand lowered slowly, though his gaze did not waver, staring into her eyes with such utter focus that she felt the blush intensifying with every moment. "Wow," he whispered. "I didn't . . . didn't think it *felt* like that."

"I didn't know either." She swallowed. "Are you . . . okay with this?"

"I . . . guess?" Dex suddenly laughed, but this was a *far* more natural sound. "I mean, it's not like you're *pretending* to be a girl, right? And you weren't planning to trick me or anything."

"No. It just . . . kinda happened."

The breath he took was very ragged, but he smiled. "Then . . . well, you know what my dad said, back when he gave me the Talk?"

"You mean about dating, sex, that stuff?"

"Exactly that stuff. He said, 'Don't let looks be what you date, Dex. Date a person. Find someone who's a *friend*. Because I married my best friend.'" He chuckled again. "I was following his advice *asking* you. I guess I was just following it even *more* than I thought."

She smiled, feeling her own shakiness starting to recede. "Guess so."

"Um . . ." Dex went bright red again. "Can I . . . kiss you again?"

She felt as though there was a spotlight shining on them and everyone was staring. "S-sure. Ummm, outside? Not in here. I did that sort of on impulse, 'cause I didn't want you to, well, doubt anything."

"Sure. Outside's great. Anytime's great, I mean, it's all up to you, I'm—"

At the start of his usual tide of nervous words, she found herself grinning. "*Relax*, Dex, or you'll make *me* more nervous!"

She texted Trayne to come pick them up and headed outside with Dex.

And they kissed exactly three more times before the minivan pulled up at the curb. As she opened the door, she saw Trayne's gaze focused rather *strongly* on Dex, with eyebrow raised high.

Dex was suddenly aware of that look, and blanched, even as he sat down. "Umm . . . Mr. Owen . . ."

"Holly?"

"Did that look forced to *you*, Dad?"

He put the car in gear and began driving. "Er . . . no. But . . ."

"Dex is now in on the whole thing, Silvertail."

The car twitched as Trayne Owen's hands spasmed on the wheel. He glanced in the rearview after a moment. "Everything?"

"Yes, sir. I know who . . . who Holly *was*, and who the other Maidens are. And I won't say anything about it."

"I . . . see. As we didn't discuss this previously, Holly, I presume either young Dexter is much more the boy genius than I thought, or you somehow gave it away."

"A little of both, Dad. Talking and some of Steve's memories just slid right in and I didn't notice, and then he connected *all* the dots in about five seconds."

"Hm." He maneuvered the car out of the lot and onto the main street. Holly sat next to Dex, holding his hand; she could feel his tension echoing hers, despite the amazing, frightening happiness echoing through her (that had caused the part of her that was still Steve to dive into his metaphorical bomb shelter and slam the door shut).

After a few moments, she saw Trayne's eyes look at her in the rearview mirror. "Holly, Dexter, this is something that needs to be discussed as a group. There are going to be questions and we need to understand how this will change things—and there may be very little time."

"Well, sure, sir," Dex said, very seriously. "I'll do whatever I can to help. But . . ."

"Yes. We cannot do it this evening—it is already quite late and it would be inappropriate to even attempt it tonight, especially as your parents are—I assume—unaware of your, shall we say, unorthodox extracurricular activities?"

"You're right. Haven't said anything to them."

"We could do it tomorrow," Holly said, thinking out loud. "It's a Saturday, and we could just say I've decided to run an extra game, right? You'd go for that without any doubt. No suspicion there."

"Yeah, no one has to twist *my* arm to get me to a game session."

"That is a good plan. Let us say early afternoon, tomorrow? Holly will call you with an exact time."

"Yes, sir."

Trayne chuckled. “No need for ‘sir’ all the time. If you are a warrior like the others, you are part of this and as much my equal as the Apocalypse Maidens.” His gaze flicked back to meet Dex’s. “However, we *will* be asking you some rather more detailed questions tomorrow. Be prepared.”

“Yes, si . . . Mr. Owen.”

“Then let’s get you home,” Trayne said firmly. “It may be a long day tomorrow.”

Part IV: QUEENS OF THE APOCALYPSE

✳ Chapter 54 ✳

"You *kissed* Dex?" Tierra whispered incredulously.

"Wow, Holly, I didn't think you'd be moving that fast. What's the Steve-part think?" Seika was nervously nibbling on pretzels, one after another, as they waited for the others to get there.

Holly winced. "Not *thinking* in that direction as much as I possibly can, Seika. And . . . it wasn't like I thought it out, it was . . . he'd just figured everything out and I didn't know if I let it just drop if, maybe, he'd start overthinking it and look at me as sort-of-Steve . . . I mean, does that make any sense? Anyway, yeah, I leaned over and kissed him before I chickened out."

"So he *knows* about us. All of us?"

"Yeah. Once he got an inkling of it, he got it all. You know how sharp he can be."

Tierra looked at her with a wry smile. "He'd just better not become the GM's pet. Not putting up with that crap."

"No way! I'd never let that happen!" Holly said, feeling embarrassed indignation burning through her.

"Never say *never*, but I hope not," Seika said. "And I'll just smack you upside the head if I think you're doing it anyway."

The front door opened and closed, and a few moments later a bit of chill air entered along with Devika, Cordy, and Trayne. Devika was already surveying them with eyebrows raised. "Dex *knows* already?"

"Yes. Look, let's just wait 'til he gets here and we're all settled in before we start going over this. It'll be a lot less confusing to do it all at once."

The doorbell rang; Trayne went to answer it.

A few moments later, Dexter Armitage entered the room. "Um . . . hi."

He was wearing a *Doomfarers* T-shirt, jeans, and white socks (he'd removed his shoes at the door, which Trayne insisted upon for everyone), and still Holly found herself thinking he looked beautiful. His nervous swallow was audible in the near silence as he set his heavy backpack down.

"Relax, Dex, no one's going to hurt you here," Tierra said. "If what Holly says is true, you saved our butts twice out there."

He looked down, embarrassed. "Well . . . Prince Twilight Dawn did."

"And he's not *you*? I know we *look* different as the Maidens, but really we're just the same, except for the few extra macros that run scripts on us."

Dex suddenly laughed, a more natural sound. "Macros! Yeah, that's a great description. Everything runs normally until you hit the right situation, then suddenly you've got a whole sequence preset for you!"

"Sit down, Dexter," Trayne said. "We have a lot to discuss today."

"Okay, Mr. Owen." He hesitated, then as he sat down burst out, "Are you *really* that white rat Silvertail?"

Everyone laughed at that, even Trayne. "I am. And as I am more comfortable in that form overall,"—there was a flash of light and the white rat was now perched on the arm of his chair—"I will demonstrate."

Dex stared, then shook his head. "Wow. Okay. So . . . what's up first?"

"Are you familiar with the situation? What has your . . . patron, Queen Lucent, told you?"

"How much detail do you want? I mean, the quick explanation is that they're all *mahou shoujo* and they're fighting against some unspeakable evil that's invading our universe, led by some woman named Queen Nyarla and the Big Bad she's bringing in is Azathoth Nine-Armed. There's more detail than that, like about how pop culture's shaping the exact presentation of the baddies and so on."

Trayne smiled wryly. "Well, it seems you've been given the basic information, although determining how much detail you were told may take some time—and probably be wise, ultimately. So you understand the position of the Maidens; what, then, is your position? Or . . . backing up, how did you first meet Queen Lucent?"

"Well . . ." Dex gave a slightly sheepish grin. "It was by email."

"By *email*?" Holly repeated, and heard the others repeating the words in an incredulous chorus.

"Yeah, I know, right? Almost deleted it as spam, but . . . well, you know how most spam's written *terribly*? This was perfect."

"What did it say? If you remember."

Dex looked at Silvertail with both eyebrows raised. "Are you *kidding* me? I read it so many times I have it memorized." He paused and looked into the distance, as though reading from a nonexistent screen. "To Richard Dexter Armitage, my greetings and salutations. Today you witnessed something you cannot explain, and both that mystery, and the desire to *act* upon that mystery, to be a *part* of that mystery, burns within you.

"I know this, for I have searched long for one such as you, with a heart that calls out for adventure, for the chance to be a hero true, to confront darkness that even now rises against your people. Know, then, that your dreams—and the perils they will bring you—can become reality, if you truly have the courage to grasp them.

"But time presses and the danger grows; this is the only contact I shall make, and if you do not accept the offer herein, never will it be made to you again; instead I must seek others, perhaps less suited but more ready.

"Thus I implore you to embrace the hopes that lie within you; I will await you tomorrow, before the statue of Lady Justice at the city courthouse, at noon.

"In hope, Queen Lucent of the Dawn People."

After a moment of quiet, Silvertail nodded. "That does sound reasonably like something she might have written, though it has been millennia since I have heard from her. What did she mean, however, about witnessing something you could not explain?"

"That whole disaster at the football game," he said. "The way the crowd went crazy— *I* felt like I was on the edge of going crazy too, but I fought it off, it felt like . . . like something was whispering in my head, something *wrong*, so I managed to push it out. Then I saw Holy Aura give her speech—"

"Whoa, whoa, hold on, Dex," Holly said. "*You* were at a *football game*? I thought that was the kind of thing you felt ruined your geek cred!"

He rolled his eyes. "You know that participation requirement the school has? I was working the concession stand. It's messy and noisy but I don't have to sit in a crowd of people. *Any*ways, so you gave your speech and I saw the bad guy confront you and then disappear. Then after a little bit the crowd started getting ugly again and I decided I *really* didn't want to be around, and got out around the time the cops started to show up."

"Ah, that explains why you retained sharp memories of the event," said Silvertail. "Your home lies outside of the circle I could cast at the time. You are at the far edge of this district."

"Right. So that's what I saw."

"Make sense, Silvertail?"

"Eminently so. Young Dexter was sensitive enough to notice an attempt to intrude upon his mind, and strong willed enough to cast the tyrpiglynt's influence out when he recognized that it was an unwholesome set of impulses. That would certainly make him a good candidate to become something such as this Twilight Dawn. Go on, then."

"Where was . . . oh, yeah. Like I said, I must've sat there waffling for . . . I dunno, an *hour* maybe, and I actually deleted the mail twice then undeleted it. I was . . ."—he bit his lip and looked down—"kinda scared, I guess. Who was this Lucent? How'd she know what I saw, or what my email was? The more I thought about it, it wasn't random spam. Too tailored to *me*. Rolled it all around in my head until I thought my brain would explode.

"But the courthouse is only about two miles from my house, and I *do* sometimes take long walks by myself, so I figured finally *why not*? I mean . . . I'm going to a wide-open public place, and someone who knew *that* much about me could've just grabbed me if they wanted, so I couldn't see it was dangerous." He laughed at their expressions. "I mean, not *mundanely* dangerous."

"Did you understand what you might be getting yourself into?"

"I kinda did, yeah," he said, looking at Silvertail seriously. "Look, games aren't reality . . . but *thinking* about the stuff in them's just as much real as any other thoughts, right? And, well, I know being a hero's dangerous. But if this person was on the level, I . . . I could *be* the

Hero." Holly could hear the capital letter in the word, and Steve remembered how Dex seemed to *shine* when the game events came together and he could be that one hero on which the world depended.

"So I took that walk and I got to the statue. Exactly at noon—and I mean *exactly*, because I was staring at my phone's clock waiting—I heard a voice behind me say, 'Thank the Dawn. You came.' And I turned around and . . . there she was."

"What was she like?" Silvertail asked.

"She was . . . you know, like the Maidens. Crazy beautiful. I couldn't keep from staring at her, though I knew I was being rude. Sometimes she had a scary . . . *distance* about her, though. Like she was something so old and powerful and maybe not-quite-human that I was talking not so much to a person as to . . . I dunno . . . a living mountain? A storm?"

"Such beings can indeed have that effect, yes. And others did not notice her?"

"I guess you know how these things work, huh? Yeah, other people hardly gave her a glance; most of 'em seemed to barely *see* her. She thanked me for coming and said she had to tell me the rest somewhere that others could not listen in. Afterward I realized she was obviously worried about this Queen Nyarla and her people."

Devika shook her head. "So you get an email from some stranger, then meet with them and go off right away to somewhere private that no one could see you at? Are you *stupid* or really just that clueless?"

"I'm *neither*, thank you very much!" Dex said, visibly nettled. "I'd made the *decision* that if there really was something behind the email I was going to follow it up. That was . . . calculated risk. And maybe just the old saying about opportunity. The chance to be part of the adventure isn't going to show up twice." He shrugged. "Besides, once I met her . . . I didn't even think about it; *you* wouldn't have, either. She said we had to go, I went; it just made sense."

"He *is* a young man, not a young woman," Silvertail pointed out. "He has not been raised with an awareness of possible danger in such situations." The others looked at each other and nodded; Holly, remembering her own horrid realization in a snow-covered alley, shivered and nodded her own understanding.

"So she took you . . . where?"

He grinned and shrugged. "A very nice house. On a street I can't quite find, like maybe it doesn't exist, or it's nowhere near where I think it should be. Then she told me the situation—including about what the Maidens were, why they existed—and that now that she could finally act she intended to provide assistance in the form of her own agent. She couldn't empower lots of them, just one, but that would be enough to help. And, well, you can see I accepted right away."

"Did she choose your, well, form?"

"Not exactly. She gave me the power to change, but she said Twilight Dawn would be shaped by me—by my subconscious and all. So I guess being a swashbuckling hero is what my subconscious wanted."

"How did you *find* us?" Seika asked.

"Oh, Queen Lucent said she would make sure that my power . . . 'resonated,' was her word, with the Maidens'. So when you activated yours, I could feel it sort of echo inside me, and it didn't take long before I figured out how to tell what direction that came from and track you. Lucent said my job would be mostly to be a support and extra resource for the Apocalypse Maidens." Dexter looked up. "Honestly . . . I'm not quite in you guys' league when it comes to power."

"Seriously?" Cordy laughed. "That sleep-zap you used on the kids isn't anything to laugh at. You could've laid out the Knights with it easy!"

"I *wish*. That power can only be used protectively—you can't use it on someone you're hostile toward, only as a defense. So the kids, yeah, or a bunch of people who're looking at some eldritch abomination and might go insane from the revelation, but not the Cataclysm Knights. Even if it'd be strong enough to do it, which I don't think it is."

"It's *probably* strong enough, if they didn't expect it," Holly said, remembering that night. "I mean, you didn't *aim* it at us, but I felt for a second like I really wanted to just roll over and take a nap anyway."

"Really? Wow. But still, wouldn't work on them; I'd be too focused on *opposing* them."

"Any other abilities we should know about?"

"Well, Twilight Dawn can use that sword like nobody's business. He's *way* stronger and faster than me, though I think not in you guys' class. He's got that ability to run through the air on stepping discs of light. That's from me, really, it's one of the ways I used to dream about flying, fantastic and precise at the same time. He's tougher than me, too—that funny Three Musketeers costume he's got acts more like armor than anything else. Haven't had a chance to learn much more yet, but I can *sense* there's more."

"Hmm." Silvertail studied him speculatively for a while.

"So . . . do you think he's a trap, somehow?" Holly asked finally.

"He *could* be, of course," Silvertail said after a moment. "I am somewhat at a loss as to *how*. If this Queen Lucent is a fake—and I am not for the moment able to imagine how that would be achieved—rescuing you *once* makes reasonable sense. But twice? Instructing your agent that he is the Maidens' ally? Unless we believe that Dex is lying about his instructions and motives, or that his Twilight Dawn persona is able to take over and perform less benign actions, this seems difficult to explain in the context of her being a villain."

"Well, our Maiden guises *do* sometimes make us do stuff," pointed out Tierra.

"True. And thus yes, it *is* possible that Twilight Dawn, himself, *is* a stealth adversary, a time bomb or Trojan horse, despite Dex's personal intentions. But . . ." He shook his head. "The *real* problem with that is that if this underlayer were to *activate*, it would have to *fight* Dexter for control. Dexter has already *demonstrated* a powerful will to resist such things, and—speaking very frankly,"—he looked at Dex and smiled—"Dex has some *extremely* powerful personal motivations to avoid doing the Maidens, and Holly in particular, any harm.

"This would make the . . . traitorous version of Twilight Dawn *extremely* weak, relatively speaking, and certainly unreliable. That leaves, practically speaking, only the possibility that Dexter Armitage is a far different young man than we have assumed—a master actor and manipulator who is as inimical as his exterior appearance is innocent."

"That's just not possible," Holly said immediately.

"Holly, you're . . . kinda biased," Seika said.

"*Holly* is biased. But I'm also Steve Russ, remember, and I've *known* Dex for quite a while. He can be a loudmouth and a clueless asshole on occasion,"—Dex winced—"but his *heart*? It's big as anyone's I know, and in the right place all the time."

Silvertail's gentle laugh prevented any argument. "I concur," he said firmly. "I had the opportunity to observe him from a unique perspective—that of an animal—and I, too, believe that Dex is a basically good person. It *is*, despite Holly's words, still *possible* that he is not . . . but I do not proceed on that assumption."

The five girls looked at each other, and even Devika smiled. "Okay then," Holly said with a grin. "Looks like we've got ourselves a real ally!"

Dex sagged back in relief. "So we're working together?"

"Yes. I would *very* much like to meet with Queen Lucent, if you can arrange it?"

"I . . . well, I'll try. But she's emphasized that she, personally, is weakened and vulnerable after what she did for me."

"Why has she done this, then?"

"Well . . . I did talk to her after our meeting before. And what she said . . ." He looked steadily at Silvertail. "She said, 'They came to the *Aili* for help . . . and instead the *Aili* fell, and so, too, Lemuria. I have a debt to pay.' From what she said, I guess *Aili* were her people?"

"Yes." Silvertail's voice was soft and sad. "Spirits of magic. Natural ones; precursors and inspiration, I suppose, to the many legends of such, the Fair Folk, nature spirits of all kinds. Elves in the older senses of the word. Perilous in some ways, but if they agree to something, they fulfill that promise. Not human, both like and unlike us. Tell her, then, that I, also have debts to pay. For her people—and she, herself—have been far reduced by the Seal itself. By our banishing most of magic from the world, she must drift in a half dream much of the time."

"I will do so, sir. I promise."

"Good. Then let us tell you what we know. For the final conflict is not long in coming."

Dex nodded, and drew his chair closer. "I know. My Queen said . . . it is a matter of weeks."

"If that," Silvertail said. "If that."

✴ Chapter 55 ✴

"Wow," Seika said, looking out at the backyard. "What a difference a week makes."

Holly's backyard was bare of snow and ice, and old brown grass shone dully in the sunlight. "Sixty degrees will do that pretty fast. But knowing the way weather works around here, it'll be back to zero and snowing next week. I remember when I was a kid there was an ice storm in *April* that almost crippled the whole region. Couple snowstorms, too."

"I don't remember . . . oh, you mean *Steve* remembers."

"Well, yeah, but Steve *is* me. At least for memories like that." She shifted uncomfortably on the porch. "And I really have to stop pretending I'm not him. I mean . . . I *am* Holly, it's not like anyone else was her. But I have all Steve's memories and stuff."

"Plus the Maiden imprints, don't forget."

"I . . . guess that does make it sorta separate. That's definitely not on Steve's side of the fence. Ugh. Let's talk about something else?"

"About how it's 'quiet. *Too* quiet'?"

"Blah. Yeah, you're right. After we whipped Nyarlathotep I figured *something* would happen. He was Nyarla's boss, right?"

"Not *boss*, precisely. Nyarla's actual superior is Azathoth Nine-Armed," Silvertail said from behind them.

"Augh! Stop that!"

"My apologies."

"It's okay, I guess. It's not like I don't know you're around," Holly conceded.

"So," Seika said, "what is or was Nyarlathotep to Queen Nyarla?"

"A . . . sponsor, one might say. Or more properly, her *recruiter*. You experienced, for a short time, his whispering in your minds, and know how powerful it is even against the prepared. He found poor Halei a far easier target than any of you; she was unfortunately all too vulnerable to the proper approach."

"So does that mean that the two of them weren't connected?"

"Oh, they were in the old days. Nyarlathotep was consolidating his hold upon her, and that meant maintaining a connection. As I mentioned, I was fortunate enough to sense the influence of that monster on her." Silvertail hopped to the polished counter and grabbed a blueberry from a container nearby. "Once she was firmly in their control, however, he had other things of interest to him and she was able to direct herself for the most part, with the guidance of Azathoth herself."

"So she won't have seen what Nyarlathotep did?"

"I do not believe so. She will not know the details. At the moment, I hope our secret remains safe. But it will not for much longer."

"We don't *have* much longer, so that's probably no big deal."

"True enough, Seika, but any advantage they gain is one less for us."

"Can't argue with that." Seika leaned down and looked closer at the ground. "Eh, still wet and mostly frozen. I guess we still practice inside."

"More secure that way anyhow."

In the distance Holly heard a familiar motor. "Oh, mail's here. Want me to get it, Dad?"

"If you want."

She ran out the front door, up the driveway, grabbed the bundle of mail from the box, and skipped back. "Umm, bill for power, local politician spam, water bill, credit card bill—hey, why do you have credit cards to pay when we've got more than enough money to buy everything with cash?"

"Helps maintain credit rating. And looks more normal overall. If you pay them off regularly it doesn't truly cost you anything," Silvertail answered.

"Huh. Never got to the point in my prior life where that was a feasible thought. Um, birthday party invite! Devika's birthday's coming up soon, I'd forgotten that. Hey, cable bill too. You know, I've been living here for like eight months now and seeing bills still makes me tense up. One of those 'you may have won a cruise' stupid-ass things. And . . ."

She paused, staring down at the envelope. It was a long, legal-size envelope, the slightly yellowed shade of white she thought of as 'ivory,' addressed in what looked like handwritten calligraphic script, beautifully done, to "Miss Holly Owen" with her address below.

What struck her most was that there was no return address.

"What is it?"

"I don't know."

She peeled back part of the flap and then ripped the back out of the envelope and pulled out the contents.

A folded piece of paper, thick and heavy, the color of light custard, was inside; something else was hidden within the folds of the paper. Holly flipped it open and read:

Dear Miss Owen,

My apologies if this missive makes little sense to you, for it will then have been badly misdirected. But I rather think you are, in fact, the proper recipient. Please find enclosed your invitation.

Invitation?

The second object was a folded, elaborately worked invitation card, with the words "*You're Invited*" inscribed in gold ink against a black background.

"I have a bad feeling about this," Seika intoned from behind her. Despite the geeky reference, her tone of voice was anything but amused.

Feeling tension rising within her, Holly opened the invitation.

* * * *

To Princess Holy Aura
And her Apocalypse Maidens
Queen Nyarla and Company
Request the Honor of Your Presence Upon the Occasion of
THE APOCALYPSE
As Embodied by
The Arrival and Ascension of Queen Azathoth Nine-Armed
Date: March Fifteenth, Two Thousand Seventeen
Place: Twin Pines Shopping Plaza

* * * *

The Stars will be Right and the Ascension take place at High Noon precisely; however, all Maidens are asked to arrive at least fifteen minutes early to participate in the opening festivities.

Call 555-7685 to RSVP

Looking Forward to Seeing You There!

She looked up slowly, to see Silvertail's ruby eyes and Seika's dark brown staring back. "They know where we are."

"So it would seem," Silvertail said slowly. "They have followed at least some set of clues; the words indicate they are not *absolutely* certain, but confident enough to send this."

"So," Seika said after a moment, "*do* we RSVP, or what?"

Silvertail twitched his whiskers as he contemplated the situation. "Of course we do," he said finally. "It would be rude not to. And, after all, this final confrontation is not one we ever intended to avoid."

Holly waited, then realized that Silvertail was looking at her again. "Wait, what, you want *me* to call this Queen Nyarla? I thought *you* were the one who'd know how to talk to her!"

"The invitation was addressed to you and the other Maidens, not to me. You *could* delegate that to me, I suppose, but—"

She shook her head, clearing away the stunned, fearful fog that had ambushed her on seeing a clear and unavoidable end to the entire long game. "No. No, I'll talk to her myself."

She pulled out her phone and dialed the number. After two rings, there was a click. "Queen Nyarla's residence-in-waiting, Arlaung speaking," said a deep, resonant voice. It sounded like the voice of a very large man, but there was a quality in it that gave Holly an eerie and creepy sensation, one that somehow echoed many of the voices of her other adversaries.

"This is . . ."—she hesitated, then realized that her name was already on the envelop—"this is Holly Owen, calling in response to Queen Nyarla's recent invitation."

Arlaung's neutral tone vanished; instead the voice was now warmer—and more alien. "Indeed? How very kind for you to call so swiftly, Miss Owen. I am afraid that the Queen herself is not available at the moment, but may I hope that you are accepting her invitation?"

"My friends and I have been looking forward to this event for months; you can count on us being there."

"*Splendid*," he said, and the undertone of his voice was grinding gravel and glass. "The Queen will be overjoyed to hear it; she, in turn, hopes very much to have the opportunity to . . . present you to the Over-Queen herself once the main event is complete."

"I'm sure she does. We will see you there."

"Indeed. I wouldn't miss the festivities for the world. Good-bye, Miss Owen."

She hung up and looked back down at the invitation. "Twin Pines . . . that's where the first battle happened."

"Indeed. Highly significant, as that was your first transformation, where the world first saw the extraordinary reborn. And high noon, of course; when the sun is at its apex is the moment that darkness shall come."

"Is 'high noon' different than regular noon?"

"Yes. High noon is the moment when the sun reaches its maximum elevation for the day. On March 15, at this location, high noon will be almost four minutes after chronological noon."

"We'd better call the others," she said. "That's the day after tomorrow."

"They will be here shortly in any event," Silvertail reminded her, "since you were planning on training. But Dexter should be called immediately."

"Yeah, you're right." She looked down at the invitation and suddenly felt a grim smile on her face.

"What is it, Holly?" asked Seika.

"The date," she said.

"Beware the Ides of March."

Chapter 56

"Well . . ." Holly said slowly, looking around, feeling her heart already beating faster.

"Yeah."

The gray March sky shed its directionless light onto the seven of them: Trayne, Holly, Seika, Devika, Tierra, Cordy, and Dex.

Dex managed a half grin. "Never thought I'd take a minivan to Armageddon."

The feeble joke broke the tension and everyone gave a small chuckle. "Hey, Sil . . . um, Trayne? Can I ask why you didn't have all the Maidens go somewhere else for the last day, to prevent an ambush or assassination?"

"It was actually Devika and Cordy more than myself that made that decision; this is, after all, Maiden business." Trayne nodded to the two girls.

"Thinking about it, leaving just didn't make sense," Cordy said. "If they knew where we were, they didn't have to send engraved invitations—which all of us got, it turns out—they could've sent monsters direct."

"Or," Devika continued, "simple technological attacks—letter bombs or something of that nature, which wouldn't be impeded at all by Silvertail's wards. So from that, I believe they either wanted us to do something right away in reaction to the invitations, or they really *meant* the invitation. The only obvious reaction you might expect *would* be for us to evacuate. Which would both confirm our identities as the Maidens, and if we didn't try to drag our families along with us, leave *them* unprotected."

"Got it. So you stuck at home as the best bet. Makes sense." Dex yanked the side door of the minivan, letting it slide backward and fully open. "Guess it's time to get in."

"Yes," Devika said. "If we leave now, we should arrive a full hour earlier than they invited us."

Trayne glanced at the sky; somehow he could sense the sun's position even through the clouds. "If nothing interferes, yes."

Holly looked at him. "Cynical today, Dad? Why shouldn't we try to take them unawares—or, being more realistic, at least give ourselves more time to beat hell out of them and maybe stop them from *doing* the summoning of Azathoth at all?"

He shook his head and sighed, a wan smile on his face. "I truly hope that it works that way, Maidens. But it is unlikely. You forget the power of the memes, the tropes, that govern the final conflict."

Dex grimaced. "You mean, it's not very dramatic if we whip the bad guys forty-five minutes before apocalypse, and then just sit around waiting for high noon, whacking them if they start twitching."

"Precisely. In no prior cycle have I ever managed to arrive in sufficient time to take the battle at my leisure, so to speak, and it was not as though I did not attempt it before; at least twice I have divined the precise location of the summoning and tried to secure it ahead of time, and in several other cases I was warned of the time and place by others, and again attempted to preempt their plans. Always something prevented me—ranging from an avalanche blocking the direct route to a temporary bout of food poisoning in the then-Holy Aura."

Holly felt a ghost of nausea and a faint impression of marble columns above her, the sensations of stone under her knees. "I think I kinda-sorta remember that."

He chuckled. "It was a . . . memorable experience, certainly. But aside from the inherent exigencies of the memetic pattern, our adversary Nyarla has shown herself to be quite resourceful, and not without various beings and people to assist her. I think we can rest assured that there is at least some mundane, if not magical, observation of our group now that they have penetrated our identities, and if Nyarla does not want us to arrive before her schedule, they are and will be quite capable of slowing us down."

Seika frowned. "Well, we've got to *try*! If we can shut this down early—"

"I do not disagree, Seika. I am just warning you not to *expect* it to succeed." He opened the doors of the van. "But let us get underway."

"You take shotgun, Dex," Holly suggested. "The rear seats are going to be crowded."

"Don't be stupid," Tierra said. "*I'll* take shotgun, Dex and you can sit in the second seat together."

Holly felt her face go red—along with Dex's—and the others laughed. But it was *warm* laughter, and she caught more serious glances between the others.

Of course. Because this is the last time I'll ever sit with him. Ever hold his hand. Or . . . anything.

They buckled in, and she felt him grasp her hand; she squeezed back so tight she saw him wince, then grin and match her grip. "Together, this time."

As they pulled out onto the road, Seika asked, "Okay, Tactics Twins, any last minute tactics?"

Devika wobbled a hand side to side. "Not . . . really. We don't know exactly what they'll be doing when we get there or when the battle starts. If Silvertail's right, we'll have to keep their schedule. If not, well, they'll be less prepared, and we should be able to start the battle early. Assuming we follow the timetable and arrive at the time of the formal invitation . . . they're keeping to certain memes, so I would expect that they won't just drop a bomb—magical or tech—on us without warning. There will be a face-off."

Cordy nodded her agreement. "Then after a little talky-talky we'll have to get down to it. We don't know what forces they'll be bringing, either, but my *gut* feeling is that they're not going to summon an army of mooks. This is the grand finale."

"So, the Knights, maybe this Arlaung guy, and Queen Nyarla, that's your guess?" Seika bit her lip but her head bobbed in agreement. "I'll bet you're right. Tactics?"

"Focus on the ones we practiced for dealing with the Knights; this is going to be a group fight that we want to pare down to the core as fast as possible. Remember the code words for our specific strategies—we don't want to tell people what we're planning. Dex—"

"Harass and distract, I know." In the relatively short time they'd had to practice, it had become clear that their initial guesses had been right; Prince Twilight Dawn, while a certainly formidable being, was not a match for any of the Maidens and probably inferior even to the Cataclysm Knights. However, his powers still offered some excellent tactical advantages which should give a considerable edge to the Maidens—at least, if the Queen didn't interfere.

"I'm worried about this Arlaung guy," Tierra said. "I'm guessing he's playing the Dragon to Nyarla's Big Bad. Either that or he's just her equivalent of Nyarla's butler, but in that case I wouldn't expect him to be at the throwdown, and he said he would be."

"You are likely correct." Trayne glanced at them all in the mirror before returning his gaze to the road. "I could hear his voice as Holly spoke with him, and he is not human at all. Unfortunately I cannot say exactly *which* inhuman being he is likely to be; phone lines cannot transmit the more nuanced sounds and impressions, alas. He *will* be extremely powerful in any event."

At that moment, the right front tire blew. Holly saw Trayne's hands go white-knuckled on the wheel as he wrestled with the van, ignoring the involuntary cries from the girls as the vehicle swayed, skewed sideways, and then finally slid to a halt at the shoulder of the road.

For a moment they sat, looking at each other, Trayne's gaze flicking across all of them, obviously making sure none of them were hurt. Then Devika suddenly laughed.

It was an infectious sound, the sound of someone accepting the absurd, and within a moment the van resounded with mirth from all seven of them. "All right, Silvertail," Cordy said finally, wiping a trace of tears from her eyes. "All right, you're going to win this one. Changing the tire's going to be, what, about fifteen minutes?"

"All told, probably," he said as he got out.

Devika shook her head, bemused. "And I suppose we'll have another forty-five minutes of delays?"

"Will you care to take a bet against it?" Trayne asked, removing the spare from its place underneath the van.

"Don't do it," Seika advised her. "Sucker bet."

"No, I will not," Devika agreed. "We will try, but I believe you will be proven right."

* * *

"Good thing you didn't make that bet," Dex observed to Devika, as Trayne turned down the detour away from a water-main break. "After the tire, there was that accident that tied up traffic, then suddenly having to stop for gas—even though Mr. Owen was *sure* he'd filled up yesterday—"

Devika held up her hands. "Okay, okay, yes, Silvertail was completely right. Do you think she'll try to slow us up *more*?"

Trayne shook his head. "If she did, *she* would be working against the same tropes. In addition, I think she has something very specific in mind, and would not want to ruin those plans by rushing them. We will get there in time, I assure you. We are, in fact, getting quite close now."

He pulled the car off into a deserted lot and drove behind the large, boarded-up building it had once served. "We will be there very shortly. Maidens, I think it is best you transform now, just in case we are wrong and they strike as we arrive. You as well, Dex."

They got out and the five girls activated their powers. Holly couldn't say she was *blasé* about the awesome beauty of the transformations, but she *had* gotten fairly well used to them, but Dex's expression of awe and joy as all five Apocalypse Maidens materialized before him reminded her of how *she* had first felt upon performing, and then witnessing, such a transfiguration.

"Wow. I mean . . . there's just no words. Just absolutely *no* words." Dex was *whispering*, a tone of voice he almost never used.

"Well? C'mon, geekboy," Temblor Brilliance said, with a wink, "we showed you ours, you show us yours!"

Trayne gave an explosive snort of laughter that turned to a fit of coughing, while Dex simply turned the hue of a brick. "Er . . . I don't think it's going to compare, but . . ." He squared his shoulders and raised his right arm, exposing an intricate bracelet of shining metal and moonstones. "In the blackest hour I call upon the Soul within, that reveals truth and dispels evil! Warrior of the World, Wielder of Sword and Will, I am he who stands between the Darkness and the Light, Herald of the Sunrise, Prince Twilight Dawn!"

The gray light darkened about him, but within the shadow brilliant sparkling luminance enveloped Dexter Armitage, rising about him, a swirl of bubbling stars to a sound of ringing bells and distant trumpets. As the brilliant sparks of light cavorted about him, his figure itself turned to light, a sketch of a young man in moonlight and starshine, delineating slender, strong limbs and outlining muscle.

The shimmering stars coalesced above Dex and then showered down; his figure stretched, taller, broader of shoulder, as a thousand of the miniature stars traced the curves of flowing hair, others spinning and dancing and darting to form a rakishly tilted hat, elaborate clothing, a cape fluttering in the nonexistent wind. The nebula of multicolored radiance disintegrated the bracelet, stretching it, reforming into a long rapier, hilt already within the hand's grasp. Prince Twilight Dawn whipped the sword down and across and up in a set of dazzling slashes, a cry of challenge and courage echoing across the lot as he brought the blade up in a salute before him, and the light scattered away, momentarily lighting up everything about him with a crystalline joy.

The five Maidens were silently staring in amazement. Then Seika began clapping, and the others followed suit. "You've got *nothing* to be ashamed of there, Prince!"

A touch of embarrassment might have shown, but he gave a deep bow to them all. "In truth, you are all too kind, but I thank you all for these words, and the thoughts behind them."

"As a fairly disinterested observer, I agree with them," Trayne said. "A different change, but equally inspiring. And it, too, fits with what I would have expected from Ruloa and the *Aili*. It . . . *feels* like her work."

He turned to the rest of them, looking at Holly in particular. "We have . . . a few minutes extra time, and we can take them now. No matter how things go, we have come to the end of our journey today. I thought you might want a few minutes to say goodbye to each other."

Even as Holy Aura she felt the instant sting of tears welling up as she faced the thought she'd been trying to avoid. Glancing around, she saw the others' faces; Seika-Radiance biting her lip and blinking hard, Tierra-Temblor with her hand up over her mouth, eyes wide, Cordy-Tsunami looking down, hair covering her face, Devika-Tempest with her gaze steady and sad, and Dex-Twilight, lips tight and eyes shimmering, about to spill over.

"Yes," she said, hearing her voice husky and tight, "yes, we do."

She didn't have to even turn; Radiance Blaze was already hugging her so tightly that she had trouble breathing. "Love you, Holly. Holy

Aura. We all do, you know. But you're my BFF, and . . . and I don't *ever* want to forget you!"

Holly couldn't say anything. Even the power of Holy Aura had no answer for the pain of a goodbye, and Steve Russ had nothing to give either. Holy Aura turned her head and kissed Seika's cheek. "Can't say it any better. But . . . I wouldn't have missed it for *anything*."

"Me neither." A touch of lips on Holly's cheek, and Radiance Blaze stepped back.

Temblor Brilliance was next to hug her, flame-red hair brushing Holy Aura's deep amethyst. "You . . . you ran a hell of a game, Holly. And . . . it's been all fun. Scary, but fun. You . . . Steve . . . you take care."

"You too. And . . . I hope Silvertail will be able to make sure you guys meet up again."

"So do I."

Tsunami Reflection took her hands. "Holy Aura—Holly, you saved me from *myself*, and I . . . I hope when I go back I won't need saving again. Sometimes I look back and wonder if I was going to become a real petty *bitch*."

Holly laughed, even though it hurt. "Oh, Cordy, don't worry about that. Everyone's got their inner bitch driving them sometimes. You're a good person and you always *were*, or your teammates wouldn't have worried about you so much. I . . ."—she reached out, touched the blue-tinged gold of Tsunami's hair—"I just wish we'd met before."

Tempest Corona stepped in front of her. "I've gained the chance to fight the *most Dharam Yudh* of all time," she said with that warrior grin that, to Holly, *defined* Devika Kaur Weatherill more than anything else. "And my soul will remember that, God will remember that, whether I do in this life or not. This is not goodbye; this is only *until later*." Then she *did* embrace Holy Aura, lifting her off the ground in the process.

Princess Holy Aura turned away from her four friends, tears now streaming completely unashamed down her face. "T-Trayne . . . Dad . . ."

And the older man hugged her and his tears made his sharp beard wet. "Oh, Holly. You *are* the daughter of my heart, and just like my first daughter, I will *never* be able to say how *proud* I am of you. I will remember you, and I will make sure your friends . . . find each other." He kissed the top of her head, as he often did when saying good-night. "And Steve . . . know that I will never forget you, either."

"He knows. *I* know." It took effort to let go, to let her father step away from her.

Prince Twilight Dawn was before her then, and he bent down and she reached up the tiniest bit. There were no words spoken, just a kiss, a contact that said everything that she could have said, communicated everything he wished.

They broke away, staring into each other's eyes. "I'll do anything I have to to protect you," he said. "I know I'm not strong enough . . . but to make sure it's not the End . . ."

". . . we'll protect each other. All of us," she said, not looking away from the crystal-blue gaze. "I'll protect you and the others. They'll protect us. And by *GOD* we'll win this one."

"A-fucking-men," Seika said, and Holly looked up, to see all the others in a circle around them.

"*Waheguru*," affirmed Devika. "The everlasting Light will be with us."

The rest added their affirmations: "Amen." "You bet." "Absolutely, Holly."

"Right," Dex said, speaking as himself, not his persona. "We'll win. We *have* to win."

"Then let's go *kick some ass*, people!" Tsunami Reflection shouted.

They all laughed. "Yes," Trayne said. "Let's do that."

✶ Chapter 57 ✶

It was . . . a little tighter fit in the van now, what with every one of them having gotten *bigger* in their transformations, and poor Devika was having to slouch down and bend her head to fit. Suddenly there was a bright flash from the front. "What . . . *Dad*, did you just *selfie* us?"

"I did indeed," said Trayne with a smile. "The family van prepared for world-saving. One for my photo album." His voice dropped wistfully. "If only I could save it outside of my memories."

"No more of that!" Holy Aura said, and she *felt* it, uncertainty and fear falling away. They'd accepted the losses; now it was time to claim the victories. "Drive on, Jeeves!"

"As you wish, mistress!" Trayne answered in his finest butler voice.

The tension grew as they approached Twin Pines, but her certainty didn't. She felt Twilight Dawn's hand in hers, reached up front and took Temblor Brilliance's, saw the redhead's answering smile. The Prince noticed, nodded, and reached behind him; Radiance Blaze's brown-skinned hand gripped the Prince's white, and then in turn she clasped hands with Tempest Corona and she with Tsunami Reflection; Tsunami's free hand came up and rested comfortingly on Holy Aura's shoulder, completing the irregular circle.

"We will stop here," Trayne said, pulling over to the donut shop parking lot across from the mall. "No point in entering the mall locked in a box."

"Right on that," Cordy said.

Holly heard Trayne lock the car behind them; a pointless gesture of habit, since no matter which way this played out, they wouldn't ever be coming back for it. *But we'll keep our habits until we're forced to lose them.*

The little group exchanged glances, and all eyes slowly turned to focus on her.

This is it. Holy Aura straightened. "Let's go."

The Silverlight Bisento came to her hand in a flare of silver light. On her right, red-gold fire transmuted to clinking chains that flowed in rhythm with Radiance Blaze's stride; on her left, rippling blue-green signaled the twin swords of Tsunami Reflection. From the far right, emerald luminance glittered on Temblor Brilliance's feet, and Holly felt a tiny smile touch her lips; they'd asked Tierra *why* she didn't have a weapon, didn't even *punch* the bad guys, blocking and striking with feet only, and she'd looked at them as though they were crazy. "I'm an *artist*," she'd said. "I'm not risking breaking my *hands*!"

Lambent purple glowed from the immense Khanda in Tempest Corona's hands, and behind them a glitter of moon and starlight told her that Prince Twilight Dawn's rapier was drawn and ready. He moved forward, swung out to flank Tierra, and on the far left, Trayne walked, a staff of crystal and silver in his hand.

Cars slammed to a halt as the seven strode with invariant rhythm across the four-lane highway. "What the hell . . . oh Christ," she heard one of the drivers say. "That's not good."

"No, it is not," Trayne said, loudly enough to be heard by all cars around him. "Do not linger here."

They reached the curb and the driveway curving down into the little valley through which stretched the Twin Pines strip mall. To Holy Aura's astonishment, there were virtually no vehicles to be seen, even though this was noon. *What the . . . ?*

Hm. Repulsion spell. I sense it as we draw closer. It is only meant for ordinary mortals; it has little effect on me and none on beings like the Maidens or, apparently, Prince Twilight Dawn. Presumably Queen Nyarla didn't want to deal with the petty annoyances of a constant stream of mortals. This works in our favor as well, and the fact that such a phenomenon would draw a great deal of attention once it was noticed (and it will *be noticed) does not matter to either side at this point.*

Holly breathed a tiny sigh of relief. At least the mall wouldn't be filled with bystanders and potential hostages.

But the lot was not *completely* empty. Besides a few cars parked on the far side of the lot, there were seven figures standing, waiting in the center of the parking lot, on the dark-black new pavement that had replaced the part ruined by the dhole.

Eclipse Umbra, leaning on his dark crystal axe, black sparkling with painful white flickering about him, taller than all the others; Avalanche Oblivion, dust of decay shrouding his brown-green armor, heavy hammer over his shoulder; wind and lightning swirled about Tornadic Gloom and his longbow was out, arrow nocked but not yet drawn; Infernal Pall's scythe crackled and smoked, red and black of lava rippling in the heat; Abyssal Night's long, ebony hair flowed out in a faint breeze, and venom-green shimmered about him and the jagged edge of his longsword.

Each of them was standing at one point of a smoking pentagram cut into the blacktop. In the center, two other figures waited; the first was a huge man, broad shouldered, muscled like a bodybuilder, dressed in a three-piece suit, no weapons evident. His hair was slicked back, black, and there was something unsettling about his eyes, slightly too round, too protuberant, and his mouth, too wide.

Beside him stood Queen Nyarla. She was slender, taller than her Knights, though not so tall as the man next to her, or Trayne, facing her with a grimly sad look on his long features. Her hair was a lustrous brown, like polished oak, and a crown of black jewels and dark metals rested upon it. She was brown skinned as well, about the same shade as Seika, but her eyes were a startling green. She wore armor as well—armor whose metal-and-crystal design echoed that of the Maidens, but was more complete, more, well, *practical* than the *mahou shoujo* costumes the memes had forced on the Maidens.

Makes sense, Holly conceded. *Big Bads get to set their own style.* And the smoothly jointed obsidian and black metal armor was certainly stylish. She didn't see any weapons on Nyarla at the moment, but she was sure they were there.

What's that?

Now that they were closer, Holly thought she saw something else in the center of the circle. *Silvertail, is that . . . ?*

Trayne's face betrayed nothing, but the answering telepathic voice was even more grim. *The covered object just behind the Queen? It looks like a figure, a body, to me. And that would mean . . .*

The Vessel of Azathoth, Devika finished. *In the center of their pentacle.*

"Welcome, Maidens, Trayne . . . and Prince Twilight Dawn, what a *surprise*!" Queen Nyarla's voice was a warm contralto. "We are so pleased to see such *promptness* in today's youth, usually so neglectful of propriety and schedule."

"Well, milady, the threat of impending Ragnarok does get one's attention," Twilight Dawn said.

"So true," Nyarla conceded, still wearing a polite smile. "Now, custom and tradition—not to mention the guiding *zeitgeist* of this era—requires I make you an offer.

"Join us. Even you, Varatraine. Especially you. This is *futile*, old friend, Maidens, Prince. Certainly you have a chance to win this battle. And even the one after that. But how *many* battles, Maidens, how many innocents sacrificed to this war? We need win only *once*, children. Stand with us, not against us, and you have no need to fear for yourselves . . . or your families."

Her smile was both sympathetic and predatory, revealing strength and threat. "For a mother who has worked too long, too hard," she said, looking at Temblor Brilliance. "For siblings and parents, such loyal servants of a temple that cannot protect them now," she said, with a glance at tight-lipped Tempest Corona, who gripped her Khanda and glared back. "For your little brother, already endangered once, Radiance Blaze, or the parents of a fine cheerleader." Tsunami Reflection merely raised an eyebrow and snorted. "I can guarantee their safety. And yours."

"What *fucking* kind of *fucking stupid* do you think we *are*?" demanded Radiance Blaze, Seika's curses sounding incongruous from the shining Apocalypse Maiden.

"There is absolutely no way *that* is happening," Devika-Tempest said firmly. "We already know what kind of *world* you would create, Queen Nyarla. Save our families to live in *that*? They wouldn't be *thanking* us for it."

"So say we all," the Prince said. "Thy speech is honey poured upon poison. It is in my mind that *we* have far more to offer."

Trayne nodded, and took one step forward. "Nyarla . . . Haleisinia. Please. This is it, the final choice, the last and only chance remaining to you. I am sorry for my blindness, for my inability to give you what you asked, but is that—is *anything* I could have done—worth what you now do? Perhaps it was, then . . . but now? These children are a thousand generations past all those, save myself, who could have or ever did do you wrong."

He took another step forward. For an instant, a shadow flickered across the Queen's face, as he spread his arms. "If you cannot forgive me, so be it, but look upon this world, the world you once loved, you told me, as much as the beating of your own heart, *anai venn shayla*, and forgive *it*. Turn away from this darkness. Please." His eyes met hers and held them, refusing to look away.

Holly held her breath; even the Cataclysm Knights looked startled, nervous, as Queen Nyarla hesitated, staring at Trayne with eyes that, for an instant, looked purely human. Next to her, the massive man in a suit tensed.

She dropped the gaze first and looked down. "And they say your powers are *weakened* here, Varatraine? Still you have the greatest of them all, your voice, the voice I loved." Her tone hardened, and Holly knew the chance had passed, had perhaps never been. "The voice that *ensnared* me, and then *rejected* me, over and over and *over*, Varatraine. You would offer me your *life*, but never what you truly *value.*" Her eyes blazed with venomous hatred. "But far more amusing to me is to take what you seek to *save*, your foster daughter and her friends!"

She laughed and looked upward as a feeble ray of sunlight flickered through a cloud. "Enough! All is prepared, the Arrival is imminent!" Her smile was fanged now, chill and savage. "Let us begin, then, and make haste, Maidens!" She held up a glittering object, a pocket watch, and it twirled coldly in the wan sunlight. "You have but thirteen minutes to the end of the world!"

✷ Chapter 58 ✷

Go! Tempest Corona's mental voice was sharp. *Do not give them the chance to take this battle's initiative!*

The Cataclysm Knights sprang forward a split second after the Maidens. A blast of venom-green enveloped and preceded them. *Poison gas!*

On it, Tempest said, and her winds blew hard, shredding and dispersing the toxic cloud, but even as the two groups neared each other Holy Aura could sense their tactician's grim mood. *That was Tornadic Gloom and Abyssal Night combining their powers. They've been training too.*

But there was no turning back at this point, no second-guessing; they had to stick with the plan. *Plan Swap and Chop, go!*

The girls crisscrossed paths, darting toward their designated opponent—Radiance Blaze toward Abyssal Night, Tsunami Reflection against Inferno Pall, Tempest Corona versus Avalanche Oblivion, Temblor Brilliance facing Tornadic Gloom.

And Holy Aura, she thought as she sprinted forward, *must neutralize Eclipse Umbra.*

The decisive movements—and, Holly thought, that split-second advantage in speed—threw the Knights off the smallest bit; from their movements, she guessed that the intent had been to impede the Maidens as a group just enough so that they could concentrate two or three of their Knights on one Maiden—possibly cycling around so that the Maidens would have a hard time countering the tactic until one or more of them was severely injured.

Seeing this was no longer feasible, the Knights braced themselves for the assault.

The Silverlight Bisento met the dark-crystal Axe with a shockwave that bowed the pavement into a crater three feet deep and twenty wide as Eclipse Umbra, eyes wide behind his narrow mask, parried her strike. Around her, four other thunderous clashes of power detonated; windows shattered in the nearest storefront and an alarm *whooped* on one of the distant cars.

Behind the Knights, she could see a glow about the pentagram, movement within; Nyarla and Arlaung were doing something, but Holy Aura could also hear Varatraine's voice invoking his own powers, calling on the carefully-emplaced geometries of will and power he had distributed around key points of the city for the past months. *They won't take him as easy as they think.*

A short contest of strength, neither Holly nor her opponent clearly winning—he had height and mass, but her strength itself did not appear inferior. They separated, circled. She could hear the other Knights fighting her friends, cursing, taunting, but there was neither mockery nor scorn on Eclipse Umbra's face; there was *caution*, and that was much, much worse. *If he respects my power and is careful, this could stretch out. Especially if his friends start doing it too.*

"What did she promise *you*?" she asked, circling to the right.

"Seriously? You wanna try psyching me while we fight?" Eclipse Umbra's smile was thin. "Sorry, busy trying to kill you, Holly."

Being called by her real name was only a tiny distraction; the swirl of his axe that summoned black shadows from the air around them was the bigger problem.

But I think I've got him beat. She spun the Silverlight Bisento and focused her spirit into it, made it a blazing wheel of pure argent light. The shadows were shoved back, torn apart, shredded to dark mist that dissipated into nothing. "You'll have to try *harder* then . . . Mike."

His mouth tightened and his eyes narrowed. "I *knew* Asshole Night had blown our cover."

So they're not all buddy-buddy? Another mark up for us. But we knew we'd probably be stronger, the real question is if we can beat them fast enough to make a difference.

As they circled each other, Holly became aware of the others, actually *feeling* what they were doing through the link that had been strengthening throughout all the months they'd been together. Steam detonated in front of Radiance Blaze, almost blinding her as she countered poison-green water with purifying flame, but the frustrated curse from within the cloud showed that Abyssal Night wasn't getting the better of it. Holly felt Devika's measured calm as she danced and spun, evading the massive, furious strokes of the Cataclysm of Decay, watching, weighing options for the strike; Holly resonated with Temblor Brilliance, leaping and kicking, her feet literally striking Tornadic Gloom's arrows out of the air in midflight as she closed the distance, the Cataclysm Knight's face showing uncertainty, even fear as she drew ever closer. Holly scarcely needed that psychic link to tell her what Tsunami Reflection was doing; explosions of steam and volcanic ash washed across the parking lot as the Maiden of Water and the Knight of Fire threw their full power at each other, a direct and unabashed contest of pure magical energy.

Too late, Holly realized the black-glowing axe was whipping around toward her. The distraction of four other points of view had slowed her, thrown her off the tiniest bit. She barely got one arm up in time.

The crystal vambrace held—barely—but Eclipse Umbra's full strength and weight had been behind that swing, and it smashed Holly's arm into her chest and sent her tumbling. She tried to roll and recover, but heard the Knight's quick footsteps approaching, knew that she would never get up before—

Silver-gold light slashed through the air, and Eclipse Umbra grunted, staggered, slowed. "And fie again, I say! Would you strike a fallen foe, and she a lady in the bargain?"

Holy Aura rolled to her feet, whipping the *bisento* around and facing her opponent as he recovered, glaring up and to one side. "Thank you, Prince!"

"Think nothing of it!" Twilight Dawn danced away through the air, darting to another part of the melee.

"I *had* you."

She shook her head, now fully on guard. "No, you never really did. There's *six* of us now, and only five of you, and with us paired up? Twilight Dawn can help out any of us when we get in trouble. Meanwhile, your Queen and her sidekick there look like they're busy with the ritual, and Silvertail's keeping them from getting involved."

She looked directly into his eyes, did not break eye contact. *Eye contact—if I can keep it up long enough—makes people feel they have a connection.*

Yeah, Seika's mind-voice added quietly, *but do you* want *a connection with these jerks?*

Wow, you're hearing *me?*

Kinda-sorta. When you're really focusing and I've got a chance to think about it—right now Poison-boy's a little afraid of getting burned, I think.

So the link's closer on all *sides.*

Clearly so, Devika interjected. *I have noticed it for some time.*

So I'm a little slow. Anyway, yes. I do not want to kill any of these kids.

They're trying to kill us, *Holly,* Cordy pointed out—in a mental tone that wasn't cruel or angry, just matter-of-fact.

I know. But I'm damn well going to try not to kill them, even talk them down if we can. Remember, if they die here, they die even after we win. They have no chance to change their paths. Steve's voice was clear, a deeper mental tone that reinforced Holly's, and for once she had absolutely no aversion to that. Steve and her were the same person, and *this* was something they were absolutely united on. *I didn't get into this job to kill people. Just monsters.*

She continued to circle Eclipse Umbra, and their eyes were still locked. *Just a little longer.*

There was a mental equivalent of four sighs in her head, but at the same time she felt the approval in her friends' minds. *All right, Holly . . . and Steve. We'll try it your way,* said Cordy.

Do or do not! There is no try! A mental grin from Radiance Blaze.

Geek, Holly thought fondly.

Suddenly she felt it; a slight shift in Eclipse Umbra's dark-brown gaze, a momentary sensation of *connection*, of feeling the other person *cared.* "Eclipse . . . Mike, I don't know what she offered you. Power, money, girls, maybe something else. But is it worth serving *her*? You heard her. The end of the world."

"End as *you* know it," he retorted, but his gaze still met hers, and there was a smidgen less contempt and wariness in it. "Not end for *us.* They'll be the rulers, but so what? It's not like *our* people have done all that great at running the planet."

Yeah, I kinda thought so. She's got a different sales pitch for them.

Maybe different for each one, like Procelli or her mentor Nyarlathotep. "Maybe so, Mike, but is it worth *killing* for? You're on the football team, aren't you? Sure you are. Did you really *like* what happened a few months back? The riot?"

That struck home. She saw him bite his lip for an instant, the eyes shift and then return to look into hers.

Holly could sense the combat still swirling around them but didn't allow it to distract her. "You didn't, did you? But that's the kind of world they *want*. You know I showed up there. You know I was fighting *their* people. That's a sample, a *tiny* sample, of what they want!"

Seconds ticked by, punctuated by shouts and impacts that she was vaguely aware of, but dared not look at. "My sister," he said finally.

"What?"

"Tammy—my big sister—is dying. Got a degenerative disease, some long name I can't ever remember, but it's incurable. Puts her in pain every day. Sometimes she cries . . ." His voice trembled. "She used to take care of me. Used to keep dad from—" He broke off, almost looked away. His gaze was defiant now, and his hands tightened visibly on the axe. "I owe her. I owe her everything, and I can't *do* anything for her. But Queen Nyarla promised she could heal Tammy."

"And she probably can," Holly admitted honestly. She saw a startled look in Eclipse Umbra's—Mike's—eyes. "But remember that game, remember what kind of things you *must* have felt when you first got this power. What kind of world is your sister going to be *living* in when they win?"

His gaze flicked from her to Queen Nyarla—who was weaving dark-emerald fire into runes and symbols that twisted the eye, hurt the mind to look upon for too long. He looked back at her, and his gaze was more human, more pained. "But I can't just let her *die*."

Silvertail?

A pause. *I . . . may be able to, after. If he has voluntarily given up this power, chosen to fight on the side of humanity . . . yes, I could bend my powers and the core enchantment sufficiently to heal one person, in the name of symmetry and balance and justice.*

"Mike, if we win . . . everything goes back to the way it was, before any monsters, any magic. Except for Silvertail. And he says that *if* you step out of the way, stop working for her, he can make sure that *afterward*, she'll be healed."

He still hesitated, wavering, though the Axe was now dropping lower.

"*Please*, Mike," she said, urgently, trying to make her voice as gentle as was possible in the chaos of battle that still swept about them. "Don't do this. Don't make me fight you. Because if I have to, I will, and I'll beat you, because I'm fighting not just for one person, I'm fighting for the whole *world*, Mike, and that means you and your sister too. Even the other Knights, no matter how much of an asshole any of them are."

There was a tiny, *tiny* quirk upward of his mouth. "Maybe *I'm* a total asshole. Maybe I'm lying."

"Are you?"

His gaze finally dropped away. "No."

He spun around and hurled the Axe, blazing with black starfire, straight toward Queen Nyarla.

For the merest instant Holly thought the attack might work, for Nyarla's eyes flared wide with utter shock.

And then the Axe halted, curved around, and spun howling straight at Eclipse Umbra.

He threw up his arms just in time, but the impact was a shattering detonation; the rebellious Cataclysm Knight was pitched across the asphalt, bouncing irregularly, shedding pieces of armor, enveloped in ebony flames.

"Eclipse—what the *hell*—" Tornadic Gloom's confusion cost him; Temblor Brilliance caught him on the chin with a perfectly timed kick that snapped his head up, body curving until he momentarily resembled a bow in profile before spinning to the ground, semiconscious. His weapon skittered away across the pavement.

Now only three Knights remained, and they, too, were stunned by the sudden betrayal of their leader; Devika-Tempest blocked the massive Hammer of her opponent and delivered a backhanded blow of such power that Avalanche Oblivion spun all the way around and fell to his knees, losing his weapon as well. The remaining two Knights retreated, eyes wide and uncertain.

"Well, well, well," Nyarla said, her voice silky yet coldly amused. "Perhaps you *are* his daughter after all. You managed to turn my Knight against me with words alone. How very . . . appropriate, I suppose."

"Drop your weapons and get out of the way," Holy Aura said,

ignoring Nyarla, looking directly at Infernal Pall and Abyssal Night. "We've got you completely outnumbered now; we can go three-on-one if you want it that way, or you can save yourselves a beating."

Abyssal Night's gaze shifted uneasily back and forth, but he raised his Sword higher. "Queen's still here, bitch. You're not in *her* league, so I'm sticking with the winning team."

Infernal Pall said nothing, looking if anything more nervous and undecided than his partner, but he, too, raised his Scythe and braced for combat.

"Such wisdom from youth. We *are* going to win this battle, little Maidens." Her smile turned suddenly fang-toothed and savage. "Though I no longer require the services of the weak and flawed, who harbor doubt in their hearts."

Abyssal Night spun around instantly, as did Infernal Pall. There was a rattling, scraping noise and Holly saw movement, made a dive to catch Eclipse Umbra's great Axe but missed; she saw the Bow and the Hammer also sliding and bouncing their way across the lot toward Queen Nyarla. The remaining Knights were struggling, trying to hold onto their weapons. Radiance Blaze grabbed hold of Infernal Pall just as he began to tip forward; the Scythe shot away from him but Infernal Pall remained where he was. No one was quite able to grab Abyssal Night, and he was suddenly dragged, cursing furiously, across the hard pavement, straight past Silvertail who leapt away to safety.

Oh, crap. They're heading for the—

The five Weapons—one still with its owner attached—stopped at the five points of the pentagram. Before Silvertail could do more than open his mouth, Queen Nyarla uttered a single alien word and threw her arms wide.

The points of the pentagram blazed up in brilliant colors that represented the Five Cataclysm Knights: black-sparkling nebula, cracked-red-black lava, swirling chill emerald, dull green and brown, cold-sky blue. The luminances flowed out, into the pentagram itself, and then funneled directly to the center . . .

. . . where Arlaung stood above the unmoving, mysterious shape beneath its cloth.

Fuck, someone's about to go all hulky winged angel on us!

Arlaung shuddered, bent over as though trying to hold something in. Then he threw back his head and roared.

The Cataclysm Knights screamed, even half-conscious Tornadic Gloom moaning. Their powers, in their multiplicity of eerie, corrupted luminance, streamed inward, through the points of the pentacle, *pouring* into Arlaung, the Knights' armor fading, evaporating, joining the stream of power flowing toward Nyarla's right-hand man, leaving behind five boys who collapsed senseless to the pavement.

Arlaung's shape expanded, seven feet, eight, almost nine, broadening, splitting the tailored suit into rags—rags that were disintegrating in the twisted, abhorrent energies that now enveloped him. Massive arms extended, the smooth skin becoming a squamous integument, blue-gray scales hard and glinting in the dimming sunlight.

Princess Holy Aura looked up involuntarily, to see more clouds forming, impossibly fast, above them, a sluggish but darkening maelstrom of clouds that now completely blotted out the sun. As the still-transforming monster stepped from the center of the pentagram toward the Maidens, Holly saw Nyarla replace him and begin an invocation that twined darkly around the cloth-draped figure.

That's the whole point of this. If we try to interrupt Nyarla's ritual, Arlaung will tear us apart . . . and if we fight him, Nyarla completes her ritual on time and Azathoth is reborn . . . here.

And she knew only a few minutes remained before it would be high noon.

Chapter 59

Silvertail studied the transforming monster bleakly. Arlaung's hands were now broad, webbed and clawed, and his head a nightmarish cross between a human's and a shark's, with a huge mouth filled with saw-toothed white fangs. *No mere Deep One, this. Something akin to Father Dagon himself, I think, and fully awakened and empowered by Nyarla's sacrifice of her Knights.*

It was a frighteningly clever gambit. The usual course was that the Knights would attempt to hold off the Maidens long enough to permit Queen Azathoth to fully manifest; thus far, the Maidens had always proven victorious and had managed to not only defeat the Knights, but also their creator—whoever had the position of high priestess of the Queen—and thus been able to banish Azathoth before her manifestation became complete. But that was because the Knights were and always had been individually inferior to the Maidens. Nyarla had recognized this, and chosen a being of greater inherent power to receive their *combined* energies and capabilities. At this moment, Arlaung Dagon-Child might be the most powerful living being on the face of the Earth.

And even though he looks like he's a water monster, I see fire and wind swirling around him. He's not going to have any weaknesses, Holly's thoughts came, tensely.

No, he will not, agreed Silvertail reluctantly. He had reverted to his true form and felt even smaller before the forces he now faced; but whatever power he had would be stronger in this shape.

Of course he has a weakness, Tempest Corona retorted sharply. *He is one being. Powerful or not, he has only so much attention to devote to each of us. Unless he's invincible, we can beat him! First—*

And then Arlaung moved.

He was a blue-skinned blur, moving at such velocity Silvertail could not follow him. His elbow—with a wicked bladed edge now projecting from it—rammed into Tempest Corona so hard she folded double, like a paper doll, and cannonballed backward, smashing and skidding across the pavement for over a hundred yards. Even before she hit the ground, Arlaung appeared behind Tsunami Reflection, his immense webbed hand grasping her entire head. Electricity writhed across the Maiden of Water as she was lifted, screaming, and thrown with casually titanic force into Temblor Brilliance; Tierra somehow stayed upright, skidding back across the blacktop with her feet digging twin trenches through the asphalt and gravel, but then fell to her knees, gasping.

Radiance Blaze moved now, her motions increasing in speed, but the sun-bright flare of fire was met by a cannon of dark, stinking water and muck drawn from the primordial ooze beneath the deepest seas. The fire *went out*, and Radiance Blaze's tall, slender form smashed *through* one of the storefront walls; the concussion brought down the roof as well, and half the store collapsed on top of her.

Princess Holy Aura stood momentarily alone, and Arlaung turned to her, his shark mouth wide and grinning. Again that blur of inhuman speed, and Silvertail cringed inwardly. *Holly!*

The impact was a shockwave that tossed the others another dozen feet, shattered the remaining storefront windows, only parting around the glowing star of Nyarla's ritual; even Silvertail, crouched low and behind intervening slabs of rubble, was nearly torn from the ground and sent flying. Fearfully he raised himself up to look.

Holy Aura still stood. Arlaung's blow had driven her backward twenty yards, but the Silverlight Bisento had parried him, and they were momentarily frozen, Arlaung staring in startled disbelief at the furious, unyielding glare of Holly Owen as focused through the power of Princess Holy Aura.

Pure argent power streamed out, encasing Holy Aura in her namesake. "You just hurt my *friends*, you *bastard*!"

Arlaung leapt back as the massive ball on one end of the *bisento* whipped around, and back again as the blade ripped the air toward his chest. Despite that, his smile was broadening again. "It's just a start, air-breather! I'll have all your hearts for *lunch* in a moment!"

He stamped on the ground, and a shockwave of earth *hammered* Holy Aura backward and down, half buried under the tumbled mass of stone and dirt, the *bisento* clattering to the side. Arlaung blurred forward, hand rising to strike—

—and moonlight-silver luminance ripped across his face. The gigantic Deep One roared in pain and tripped, somersaulting involuntarily across the parking lot and fetching painfully up against a light pole, which bent and fell on him.

"Rest assured, monster, thou shalt not touch Princess Holy Aura, unless it be through me," the Prince said; but though it was the Prince's voice, Silvertail knew the fury in that voice belonged to Dexter Armitage.

"Oh, you'll get yours too, posturing little second-rate surfacer," growled Arlaung, levering himself to his feet. With that hideous speed he snatched up the fallen light pole and lunged forward. Caught unprepared, Twilight Dawn barely raised his sword before the pole whipped around and *batted* him across the entire span of the lot, to fall with a cry of pain somewhere in the depths of Fashion Post.

But even at that, Silvertail suddenly felt a rodent smile on his face, because he heard the whisper of mental voices, thoughts as fast as lightning joining together, Devika's voice the conductor of an orchestra of the elements. *I shall begin, and then Tierra, and the rest of you . . .*

Mist and fog rose up from nowhere, enveloping Arlaung in an obscuring haze. He clawed at the air, wind at his command dispersing the fog, but dust and gravel *fountained* from the ground in a blinding cloud; he choked and snarled, lunged furiously upward in an immense bound, clearing the air and rubbing the grit from his eyes—

—only to see Radiance Blaze's chain-whip screaming through the air, its saw-toothed length flaring with red-gold fire. It coiled about Arlaung and retracted, yanking him downward, spinning, roaring his fury—

—Straight into the twin blades of Tsunami Reflection and the gigantic counterweight ball of the Silverlight Bisento.

Arlaung hurtled, spinning end over end, up and over the top of the

Twin Pines Mall, to come down with an apocalyptic *crash* into one of the massive air-conditioning units above the anchor store's main building. The combined concussions and impacts proved too much; the roof caved in, and with an earthshaking thunder the center of DIY Home collapsed.

That won't have stopped him, guys, warned Cordy.

No shit, Seika answered.

Crashing sounds reverberated from within the remaining interior of the huge hardware emporium.

Maidens, Silvertail thought, *It is time.*

Way ahead of you, Dad, thought Holly.

Three should suffice, Devika said. *Now!*

Devika—Tempest Corona—spoke aloud then, and even as Arlaung burst from the wreckage of the store her voice echoed out, pure and hard and certain: "In the name of justice, by the power of the storm and thunder—RELEASE!"

Behind her, Tsunami Reflection was also speaking: "In the name of trust and faith, by the power of the endless seas—RELEASE!"

And Radiance Blaze spoke as well: "In the name of hope and courage, by the flame of the human spirit—RELEASE!"

A lambent violet corona flared up, sharp ozone scenting the air, even as blue-rippling light enveloped Tsunami Reflection and Radiance Blaze's fire ignited into pure gold. The three girls were meteors, blazing through the air to meet the mighty charging figure of the transfigured Arlaung.

And now his face was uncertain.

Speed matched speed, and the huge Khanda sword, one of the three great weapons of a Sikh, parried the blue-scaled fist, edge piercing the shining armored skin and drawing dark blood. Arlaung's other hand was caught by a scissors block from Tsunami Reflection's twin swords, and the flaming whip coiled about one leg.

Instantaneously he called upon the earth, reinforcing himself, bracing and holding him against the powers of the Maidens with the mobile yet intransigent strength of the stone and rock around him. Black sparked with cold white enveloped his hands and Silvertail could sense it grasping hungrily at the girls' spirits, feeding on the power that was, itself, burning at the essential boundaries of their souls.

But the very reinforcement Arlaung called halted him, made him a bulwark but a target as well, and Devika Kaur Weatherill knew what to do with a target. From the lowering clouds gathering overhead came an actinic blaze of lightning, the power of the storm incarnate striking Arlaung directly, his own firm anchor to the earth making him unable to evade or dodge the implacable laws of physics behind the magic. He roared in agonized fury, convulsing under the hammer of thunderbolts that rained from the sky, and throwing up one arm desperately as Tempest Corona's crackling sword came down.

With a shattering report like a mighty oak splitting in a thunderstorm, the Khanda cleaved through Arlaung's arm. He screamed then, a whistling, screeching sound that was utterly inhuman, and tried to escape, lunging backward. Her face pulled tight in fury and the pain of the Release, Tsunami Reflection sent out twin torrents of water that curved about and froze yet still moved, two hurtling juggernauts of ice that converged on Arlaung and smashed him between hammer and anvil. Without even a pause, Radiance Blaze's fire rose up, a coiling dragon of flame, and dove in a curving parabola of doom onto the ice-covered shape. There was a detonation of steam and smoke and melted rock, and the massive form of Arlaung tumbled away limply, a one-armed doll cast aside by a careless child.

Silvertail heard a curse and a cry of "*Arlaung?!*" from the circle; at the same time, the three Maidens dropped to their knees, letting the Seals reestablish themselves before the power of the Release could damage them.

Arlaung lay still, wisps of steam and smoke rising from him, black blood still flowing from the stump of his severed arm.

The three girls stood, and five Apocalypse Maidens turned as one and faced Nyarla.

She glanced at Arlaung, then gave a wintry smile. "You are stronger than I imagined, Maidens. Yet he gave me the moments I needed."

Swiftly, she reached beneath the cloth before her and drew out . . . something. It wasn't a figure—it was something much smaller, barely the size of a clenched fist, but it glittered with a smoky, prismatic hue that shifted and *twisted* the gaze. "Only a few moments remain before the stars are right, and you, poor children, have not a chance of defeating me in *that* time, not now."

Oh, great Lemuria . . . "Beware, Maidens. I believe . . . that is the Trapezohedron, once called the Eye of Azathoth."

"You mean that thing was *real*?" Holly said, staring at it and then averting her gaze.

"Yes and no. It is not a channel to Nyarlathotep, though that being made use of it; it is said to be a link to Azathoth herself. I had never expected to *see* it."

Nyarla laughed. "And well you should not; it was guarded by every generation, a weapon and source of knowledge, but one they feared to lose or have destroyed. But this time I have chosen to unleash its full capabilities—and tailored them to your beloved Maidens!"

Silvertail felt a moment of doubt. The Trapezohedron's powers had been the subject of wonder, rumor, and confusion for centuries, but his impression was that it was more a scrying device than anything else, an oracle with Azathoth's power guiding it. It *shouldn't* be a weapon of formidable power . . . yet Nyarla radiated confidence. *Be cautious, Maidens. I admit I do not know what she might be able to do with that stone.*

Understood. Guys, we'd better fan out—

"Tailored to them indeed, Queen Nyarla," said Prince Twilight Dawn from behind them all.

A brilliant crescent of light the color of the moon and silvered clouds streaked across the parking lot, past and through the Maidens and Silvertail, to splash harmlessly against the spell wall surrounding Queen Nyarla.

And Silvertail felt, to his horror, a tremendous drowsiness fall upon him. He sank to the pavement, fighting with all his will, but his eyelids began to sag. And with a clatter and sigh of armor and gauzy garments, the Apocalypse Maidens, too, collapsed, their limbs gripped with weariness, their eyes closing, sliding face-first toward the ground, beckoned to sleep . . . a sleep from which they might well never awaken.

✴ Chapter 60 ✴

The only thing that kept Holly's eyes open was the overwhelming feeling of horror and betrayal; and even that only kept her aware, but unable to move anything except her head and eyes, and those only enough to look up at Nyarla. *No, Dex! No, you couldn't!*

"Tailored to them," repeated Twilight Dawn, and now he strode forward, past the unmoving bodies of the Maidens, fully into Holly's view. "But *not* to me."

Holly thought Nyarla's face was too controlled, her raised brow a bit *too* casual. *What . . . he didn't betray us?*

"*You* are only a factor when *combined* with the others, little Prince," Nyarla said, beginning to raise the Trapezohedron. "Compared to any of them, you are scarce a child."

"Normally yes," the Prince said, but he was smiling. "Yet my Lady said that once, and once only, would I surpass them, and that would be in the moment they were in greatest danger, when one would be needed to save them—to save them all, as I had sworn." His sword pointed toward Nyarla, steady and gleaming, an arrow of silver awaiting the command to fly forth. "She knew of the Trapezohedron, and guessed your intent. Its power will not avail against that of Queen Lucent, who I now know to be Ruloa of the *Aili*."

A twisted coil of darkness and light *pulsed* from the Trapezohedron, and flew toward Twilight Dawn; but the rapier in his hand caught it, carved it apart into remnants that dissipated harmlessly. "We knew that if the Maidens faced that power, they would be weakened, perhaps slain, for she saw them felled in her vision, a vision she showed me."

Of course. He said it could only be used to protect. *He's defending us—*

—or, Devika's grim mind-voice finished, *he* thinks *he is.*

The Prince's voice was confident now, as he advanced on Queen Nyarla; the Queen hesitated, her face no longer smiling. Holly recognized the ringing tone in that voice; Dex saved it for the climactic confrontation in every game, when his character finally had its chance. *This isn't a game, Dex! Watch out for her!*

Silvertail's mental voice came to her, weakly. *Holly, Maidens, you* must *get up, somehow. There is something very wrong here.*

"And she told me what to do."

With the speed of cloud-shadows in moonlight on a field, Prince Twilight Dawn darted about the pentacle; the Twilight Rapier dipped and danced, carving holes and gaps in every part of that pattern that he passed. "Your summoning and focus are disrupted, and I shall give you no chance to renew them!"

Holly threw her will against that inert, lazy, seductive sleepiness. With aching slowness, she forced a finger to move. Then her hand. In the back of her mind, she felt her friends also straining against the soft simplicity of sleep, a sleep that lay upon them as though they had spent a week awake. *Got . . . to get . . .* up!

Yes, Maidens, you must! What he says does not make sense *to me!*

Now Twilight Dawn advanced, and his rapier slashed three times, the spell wards around Queen Nyarla shattering. The woman backed away, throwing three more braids of dark power at the Prince—dark twists of energy that came apart in the shimmering moon-touched starlight that surrounded him. "And now your hostage, too, is no longer in your control."

I . . . can almost . . . move . . . Holly dragged one arm in, trying to focus. *If I can just get* up *I think this will go away—*

And as the Prince knelt—rapier still pointed at Nyarla—to touch the cloth, Queen Nyarla's face suddenly broadened with a brilliant smile, and she threw her head back and laughed.

Oh, fuck, Seika's mind-voice said.

Prince Twilight Dawn had leapt back to his feet, and his face showed uncertainty. "What—"

"Oh, Prince, you child, so easily led." She raised her hand, and there was a screaming in the air, as of something falling unguessable distances through the protesting atmosphere—

Impact!

Holly would have screamed, but the shock of pain was so great that the breath was driven from her completely. Red haze obscured her vision and the tearing, burning agony consumed her chest and echoed back to her from the other Maidens. *It . . . got all of us . . . what the hell?*

Forcing her eyes to look to the side, she felt the horror intensify. They had been *impaled*, struck through from above by black, spike-covered things like jagged collectors' pins through gigantic insects. A tiny one had even fallen on Silvertail.

Twilight Dawn had whirled and was staring in open-mouthed horror. "What the . . . No, no, this wasn't supposed to—"

He gasped and fell to one knee, face as white as the moon itself. A thin whine of pain escaped his lips as the sword clattered to the pavement from his limp, nerveless fingers, and one hand went up, clutching at his chest.

That sight drove her own pain back, if only for an instant, and breath flowed into her, edged with fire. "D . . . Dex! What's she . . . doing . . . ?"

His eyes met hers, wide, uncomprehending. "Not . . . her. Feels . . . like my chest . . . ripping apart . . . inside me . . ."

Her own heart almost stopped. *No.* "Oh, God, no . . ." she heard herself whisper.

"It was *I* who gave you this power, Prince," Nyarla said sweetly, and for a moment another woman stood there, a beautiful near-human figure of moonlight and silver. "I who showed you that vision—that you now see has come true, with *you* the one ensuring it would come to pass." Her smile widened further as Twilight Dawn's eyes widened in the realization of his failure. "It was *I* who arranged the ambush of Ruloa and took her power—and saved it for all these ages, for it was of little use in the other world, but of great power here.

"And here, at last, I found the right time, the right place; I found a foolish boy who was oh-so-noble, but with one tiny, pitiable flaw . . . a flaw that, exploited properly, would ensure the Maidens' defeat . . . at the hands of their would-be champion, would allow a power meant for defense to lay them low, a power weaker than theirs to strike them from behind . . . all in the name of *protecting* them." She threw back her head and laughed again, and there was very little human in that amusement.

Shit. His grandstanding. Dex always wanted to be the Hero, the one standing at the finale . . .

With a tremendous effort Dexter Armitage forced himself upright, tried to lunge with his sword at Nyarla; she simply struck him down with a gesture.

"And now the stars are right, and as I foretold,"—she smiled down at Holly and the others—"I will be able to present you to my Queen in person."

Twilight Dawn looked straight at Holly, meeting her gaze, his face bleak with acceptance of the truth. "Oh, God, Holly. I'm sorry, I'm so sorry, it's my fault, and now—"

He screamed again, and then blackness *fountained* from his mouth, his eyes, his chest. Even as that happened, the swirling clouds overhead . . . *opened*, and a darkness blacker than night rippled and flowed within, streaming down and joining the pitch-blackness now writhing about Twilight Dawn's body.

No, no, no, no . . .

The blackness condensed to an ichor, a flowing, sluggish tide of pure night that enveloped the screaming, struggling form, dissolving the trappings of Twilight Dawn and leaving, for just an instant, the staring, terrified eyes of Dexter Armitage before even that was obscured. Lightning played through the clouds above and the tide of onyx slime rose higher, became a vague, viscid figure, a rippling gelatinous mass that had an obscene hint of head and feet and arms, that stirred and rose to all fours; Nyarla placed the Trapezohedron within that flowing obscenity; it began to stabilize then stood, wobbling at first, the head towering ten feet above the ground and still rising.

"Lemuria's Memory preserve us all," she heard Silvertail murmur, even against the agony of impalement.

Darkness was now spreading across the land—not just from the clouds, but a darkness that brought with it a rustling crepitation as of *things* waiting in the dimness, *things* that were approaching through the cloak of dim night about them and that, if seen, might drive one mad.

And suddenly she *saw*, through that connection she had felt to her world and her universe, *saw* the world:

—*saw* the buildings of nearby Albany twisting, becoming knife-edged towers of blood-touched onyx under a boiling red sky

—*saw* a boy and his mother walking on a beach far away, at night, Hawaii perhaps, and the stars above winking out, wavering, a few becoming pitiless white orbs, dead and cold, and the palms distorting, rattling like bones and grasping the air without wind, as the beach grew cold and *something* heaved itself from the sea before them and began to slowly make its way, with chitinous limbs grating and insectoid mouth working, toward the terrified child

—*saw* a field in distant China shaking, and long-dead arms thrusting forth from the soil, animated not by the spirits of humanity but something infinitely more horrific

—*saw* the three-lobed Eye of Nyarlathotep blink and smile an impossible mouthless smile as it found Holly's spirit and her world and knew it could return

—*saw* some ancient, indescribable ruins far beneath the ocean as they suddenly thrust upwards, rising, water cascading away from them, carrying eons of ancient foulness away, and within the ruins *something* stirred and tried to open a tomb sealed so long stone had formed across the door . . .

From the sludge-like figure more arms extended, two to a side, three, four, and then a final arm protruding from the thing's back, reaching up and over the head, a hideous tentacular scorpion tail. The shape began to solidify, manifesting something horrifically alien yet undeniably humanoid and female, and it raised the arms and gave a bubbling, echoing cry that almost broke Holly's will to fight, to struggle.

"The stars are *right*," Nyarla repeated, voice filled with ecstatic triumph, "And Azathoth Nine-Armed is come again!"

✴ Chapter 61 ✴

For a moment, Holly lay there, complete and utter despair flooding her, looking through Steve's eyes as everything they had tried to accomplish—that *he* had tried to accomplish—fell away, demolished by the enemy's foresight and planning.

Azathoth's here, *and we're just bugs in her collection. We were supposed to* stop *this, seal her away, and now it's over. Nyarla* said *we only had to lose once . . . and now we have.*

Steve let her head loll back to the ground and Holly's tears of pain and defeat flowed down his face. *My friends are all going to die, my* world *is going to die, and it's too late to stop it.*

And then a tiny voice finally penetrated her consciousness.

Holly! Holy Aura*! It is not too late! Until Azathoth is fully manifest—completely formed—and the world utterly under her sway, she can still be banished! But we must act* now*!* The little white rat's agony was clear beneath the calm words, but she could sense the truth.

It's not too late.

Those four words were the ones they needed, and the will—*her* will—united, banished the enervation of despair. She forced her head up, glaring at the laughing Queen Nyarla, gathering her strength. "You . . . *bitch*."

"Curse at the boy, not at me, Holy Aura," Nyarla said with another laugh. "*He* was the one who defeated you."

"You *played* him," Seika said venomously.

"And you, as well, yes, and darling Varatraine. How *delicious* that you had enough hope left, Varatraine, that you could bring yourself to believe Ruloa still lived."

Silvertail's voice was thready with pain, but still unwavering. "You used her own power; that was, I admit, brilliant, and convincing. No wonder I did not sense darkness within him; his nature as the Vessel was concealed within the genuine, untainted power of the Aili."

While they spoke, Holy Aura tried to assess her condition. *This . . . thing impaled me through the chest, but somehow missed vitals. I guess that was intended—she said she wanted to present us to Azathoth. But it's gone all the way through me and who knows how deep into the ground!*

Devika's mind-voice was grim but certain. *Then we must pull them* out *of the ground.*

She could feel Seika and Tierra cringe at the thought, and she shuddered, feeling fresh spikes of pain even with that tiny motion. The shafts through them weren't smooth pins or stakes, they were covered with sharp spines. Any movement would be . . .

We must, Devika said.

Holly realized she *could* move again, the agony and fear—and perhaps the rebirth of Azathoth and thus dispersal of Twilight Dawn—having banished the lethargy and sleepiness. Now the only paralysis was the pulsing pain and fear of even greater agony weighting her limbs.

"We . . ." Devika ground out, and slid her arms in, hands beneath her, flat to the shattered blacktop, "are not . . ."

She began to push. ". . . yet . . ."

Nyarla's laugh rang out again. "You can't possibly mean to fight me *now*!"

There was a faint grinding noise. Though Devika's brown skin was graying, her expression did not change, and Holly bit her lip in sympathetic horror and hope. *Did she move? Is she—*

The rough grating noise was louder, and now there was dim light beneath Devika's chest. ". . . finished!" Devika said, and though her voice was quavering with agony, it was determined, unyielding, certain.

We can do this! It was Cordy's mind-voice, calling to them, reminding them that they were not alone, that they were *together*.

I won't let Devika be the only one, Holly thought, and without letting herself hesitate, put her hands on the rough parking lot and *shoved*.

Agony exploded from her chest, from the shuddering vibration of the shaft trying to grip the ground with the spikes along its length, from the wriggling of the spine-covered shaft within her body, from the longer spikes that blossomed above her and made the nightmarish head of this gigantic collector's pin, but somehow she held the agony at bay. Her memories as Steve helped, memories of the injuries and pain he had suffered as an adult—a broken ankle and having to hobble on it half a mile through a storm, a twisted back, a kidney stone. None of these quite *matched* this pain, but they reminded him that pain *passed*, that pain was part of *life* sometimes, and that as long as Holly Owen *felt* pain she was still *alive*.

The black-spined shaft tore free from the pavement and Holly—somehow—forced herself upright, standing with the thing still through her body, held immovably by the spines within her flesh. To her amazement . . . and utter pride that made her tears at least as much joy as agony . . . she saw that not just Devika, but the other three, too, were standing, facing Queen Nyarla, who for the moment was not laughing, but staring, eyebrow raised, at the unexpected sight. A tiny sound to the left, and Holly realized that even Silvertail had managed to tear himself free.

"We . . . aren't done . . . yet," Holly forced out, realizing that at the moment she wasn't getting much air. *Punctured a lung? Diaphragm, maybe? I'm getting some in, but it's really limited.*

Nyarla had recovered, and laughed again. "Oh, dear, how very heroic of you. But you *are* done, children. But a few minutes before the Queen is fully manifest, and you want to fight *me* when you can barely *stand*?"

Much as she wanted to deny Nyarla's words, Holly couldn't. She was using the *bisento* to support her; Devika leaned on her Khanda, and Seika, Cordy, and Tierra were supporting each other in a sort of wavering way. *We can't fight like this. We couldn't beat that guy that followed me down the* street *like this. We have to heal up!*

"But even so," Nyarla continued, "Why should I risk it?" Her smile was fangs and hatred. "Do you not realize you are *entirely* at my mercy?"

She snapped her fingers, and black lightning danced its way along the impaling black spikes, draining Holly's strength, pain turning her knees to jelly, making her drop, kneeling, almost on all fours, the point of the spike scraping with vibrating agony on the blacktop.

We can't heal with these things in us. And they'll kill us with that power anyway. Which means . . .

She could barely contemplate what she had to do; even the memories of Steve weren't enough to help.

But the screams of her friends, and the knowledge of Dex, entombed in that towering, condensing form before her, were.

She grasped the shaft as far in front of her as she could, gripping hard, heedless of the sharp points of its thorny exterior stabbing deep into her hands. *One shot. Gotta do this in one shot or I'll never have the guts to try again.*

With a supreme effort, Holly Owen—Princess Holy Aura—refused the weakness of pain, denied the dark power trying to drain her strength, and *pulled back* towards her with all the strength of both arms.

With a sucking, tearing sound and a paroxysm of unendurable agony, the spike was torn from her and hurled backward, clattering impotent to the ground.

For a moment, all was silent . . . then there were four more cries of fury and pain, and around her, four more spikes hit the ground as well, echoed by the higher tinkling sound of a much smaller spike being cast away.

Red was filling her gaze, the crimson haze of agony threatening to take her consciousness, but without Nyarla's black, soul-draining spike through her, she *felt* the power of Holy Aura once more, drew it in, called on it to lift her up. *Tsunami Reflection,* she thought, and focused, trying to channel what she could into the other girl. *If I can just get her moving . . .*

She began to fall.

Cordy caught her arm, and there was a liquid glow of sapphire. Pain began to recede, and as it did, Holly felt more strength flowing into her, and sent it back out, into Cordy and Seika and Devika and Tierra. The strength of Earth and Water flowed back into them, knitting torn tissues, shoring up the weakened flesh, driving out pain, and Holly felt her head coming up.

Queen Nyarla's eyes were wide, disbelieving, as the five Apocalypse Maidens straightened, their wounds healing, their armor rebuilding itself before her eyes, and now for the first time Holly saw real doubt, a touch of actual fear, in those ancient, young eyes.

Princess Holy Aura raised her arm, sensed the arms of her comrades doing so at the same time. "Queen Nyarla, you have deceived and betrayed our friend, turning his wish to be a hero into destruction, and him into the instrument of the world's obliteration! In your own Knights you have corrupted courage and twisted hope, but *we* are the Apocalypse Maidens!"

Five fingers pointed directly at Nyarla, who gripped the hilt of the sword at her side with white-knuckled fingers. "And the Apocalypse Maidens say that *you*"—the hands formed fists, and the thumbs thrust toward the earth in finality—"are going *DOWN*!"

Chapter 62

Radiance Blaze moved first, her chains lighting the eldritch night with purity of flame. Nyarla snarled something in Lemurian and the chains rebounded, the impact momentarily outlining a wall like an unsubstantial beehive surrounding Nyarla with a multiplicity of hexagonal shields. Tentacles of night-dark snatched at Radiance Blaze, but her fire incinerated them before they could even touch her armor.

Tsunami Reflection made a double-cut and brilliant crescents of high-pressure water slammed into the shield; pieces of the insubstantial barrier shattered, and Nyarla gestured again, reinforcing it and sending a fluttering cloud of nightgaunts screaming at Tsunami and Temblor Brilliance, but even though these creatures were four times the size of the ones Steve had fought on that faraway night, and glowed darkly with the power of Azathoth's rebirth, the two Maidens brushed them aside like gnats, fury and determination writ coldly across their faces.

We have to finish this fast, *guys*, Holly thought grimly. *That . . . thing's starting to solidify.*

Understood. Silvertail, we'll be making a delivery, can you arrange a container? Devika's mind-voice was as matter-of-fact as if she were planning a play on the basketball court.

Holly launched herself at Nyarla, and the impact of the Silverlight Bisento cleaved half through Queen Nyarla's shield, forcing her backward. For a moment she wondered why Devika was talking like that, then she understood; Devika was taking no chances that this, their strongest enemy, could possibly read their mental messages. Even if Nyarla could, she would gain nothing from it.

A . . . ah, yes, of course. All the materials are to hand. I will need a few moments.

"Oh, I shall give you *none*!" Nyarla's voice was unsteady, high pitched and filled with disbelieving anger, but her hands and power were deadly controlled. She ripped her black-crystal sword from its sheath and cut; shards of edged night screamed outward, summoned from the very air, fanning out to completely encompass Silvertail and everything for a dozen yards around him.

They never reached their target; the earth itself reared up, an impassable barrier against which the razor-shards broke harmlessly.

Holy Aura threw a salute to Tempest Corona. *Good call, Dev; she* can *read this!*

Tempest Corona grinned, a flash of white in the gloom, and her great sword came down, surrounded by the crackling aura of the power of storms. Nyarla gave an inarticulate scream of hatred and flung her arms outward.

The barely visible shield *expanded*, a controlled and solid explosion that rammed into all five Maidens like a dozen sledgehammers. Holly tasted blood in her mouth as she smashed through one of the remaining storefronts, scattering cold cuts, cheeses, and bread in all directions. Nyarla summoned the darkness to her, armored herself in night and alien power, and gestured again. Half-seen gateways shimmered in the air, and *things* began to come through them.

Even with the strength and power of the Apocalypse Maiden surrounding her, Holly felt her mind recoil from what she was seeing. The creatures made no *sense*; she could somehow see them from in *front* and *behind* and *below* and *above* at once, and all sides were hideous assemblages of mad eyes and slavering orifices, sucker mouths hungry and champing and howling.

Silvertail's mind-voice spoke then. *Ready.*

Even as the creatures began to pull themselves all the way through, Devika shouted, "Combo Platter in a Box!"

Nyarla blinked—and then whirled as she saw a complex spell wall surround her, one open only in one direction—toward the Maidens.

Ignoring the creatures now slitherwalking toward them, Cordy called out, "*Raging Tsunami—*", and before her a gargantuan wave, shining with the blue-green of the tropics, rose up . . .

"*—Volcanic—*" Tierra and Seika said together, and the wave began to boil and steam, while black and red seethed in its depths . . .

"*—Thunder—*" said the implacable voice of Devika Kaur Weatherill, and lightning played across the mighty breaker as it roared across the pavement, straight toward the disbelieving Nyarla . . .

"*—Star-Strike!*" Into and behind that immense wave, that shuddered with the power of four Apocalypse Maidens, Holly threw every ounce of Holy Aura's strength, calling on that singing starlight she had seen in her first true awakening.

Nyarla tried to dodge, realized she had no time to break the wall, and then with an insane shriek of denial, hurled a coiling bolt filled with twisting *colors* that Holly's eyes and mind could neither imagine nor describe.

But the combined attack of the Maidens absorbed that abominable energy as though it were a pebble, and the roiling holocaust of power rose and then came down upon Queen Nyarla.

The impact of the wave knocked them all to the ground, and scoured the pavement away, stripping it from the earth beneath as though it were nothing but the thinnest coating of dust. It continued on, bulldozing the bank and leaving nothing behind, to end only after wiping away the far end of Twin Pines. The wave faded away, leaving only a confused and immense pile of debris.

The creatures—and their gateways—were gone as well.

For a moment the five girls stood, watching, waiting to see if somehow Nyarla had survived even *that*. But there was no movement.

Then Holly looked up. A face was beginning to emerge from the formlessness, with eyes that glowed with those impossible, unspeakable *colors*, a glow that pierced the eyes yet shed no light in the gloom that still deepened. And below, where Azathoth's stomach should be, two *more* eyes, and a mouth opening, a fanged orifice large enough to consume an eighteen-wheeler in one bite.

"Now, Maidens! As you did with Nyarlathotep!"

The old pentacle had been erased from existence, but the Maidens did not need it; they could form the five-pointed star themselves. Azathoth Nine-Armed stirred, made an abortive gesture.

"Pay her no heed!" Silvertail said. "She cannot act until she is fully manifest—and it is that which we must prevent at all costs! *Hurry*!"

Holly reached her point. *North, I'm supposed to be north . . .*

There was neither sun nor star to guide her, and even if she had *had* a compass she wasn't sure it would be working. But she *did* know that the road running *past* the mall went north-south along this stretch, and that was good enough. "Ready!"

The Maidens extended their arms, the light streaming from them once more, and the brilliant star appeared; then the arms stretching back, back, turning the figure to the broken-pointed shape of the Elder Sign that was on each brooch.

Azathoth gave a distant, furious double roar from both mouths, but Holly realized there was nothing else the Nine-Armed *could* do. All her energies were bent on her manifestation, and if she stopped to try to *act*, she would release her anchor on the world itself, and disappear.

"Now you must put another Seal about the gateway through which she comes!" Silvertail shouted, over a wind that was now rising. Crackling, deep-violet lightning ripped through the clouds above, accompanied by thunder that sounded like roars and screams.

Tierra stared upward at the blacker-than-black eye of the storm. "What? That's like . . . twenty thousand feet up or something!"

"Your powers are strong enough and more than strong enough, Maidens!" Silvertail said. "Keep the Seal between you and *rise*!"

Rise?

Wait, Tierra thought. *I could make the earth* stretch *up . . .*

I can be a rocket, Seika thought with glee.

A waterspout could carry me aloft, Cordy added slowly.

And the winds can of course lift me. Perhaps I could also lift you, Holly?

She shook her head. *No. No, we have to do this ourselves, not divert our energies outside.* She smiled suddenly. *I kept jumping, but never thought about* flying, *even though sometimes I seemed suspended in air. But if I'm the power of spirit and the stars themselves . . .*

Holly concentrated, and reached *within*. Instantly she felt the power, and looked at it more closely. *Yes. I'm . . . this body, it's* made *of magic, of the power of the spirit. And spirits are not bound by gravity.*

Still holding her arms in a sharp V behind her, Princess Holy Aura leapt into the sky, and pure white light trailed behind her. On her right hand, Radiance Blaze climbed upward on a stream of fire; to her left, a rising column of earth and stone propelled Temblor Brilliance skyward, while across from her she could see a crackling storm driving Tempest Corona to her destination and a whirling maelstrom stretching to the heavens with Tsunami Reflection at its tip.

They reached the hissing, crackling clouds, and as they came level with the edge of that black hole, the gateway through which streamed the essence of Queen Azathoth Nine-Armed, Holly felt a *shock* go through her, a sensation as of a bolt sliding back.

Instantly the rainbow of light—white, red, blue, green, violet—that had followed them *solidified,* became a brilliant *pillar* of crystallized energy that rippled with all colors of the Earthly rainbow, a mute yet absolute argument against the alien, obscene glow of Azathoth's rage-filled eyes.

Perfect, *Maidens! Now swiftly, to the points on the ground and banish her! Send her back whence she came and we will have won, the world will be safe once more!*

Holly released the power that had buoyed her up, plummeted back toward the ground, then accelerated that drop, somehow *sensing* how fast she could—and must—return without risking her own injury. The other Maidens were but an instant behind her, and all five stood now secure in their places, the obdurate power of the Seal holding Azathoth for the moment, and its Light even keeping the creeping, alien monstrosities that were growing from the landscape from approaching.

The same invocation that sent back Procelli, Holly thought. *With a different ending, but basically the same.*

Your instincts for this are right and true, Silvertail said.

Tierra nodded and her voice echoed out across the battleground: "By the Earth, the world on which we stand—"

Holly looked around at the others as they began the last ritual, the final act that she would ever do with the Maidens . . . with her friends.

"—by the Water that cradles all that lives—" said Cordy Ingemar.

She looks so tired. Even after healing, we're so battered, bloody . . . Steve felt his heart aching, seeing what these girls—*children*—had been put through, while the adults could do no more than stand by. *And so* thin, *we've burned pounds and* pounds *in this battle . . .*

"—by the Air, that gives us breath and life—" intoned Devika, ignoring exhaustion and injury and standing so proudly that Holly could barely look at her. Holly let her gaze slide outward, across the shadow-haunted nightmare the mall was becoming. She saw the sprawled figures of the Knights, smaller and more helpless without their armor, each in a slowly shrinking circle of earth surrounded by nightmare. *More kids. More victims of these* things.

"By the Fire that burns within, that warms us in the night—" Seika said firmly, but Holly could see the tears on her cheeks and felt her own throat burning, her eyes stinging. *This is it. This is the end. But we've won.*

She forced her voice to be strong and pure as she spoke, "And by the power of the Spirit, the foundation of all . . ."

So why don't I feel like we've won?

She raised her eyes and looked at the towering figure of Azathoth. *Dex.*

But the ritual had to be completed; Azathoth had to be banished. "By all the Powers we banish thee, we abolish thee, we drive you hence from all Time and Space!"

Azathoth roared again, and this time there were *words* in that sound, in a language Holly could not imagine and yet she *did* understand, threats and imprecations, offers of power and of obscene delights to shatter a human soul. *No, you invading abomination, we're sending you away, and hope you can't come back for a thousand years!*

Come back . . .

"So say the Apocalypse Maidens, and by our power it is *DONE*!"

The earth shuddered, then *heaved*, and Queen Azathoth Nine-Armed bellowed her fury. But the gateway above her turned to *Light*, and she began to be drawn *up*, her substance being pulled back and hurled into the Void from whence she had come, shrinking as her very form was dissipating back to the Void from which it had come . . .

. . . and from which she will one day return.

There *was* something wrong, and that sense of wrongness formed itself into a question. *Why did this all start? Why did Silvertail choose me?*

Holly suddenly felt an implacable fury rise in her as she thought about what had happened, what was *going* to happen . . . and just as suddenly, she felt a revelation burst in on her, a decision so *obvious* that she should have realized it ages ago.

And Princess Holy Aura stepped back, away from the pentagram, and the Seal shattered, the portal above went darker than darkest night.

Queen Azathoth Nine-Armed was free—and it was far too late to perform the Seal again.

In a few moments, Azathoth would have the victory she had awaited for untold thousands of years.

✶ Chapter 63 ✶

"*Holly?!* What the *fuck* have you *done*?" demanded the exhausted, terrified, confused voice of Seika.

But Holly wasn't listening, couldn't allow herself to listen. There were only a few dwindling moments remaining, and she had to do this, do it *right*, because that was why they had begun, why *Steve* had begun this journey, and they were the same person, really. Holly/Steve nodded to themself and bowed her head. *We began this . . . Silvertail and I did this because we wanted to do the* right *thing.*

The others were calling, even starting for her, but she shook her head, felt two tears fall from her eyes. She folded her hands as if in prayer, head bent over them, and spoke, letting the words come from within, where the wills and spirits of her predecessors awakened and felt hope once more:

"By the sacrifices of those who have gone before, by the courage of those who stand with me, in the name of the future for which we fight, I call upon the power of the Maidens! Strength of Earth, the foundation of the world; strength of Air, the power of storm, the breath of life; strength of Water, the essence of the blood; strength of Fire, that nurtures and protects; and the strength of the Spirit and the stars beyond!" Her head came up, flinging back the midnight-violet hair with a sparkle of pure white light, and she finished the invocation, "I call to you all and command you—*RELEASE*!"

The other four Maidens staggered and fell to their knees, as brilliant-glowing power streaked from them to Holly; flaming red-orange-gold and the sense of love and fierce devotion, thunder-corona purple and determination of a warrior, rippling blue with sympathy and support, green and the singing, dancing spirit of the artist, all converged on her as her own power flared up, star-bright argent.

It was a silent explosion of pure force, a detonation that knocked her friends down, sent the encroaching monsters tumbling away like dust, even limned the still-looming form of Azathoth Nine-Armed, outlining the shield that protected the forming Queen of the Elder Beings. Holly heard a scream, realized it was her own, as the powers combined ignited within her, filled her body and soul with an inferno of agony that was also so ecstatic she could barely remember who she was, what she was trying to do.

And then a single, quiet voice: *Holly . . . why?*

Because we promised we would do the right *thing,* she answered, glad that it was telepathic or she knew she would scream, or cry.

But if you had completed the banishment . . .

. . . I would have just shoved the problem off, onto the next group of kids. And the next, and the next. If there's a chance, I have to try. It's the ethical, moral choice . . . just like you taught me.

Silvertail looked both stricken and vindicated. *And if you fail?*

She managed a smile, knowing that by now her whole *body* must be glowing, it would be a hint of a smile in the midst of a rainbow furnace. *Nyarla was right. All we have to do is lose* once, *and it's over. And if they keep* trying, *some day they'll win . . . unless, somehow, we can put an* end *to it. Put an end to* Azathoth *herself.*

A private thought, to Silvertail only: *And Dad . . . you were the one that said we might be the strongest Maidens that have ever been.*

A pause, filled with that mingled aching pride and fear that truly made him her father: *Yes. Yes, you are, daughter of my heart and spirit. Strongest in every way, so that even Aureline would know her truest sisters could stand at her side and none be less than her equal. But to see you do* this . . .

Then she saw the four others slowly standing, summoning the remaining powers of the Maidens to them, and weakened or not, the energies lit up the horror-night about them with certainty and courage. "She's right, Silvertail," Devika said.

God, no, Holly . . . but . . . Seika's horrified thoughts caught, and she somehow gained control. ". . . but yes," she said aloud, her voice thick with tears but as hard and certain as it had ever been. "Let's stop this. Forever. Never again. Never *fucking* again."

Cordy and Tierra echoed it. "Never again."

She could barely make out the tiny white form through the energies that shimmered around her, but the voice was clear, sad and yet trembling with pride for her. *You know that if you do this, you and Steve will—*

"I know," she said aloud, and looked up, at the towering figure that was now almost fully formed. "But I'm okay with that, completely . . ." —her voice rose, echoing through the darkling gloom—"as long as children *NEVER* have to pay this price again!"

She raised the Silverlight Bisento and pointed it directly at Queen Azathoth Nine-Armed, even as the eyes focused on her, poisonous wells of malevolence within the nearly solidified form. "You're going *NOWHERE*, monster!"

Through the mystic weapon she channeled all the rage, the pain, the *prices* she had been chosen to pay . . . and the joy, the love, the wonder she had gained in return. "*APOCALYPSE SPIRIT!*"

Pure white light, so brilliant it turned the eldritch night bright as day, blasted from the Silverlight Bisento, and the holy weapon began to *melt* from the energies it carried, silvery-glowing metal dripping from the blade. The spear of intolerable brilliance struck as a quasi-solid mass of pure power, shattering the shield about Azathoth, then eradicating a second shield like paper before a blowtorch, and finally blowing a hole in a third shield not an arms' length from the alien god's form, to burn its way deep into the monstrous black shape.

Even as Azathoth gave vent to a dual scream that shook the world itself, Holly was thinking to the others: *Please, all of you—*

She saw, suddenly, that Tempest Corona already understood. *We know. Everyone—*NOW*!*

Fiery tears trailing behind her, Radiance Blaze was first, and her chains stretched, coiled out and around, and suddenly the four arms on the left-hand side of Azathoth were bound together, being pulled back by Seika's remaining strength. Tempest Corona flew, enveloped in crackling storm clouds, and threw her arms around the scorpion arm, preventing it from reaching down. Cordy's water encircled two of the remaining arms, solidified, steel-hard ice encasing and immobilizing, while Tierra caused the very dust in the air to condense and coat the last pair, jacketing them in unmoving stone.

The way was clear.

"Go, Holly!" shouted Seika, and Radiance Blaze's tears were streams of glittering fire. "*GO!*"

Go, came Silvertail's thought. *I love you, Holly Owen.*

Her own tears evaporating in pure power as she gathered herself, she replied. *I love you too, Silvertail. All of you. I love you and . . . I think this really is goodbye.*

Then Holy Aura lunged forward, a streak of whitest sunshine arrowing through the murk, closing her mind against everything except what she must do. "*IT'S OVER!*" she shouted, and her voice was a clarion cry, a sounding of trumpets and drums, a roar of challenge.

Azathoth saw her coming, gritted two sets of fangs and threw up another shield. But both that shield and the Silverlight Bisento shattered on impact, and Princess Holy Aura drove onward, her body crackling with unspeakable pain and unendurable ecstasy and power enough to rend worlds, an unstoppable projectile driven by will and hope, to smash into and *through* the dead-bone fangs and plunge irresistibly into the noisome depths of Queen Azathoth Nine-Armed.

She screamed again in concert with Azathoth herself, one a scream of outraged agony and fury and fear, the other of revulsion and denial and hope and love in extremity, and her light made the very *substance* of Azathoth recoil, evaporating before the absolute force of the radiance of the first Apocalypse Maiden. Holly felt herself buoyed up by the echoes of the past, even, she thought, a sense of another girl who had looked very much like her, who had made the decision for herself—just as Holly did—and had once called a man named Varatraine "Father."

The substance of Azathoth grasped at her now, each spined and acid-dripping tendril vaporizing on contact yet each slowing her. A dozen, a hundred more, and she felt the pressure, the noxious strength of unutterable hatred and alien hunger clawing at her, but she drove onward. *You will not stop me,* she thought, and she felt a shudder throughout the immense form, and the first intimations of doubt entering a mind that had never known the possibility of threat.

And before her she saw a figure entwined in vile blackness, organic web of dark veins and ebony flesh, pulsing as it slowly sapped the figure within of all it was.

She tore free of the last attempts to impede her and plunged directly into that heart of darkness. The obscene cocoon shuddered and then *vaporized* at her furious assault, and she caught him as he fell forward. Azathoth thrashed around them, but for that instant it was still in the tiny space, and she enfolded Dexter Armitage in her arms, curling her body around his.

She gave him a single kiss on the bedraggled, vileness-soaked hair. "Remember me," she whispered.

Then Princess Holy Aura, First Maiden of the Apocalypse, unleashed everything she had to give, and the universe turned to pure light.

✳ Chapter 64 ✳

Silvertail gripped the stone beneath him so tightly he felt his claws might shatter. Holly—Princess Holy Aura—said her farewells and he told her the truth that she had known, but that can never be said enough, and then she was up, she was burning away the night, a meteor of purest argent against a figure of malevolent black.

She struck and disappeared within, and Azathoth went mad. She thrashed and struggled with rage and, he thought, the realization of that alien emotion, fear. Radiance Blaze and the others were cast aside in that paroxysmal convulsion, unable to hold the Queen of Elder Things in the full power of her fury. Seeing them felled and then struggling to rise, he regained his voice. "No, Maidens, stay down! There is no more you can do, except hope and pray to whatever you believe in!"

Aureline, he thought, *help your sister. Ruloa, whatever remains of you, protect her.* He hesitated, then closed his eyes. *And you, the Five Gods that I have spoken not to in all the years since my world fell . . . help her, if you exist, if ever you cared. Give her this victory.*

Let her teach a god how to die.

For an instant, he *felt* a presence, many presences, a dozen, a hundred, ten thousand and more, as Azathoth froze. The world—a *thousand* worlds—held its breath as Reality paused, balanced between the Queen of Monsters and the will of a single Maiden.

Brilliant rays of pure white *speared* outward from within Azathoth Nine-Armed, and the *things* that had materialized from alien, eldritch realms *screamed.* They scuttled-crawled-oozed backward, away from the incomprehensible, but there was nowhere to run, for in the next frozen fraction of an instant, Queen Azathoth Nine-Armed *exploded.*

The blast was a shockwave of white, of purity that *sang* as it ripped across the landscape, and where it touched the black, alien corruption was wiped away, sent back to the nameless realms from whence it had come. Silvertail *sensed* its passage outward, and like Holly he *saw.*

—*saw* the obscene red-black towers suddenly wiped clean, edifices of concrete and steel with sharp and proud lines standing tall and unmarred in the sunshine that now shone down, undimmed, upon the South Mall and all around it

—*saw* a nightmarish *thing* looming over a child and mother, claws extended to rend and crush, suddenly freeze, and then light shine *through* the creature, turning it gray and transparent, a luminance that erased the creature, turned the bone-rattling trees to palms waving in a gentle breeze beneath a night sky, and enfolded mother and son in a reassuring nimbus that said *it's all right, it's over*

—*saw* an army of skeletal monstrosities pause as though hearing some terrible cry, and then collapse, falling to dust long-dead, and the soldiers and citizens staring in unbelieving relief and gratitude

—*saw* a cyclopean tomb door grinding shut against its furious occupant, and the ancient, impossible island shudder as the ocean reclaimed it, plunging its obscene bulk beneath ten thousand feet of serene ocean.

For a moment he could do nothing but stare, blinking at the sunlight that warmed the shattered stone and the very air around him, trying to grasp the fact that the impossible had *happened.*

Then the triumph and tragedy struck him, and as Trayne Owen he stood, tears streaming unashamed down his face even as he smiled a smile of inutterable pride and joy, and shouted, "She has *done* it! Azathoth Nine-Armed, the Undying Queen, is no more!"

Where Azathoth had stood was a boiling cloud of light and shadow, slowly dissipating in the sunshine. The girls—no longer in their Raiments, but merely themselves now— gathered about it, crying, and he joined them.

Then he heard Seika's breath catch, and he looked up, to see the faintest hint of a figure within the ebbing light, a human shape wavering at the center of the crater, a blurred sketch in pencil and wash.

The girls held their breath, and Trayne, too, found himself not breathing, waiting to see what impossibility awaited within that evaporating, luminous cloud.

Then the light blew away, the last shreds of mist in a sunlit morning.

Seika and Tierra caught the thin, wasted figure of Dexter Armitage before he could hit the pavement. He raised a hollow-eyed gaze to see who had caught him, looked around.

Then Dex covered his face with his hands and began to cry.

A part of Trayne wanted to be angry at the boy, for his vainglorious act that had led to this ending. But he knew—none better—that all humans had weaknesses. *He is punishing himself far more than I could manage.*

"Come," he said. "Let's go home."

"Home" was, of course, his own house. He had nowhere else to go, and he did not think that the remaining Maidens were ready to go to their own homes.

The journey back had been silent, broken only by Dex's quiet but constant sobs. Trayne tried to conceal the heartbreak that he felt; it would be pointless to add anything to the younger people's burdens. He busied himself instead with ensuring that none of the many police, firemen, and others now surrounding the area noticed or interfered with their passage.

The quiet in the Owen home was itself oppressive, a reminder that its brightest and most-beloved resident was not coming home again. He busied himself by putting together a mass of sandwiches and other food.

Despite initial gestures indicating they didn't want anything, the Maidens, and eventually even Dexter Armitage, began to eat, which afforded Trayne the slightest bit of relief. All five of the youngsters were frighteningly thin, having expended incredible amounts of their own mass in the use of the powers in that final battle; Dex, of course, had lost some of his to Azathoth, although the very fact he still *had* a body indicated that some of that power and mass must have been returned to him when the Nine-Armed had been defeated.

"Why do we remember?"

The sudden shock of Devika's—or indeed anyone's—voice made

everyone jump. A shuddering sigh ran around the table, but Trayne felt a tiny trickle of warmth reentering his heart as he saw that by breaking the silence, the tall Sikh girl had also forced her friends out of their isolated gloom. The heads that raised and looked at him had gazes that were filled with pain and loss, but also, now, a touch of curiosity, of interest, and less of despair, even Dex looking *at* instead of *past* Trayne.

"Yeah," Seika said after a moment. "I thought once that *monster* was beaten, everything was going to rewind."

Trayne frowned. "That . . . is an excellent question." But even as he said that, a slow and wondering understanding—and, behind it, a new worry and weight of responsibility—emerged. "But . . . she was not *beaten*. She was *destroyed*. As Holly . . ." His voice wavered, but he forced himself to continue. "As Holly intended, Azathoth Nine-Armed was not sent back to her continuum to try again, but eradicated, wiped entirely out of all time and space. Traces of her *power* may remain in various parts of the cosmos, but the *entity*, and the vast majority of her might, is gone, destroyed by the will and courage of Princess Holy Aura."

"So . . ." Dex's voice sounded rusty, thick and rough, but he spoke. "So this never-ending cycle you told us about . . . it's actually *ended*."

"I . . . suppose so. It *must* be, since we are still here, speaking of it." Trayne heard the wonder in his own voice, and for the first time since the battle managed a smile that was not immediately filled with sadness. "I must confess, I have never even contemplated an 'after' for this."

"So . . . we won't forget?"

Trayne roused himself, began to think clearly on the subject. "Allow me a bit of time to think on that. This is, as I said, utterly unprecedented; I never imagined this particular scenario, not at least since the last time it was attempted and the failure demonstrated that it was, as far as I knew, impossible."

"Well, it *happened*," Cordy said bluntly. "So why did you think it was impossible, when it obviously *wasn't*?"

"That is *part* of what I am considering, though some of it was obvious enough."

"Give him a minute, will you?" Tierra said. "We lost our friend, he lost his daughter. None of us are really thinking straight right now."

"Sorry," Cordy said.

"Think nothing of it." In the ensuing quiet, he contemplated the entire situation, in the light of everything he knew. He finally shook his head in amazement.

"The fact is," Trayne said, "it was a concatenation of factors, all of which were unlikely, and at least two of which I truly had never considered before this cycle.

"First, of course, was the fact that Stephen Russ had sacrificed essentially the entirety of his self-identity for the purpose of this mission. As I had hoped, this made Holy Aura—and through her connection with you, the other Maidens—far more powerful than she had been in most other cycles. Second, the decision to bring your *families* into it, and their *unanimous* decision to accept this risk and to support us, represented a risk and sacrifice in and of itself.

"But third was Holly Owen herself. While she and Steve Russ were in essence the same *being*, each of them was a different *identity*, a different lifestyle, a different set of life-experiences despite the common thread of essential existence, and thus were ultimately different *people* even though they were, in another sense and quite consciously, the same person.

"Thus, when Holly made that decision, she was deliberately and with full understanding sacrificing herself a *second* time, and that once more increased the power of the Maidens, and Holy Aura in particular."

He looked down, then up, and smiled sadly at them all. "That was, of course, not quite all. Steve and Holly made that decision *because* I had made the decision to try to act within the most ethical and moral bounds that the enchantment allowed—a decision that strengthened the entire enchantment, as it brought it even more closely in alignment with the ideals that we were fighting for."

Devika nodded. "Like the difference between trying to pull or push something from the side instead of straight ahead; the closer to the centerline you are, the more of your strength you can actually apply to the job, and the less chance you have of hurting yourself."

"Oh, very good, Devika! You have excellent instincts for this sort of thing. Exactly. You might think of it even better as a structure—if you put a support beam in and it is not as close to vertical as possible, it is much more likely to collapse under pressure. Now where was I . . . yes.

"So when Holly made that final decision, it was the continuation, and culmination, of our attempt to, as she said, 'do the right thing.' She was refusing to allow this endangerment of children to continue, and demanding that we no longer keep risking the future by leaving the next battle *to* the future."

"And," Dex said, with a tremulous, very tiny, smile, "Steve also had a lot more weight to throw around."

It was a small, painful chuckle, but Trayne did laugh the smallest bit at that. "Yes, that was the final point. Holy Aura's maximum mass in any prior incarnation never exceeded, perhaps, a hundred and forty, a hundred and fifty pounds, and you girls have endangered yourselves by losing, perhaps, twenty pounds each. Though Holly herself was no heavier, the *true* mass of Stephen Russ—that she had to support in addition to her nature as a Maiden—was over three hundred pounds, and she used *all* of that mass-energy.

"Overall, that made her final assault quite literally orders of magnitude more powerful than any prior Maiden could have managed . . . and sufficient, in the end, to destroy even Azathoth Nine-Armed."

The girls and Dex were quiet for a moment, but it was a less . . . *tragic* silence. The loss was not forgotten—likely never would be—but all of them realized that they had not *failed* in their missions, and even Dex seemed to be regaining some of his *self.*

"So the world really is *safe* now," Tierra said slowly. "I mean . . . no more invasions, no more Cataclysm Knights, no more tyrpiglynts, all that. Back to normal."

"I would not say *that*," he answered. "The world is safe from *Azathoth*, and most of those who served her; and if there exist others like Azathoth, her utter destruction will serve to give them pause.

"But by destroying her, the cycle is, as you have said, *ended*. There is now nothing sealing off the world from the cosmos, nothing preventing magic from filling the Earth as it once did. There will be other threats, large and small, and the world is certainly going to change." He frowned. "And now I will have to think on *that*. We made *so* many of our plans on the assumption that we only had a year, at most, to concern ourselves with, and now it seems time will march on."

Another moment of quiet, broken only by the continuous sounds of eating, and then Seika looked up slowly. "Silvertail . . . ?"

"Yes?"

"Why are *you* still here?"

He raised an eyebrow. "Did you think I would just *desert* you after all we have—"

"No, no, I mean why are you still *here*, as in, why didn't you die or something? Not that I want you to, but you said you were the linchpin, the key, to the whole enchantment, the cycle. With the cycle broken, shouldn't it have broken *you*? Especially with Holly . . ."—her voice caught—"with Holly . . . Princess Holy Aura, the first Maiden, gone?"

". . . Silvertail? Earth to Silvertail! Hey, Mr. Owen, are you okay?"

He realized he had been sitting there for long moments, just staring at her blankly, mouth hanging foolishly open. He closed his mouth, then looked around and shook his head. "I . . . confess, I had not even thought about that, but . . . you are absolutely correct as per usual, Seika."

Dex tilted his head. "Huh. Yeah, and didn't your summary to me say that the other Maidens basically centered on Holy Aura? Wouldn't that, like, all come apart when there *wasn't* a Holy Aura?"

"Yes," he said with slow incredulity. "Yes . . . exactly, it should. You should no longer be Apocalypse Maidens, but ordinary girls, now, and I should be nothing at all; the only reason I still existed was to be the single flaw and keystone in the enchantment that created the Maidens, and my service should be over."

Dex stood, shaking, but his eyes held a sudden, fearful hope. "Maybe it isn't. The last thing she said . . . I remember her, she *spoke* to me, just before . . ."

Seika caught his hand. "What? What did she say?"

"Just . . . just 'remember me.'"

Remember me.

Trayne felt his heart beating painfully, hope and denial competing in compressed agony within. "Maidens . . . Seika, Tierra, Devika, Cordy . . . *are* you Maidens still? Can you feel the power, reach for it within you?"

They looked at each other uncertainly, and then as one, they rose and took each other's hands. "To avert the Apocalypse, and shield the innocent from evil, and stand against the powers of destruction, I offer myself as wielder and weapon, as symbol and sword," they began, and then continued each with their own invocation of power and symbol, to finish, ". . . the Apocalypse Maiden, Radiance Blaze!"

". . . Tsunami Reflection!"

". . . Temblor Brilliance!"

". . . Tempest Corona!"

Four simultaneous detonations of pure luminance erupted across from him, and from fire and water and thunder and shuddering earthlight emerged four Maidens, looking at him with eyes filled with such wonder and newfound hope that it almost broke his heart.

"Oh, by forgotten *Lemuria*, by Ryumi's memory . . . maybe, just maybe . . ." he heard himself murmur. "Children, you have . . . you had a bond, all five of you to each other. If her spirit lives, if *she* lives, somewhere in the infinities of the cosmos she touched in that moment, that bond just might draw her back. But to summon her . . . would require five, in addition to the one in the center that would receive her, if such could be done. And all would need the power, need to resonate with the essence of—"

"In the blackest hour I call upon the Soul within," said a trembling voice, but a voice that grew stronger as it spoke, "that reveals truth and dispels evil! In the name of the ones I betrayed in arrogance I call upon that power to right that which I made wrong! Warrior of the World, Wielder of Sword and Will, I am he who stands between the Darkness and the Light, Herald of the Sunrise, Prince Twilight Dawn!"

And there was a flare of darkness and stars and a singing sparkle of light that Varatraine remembered from the days before the darkness, and Prince Twilight Dawn looked at them with the apologetic yet desperately hopeful eyes of Dexter Armitage. "Please . . . I know I'm not really one of you, but . . . if I could be the fifth . . ." There was no trace of his playacted persona; only the words of a remorseful teenage boy.

"Your power remains as well," Trayne breathed, hardly able to believe what he saw. "Then it *was* truly Ruloa's power, and Azathoth did not, or perhaps *could* not, entirely strip it from you. Not the fifth, young Armitage, for the five must all be bound by the enchantment that is to call her back, but the one in the center, who would receive . . . yes, you could take that position. If," he added, looking at the Maidens, "they will accept you in that position. For if there is any hesitation, uncertainty, or disruption, there is no hope whatsoever in this impossible enterprise."

Twilight Dawn looked down, then visibly steeled himself and looked up. "W-will you let me help? Please? I know I fucked up completely, but . . ."

Seika looked around at the others; they, even Devika, looked back at her, clearly waiting for her decision. *She was, as they say, Holly's "BFF." They're letting her call this shot.*

Princess Radiance Blaze stepped up and looked into Twilight Dawn's tortured gaze.

Then she backhanded him across the room, through the wall, into the next, to fetch up painfully against the reinforced far wall. She followed, tearing a hole large enough for the others to see her as she hauled the stunned Prince to his feet, plumed hat falling to the ground. "*That* was for being so *stupid* as to let that *bitch* fucking set you *up*, you *fucking idiot*," she said, shaking him. "If you *ever* do something that *fucking stupid* again I will take that rapier and break it off in your *ass*, do you get me, Dex?"

Twilight Dawn made not the slightest effort to protect himself or resist her, he just nodded painfully. "Yes, Seika, *God* yes, I'm so sorry, I know how stupid I was, I'm sorry, I—"

Then Radiance Blaze kissed Dex on the cheek and hugged him so hard he gasped. "And stop apologizing, dork. We know you'd never hurt any of us, ever, and that you're about that far from doing something even *stupider* to yourself. Come help us . . . and even if it doesn't work, I'm done being mad at you. 'Kay?"

He was touching the cheek where she had kissed him (which also showed the angry red where she had struck him) and staring at her in wonder. "Yes. Yes!" He looked up at the others.

The three smiled at him, and shook their heads. "It's over, Dex. *She* forgave you, and if she did, we're okay," said Cordy, and went over to him. One after the other, the three Maidens hugged Twilight Dawn, and he them, and none of their faces were quite dry; his was utterly soaked, but as he finally reentered the dining room he wore a pained smile that warmed Trayne's heart.

"Then come, Maidens, Prince. I will be honest . . . I do not know if this is possible; were it not for these . . . anomalies you have shown me, I would not contemplate it at all. But if it *is* at all possible, it must be done *now*."

"Where? The Discount Danger Room?" Seika asked.

He chuckled. "Yes, that will do as well as anywhere."

Forming a pentacle around Dexter Armitage was simple; the five Maidens had practiced such maneuvers frequently, and Varatraine of Lemuria had spent millennia using the mystical figure with and without others. Dex, still as Prince Twilight Dawn, knelt in the center, eyes closed, and as they all formed the five-sided figure Trayne was able to sense that he was already focused on memories of Holly exclusively.

He called forth his own power, and the Maidens theirs, and the rainbow light dazzled the eye. "Now, all of you: You must concentrate on our bond with Holly, with Holy Aura, on your memories, on your feelings, on your desire to see her once more, to call her *to* us. Let *nothing* interrupt your concentration."

And he bowed his head and remembered.

What the . . . did you just talk? Stephen Russ, staring at the white rat before him in disbelief.

Then perhaps you can see why the word "Princess" isn't exactly appropriate.

Twin Pines Mall, and a gigantic rock-worm towering above. *Dammit, yes, I'm sure! I can't stand here and let people get killed! I'd never be able to live with myself! Now, Silvertail! I accept this mission, this calling, whatever it is, I'll be this, this . . . Princess Holy Aura! Tell me what to* DO*!*

Then Holy Aura . . . Holly Owen. The insistence in staying in that form, in learning what it *meant* to be a teenage girl in this society. In *becoming* a teenage girl, so that she could do what must be done.

Her insistence on doing what was *right*. The small form shaking beside him, in fear that her best friend's parents would reject her.

And the impossibly painful thrill of remembering what it felt like to be a father once more.

Now he *felt* the resonance, the echoing of thoughts and memories around the mystic circle that was also a summoning pentagram. Seika, heart pounding but suddenly, incredibly sure of what was happening, diving in at the last minute to protect her friend Holly Owen. The wonder at discovering the truth, at becoming *part* of the truth. *Holly, come back, please come back . . .*

Tierra's memories were strong too, of Procelli's venomous hatred and power, and of her wondrous rebirth into an Apocalypse Maiden . . . of the games that had filled their afternoons and the way in which her mother's life had become something other than a grinding, slow death. *We* need *you, Holly, please be alive!*

Devika's had the intensity of the warrior she had been born to be, and she was praying to her own vision of God, a pure light that lay beyond any light, and remembering the joyous, incredible moment that she was given a chance to strike a blow at true evil, and the way that Holly Owen had warmed to her, brought her into her circle of friends without hesitation or question, when so many others had looked at her as a freak. *You are our* spirit, *Holy Aura, Holly Owen, and if God wills it, please, come back to us!*

And Cordelia, tears sensed on her face, remembering the terror of being trapped within impossibility, the girl she had hardly even *seen* before promising help, becoming something radiant and beautiful beyond comprehension, and then she *herself* being given this strength, striking back at Procelli, sending the tyrpiglynt back to the void; her own father's simultaneous joy and horror at learning the terrible responsibility she had; her own realization of what a weight Holly bore, and how her past as Steve was both helping and harming her; and these, her new and best friends, becoming something closer to her than family. *Don't leave us forever, Holly! We won! Come back!*

And . . . *and was that a response*? Something distant, faint, something weak and dissipated beyond imagination, but for a moment he thought he *felt* something, something that asked with a soundless voice so faint that the whispers of the wind would be shouts, *Silvertail?*

The girls stiffened; they had sensed something too.

Their power ignited anew, and Trayne Owen held himself back from calling out a warning; their bodies were already so thin from the battle, they could not survive much more, but he could not stop them. He let his own meager power flare up, felt his form dissolve to the white rat, *threw* his full strength into the enchantment. *HOLLY!*

Again, the sense that—just perhaps—there was *something* there, and the Maidens redoubled their cries, reaching out their power through a bond that might still exist, that hope *demanded* must exist, and in the center he heard Twilight Dawn shout out, "*Holly, come back!*", and his own power rang out, the chiming crystal calm and mysterious shadow of the dawn twilight made manifest.

The girls *focused* now, *drove* their power outward, energies shaking the foundation, vibrating the house, and Varatraine of Lemuria heard them calling to that phantom echo of a memory, to the friend they had thought lost, and their calls were no longer wistful or hopeful but demanding, certain, disregarding thoughts of failure; Dexter's face beneath the manifestation of Twilight Dawn was set in absolute determination.

Silvertail Heartseeker read the hearts that had been sought, and realized that the five young people would never give up, even if what they heard was just a reflection of their own hope and desire. With the intensity that only the young can master they had decided on the only truth they would accept, and they would live—or die—with that hope.

For the merest instant he hesitated, his long, long life streaming through his mind, his memory of all the efforts he had made to survive, his struggle to ensure that he would, somehow, continue so as to protect the world. But he remembered both Steve, reaching up to clasp a brooch that would change his life forever, and Holly, hugging him tightly and calling him *Dad*, and he closed his eyes with a smile. *Seven of us shall return . . . or none.*

He released the entirety of his *self* into the circle, and his consciousness shot outward, beyond all time and space, and he felt the Maidens before him, and the dwindling yet obdurately immobile anchor that was the will of Dexter Armitage behind, and something *was* there, something glinting in the Void beyond all other things, something that sang and called and reached out—

And there was a cataclysmic *shock* that blew him flat on his back. His eyes snapped open, and he saw the four Maidens also groggily raising themselves up, staring into the center of the pentacle.

Twilight Dawn was gone, with Dexter Armitage's form—now as frail and thin as the girls'—kneeling, gazing up with incredulous hope.

Above him, there was a mass of glowing light, a bubbling, moving cloud of rainbow radiance eight feet across, slowly drifting downward, emanating an absolute force that raised the hairs on Silvertail's back. But as it descended, it began to shrink, to condense. Within the cloud a figure started to become visible, a sketch of a girl made in fire and shadow and starlight. It floated farther downward, and then it *evaporated,* the light dissipating, a soap-bubble popping and vanishing . . .

And into Dexter Armitage's arms fell the limp form of Holly Owen.

"*HOLLY!*"

The joyous yet disbelieving shout came from all of them. Silvertail, to his own surprise, was there first. "Put her down, Dex," he said, transforming to his human shape, and the boy reluctantly lowered her. Trayne touched her face, then examined her quickly, checking . . . *No pulse? No, by the Gods, I refuse to accept that!*

"Tempest Corona, I need your power!" Devika's hands were on his own instantly, and he felt it, the crackling of electricity. *Just the right amount . . . millivolts only, precisely applied . . .*

"*Clear!*" he shouted, and the others pulled back.

Holly's body twitched, fell back. They gathered around again, and his shaking fingers touched her neck again. For a moment, he still felt nothing.

But then he saw all the others placing their hands on their friend, Dex gripping her hand, and all of them murmuring her name, and something jumped, quivered under his fingers . . .

And Holly Owen's eyes opened.

Trayne found the room blurring, and once more tears streamed down his face.

But this time, they were tears of joy.

✴ Chapter 65 ✴

"I still cannot believe it," Silvertail said.

Laughs ran around the little group. Holly was glad to see that all of them were finally starting to look less like skeletons; it had been a difficult few days for all of them, given the various parents' reactions.

The chaos of The Event, as the news was calling it, had at least made one part easier; schools had been closed for a week and might be for another week or even two, and while most businesses were operating, the various police and military forces investigating were encouraging people to minimize their travel and such until they had come to a decision about how to handle the mess.

"Why not? I mean, yeah, we thought she was gone for a while, but it's magic, so—"

Silvertail rolled his eyes, something relatively hard to see in a rat. "*Magic* is not some arbitrary word that lets you do *anything* without limit. You cannot get something for nothing, and I would stake my thousands of years of experience that even with all of the factors aligned in her favor, Holy Aura had to have expended at least three hundred pounds, perhaps as many as three hundred and twenty, of her mass to accomplish that final attack. That was *all* of the mass that Steve had, or at best would have left perhaps twenty to twenty-five pounds behind—not enough to leave you alive, Holly."

"No, I'd guess my *bones* weigh about that, let alone everything else," Holly agreed.

Seika leaned back and grinned. "But *I* think I know how it happened."

Holly stared narrowly at Seika, but the black girl with her poofy hair wasn't joking. "Okay, Seika, let it out!"

"Well, you know that all us Maidens are basically eating machines, right? Especially after we use the power, we just have to pretty much go on that old seefood diet—"

"Yep," said Tierra, "I see food, I eat it."

"Well, something *I* noticed was that compared to the rest of us, Holly outdid us at the table. Even Dex mentioned it. At first I thought it might be because her 'real body' was bigger than ours, but you know, it wasn't *that* much bigger, and anyway, even a thirty-five-year-old big guy isn't going to be eating two or three times what a growing teenage girl does just to maintain his weight."

Silvertail looked thoughtful. "I see your point. But she threw *everything*, by her own words, into that attack. If her . . . *Steve's* . . . body had been getting bigger, then she should have just used that extra mass. Yes?"

"Maybe, but check this idea out. We've seen all the memes and such affecting us *and* our enemies, right? So what about our *own* beliefs? Steve was *born* a guy, and as Steve he was completely down with that—it was the way he thought of himself. But for *Holly*, being a girl was normal. They were the same person, but they had completely opposite . . . *self images*, get it?"

Silvertail was staring at her, and then suddenly broke into high-pitched squeaky laughter. "Oh, my, now, that *is* brilliant. You are saying that her and Steve's *subconscious* was in a basic conflict, and the magic took that as a demand that they *were* in fact different people . . ."

". . . and so what she was doing was eating to maintain Steve's body, *and create Holly's*."

"By Lemuria, that's ingenious. And it fits with the way magic works, and does not demand that we get something from nothing. Yes, Seika, I believe you have hit upon the explanation." He looked at Holly. "You are, in the most literal sense, a self-made woman."

Somehow, that *fit* for Holly. "I think you're right, Seika. I feel . . . *new*, I guess. Like I was reborn, even though at the same time I feel the same." She thought a moment. "Well, one obvious way to test it."

She concentrated in a familiar way, and there was a tiny quiver, a shimmer . . . and then nothing. A huge, empty void filled her for a moment, and she knew from the looks of the others that her face had fallen. "Steve . . . I can't turn back into him."

The sad emptiness was all the more poignant because she remembered, only a few days before, thinking how wonderful it would be if she had never *been* Steve, had always been Holly.

"You've just lost a part of yourself," Silvertail said gently.

Her head snapped up to look at him, startled.

"Of course I know, Holly. And so, too, does Seika, and your other friends have at least an inkling of it. You *were* Steve Russ. He's your history, your . . . memory trace, as modern psychology might put it. You may have *become* Holly Owen, but Holly is just as much Steve's creation as she was mine, or that of her predecessors. More so; it is Steve's spirit that infuses you; you were Steve, and he is still you, and to have lost the ability to call upon the *self* you lived with for thirty-five years? It would be a great tragedy indeed if you could not mourn that."

She managed a smile, patted Silvertail. "I . . . guess. And now I have the life I thought I was giving up."

"With some rather greater complications, I am afraid."

The five girls faced Silvertail with more serious looks. "Okay, boss-rat, drop it on us," Tierra said.

"As I had suspected, magic is no longer barred from the world. I have carefully examined the structure of the remaining magic upon you and myself. The part of the enchantment that created the Maidens remains, but the part that was tied to Queen Azathoth herself was also the part that sealed the world away from the forces of the supernatural—for the most part, that is; obviously as the spirit itself partakes of the forces we call magic, it could not be entirely barred."

"So is our world about to turn into Lemuria?"

He gave a faint, squeaking laugh. "Not precisely, no. The . . . *potential* to rebuild that which was lost is now there, but my world was destroyed; it will not reappear in a blaze of light and utopia. Your world *is,* however, changing in an irreversible fashion. The Event, naturally, has begun that—even the most steadfast of skeptics came face-to-face with manifestations of Azathoth's presence, and can no longer deny that there are things beyond those dreamt of in your philosophy, to paraphrase the Bard.

"More importantly, the forces which were hidden or limited in your world will reemerge. The *Aili* may be truly gone, or may be reborn;

your friend Dexter may find he has another mission besides merely guarding his friends, if Queen Ruloa's power truly lives within him."

"You say 'forces,'" Holly said slowly. "You mean . . . what? Monsters? Wizards? Other species like, oh, dwarves? Are we doing a Shadowrun, chummer?"

She suspected that a year ago the last line would have caused him to blink at her with complete incomprehension; now, he simply bared his chisel-like teeth in a rat grin. "Something of all of them and more, I am afraid. Ancient races will awaken. People will discover they have the talent for magic, and will begin to figure out what parts of the various traditions are utter balderdash and which ones hold real promise. Beings from *outside* will sense this world, and as they always have, hope to find a way in through the cooperation or seduction or corruption of humans in search of power of one sort or another."

"And some of them are going to be as rotten as Azathoth's crew, aren't they?"

"Undoubtedly. Humanity will face many new adversaries . . ." He hesitated, then sighed. "And even some we have seen before, perhaps."

Devika's eyes narrowed. "What have you discovered?"

"I have spent most of the time in the last week—when I did not have to tend to you or your parents' concerns—tracking the activities of various organizations, especially around our battleground." He gazed at each of them in turn. "Neither Arlaung's body, nor that of Nyarla, were found in the rubble."

"*Fuck!*" Seika said instantly. "I *knew* they'd get away! I just *knew* it!"

Holly felt a slanted grin on her own face. "Well, fits some of the memes, doesn't it? The Big Bad went down, but her Dragons get away to be problems later. But probably not for a season or so, anyway. Gotta have other adversaries in between."

"What about the Knights?" Cordy asked. "I mean, Mike had changed sides and all. Then they got backstabbed by their own boss."

"All five of them were found unconscious, some in very poor condition. However, they have been recovering. How much they remember I do not know; while undoubtedly the Knights' basic personalities were similar to those we saw, I am certain that the Armor enchantment each was given was designed to work upon their weaknesses and faults, directly affecting their minds. With that removed? They may not be clear on what happened for quite some time."

He looked momentarily grim.

"What *is* it, Silvertail?" Tierra asked. "Something else is worrying you."

"You may recall that earlier this week I came home, and went to bed almost instantly?"

Holly nodded; so did Tierra, who had been there at the time.

"Let us say that I have also been working to *minimize* the effectiveness of certain organizations which would otherwise be seeking to cover up, or capture, the various principals in this event."

Holly's lips tightened and she felt a pang of anger. "You mean the OSC."

"Exactly. Agent Kisaragi . . . may be able to be reached. But with the scope of this disaster, there were many other OSC teams present, and they were not all under her direction. And the OSC is not the only such organization, only the one with the longest pedigree; given what is to come, I expect that intelligence and military as well as more local police forces will quickly either form liaisons with such, or develop their own . . . paranormal response units, we might say."

"So what were you doing, exactly, that wore you out?"

"Preventing them from administering amnesiac and mnemomorphic treatments to people, among other things. I believe they would have taken at least one or two of the ex-Knights into custody if they could have erased or modified the appropriate memories in various people including their parents."

"Jesus!" Holly was appalled. "Are you serious?"

"Obtain and Secure are two of the three words that define their mission, Holly, so yes, deadly serious."

"Wasn't that dangerous, Silvertail?" Cordy asked, concern clear in her voice. "They could have caught *you*!"

The little white head nodded. "It was indeed a risk, Cordy, but one I had little choice on."

"Why?" asked Devika. "Not meaning to sound cruel—and in fact, I would have done the same thing—but practically speaking, risking *you* for those who were our enemies does seem ill considered."

"On the surface, yes. But if they could get away with it on your counterparts, there was no telling what they might learn from them—and also it would encourage them to continue to think in those terms. That is, they would continue to attempt to capture and seal away anything they viewed as a potential threat to humanity, including, naturally, the Maidens, unless and until they felt *they* could control them."

"Got it," Seika said. "You had to make 'em understand that they were going to have a hell of a time pulling off that stuff around here—without giving away why—so they're forced to back off and think about it instead of just charging in here to grab us a little later."

"That is essentially it, yes. I also *hope* that we can find a less adversarial way to communicate with them; they are, as I said, one of the oldest, if not *the* oldest such organization on the planet and could do a great deal of good if we can keep them from thinking that this is something they can cover up or control."

"Which they won't be able to do anyway, if what you say is right," Holly said. "There's going to be monsters and wizards and maybe fairies and aliens and who knows *what* showing up. They'll need to have more tentacles than Nyarlathotep to plug all *those* holes in their cover-up!"

Silvertail laughed. "Indeed!"

"What about us? Are we going to be . . . any different?"

"An interesting question, and one I cannot yet answer, Maidens," Silvertail said after a moment. "You *were* a weapon with a single purpose, paired to the opposite pole of the Seal that is now no longer. This may well affect you in some way over time. You may age differently; you may find your power to be weaker—or perhaps stronger, or change in some other fashion.

"However, your essential link remains unbroken. No matter how things may change, you will still be connected and, in one way or another, empowered by that spell."

"So we'll stay the Maidens, even if the specifics change around a bit."

"That is my belief, yes."

"How about you? Are you going to be stronger? Maybe get your old body back?"

Others might have had a hard time reading the expression, but Holly and her friends had spent a lot of time around Silvertail; she could see the wistfulness suddenly cross his face. "I wish it could be so. But . . . in a sense, yes, I suppose. I will indeed be stronger than I was, as there will be more magic in the world for me to manipulate; that means that I should be able to remain human for longer periods, under more situations." He managed a smile. "In fact, I have already demonstrated my strength to myself; in addition to all the rest I have told you, I have fulfilled our obligation to Michael, *née* Eclipse Umbra; his sister is now recovering and will regain her health fully, and that required far less of my strength than I had expected."

"Good," said Seika emphatically. "It's great that she's going to be okay, and even better that you're going to be stronger. We're going to need you."

"Right," Holly said, looking around the room. "Because all this means one thing: the world's still going to need *us*."

Tierra laughed. "Right! The Apocalypse may be over—but the Apocalypse Maidens aren't going anywhere."

Cordy bit her lip. "We'll have to talk to our parents all *over* again. Because it's not temporary anymore."

Holly looked at her. "You want to stop? You guys all signed on just for the Apocalypse, and we kicked Queen Azathoth's ass, so if you—"

Devika laughed, and so did the others. "We won a *battle*, but the *war* against evil isn't over. Arlaung and Nyarla are out there somewhere, and Silvertail says there are other enemies to come."

"Holly, I know you really *mean* it," Seika said, and Cordy continued, "but really, you think we'll let you try to defend the world *by yourself*?"

Tierra punched Holly in the arm lightly, then took her hand; the others all linked hands with her. "We *are* the Apocalypse Maidens, right?"

Holly felt a burst of gratitude. "Yes, we are. *All* of us."

"Then we keep doing what you said: the *right* thing," Seika said.

Silvertail chuckled. "The ethical magical girls," he said with a smile, and transformed to Trayne Owen. "Yes. We will. If your hearts are resolved—"

The five smiled, exchanging glances, and then, as one, they began, and the rainbow of holy light answered:

"To avert the Apocalypse, and shield the innocent from evil, and stand against the powers of destruction, we offer ourselves as wielder and weapon, as symbol and sword . . ."

FIN.